Nodding, he said reluctantly, "All right. You and the boys go east and the gold is mine."

"Get us there safely, and it is yours."

With a smile, he held out his hand. "You have yourself a deal, Miss Buchanan."

Lizzie did not hesitate as she solemnly placed her hand in his. His grin widened, and his eyes led hers to her slender fingers resting in his palm. Slowly his other hand began to settle over them. She pulled her fingers away with just enough poise to show him that he could not daunt her. It was his turn to laugh when he turned to go outside.

"One other thing," she said cooly.

"Yes?" He filled the doorway as he looked back at her.

She stood straighter to prove she was not awed by his impressive size. "I am not your slave, Mr. Hollister. You will be served meals at the same time as the boys. This is a partnership. Do you understand?"

"I understand exactly how it will be when we are on the road east." All good humor left his voice. He leaned forward until his nose was bare inches from hers. Glaring, he stated icily, "This is *not* a partnership, Miss Buchanan. There can be only one boss on the trail, and that is me. You don't know all the dangers. Play games, and you will end up dead."

Jo Ann Ferguson

NOTHING WAGERED

Tudor Publishing Company
New York and Los Angeles

Published by
Tudor Publishing

ISBN: 0-944276-03-2

Printed in the United States of America

First Tudor printing—April, 1988

To my kindest, most critical critics—
Carol, Irene, and especially Carolyn, who has
Golden Dreams of her own.

CHAPTER ONE

DEAD DRUNK. WITH A MOAN, HE GRASPED HIS head. He understood the phrase too well. He was the latter and wished he could be the former. His head felt as if a tombstone was grinding down into his shoulders.

Damn!

He dropped back into the mud after trying to gain his feet. That rotgut was becoming too much for a man with as many miles behind him as Cliff Hollister had. Even a few trips ago, he could waste his pay and walk away with a whistle on his lips.

Damn! he thought again. This was a young man's game, and he was not getting any younger.

When he felt a hand on his shoulder, he cracked one eye open and fought to focus it. With the glare of the sun in his eyes, he stared at the wavering form before him. Irritably he wondered why the sun was out. He could not remember any of last night . . . or the night before . . . or the night before that. . . .

"Mr. Hollister?"

He smiled as he heard the feminine voice. Maybe it was not so bad after all. One of Delilah's gals must be feeling sorry for him. He could enjoy some female sympathy right now. As he tasted the mud in his mouth, he doubted if he would be able to savor much else with her.

Then he remembered the state of his nearly empty pockets. Gathering the remnants of his tarnished dignity, which was all remaining to him, he managed to struggle into a sitting position. He leaned against a watering trough, with one arm dangling in the water. The dampness climbed the flannel sleeve of his shirt, but he paid it no mind.

"Are you Mr. Hollister?" Disbelief heightened the voice.

He smiled again, then moaned as the simple motion wrenched his too tender head. Squinting, he tried to bring her into focus. If she looked half as fine as her sweet voice sounded even through his aching skull, she would be a lovely lass. Not too old either, by the lilt of her voice. He did not recognize its warmly husky tones, which surprised him, for he was sure he would know any of Delilah's gals.

"Yeah, I'm Hollister." He winced. Dammit! Why did his own words have to twirl through his head like heated winds across the desert? Irritably he snapped, "If you are looking for a customer, honey, you are two days too late. My gold is gone."

"Are you Cliff Hollister, the wagon master?"

Finally he found the stamina to stand. He

wiped his hands on his mud-caked pants and staggered forward several steps before he could secure his balance. Looking down into her face, he saw it for the first time without the sun burning his eyes. He swayed as he bowed but avoided falling on his face. Even through the blur in his mind, he noted she did not put out her hands to break his fall. The lass had been around too many drunks to worry about another.

Easily he appraised her. To his drink-gazed eyes, she had seemed like a blob of dark against the sky. Closing one eye, he tried to bring her form into some sort of recognizable shape. He nearly laughed as he noted her ragtag clothes. None of the whores at Delilah's would be dressed like that. Her flannel shirt had a tattered hem and was thread-bare at the elbows. Beneath it, she wore a pair of the denims favored by the miners in the hills. A felt hat sat on the back of her head and was tied under her chin with a piece of twine.

"I am Cliff Hollister, honey. Who are you? You certainly had better get yourself some nicer working clothes if you want to make a living here in Hopeless. The boys like to see a woman dressed in lace, not decked out like one of them."

Outrage tinged her voice. She spoke with an accent far too cultured for any woman wearing the uniform of a miner. "My name is Lizzie Buchanan, sir. And I am not . . . Never mind! If you are Cliff Hollister, I am looking for you."

Irritably, he stated, "I told you that already, honey. And I told you I had no money to pay a whore, nor at the moment do I have any desire for your company. Go on, lass, and leave me alone until I find my head and rid myself of this boulder."

As if he had not spoken, she continued, "Mr. Hollister, I have to get back east."

"Take a ship. They leave weekly from Frisco."

"I have too little money to pay for passage for the three of us."

He shrugged. "Well, earn it, honey." He placed his face close to hers and laughed as she quickly stepped back several paces. Flighty little thing, she was. Pretty as a prairie morning with her hair the color of wind-dried grass and her eyes the same shade as bottomland soil.

"I thought I could hire you to escort us back."

Cliff roared with laughter. The sound reverberated inside his skull, and his laugh abruptly changed to a moan. He started to wander away in search of a place to finish sleeping off his drinking binge. He had staggered a half dozen steps when he stumbled and fell.

Spitting more mud from his mouth, he heard the light sound of female laughter. He erupted from the mire to glare at the wisp of a woman with her hands on her hips. When she giggled again, he wiped his face on his equally filthy shirt. His nose caught in a rent in the sleeve, and he swore imaginatively.

"Forget it, Mr. Hollister!" she called as he rose unsteadily. "You cannot find your way along the street. I doubt you would be worth a day's panning, as far as taking us home is concerned."

He rounded on her and grasped her by her surprisingly slender shoulders. The wide sleeves of the work shirt had led him to believe she was much bigger than his hands told him. Shaking her, he watched as her hair filtered from beneath the hat. Mousy, he decided. He liked his women well rounded, with raven locks.

"Listen here, honey. I am the best damned wagon master this country has ever had. In my last three trips, I lost not one weak-bellied settler to a trail accident. I always arrive with at least three-quarters of the wagons we had when we left St. Louis."

Gazing up at his gray eyes, she smiled coolly. "You smell like a three-day-old corpse, sir." She laughed again at his shocked reaction to her response to his pronouncement.

Lizzie Buchanan did not need to hear a recitation of Cliff Hollister's qualifications. She knew from firsthand experience his capabilities. When she had come with her sister, her sister's husband, and their young sons to the gold fields of California three years before, this man had been the assistant wagon master of their caravan of canvas-topped farm wagons. She had seen his prowess in the sometimes sensitive administration of the wagon train.

As she regarded him, she knew when his dirt-encrusted hair and beard were clean, they would be a rich walnut brown. Lizzie had not forgotten, during those intervening years of hard labor, the sparkling smile of Cliff Hollister when he stopped to talk at their wagon. Not that he had noticed a gawky teenager among the women of the train.

There had been stories of him and that Birley

girl. . . . She shook her head. That did not concern her. She needed help, and this man might be the only one able to give it.

"Look, Mr. Hollister, I am willing to hire you to take me and my two boys back to Independence or St. Joseph. You have to go there anyway to meet your next wagon train. Why not make a few dollars on the way?"

"I am in no mood to be doing business, honey."

"You are in no condition, you mean!" she retorted tartly. Shoving him away from her, she called over her shoulder, "I will find someone else."

"Good! I hope—"

When she heard a crash behind her, she nearly did not turn around. With a sigh, she saw he was again face down in the awful mixture of mud and unsavory town litter. She knew she should leave him in the swill with the rest of the swine.

The only problem was she needed him. It was deep into September. If they did not leave soon, they would be imprisoned in Hopeless for another winter. She cringed as she imagined living in a shack on the hillside. More wind came through the unchinked walls of the primitive cabins than was kept out during the damp months of the winter.

Squaring her shoulders, she wondered if she was up to this task. In the months since the accident in the mine, she had learned she could do things she would once have scoffed at as impossible. If she wanted to go home to Kentucky, she had to depend on herself to make it happen.

The one thing she could not do alone was find

the way east through the trackless lands inhabited only by wolves, prairie dogs, and Indians. She went back and picked up Hollister's arm. With it wrapped around her, she put her shoulder beneath him. Straining, but with strength garnered from hard hours of working in the mine, she raised him to his feet.

His head lolled and came to rest on top of hers, and she sagged under his weight. Fiercely she fought to straighten her knees. Asking herself why she was bothering but knowing there was no other alternative, she half carried him down the street, which was only two storefronts long.

Those two buildings were all that was needed in Hopeless—the saloon and the assayer's office. They served everyone's needs. There was a store and a blacksmith to repair tools on the other side of the ridge in Mud Hollow.

At the end of the street, she turned toward the rising sun. The hut stood alone. It had cost a great deal to rent it for the last three weeks, and by the end of the month they would have to vacate it. To pay Mr. Emory's exorbitant rent would take the last of their money, which they needed to return East.

"Open the door, Tommy!" she called to the larger of the two boys sitting in the mud by the cabin. She sighed with exhaustion. Not only would she have to tote water from the creek for Mr. Hollister, she would have to wash the boys again.

Mud. She wondered if every bit of California was covered by it. All she had seen of the state was. Mud and rock and useless dreams of glitter that did not exist for this family.

The child leapt to his feet, knocking his little brother into the dirt. Lizzie soothed the little one even as she was aiding the man over the threshold and into the cabin. As if she were manipulating a puppet, she had to control his every movement by telling him what she wished him to do.

"Pick up your right foot, Mr. Hollister. Step through the door."

She bit her lip as she heard the children laughing at the man's inept attempts to follow her orders. His foot hit the raised board of the doorsill for the third time, nearly knocking them both on their faces. Only because she had to concentrate did she restrain the giggles bubbling in her throat.

Entering the house's one room, she glanced at the yellowed sheets on the bed and shook her head. Her hospitality did not extend to allowing this filth-covered drunk to sleep in their clean bed. A grim expression of satisfaction settled on her face as she let the man drop heavily to the uneven planks of the floor.

He groaned as he hit the hard surface, but he didn't move. She looked at him, rubbing her aching shoulder, and wondered if she had been foolish to drag him here. When he had slept off his whiskey, there was no guarantee he would help her and the boys. All she might end up with were these sore muscles. If she did not have to get home so desperately, she would have found someone else. Right now, right here, no one else could help her. Few came to Hopeless, for the settlement had been appropriately named. The covered wagons went elsewhere. That was why she had been so excited to hear that Cliff Hollister had been sighted in the saloon.

As she regarded the man lost in his drunken hallucinations, she wondered if salvation always came clothed in mud and reeking of Delilah's cheap whiskey. She stepped over him and put a tentative finger to the coffeepot on the cast-iron stove. The pot was still warm. Taking it and stretching for one of the two chipped cups on the shelf, she poured herself a serving of the bitter beverage.

She leaned against the wall and wondered what was going to happen. One side of her mouth tilted up wryly as she heard the thunderous sound of Cliff Hollister's snores.

"No wonder Delilah threw you into the street," she said with a chuckle. "That noise would rattle the walls of her place and scare off her customers."

No response came from the man. She decided there was nothing to do but let him sleep. Pouring water into the tub, she centered it on the table, which, with two benches and the bed she shared with the two children, filled the tiny house. She began to rinse the breakfast dishes. It was a simple task. Three bowls, two mugs with no handles, and a trio of wooden spoons were all that had to be cleaned before they could be used for the next meal.

The two boys wandered in to stare at the prone form. "Who is that, Lizzie?" asked the younger.

"That is the man who is going to take us

home, Pete." She tousled his hair with her wet hands as he wrapped his arms around her leg. The water darkened his flaxen hair and spiked it to stand at odd angles.

"But we are home."

Her lips tightened. This was the only home these boys knew. Tommy could barely remember the trip west, and Pete had celebrated his first birthday here on a blistering summer day that baked the mud and turned it into hard patches of cracked earth. This was not the world they were going to have all their lives. They deserved something much finer, and she intended to see they would have it.

Gently she said, "I have told you we are going east."

"I don't want to go," whined the child. "I want to go home to Pa and Ma."

Lizzie knelt by him and pulled his head against her chest. Like her, the two boys were dressed in flannels and denims. She had cut their shirts and trousers down from the last of their father's clothes. Already Pete was outgrowing the shirt, and the hems on the sleeves had been turned down as far as possible. She did not want to think of how she would be able to dress them all if they were forced to stay in Hopeless through another winter.

"You can't be with your Pa and Ma, Pete. They are in heaven. Remember?"

"Yeah, remember the bad boom?" added Tommy with the wisdom of his six years.

As the younger one nodded, Lizzie felt a

burning at the back of her eyes. Lowering them to the rough floorboards, she knew she could not meet the innocent gaze of the two pairs of brown eyes, so like their father's candid ones. She could not share their easy acceptance of the abrupt alteration of their lives, from a happy family struggling to grasp a dream to a spinster and two orphans.

It had been so sudden. Two sudden, but overdue, for they had teased the vagaries of luck too long. An ear-wrenching crash and two people buried in the side of a mountain, never to be rescued. If she had been with them that day . . .

The man on the floor groaned, drawing her attention from the past. She rose and went to the tub on the table. "Go on and play, boys. I will call you when it is time to eat. Don't wander away or go near Delilah's!"

"We know, Lizzie," said Tommy with the tired disgust of a child who hears the same rules every day.

More than once Pa had told him that if something happened in the mountain, he, Tommy, would be the man of the family. Just once he wished Lizzie would let him assume that role. He grimaced as he tripped over the boot of the sprawled-out man, who had not moved during the conversation.

Why did she have to bring this whiskey-soaked fool home? Neither he nor Pete wanted to leave the Whitney's Dream mine. Gold waited in there. If they could stay a few more years, he would be big enough to break the rock to set the charges himself. He knew how. Pa had let him help count them more than once.

He glanced at Lizzie. Pa also had told him to obey her. There was no choice but to go to Kentucky. Later he would return. The claim belonged to him and Pete. They would prove to everyone that Pa was right when he said a fortune in gold was hiding in there.

Watching the youngsters go out into the warm sun, Lizzie sighed. She understood how frustrated they were about departing from the only world they knew. Three years ago she had felt the same when she was told they were leaving Kentucky, so she knew that no words she could say to the boys would convince them she was right. The mention of school, fine clothes, and a comfortable house with playmates next door would not appeal to them.

Throughout the day, she did her chores. In a surprisingly short time, she grew accustomed to stepping over the broad shoulders of the man on the floor. Soon he seemed to be no different from any other permanent feature of the cabin.

With the last of the yeast she had bought from the man who sold beer to Delilah, she made bread for their supper. Setting the dough on the doorstep to rise, she kept a watchful eye on it. With no window in the cabin, this was the warmest spot in the house. More than once, her dough had been tipped onto the ground or stolen by some four-legged creature. She would bake the bread in the cast iron Dutch oven.

As twilight approached, the road in front of

the house became busier. Clusters of miners came
strolling along the path from the hills. Their deep
voices reached into the cabin as they noticed their
anticipation of the entertainment available for a bit
of gold at Delilah's.

Their arrival signaled to Lizzie it was time for
the boys to come inside. She did not want to risk
them incurring the wrath of a woman eager or
whiskey befuddled miner. Tommy had inherited
the Buchanan outspokenness. If he opened his
mouth to one of these men, tragedy might result.

After the boys had washed in the water from
the bucket on the bench closest to the door, she told
them to sit at the table. Her eyes went from the pail
to the man who had spent the whole day sleeping
on her floor. She picked up the bucket and tilted
the dirty water over his head.

With a sputter, Cliff came awake. As the
water pooled on the floor and dripped through the
cracks in the boards, he rolled over to stare up into
the smiling face of a woman. She seemed vaguely
familiar. When he heard childish laughter, his eyes
moved slowly to view two boys bent over with
mirth.

Why in hell did you—?"

"Mr. Hollister, we have business to discuss,
and it will be transacted only if you are sober and
awake. You have been senseless for the whole day. I
think it is time you woke up and acted human
again."

He sat up and leaned against the foot of the bed.
His bleary eyes cleared, and he recognized the
cabin. This was Carson Emory's place, which he

leased at ridiculous prices to those newly arrived in Hopeless. He wondered why this woman and her brats were living here.

"How did I get here?" His last memory, blurred by the whiskey, was of talking to her in the street in front of Delilah's.

"I carried you." She smiled superiorly. "Fortunately, you are a compliant drunk, Mr. Hollister. You cooperated well, although it took several tries for you to lift your big feet through the door."

He frowned as he heard the youngsters giggle louder. Salvaging the remnants of his pride, he snarled, "You are a damn persistent woman!"

Not knowing whether that was an insult or a compliment, she said quietly, "If you prefer, I will take you back out into the street, and you can eat mud. Otherwise, you can stay with us and share our dinner."

"Why?"

She smiled, and he was shocked by the transformation. The brown of her eyes glowed with a light that brightened her tired face. For the first time, he wondered if she could be these children's mother. She looked far too young, not much more than a child herself. Maybe nineteen, maybe twenty. Certainly not old enough to have a son the age of the towhead gazing at him with the same lack of innocence he had seen in many children raised in these rough towns.

"Because I want to strike a bargain with you, Mr. Hollister. You are out of money. Delilah has thrown you into the street, which I would guess is because you have run up a tab even too high for her generosity." When he snorted in derision, she laughed lightly. The owner of the saloon had fully earned her reputation of being closefisted. Lizzie continued as if he had not interrupted her. "It is September, and the high passes will be closed by snow in another few weeks. All of which means you must be thinking of heading east to meet your next group of idiots traveling west."

"And you want me to tote you and these boys back with me." He swallowed his groan. Not only was she demanding, obstinate, and dressed like a man, but she seemed to have intelligence. All in all, everything he detested in a woman. Smart women required more attention than he wanted to give to any female.

"That's right."

"Out of the goodness of my heart?"

Her laugh became bitter. "Of course not, Mr. Hollister. I would not impose upon whatever bit of kindness you might have hidden in that rock-hard place. I can pay my way."

Leaning his elbows on his drawn-up knees, he asked, "How much?"

"That all depends."

"On what?" He hid his smile. This gal was sharp. She was trying to keep control of the bartering. Maybe she would be fun after all. It would be interesting to have someone beside his own thoughts as company on the trail.

His eyes slid along her but could guess little about what she would look like in a suitable woman's dress. Recalling the slim line of her shoulder, he wondered if she would be as dainty elsewhere beneath the heavy shirt and baggy pants. Even her waistline was hidden under the tails of the shirt, which reached almost to her knees.

Lizzie drew a bag from under her shirt. Untying it from the string around her neck, she tossed it to him. "It all depends on whether this is enough."

He did not bother to untangle the knotted cord to open the bag. Balancing it in his hand, he could tell fairly accurately how much gold dust was inside. Not a fortune, but enough to provide for him comfortably until the next wagon train came west in the spring. He could enjoy it in St. Louis or go south to Natchez-Under-the-Hill and have a grand time.

"Just the three of you?"

"Yes. You must provide us with horses and take us safely to the Mississippi. It should not be too onerous a task, seeing as you are headed in that direction anyhow."

"Not directly." He watched her face as he said, "I must go south to pay off an old debt in New Orleans."

With a smile she said, "Then take us there. We can get from there to Louisville with little effort. We are not that choosy, as long as you get us out of this mudhole and back to civilization."

"We can discuss those details later." He stood up, and his head brushed the low rafters of the primitive cabin. "First I want to clean up." He stared at the dark puddle on the floor where he had been sitting. "I assume that was all your clean water."

" 'Tweren't clean!" Pete put his hand over his mouth as he chortled with delight. He was enjoying this show tremendously.

Cliff glowered in the child's direction, but his expression only increased the amusement in the cabin. He picked up the now empty bucket. "I'll get some clean water from the creek. Then I'll have some food."

As he walked past them toward the door, Lizzie grabbed his arm. He shook her off easily but paused. His eyes narrowed as she stood between him and door. The gal was up to something.

Holding out her hand she asked, "Do you think me a total fool, Mr. Hollister? Give me back my gold. I am not about to let you wander out of here and spend it at Delilah's."

"Look here, Mrs.—" He realized he could not remember what her name was. That surprised him, for he could recall most of the other details of his earlier conversation with her.

"Miss Buchanan. Lizzie Buchanan."

"Buchanan? Lizzie?" he gasped. "You are Lizzie Buchanan?"

"Is there a problem, Mr. Hollister?"

He shook his head as he wondered how he could have forgotten that name. "I am just surprised to see *Miss* Lizzie Buchanan with two boys."

"It is easy to explain." When she saw his upraised eyebrows, she went on tartly, "Tommy and Pete are my nephews. Their parents are dead, and they are my responsibility—if that is any of your business."

"If we are traveling together, it is my business. Everything about you will be. This won't be a lark, Miss Buchanan."

"I did not expect it to be." She held out her hand. "My gold, please."

He thought briefly of pushing past her. Already he was regretting his unspoken agreement to her bargain, but that gold refused to be ignored. He placed the leather bag on her outstretched palm. His eyes remained on the bag as she tightened her grip around it.

"When do I get to call that mine?" he asked with eager greed.

"At the end of our journey. You will purchase our mounts and our supplies. Keep a record of it, if you wish, but take us east and you may have all this."

Nodding, he said reluctantly, "All right. You and the boys go east and the gold is mine."

"Get us there safely, and it is yours."

With a smile, he held out his hand. "You have yourself a deal, Miss Buchanan."

Lizzie did not hesitate as she solemnly placed her hand in his. His grin widened, and his eyes led hers to her slender fingers resting in his palm. Slowly his other hand began to settle over them. She pulled her fingers away with just enough poise to show him that he could not daunt her. It was his turn to laugh when he turned to go outside.

"One other thing," she said coolly.

"Yes?" He filled the doorway as he looked back at her.

She stood straighter to prove she was not

awed by his impressive size. "I am not your slave, Mr. Hollister. You will be served meals at the same time as the boys. This is a partnership. Do you understand?"

"I understand exactly how it will be when we are on the road east." All good humor left his voice. He leaned forward until his nose was bare inches from hers. Glaring, he stated icily. "This is *not* a partnership, Miss Buchanan. There can be only one boss on the trail, and that is me. You don't know all the dangers. Play games, and you will end up eating your dead as the Donner party did when they foolishly struck out on their own."

Lizzie fought to hold her exterior serenity in place. She wanted to cringe before his vicious stare. To let this man learn he could intimidate her would be to lose any bit of control she would have while they traveled. His tacit threats must be ignored.

She had enough sense not to attempt to repeat the tragedy of the westward-journeying wagon train that had been snowbound in the high pass that later took its leader's name. If she wanted to risk death and the other horrors those desperate people had suffered, she would not have sought out this arrogant man.

"Mr. Hollister, I am aware of my own ignorance of the California Trail. You will find, however, that I am as capable as any man of surviving the rigors of the trip."

A snide smile tipped the corners of his mud-caked mustache. "Is that why you dress like one, *Miss* Buchanan?"

Sputtering with aggravation, she watched as

he left the cabin to go to the creek gurgling behind it. She sent the boys after him. With Cliff Hollister, they would be safe and able to get a good cleaning. She knew enough about the man to be sure of that. He might be fond of liquor and loose women, but he would not mistreat a child.

All of them had to wash up before they could sit at the table in the little cabin. Even after the worst days of working in the mine, Lizzie's sister Whitney insisted they come to her table clean. The habit remained with the family after the disaster.

Her anger at Cliff's cruel comments could not keep the echo of the tragedy from resounding through her head as she thought of that day. Sick in bed, she had known instantly there was something different about the crashing of the rocks along the hillside. She could remember too well telling Tommy to watch his brother as she raced on unsteady legs to discover the mine entrance had disappeared.

Forcibly putting those thoughts from her mind, Lizzie went to the packs that contained everything they would take when they returned home. There was not much. As she rehooked the gold-dust pouch around her neck, she checked the saddlebags. A change of clothes for each of the boys, a hairbrush, and the miniatures of Whitney and her husband Zach Greenway, which would one day belong to their sons.

Out of all they had brought with them to California, only this remained. The rest had been sold to grubstake their only mining claim, which had proved barren. Its fine name forecast only sorrow.

The Whitney's Dream became a nightmare. Sometimes Lizzie wondered if Whitney and Zach's deaths were really accidental or simply a dual suicide when they learned their hopes would never be realized.

Rising to her feet, she busied herself to hide from the memories of the day she never wanted to remember. It was simpler to concentrate on rewarming yesterday's soup than to think of clawing at boulders taller than her head as she struggled to find a way to rescue the two trapped within the mountain.

The boys returned before Cliff. She set them to work putting dishes on the table. When the soup was hot, she poured them each a bowlful. Next to their spoons, she placed a slice of bread. As always it was scorched, for the stove was inconsistent at best. There was no butter. Such luxuries they had not had for the past year, and only Lizzie missed it.

She paused as she prepared to fill the third bowl. She reminded herself she was going to let Mr. Cliff Hollister fend for himself. If he was not there when she served the meal, he could get his own food. She scooped out a portion for herself into the last clean mug. There was not enough bowls for each of them to have one, and some vestiges of etiquette urged her to give her guest the one she normally used.

When Tommy paused in the middle of a word, she followed his eyes to the doorway. Not one of those at the table spoke as a red-haired man entered. She rose to her feet with a futile, protective gesture.

"Lizzie, what's this I hear? You are serious about taking the boys and heading east? I was just in Delilah's. There is plenty of talk about you asking about the trail masters going east. Gal, are you crazy?"

"Get out of here, Sam. I do not want you in my house."

He swaggered toward her. When she heard the boys' bench scrape on the floor, she took her eyes off the man to warn the youngsters not to react to his blustering. In an eye-blurring movement, he reached out and pulled her into his arms.

"Take your hands off me, Sam Winchester. Take your hands off me, or I—"

"Gal, you know you can't resist me," he drawled.

The sharp edges of his belt buckle cut into her as he pressed her close. Paying no mind to the shouts of the children, he forced her lips under his. Although she struggled, she could not break his hold around her. The sharp taste of cheap whiskey invaded her mouth as he attempted to subdue her.

"Get out of my house," she repeated as she wrenched her mouth away.

Laughing, he watched the fury across her volatile features. "This ain't your house. My pal Emory sent me over to tell you to get out. Now. Today."

"We paid him through the end of the month!" she retorted.

"Sorry. Your rent was just raised."

"Since when have you become Carson Emory's errand boy?" She dared not lower her guard to show her disquiet. From past experience, she knew Sam would pounce on any misstep she made.

"Since now." He laughed easily as he ran a hand along the length of her arm. Few men had looked past the ugly clothes to see the fine woman beneath the rags. Sam philosophically saw that as their loss. He wanted Lizzie Buchanan, and he had arranged to back her into a corner so he could have her.

Lizzie jerked her arm away from his too-rough fondling. "Get out. Now!"

"Where are you going to go?" He answered his own question as she glared up at his unshaven face. "You have no choice. Now you have to come up to the Dry Gulch Mine with me, Lizzie. Come on. You can't sleep in the street. Hell, I'll even take Greenway's brats with us. As long as they stay out of our way at night." He bent to nuzzle her neck.

Her hands pushed against his broad shoulders. Like all the men in the area, he was as unyielding as the rocks he worked to break. The reek of his unwashed hair gagged her. She ignored the retching feeling in her stomach as she fought him.

"I will not go to the Dry Gulch with you! I am not going anywhere with you! Get out of here. Even if Emory has raised the rent, I have possession of the cabin for tonight."

He grinned, displaying craggy and missing teeth. Sam Winchester enjoyed fighting; like an old tomcat, he carried the scars of many battles with him. "No, sweetheart. Emory told me you should have been out last night."

"You put him up to this! This is all your idea!"

He laughed, not bothering to deny her accusation. There was no reason to when it was the truth. "Come on. Stop being so muleheaded. I will treat you fine and teach you what a woman like you should know."

"Get out!" she snarled through clenched lips.

"I think the lady has made her wishes clear," came another voice from behind them.

Glancing over his shoulder, Sam did not lose his triumphant smile. Just two nights ago he had enjoyed a few drinks with Cliff Hollister. They had spent some time wagering on what man would choose which whore at Delilah's before they separated, each to buy the one he wanted. Hollister had been much the worse for the drinks they were swallowing as quickly as they could be poured. The miner had won nearly fifty dollars from the dark-haired man.

"What are you doing here, Hollister?"

The jovial man he had seen days ago was gone. Gray eyes drilled into him like explosives into a wall. "Let her go. She says she does not want you here."

"Lizzie? Ah, you can't believe everything she says. She's just trying to sweeten my desire for her, ain't you, sweetheart?"

"Will—you—let—me—go?" She enunciated each word clearly as she arched her shoulders to break his hold on her.

Cliff stepped into the room, filling it to capacity. "I think Miss Buchanan has expressed herself well. She wants you gone, Winchester. I suggest you go before my gentlemanly instincts force me to throw you out."

Comprehension darkened Winchester's face. She had done what she had been threatening to do since Greenway's death. She was going to take the brats and go back east by hooking up with Hollister. Go back before Sam could convince her to live at the Dry Gulch mine with him.

When the taller man stepped toward him, he decided this was not the time to press the issue. They could not be leaving immediately. Hollister was not familiar with Hopeless. The dark-haired man had been here only the past week as he paused on his journey east.

Many in the settlement owed San Winchester a favor or money. This would be a good time to collect for all the times he had used his muscles to intimidate a weakling for his pals.

"Hell," he breathed. "If you feel that strongly about it, Lizzie, I'll leave. One of these days, you are going to be sorry you did not take me up on my offer."

Coldly, she stated, "I doubt that. Good-bye Mr. Winchester."

He swallowed his retort. If she thought he was going to accept defeat so easily, she would learn her lesson. Without another word, he pushed past Cliff to go out the door.

"Thank you," said Lizzie sincerely, as she watched Sam stamp away. She expected he would find solace at Delilah's. Turning to the wide-eyed children, she urged. "Finish up, boys."

"May I join you? I believe I was invited."

After all the upset of the day, it took her a moment to remember her sharp comment to him. "Of course you . . ." Her voice disappeared into shocked silence as she looked directly at him for the first time since he had returned to the cabin.

Here was the Cliff Hollister she remembered from her adolescent fantasies. Damp hair curled across his forehead and glistened with dark lights in the last glimmer of the sunset. Although his clothes bore stains the pale color of dried mud, they were cleaner than those worn by the miners who patronized Delilah's. Open at the neck, his flannel shirt beneath his buckskins revealed the strong muscles of his body. He had been honed by his hard life of leading settlers through the maze of potential disasters to the lands along the western ocean.

Suddenly she wondered how she had managed to bring him to this hut alone. Her head would barely touch his chin. Even if she stood on tiptoe, she would not be able to meet his level gaze. He must have been aware of far more than he pretended when she helped him to the cabin.

As her eyes rose to meet the laughter in his, she turned away. She did not want him to see the flush brightening her cheeks. That he was aware of her appraisal should not have surprised her. With his quick mind, he was her match and would not give her any chance to gain the upper hand in this precarious relationship.

Her voice quivered as she spoke, despite her efforts to appear unruffled. "Sit down, Mr.

Hollister."

"I think you should call me Cliff. We are going to be on the road for a while, and it would be easier. I never have liked being called Mister." He winked at the boys. "You two can call me Cliff too. What are your names?"

As always, Tommy was the spokesman. "He's Pete. I am Thomas Zachary Greenway." He paused as he stared at the man who looked so different from the drunken hulk who had careened into the cabin with their aunt. Cleaned up, Cliff resembled the few men who actually made a successful strike in the mountains. The silver of his belt and the cold steel of his pistols he wore at his hip shone in the sunshine seeping through the open door.

"It's good to meet you, Pete." His smile broadened as he added, "And you, Thomas Zachary Greenway. I understand you are going to be aiding me on the way to the Mississippi."

Lizzie smiled as she went to the stove to get the soup pot. No matter what else he might be, Cliff Hollister was undeniably charming. He knew exactly how to gain the boy's admiration and allegiance. Since the accident, she had struggled to find a way to make Tommy feel he was the man of the family as she knew he longed to be. In their precarious world, it was not easy to find decisions a six-year-old could feel he helped make. Cliff had discovered the perfect answer.

As she served him, forgetting, after the confrontation with Sam, her resolution to make Cliff take care of himself, she asked, "How soon can we leave?"

"Winchester wasn't bluffing? Emory will
throw you out?"

"I'm surprised he hasn't been here yet. As
soon as Sam talks to him, we will be sleeping in the
street. The two of them are drinking partners, and
if Sam wants us out, Emory won't hesitate to do as
he asks."

"Sounds like Winchester. He's a cheat." Cliff
rubbed the back of his still-aching head as he
thought of how the man had managed to take some
of his hard-earned money. "He must really be
anxious to have you around; he's cooked up a
complicated plan, considering that all he wants is
to have you sleep with him."

She colored at his words. When she was
tempted to retort, she remembered the boys and
swallowed her anger. Instead she said, "We are not
going to the Dry Gulch. What I want to know is
how soon we can leave Hopeless."

Taking a spoonful of the soup, thick with
vegetables and unidentifiable meat, he murmured,
"It'll take several days at least to get the supplies we
need."

"Oh," was all she could say. She dropped into
her place on the bench.

"Don't worry, Miss Buchanan. Delilah has a
few empty rooms. A couple of her gals ran off to
get married."

She nodded. "I know, but I don't have—I
mean, I don't want to waste my gold to pay
Delilah's prices."

"All part of the service." He waved his spoon

at her. "Eat up and we can go over there. She'll be willing to help me. I have enough gold to coerce that gal to give us a room. I owe you one for rescuing me from the mud." Without giving her a chance to respond, he turned to the boys. "Did anyone ever tell you the story about the time I led a wagon train through the high passes in a blinding blizzard and we found shelter among the Indians?"

As the children listened raptly, Lizzie ate her soup. She smiled indulgently as Tommy reacted to the story with shouts of excitement. Her happy expression faded as she thought of having her nephews in Delilah's place for even a single night. They had little innocence after what they had seen during their short lives, but she wanted to safeguard what remained.

She sent them out to play in front of the house one last time and turned back to the table, intending to gather up the dishes. Instead she left them where they were. Emory had reneged on his share of their bargain. Under no circumstances would she clean up before departing. She could not leave the cabin as filthy as it had been when they arrived, but she would let the crook wash the bowls and cups himself.

She picked up the two saddlebags. "Whenever you are ready, Cliff."

"Is that all you have?" He looked about the stark cabin.

"We travel light."

He nodded. "That's good. I figured you must

be a sensible woman. After all, you could have left with Maxwell last week."

"He is unreliable," she said as she let Cliff take one of the bags. "You heard about what happened last year."

"I heard." His mouth formed a straight line behind the darkness of his beard.

Everyone had learned about Maxwell's fiasco. Twelve wagons destroyed. Fifteen people dead at the ford, and nearly as many dying during the rest of the trip of injuries or starvation. His foolish attempt to cut days from the trip had resulted in disaster. Only those desperate for a share of the gold rumored to exist in these ridges would travel with Maxwell.

"May I ask you a question, Cliff?"

He grinned roguishly as he stood up and placed the saddlebag over his shoulder. She was using the table as an effective barrier between them. That she used his given name but had not asked him to reciprocate warned him that she would be unlikely to lower it. He leaned forward and heard the rickety table creak.

"I think you already have, Miss Buchanan."

"Another then," she said seriously. She did not dare respond to his teasing. Only if she was cautious could they arrive at the Mississippi safely. She needed him, but she did not trust him. "Why are you being so kind to us?"

"The truth?"

"It usually helps," she said tartly, but she felt

the corners of her mouth twitching.

With a shrug of his shoulders, he replied, "It's lonely on the trail. It will be nice to have company. No, no," he added when he saw her smile become a scowl, "I didn't mean *that*. Don't read Winchester's motives into mine. You are a survivor. That is clear. You will do well. Besides, any girl who can control a runaway team and bring her family's wagon back in one piece will not be a liability on the way east."

He followed his laugh out of the cabin. Lizzie stared after him. That incident had occurred over three years ago, as they drove in the train to California. Never had she suspected he would remember it. Grim resolve filled her.

Cliff Hollister was a man to be reckoned with. Although he acted like a sailor newly ashore when he reached the trail's end, he assumed another character on the journey west. If he remembered that time when the team had been spooked by gunshot and she was the only one who could bring them to a stop, there might be other things he recalled.

She flushed as she wondered if he had ever discovered her childish infatuation with him. Then she had thought he was the strongest, handsomest, smartest man in the world. Many things had changed in three years, including her and her opinions of men. She knew this man for what he truly was, and she would be able to resist his charm.

That was one thing she had to be sure of before she headed into the wilderness with him and the two boys she loved as much as if they were her own. Never again would she pine for Cliff Hollister and pray he would look her way.

CHAPTER TWO

IT DID NOT SURPRISE LIZZIE THAT BOTH YOUNG-
sters became silent as they entered the saloon. As
long as they could remember, they had heard
stories of the horrible happenings at Delilah's Den,
as it was affectionately called by its patrons. At one
time it had possessed a far more lyrical name, but
that had long since been forgotten by everyone.

It was a dim, dingy place. Nothing like the
finely appointed bordellos of San Francisco or
Sacramento. There was not even a stage for
traveling players. At one time an untuned piano
had stood in a dark corner, but it had been
destroyed during one of the more violent brawls
that erupted irregularly. Delilah never replaced it,
for the men did not come to the saloon to listen to
music.

A dozen tables leaned awkwardly at every
angle throughout the room. Chairs, some with

backs, others broken, surrounded the tables. Most were occupied by miners as dirty as the building itself. Before them, between soiled glasses and quickly emptied bottles of gut-burning whiskey, were piled cards and nuggets of gold. Clustered around the men, gaudily dressed women tried to relieve the luck of their winnings and consoled the losers by taking their last glitter of gold.

The bar itself was a masterpiece. Of solid mahogany, it had been brought from the faraway Sandwich Islands. Backed by a wall of mirrors, the brass-edged bar showed signs of its hard use. Notches along its top marked spots where bottles had been broken against it.

Over all this, Delilah ruled with an iron hand. Her place was the only one within miles, and her customers knew the rules of the house. Posted prominently behind the bar, they were very simple. Pay for what you enjoy or break. No shooting inside. No abusing the girls unless Delilah was informed in advance.

Lizzie's grip tightened on the boys' hands as her wide eyes noted the number of men in the room. Because the mining claims were so spread out across the hillsides, she had had no idea so many miners lived in all the valley.

The wave of murmurs that had started with their entrance gave way to silence as the man behind her put his hand against her back. Those who might be eager to make trouble for her would be less willing to tangle with her companion. Cliff steered her toward a woman who was coming down the stairs to the left of the bar to see what had caused the sudden hush in her place.

"Cliff Hollister!" She frowned as she adjusted the deep neckline of her blue satin dress, which was stained with an abstract pattern of splashed whiskey. "I threw you out of here once today. Do I need to do it twice?"

He grinned, and Lizzie was shown the most public side of the complex man. The charm he had lavished on the young ladies in the wagon train and the youngsters at the table tonight was not wasted on Delilah. Because Lizzie had not been a recipient of that enchanting smile, she could see how calculated it was to gain him exactly what he wanted.

Slowly the blowsy woman began to smile. Her blue eyes twinkled as she pushed the tangled strands of her too-pale blond hair over her bare shoulder. To Lizzie's coldly appraising eye, the movement was as lacking in spontaneity as was Cliff's enticing expression. As Delilah walked toward the foursome, her hips swayed in an exaggerated motion that made Lizzie extremely uncomfortable and very aware of her tattered clothes.

Despite herself, she glanced up at the bearded face of the man next to her. She was not surprised to see him smiling with the same predatory grin as that which decorated Delilah's face. She felt as if a message was being passed between the two of them to which she would never be privy. A sense of uneasy disquiet invaded her.

"Now, Lila, you know you want my money."

"That's not all," she purred as she stepped

closer to him. She ran her fingers along the front of his shirt.

Lizzie had stepped back to avoid being trampled by the madam whose brothel, connected to this saloon, was the most profitable part of the business. As she watched, aware of the many questions forming in the minds of the boys by her side, Lizzie wondered what her eagerness to escape from California would do to them.

Cliff chuckled but pushed Delilah's eager fingers from him. His action did not seem to bother her greatly. "I have a business proposition for you, Lila."

"All right," she said with her mouth pursed in a moue that would have better suited a woman not wearing the garnish lip coloring she had chosen. "Tell me."

"I'm taking Miss Buchanan and her nephews east with me. Emory has evicted them, so I thought we could rent your extra room while we are making our preparations."

With a sniff, she turned to look at the others. Quickly she dismissed the boys as urchins she had seen playing in the street. The woman interested her. "*Miss* Buchanan, is it?" Rudely she eyed Lizzie as if she was a colt to be bought in the market. "I thought you were a boy, I did. Girl, you should do something to make yourself look like a female." Before Lizzie could respond, Delilah turned back to Cliff. "Hell, honey, I don't run a nursery for wayward children. My customers come here to avoid their families, not be surrounded by one."

"We can pay. We'll pay in gold, Lila," Cliff

responded. When Lizzie started to remove the bag from beneath her shirt, he signaled her clandestinely to leave it where it was.

Instantly Lizzie understood. As much as Cliff acted as if this businesswoman was a friend, he did not trust her any more than Lizzie trusted him. It would make for a most uncomfortable stay.

"Just the room?" Delilah demanded greedily.

"Food too."

She grumbled but nodded slowly. "All right. All I can spare is Patsy's room, so you'll have to sleep with the three children here unless you can make other arrangements of your own."

"Sorry," he said with a return of his engaging grin. "Empty pockets."

"Cliff—" began Lizzie, trying to submerge her fury at being grouped with the boys as a child. She did not want to share a bedroom in a brothel with him. Although they would be sleeping side by side on the trail, there was something totally different about this arrangement.

He ignored her worried face. Motioning to the stairs at the back of the bar, he urged, "Go on up, Miss Buchanan. You and the boys can make yourself at home. "It's the second door on your left."

Lizzie noted his familiarity with the place but said nothing. All the single men and many of the married ones frequented Delilah's Den. She was not so naive that she did not know exactly what happened here. Simply, she had never thought she would be sleeping under this roof. Nor had she expected to be staying in the same room as Cliff

Hollister.

Every eye in the saloon focused on her as she went to the staircase. The first stair tread creaked threateningly, making her leery of putting her full weight on its rotted surface. Hushing the questions erupting from the boys, she climbed the steps ahead of them. She did not touch the railing; it appeared to be in worse condition than the stairs. The next reeling customer who came up this way was sure to knock it down into the main room.

"Ho, Lizzie!"

Involuntarily she turned at the calling of her name. When she saw it was Sam who was shouting to her, she shook her head to quiet the youngsters and told them to keep walking. Her back stiffened as she continued up the steps.

Sam was determined to shame her, for he called, "Is this how Hollister is letting you pay your way? Does he get you just tonight or all the way back to the Mississippi? That useless mine Greenway staked could not have given you enough to buy your way. Why sleep with just Hollister, darling? We would be willing to help you make your grubstake. Right, boys?"

She intended to ignore him until she heard the harsh sound of Delilah's laugh over the enthusiastic replies of the men clustered in the room. Tightening her grip on the children's hands, she turned to face them all. From her perch halfway up the stairs, she commanded a view of the whole room.

"Mr. Winchester, as usual, you are wrong about everything. The mine did produce. Enough for our trip and to start anew." Her smile grew cold as she looked from him to the other men in the room.

She recognized several of the men by sight, but all the faces were blurred in the heated mist of her anger. Finally her eyes rested on Cliff, who was enjoying the performance as much as the others. His grin broadened as she scowled at him. It did not astonish her that he found this public ridicule amusing.

Although she cursed all of them in her mind, she continued calmly, "If I needed money, I must admit I would be willing to sleep with a real man to get my boys home safely. Unfortunately, in either case, Mr. Winchester, that leaves you out, doesn't it?"

The roar of laughter this time was at the man's expense. Applause from Cliff's direction tightened her pursed lips. She heard Sam's oaths at her back as she led the way up to the second-floor corridor and out of view of the saloon.

Second door on the left, she repeated over and over in her mind. She did not want to let her rage at Sam's words blind her into choosing the wrong door in this brothel. That would be more than embarrassing.

Even when she stood before the one she knew must be the correct door, she hesitated to touch it. She looked at the trusting faces of her nephews and realized she could not stay in the hallway. There was no telling what they might see if any miners came upstairs with Delilah's girls. She did not admit, even to herself, that she was as concerned about her own comparative innocence.

The door opened with a simple turn of the knob. Inside was a large iron bed and a settee. A chair stood on the other side of the room next to a rickety washstand that held a chipped basin with a little water in it. She guessed the rug's pattern had been a rose print at one time, but it had worn to a dull brown like the rest of the room. Nothing hung on the dirty walls. It was a depressing room, even compared with the wretched quarters she had been accustomed to living in since their arrival in Hopeless. She wondered why any man would pay to love a woman in it.

Telling the boys to sit on the settee, she put their bags on the chair. She went to look out the window, but it was so covered with dirt she could not see through it. Not that it mattered. She was too familiar with the scene outside.

To her, the pine-covered mountains no longer appeared beautiful. They had become the walls of her prison, holding her from everything she wanted. Before the accident, she had pleaded with her sister to leave. Always she had promised, "As soon as we make our strike," but that had never happened.

She spun as the door opened. Her intake of breath exploded out, but not in a scream, as she saw Cliff at the door. His eyes swept the room, settling lastly on her. She expected some comment on her actions downstairs and was shocked when he began to speak on a totally different topic.

"Keep this door locked, Miss Buchanan."

"I will. I meant to, but we just got inside." She was clearly flustered, but she could not avoid her confused feelings. Nobody had taught her how to act in a brothel. Taking a deep breath, she fought to calm herself. In a more normal tone she said, "If you wish, you may call me Lizzie."

"If I wish?" he echoed and chuckled as he dropped his hat onto the bed. Unhooking his gun belt, he placed that on the ragged edged coverlet as well. "You sure haven't had your smooth eastern edges roughened out here, honey. Are you sure you wouldn't rather stay and work for Delilah? With those ladylike manners and the obvious number of admirers you have downstairs, you would have them standing in line to hear you whisper in their ears as they—"

"Cliff!" she gasped. "The boys!"

When he saw the blush climbing her cheeks, he wondered who was more upset about the remark; her or the boys. She was an odd little thing. While he was washing at the creek, he had quizzed her nephews. They told him of how hard she had worked to search for gold before their parents' deaths and how she had slaved to make a home for them in the aftermath of the tragedy. Although her hands were as calloused as his and her skin so darkened by the sun it would make an eastern lady cringe, she remained a gentle spirit more suited to tending roses than digging for gold in the mud.

She watched as he sat on the bed and, leaning against the headboard, put his feet up on the covers. With a gasp of outrage, she knocked his boots off the bed.

"What are you doing?" he demanded.

"We—the boys and I have to sleep there. We would prefer to do it without your filthy boot marks on our covers."

Leaning forward, he captured her eyes with his glare. "Didn't I tell you that you were not the leader on this expedition? Maybe *I* want to use the bed."

"Didn't I tell *you* that I would not be your slave?" She refused to let him give her orders. The remembered sound of his amused applause echoed through her ears. "There are three of us. We are used to sharing a bed. You can have the settee."

"It's a foot too short!"

She folded her arms across her chest. "Then find somewhere else to sleep, Mr. Hollister!"

"I paid for this room!" he stated in a low tone that did not lessen its threat.

"And I am paying you for the time it takes to get us back to Missouri." She smiled with the same iciness with which she had confronted Winchester downstairs. "As I figure it, Mr. Hollister, that makes me your employer, since I am paying your wages."

In one smooth motion, he leapt off the bed. Its squeak sounded sharply in their ears. Grabbing his hat, he shook it in her direction. "That's it. I'm calling this arrangement off right now. I do not need you or your gold, Lizzie Buchanan. Find your own way back to the Mississippi."

"Good! Renege on our bargain. I shouldn't be surprised. You haven't changed, have you? All you care about is getting your own way in everything!"

He stopped as he was about to open the door. Turning to face her, he demanded, "What in hell are you talking about, girl?"

"Nothing," she replied quietly. She went to the bed and pulled back the covers. Already she had said more than she should. So had he, but none of it hurt as much as when he called her "girl." She could not ignore his lean masculinity, and he saw her only as a child still. In that he had not changed, and she was sure he would not.

Calling to the children, who had been watching the arguing adults, she told them to ready themselves for bed. She looked over their heads to see the man's eyes on her. The queer expression on his face was met by her blank visage. She would not let him see how much his words had affected her.

"I hope you don't mind us taking advantage of your hospitality now that our agreement is off, Cliff. We will vacate the room in the morning, but I do not want the boys sleeping outside tonight. Not that it is so cold, but it looks as if it might rain. It is too late to find shelter, and—"

"Do you ever shut your mouth?" Irritation continued to color his words. "Stay here, Lizzie! The room is paid for through the end of the week. Whatever other faults Delilah might have, she wouldn't cheat me in a business deal. You can stay here safely for the rest of the week."

"Thank you." She meant the words sincerely. In just this one day, he had come to her rescue too many times. She picked up his gun belt. "Don't you want to take this with you?"

Silently he took it. When his fingers brushed hers lightly, she drew away, frightened by the power of the feeling surging through her. She had not changed either. The years since she had last seen him had not muted her desire to have him notice her as more than someone's younger sister.

Neither of them spoke as he buckled the belt around his lithe hips. When he moved to go, Pete threw himself toward the tall man and demanded a good-night kiss. Cliff glanced in surprise from the towhead to Lizzie.

She said quietly, "Their pa always tucked them in if he wasn't at the mine. Pete and Tommy were very close to Zach and Whitney. They miss them." Her dolorous statements revealed her own grief.

"How long has it been?" He patted the child awkwardly on the head, but his eyes remained on Lizzie's sorrowful face.

" 'Twas in the late spring."

Softly he asked, "And you've been alone since then?"

She shook her head as she placed her hand on Pete's shoulders. "We are not alone. We have each other." Turning the youngster toward the wash-stand, she said, "Under the covers, now. It's time for you to be asleep."

While she competently washed dirty faces and checked that the boys had taken off their shoes, Cliff watched from the door. Her tenderness with the children was in direct contrast to the prickly temperament she showed the rest of the world. When she kissed each damp face and hugged both children tightly, he walked over to the bed. He was drawn by some force he could not name.

Lizzie moved away smoothly as he bent and found the younger boy's arms wrapped tightly around his neck. The pudgy cheek moved against his face, and he felt a moist kiss on his face. Startled at first, Cliff chuckled. He had been kissed good-night many times but never with such guileless giving. He looked at Tommy, who was watching the scene somewhat enviously. With a laugh, Cliff held out his arms to him. The six-year-old did not hesitate.

Behind Cliff, Lizzie bit her lip as she saw how much the boys missed having a man in their lives. Tears in her eyes made the happy scene waver as she realized that as much as she could give her nephews, it would not be enough. Perhaps she could find some man who wanted sons and would take her with them. Never would she allow their small family to be separated. She did not think any man would want her, except Sam Winchester who offered her only a life of degradation as his bed partner and a slave in his mine.

Fiercely, she told herself not to be so dreary. Back east, things would be different. She would find a life there that would make them all happy. All she had to do was discover a way to get them there.

Telling the boys to go to sleep, she followed Cliff to the door. She nodded wearily when he told her to be sure to keep it bolted.

"No telling who might try to get in here."

"I know." She leaned against the splintered

edges of the door as she looked up into his face, shadowed by the dim light in the hallway. Suddenly she was too tired to care about anything. She'd been so close today to finding her dreams, only to have them snatched away again by this capricious man.

"Use the room as long as you wish. As I said, you have it until the end of the week."

"Thank you."

Uneasily he shifted. There was nothing left to say. "Good luck, Lizzie, to you and the boys."

"Thank you. Good-bye, Cliff."

"Good-bye." He started to turn to walk away, then paused. "Maybe sometime I will look you up when I am wintering back east."

She tried to smile and failed, but she said, "That would be nice."

For a long minute they stared at each other, not sure how to end their short partnership. They were not yet friends, but they were no longer strangers. No trite phrases would work at this leave-taking.

He put his fingers out toward her, but whether to touch her or to shake her hand as partners should she would never know. From the staircase end of the corridor came the lusty sound of a man's laugh followed by a loudly spoken lewd suggestion that turned Lizzie's cheeks crimson.

"Good night, Cliff, and good-bye."

Before he could reply, the door closed in his face. He heard the bolt slide into place. With his back against the wall, he watched a miner pass by in the narrow passage with one of the women from the saloon. He noted, as if he had never seen it before, the woman's bored, resigned expression.

He thought of the honest emotion in three pairs of eyes on the far side of the door. What Lizzie and her nephews had was what these men longed for but could not find.

Damn! He was not going to let two youngsters and a half-grown wildcat interfere with his fun. Downstairs whiskey waited to be drunk, and he would find entertainment at the card tables or in one of the rooms along the hall. As he walked rapidly toward the stairs, he was determined to enjoy himself to the fullest tonight.

Lizzie sagged against the door and stared across the room. Moonlight filtered through the dirty window. Sitting on the settee, she loosened her boots and removed them. She wiggled her toes, glad to be rid of the burden of the too-large shoes. Zach had bought them for Whitney, but Lizzie took them when her own wore out during the winter. She curled up on the cushions, moving to avoid the sharp poke of a loose spring.

What they would do in the morning, she did not know. She had until the end of the week to decide her future. If nothing else became available, she would have no choice but to go to Sam and become his mistress. When the alternatives were that or starving, the decision became easier. By herself, she would have considered striking out across the mountains. She could not risk the boys' lives on such a foolish quest, which was sure to end in death.

Around and around her thoughts raced until

they became as fatigued as her body. Her unhappiness followed her into sleep to torture her with horrible nightmares of the days and nights she would spend as Sam Winchester's woman.

In the morning, despite the rain rolling muddy paths along the window, Lizzie awoke with a brighter attitude. Through Cliff Hollister's generosity, they had two days to find a way to leave Hopeless. A knock on the door announced the cook with a breakfast tray.

Thanking him, she woke the boys and urged them to eat. They sat on the floor and chatted about everything that had happened the night before. Although she smiled, she was able to contain her laughter at their misunderstanding of all they had seen and heard. It pleased her that their innocence was unchanged.

She opened their pack and removed her hairbrush. While they ate, she undid the bun at the back of her neck and released her hair to flow down her shoulders. Leisurely she brushed it as she did every day. She paused when Tommy offered her a bite of his biscuit.

Another knock sounded on the door. Urging the boys to take anything else they wanted, she picked up the tray. She placed it against her hip as she opened the door. "Here it is. Thank—Cliff!"

He leaned nonchalantly against the doorjam. It was as if they were continuing the conversation she thought had ended with their farewells. "Good morning, Lizzie. May I come in?"

"It's your room," she said reasonably. She put

the tray back on the floor. The simple motion gave her time to regain her shattered composure. "I thought you were the cook coming for this. As soon as we are finished eating, we will be out, if you want the room."

"No, no, I don't want the room." He stared at her as he closed the door. Absently he replied to the boys' greetings as his eyes remained glued on her. "You've grown up!" he blurted.

"It has been three years."

"Not that. Just since yesterday." He reached out to touch the strands of her hair, which was the shade of corn silk waving in the vagrant breezes of the plains. "Why are you hiding this beautiful hair?"

"It's not hidden. No one has bothered to look." She went to sit on the settee to evade his touch; it disconcerted her deeply. Trying to maintain her serenity as a guard against his charm, she asked, "If you do not want the room, then why are you here?"

Mentally he shook himself. With her hair soft around her, she looked sweet and feminine despite her ugly clothes. Only when she spoke did he remember her forthright nature.

"I thought we should discuss arrangements for our journey."

"Our journey?" Suspiciously she demanded, "What do you mean? You made yourself quite clear last night about not wanting to be tied down with us on your trip."

There was a boyish guiltiness in his smile, as if he had been caught by a schoolmaster skipping classes. Wryly he explained, "I nearly lost my very last coin last night at the card table. I have enough to pay for my supplies but nothing to live on until the spring when the wagons roll." He shrugged. "I guess I need you now as much as you need me, Lizzie. What do you say?"

"Say yes!" urged Tommy eagerly. "Say yes, Lizzie. I want to go with Cliff."

Pete pied up. "Yes! Yes!" He began to jump up and down in a wild dance across the floor until Lizzie ordered him to stop before he stepped in the food.

She looked from the man's studied demeanor to the children's enthusiastic faces. Never again would she trust Cliff not to abandon them on a whim, but this was the first time she had heard either child speak so happily about leaving Hopeless.

"All right," she answered slowly. "We will have to depend on one another during the trip."

"The payment will be the same at the end of the trip, of course," he said, reassured by his easy victory.

"Of course."

"Good." He held out his hand to her. "Partners again."

"Yes, partners again." There was a visible lack of enthusiasm on her part as she shook his hand for the briefest possible time.

He smiled broadly as he dropped to the floor to sit next to the boys. Picking up a sourdough biscuit, he spread it liberally with honey. He began another of his stories to entertain the youngsters and soon had them crowing with delight at the wild episode.

Lizzie said nothing as she listened to the fantastic tale. It was as if there were three boys on the floor. She paid scant attention to their conversation as she finished brushing her hair. Twisting the long strands, she arranged it in her normal style. She jabbed the bun with hairpins to hold it in place.

"Do you have to do that?"

"Pardon me?" she asked as she realized Cliff was speaking to her.

"Do you have to bind your hair up like that?"

She shrugged. "It keeps it out of the way. I suppose I could braid it like an Indian."

"That would be an improvement. At least then it could be seen instead of being hidden beneath that horrible hat."

"What?" she gasped. She had been joking. For years she had been wearing her hair in the same sedate style. Next to Whitney's golden locks, her hair seemed to her to be so plain, its color so washed out.

She pulled away as he squatted in front of her. "Don't be so shy," he ordered with a laugh. "It's not as if I would do anything that would make you say, 'Cliff! The boys are here!' "

Despite herself, she began to smile at his easy imitation of her own skittishness. Her grin grew into a soft chuckle, gentler than any she was used to hearing from her throat.

When she reached on either side of her head and withdrew the pins from her hair, she did not move. His face was so close to hers, his breath warmed her face. She stared into his eyes, not sure what emotion showed on her features. As he loosened the strands, his fingers lightly touched her skin, sending lightning-hot sparks along her.

He handed her the brush. Lowering her eyes to be able to see her fingers untangle her hair, she noted his broad hand resting on the arm of the settee so close to her. Even though he did not touch her, a warmth reached out from him to caress her.

It did not take her long to coax the hair into a pair of braids. The ends rested in her lap. She leaned over to put the brush in her bag but halted as her nose came within inches of his face.

"Excuse me. I don't want to lose my hair-brush."

Picking up one of the braids, he smiled. "A flaxen-haired squaw is a strange sight."

She stood up after pushing his hand away from her hair. Jamming the brush into the bag, she said, "If we are going to leave, I think we should spend more time making plans and less being frivolous." She looked in the cracked mirror above the washstand. She twisted the braids around the crown of her head and pinned them into place. "What do we do first?"

"*We* do nothing. I have to go and see about some horses for you and the boys this morning. All of you are small, so I think I'll get only two." There was no humor in his smile as he said, "The less I spend of your gold, the more there will be for me at journey's end."

"And that gold is all important, isn't it?" she

snapped with sudden heat.

He laughed, breaking their temporary truce. "I would not be willing to be slowed by a family of youngsters otherwise." He placed his hat on his head, grabbed the last biscuit, and mumbled a farewell around his full mouth.

No one could respond before he was gone. Lizzie ran to the door and locked it. Enraged by his taunts, she was not sure if she would reopen it when he returned. Then she knew she had no choice. Cliff was right. They were dependent on each other, even if they despised the circumstances.

Of one thing she was sure. She would not be taken in by his easy charm again. For one wonderful moment, she had thought he was being honest with her when he complimented her on her hair. She wondered if he could be honest. Like Delilah, she would have to learn not to be swayed by the sweetness of his words and his too-warm smile.

"Lizzie?" The young voice drew her back from the morass of her thoughts. Tommy asked quietly, "What gold is he talking about? We don't have any gold to pay him."

"Shh!" She put her finger against her lips. "Never say that aloud. Cliff and I have a bargain. He gets the dust in my bag in exchange for taking us east."

"Dust? Lizzie, that—"

Hating to lie to him, she knew it was the only way to satisfy him. "I have enough to pay him. Don't worry. Our bargain is struck, and we are both pleased with it. Now no more talk of gold. It is not smart to speak of it, for there are many who would try to rob us."

The two lads could understand that. They had been raised on tales of murder and betrayal where partners would do anything to gain sole control of a lode. Never would they say anything to hurt their beloved aunt. That they would keep silent was enough for Lizzie. Some things had to be kept a secret until their journey's end.

CHAPTER THREE

THE HOURS PASSED SLOWLY IN THE SMALL ROOM. For people used to fresh air blowing in their faces and the open vistas of the forested ridges, it was a prison. Only the cook came to the door when he reappeared to collect their tray. From below oozed the sounds of the saloon being readied for the evening's crowd. On the second floor, solely silence. The whores were asleep after their night's work.

Once Tommy and Pete had exhausted the delights of bouncing on the thick mattress of the narrow bed and examining every corner of the room, they grew restless. They were not interested in listening to a story.

"Lizzie, you don't tell good ones like Cliff," Tommy criticized. "Do you know any stories about Indians?"

She shook her head and smiled. Inside she

fumed. Even before they had begun their journey, Cliff was interfering in their lives. Never again would there be the oneness she and the boys had known as they depended on each other to survive their grief.

Her anger faded. Perhaps the time had come to let the sorrow go. To escape it, she wanted to return to a life she had known in simpler days. If this was the way Tommy and Pete had chosen, she could not disparage it.

Lizzie had despaired of devising any way of entertaining the boys at the time Cliff returned. He was smiling, so she knew the news must be good.

"I have two fine horses for you. Flatfoot Hans was looking to sell his team to refinance his claim, so I was able to get them for a better than fair price."

"Then we can leave in the morning?" If she had to spend more than one more night in this place, she was sure she would become insane.

"Tomorrow?" He laughed. "Impossible. I still have to go over to Mud Hollow and get some supplies for us. We can shoot meat along the way, but I need bullets and you need clothes."

Her eyes widened. "Clothes? These are serviceable. If you mean a dress, I don't—"

"A dress?" Shaking his head, he turned to the two boys. "Is your aunt always this contrary?"

Pete giggled at the comically confused expression on the man's face, while Tommy nodded with delight. She saw they were totally won over by Cliff's charismatic presence. Not that it mattered, now that her eyes were wide open to his subterfuges.

Looking back at her, he went on, "Those clothes are fine for mucking through the rubble of a hard rock mine or for panning, but the trail is rough. I'm going to get you and the boys some buckskins."

"Won't that be expensive?" She regretted the words as soon as she saw the flicker of displeasure in his stone gray eyes.

"I think that's my concern, Lizzie. I won't have my trip delayed and risk getting caught by high-country snowstorms simply because your tender backsides get saddle sore." With a loud laugh, he pointed at her face. "Do you always blush so much, girl?"

Refusing to be caught up in the amusement of the other three, she demanded, "How long will you be in Mud Hollow? It's very boring here."

"I'll be back before sundown. You don't have to stay in this room."

"Where can we go?"

He shrugged. "I don't know. Look, if it will help, I'll take the boys with me. It's an easy trip over the ridge. That way I can see how the horses do along the trail."

Eager shouts answered his offer, and Lizzie nodded reluctantly. She couldn't tell the boys they would not be allowed to go with him. Simply because she was not included in the invitation was no reason to refuse them their fun. She should be happy Cliff seemed willing to be so kind to Tommy and Pete. Most of the men in town despised the youngsters, who got in their way and reminded them of ties left far behind.

"As long as you are back by sundown, they can go," she muttered grudgingly. Her words were swallowed by the cheers of the boys.

Doffing his hat, Cliff bent deeply at the waist. "Your wish will be etched upon my heart, dear lady."

"Enough!"

Each resolution to treat him coldly was broken when he teased her. Although it was the same way he jested with the youngsters, it created a warmth inside her that had been missing in her life. Since the accident, she had had no friend to share the pain of her loss and her fears of the future.

Startled, she realized she needed a friend. Cliff Hollister might be the one she could depend on to help her reach her goals. That he would never be more she could accept, for he filled an empty spot in her life.

Squatting to face the boys, she rebuttoned their shirts and ordered them to tuck shirttails into their trousers. She handed each one his battered hat. "You listen to Cliff now, and behave yourselves so I would be proud of you."

"They'll be fine," Cliff stated. He was rewarded by grins from the children.

Rising, she watched as they raced to the door. They spun about to come back for a kiss before they left. With a laugh, she urged them to have a good time.

"They'll be fine," Cliff repeated as she glanced at him. "I promise to take good care of them. I know they're all you have left."

"They are the most important part of my world," she answered with sudden honesty. "I don't want them growing up here. I want them to have schooling and a home where there is food instead of scraps costing more than most men make in a year."

His reply was interrupted by Tommy calling, "Come on, Cliff!"

With a smile, he waved to her. Taking each boy by the hand, he walked out into the hall dappled by the gray light of the sun peeking through the clouds. By the time they returned, they would be wet and filthy, but it was good for the boys to get out of the close confines of the brothel.

She went to the window to watch them through the rain-washed streaks. The thin walls could not mask the sound of childish laughter as they mounted the three horses. Neither boy rode exceptionally well, but the road between Hopeless and Mud Hollow was not rough. There were many things she did not know about Cliff Hollister, but the affection he already shared with her nephews could not be faked.

The silence in the room grew ever more oppressive. Within minutes, she knew she could not stay there for the rest of the day. Curiosity led her feet along the corridor and toward the saloon on the floor below.

Lizzie paused on the stairs to view the room, which was even more depressing in the daylight. Without the multitude of candles that attempted to brighten it at night, it had changed into a maze of shadows and dust. She was surprised to see damp spots from the swath of a mop on the floor.

"Come down, Miss Buchanan."

She did not smile as she heard what was nothing short of an order. Her eyes pierced the gloom to pick out Delilah at a table in the far corner.

"Don't just stand there speechless, girl. Come here."

Mostly because she had nothing else to do, Lizzie followed the voice to its source. She did not scurry to obey the command, for she did not want the older woman to think Lizzie Buchanan was hers to rule as were the women who worked in the saloon. Pausing by one table to compose herself, she noted several decks of cards. Absently she picked up one pile. With it in her hands, she could hide her unease from the madam's sharp eyes.

Delilah had changed from her working dress to one much more suited to her full figure. The gray serge was decorated with pearl buttons along the high-necked bodice. Narrow black braid outlined the stovepipe-thin sleeves and accented the skirt of the conservative gown.

The owner of the saloon pushed a chair in her direction. "Sit down. I need a break from bookkeeping."

"Yes, ma'am." Lizzie was overwhelmed by the change in her hostess and fell back on the etiquette she had learned as a child. Except for her brassy blond hair, Delilah reminded her of a church-school teacher in Louisville. Both had the same overpowering presence that made it clear no nonsense would be tolerated.

Delilah cackled her ear-shattering laugh. " 'Ma'am'? The last man foolish enough to call me that got a bottle broken over his head. Deserved it, he did. I know what I am, dearie, and 'ma'am' is not the proper title."

"What do you want me to say?" demanded Lizzie, piqued that her polite words were being thrown back into her face. "Do you prefer whore or prostitute?"

"Good. You have spirit." Again Delilah laughed as the younger woman stared at her in bafflement. "You'll need that if you intend to drag those boys after Cliff Hollister."

"We will manage."

Delilah rested her elbows on the tabletop and leaned forward. "What do you have waiting for you back east? Any family?"

"None but the boys and me."

"A home? Money?"

"No."

"A lover?"

Lizzie could not control the heat beneath her collar that climbed to her cheeks. She kept her eyes lowered to the cards in her lap. In a whisper she said, "No, no one, but we will manage."

"I thought so." There was satisfaction in Delilah's voice. "You're running off without thinking about what you're leaving behind."

"Leaving behind? A mine that is a tomb for my sister and her husband? Mud and rain, heat and cold?" Lizzie smiled ironically. "I don't think I will miss any of it—" Lizzie paused, not knowing how to address the older woman.

"You can call me Delilah, dearie. It won't compromise any of your highfalutin ways." Delilah's brow wrinkled as she concentrated. "I saw the way the men reacted last night to Sam Winchester's words. Even in those clothes, you don't look half bad."

Hesitantly Lizzie replied, "Thank you."

Delilah stood up and went to the bar. Grasping two glasses and a bottle, she came back and placed them on the table. "It wasn't a compliment, dearie. Have a drink. You do drink, don't you? I am afraid I don't have sarsaparilla. My customers like hard liquor and soft women. Not the other way 'round."

Lizzie took the glass, still streaked with the dirt from the hands of its last user. In dismay, she looked at the amount of liquor in it. She sipped it daintily, but set it back on the table abruptly as the fire from the whiskey scorched her throat.

The other woman laughed before draining her glass. "Girl, you'll have to do better than that if you accept my offer."

"Offer? What offer?"

Delilah's chair protested beneath her as she sat down. She swore imaginatively, got up, pushed it away, and grasped another all in one smooth movement. With her glass in her hand and moving in rhythm with her words, she said, "Miss Buchanan . . . Lizzie, isn't it?"

"Yes." Even that word was spoken reluctantly. Lizzie gripped the edge of the table and could feel her feet beneath her tense, ready to race away from this wicked woman. Only the knowledge that

Delilah could throw them out into the street with as little compassion as Carson Emory had shown kept her from leaving.

"You saw how the men want you."

"That was only because they were drunk and Sam was egging them on."

In disbelief, the blond shook her head. "You believe that, don't you? Dearie, haven't you looked in a mirror in the past few years?"

"I have, and I know I'm no prize."

"You're blind." Delilah swallowed the glassful of whiskey and poured another. "You are as pretty as your sister, perhaps prettier; she was not as delicate as you. She did well. You could do better, for the men know you don't have a husband and two brats living on the north ridge."

Lizzie tried to speak, but the words burned in her throat as harshly as the whiskey had minutes before. Delilah's face wavered in front of her as she tried to control the nausea in her stomach. When the glass was pressed into her hands and she heard a far-off voice command her to drink, she compliantly lifted it to her lips. The searing power of the liquor cut through the cobwebs of her shock.

"You didn't know!" This time Delilah's laughing words did not reverberate as if from the far end of a tunnel.

"No," Lizzie whispered. Suddenly her strong will reasserted itself. In a louder voice, she stated, "And I don't believe you! Whitney was not—she was not—"

"A whore?" Delilah finished. "No, she wasn't, but she worked for me the summer after she weaned that little one. The mine had taken all their money, and you would have starved otherwise. She worked only long enough to earn the four hundred dollars she needed to buy a barrel of wheat flour so you could make it through the winter."

Lizzie closed her eyes in pain. It was easy to recall how Whitney had dragged herself about that summer. Zach had been working nearly twenty-four hours a day at the mine, so he had no idea where his wife was when he thought she was home with her children. Lizzie remembered taking care of the baby while she thought her sister was helping out at the Morgans' household with Mrs. Morgan's latest baby. That was the story Whitney told everyone when she gave Zach the money for the flour.

Not once had Lizzie suspected Whitney was lying and living a life so different from the one she had been raised to expect would be hers. Lizzie wondered if her sister had ever told her husband. She doubted it, for Zach would not have been able to conceal his rage.

Hiding her face in her hands, she asked herself how she could have been so stupid. No one made that kind of money helping a neighbor. She had not wanted to know what Whitney was doing, and she did not want to face it now.

Delilah's harsh voice cut into her thoughts. "Come on, dearie. It's not so horrible. She did a good job for me and quit as soon as she had her four hundred dollars." With a wave of her glass she ordered, "Forget that! It was two years ago. What

I want to know is if you would like to replace Patsy."

"Me?" Lizzie squeaked.

"Why not? You would look right pretty in the gowns the girls wear. You get to keep half of what you earn. If you want to provide for those boys of yours, this is the best way." Grimly Delilah added, "What else are you going to do but sell yourself to some eastern gent anyhow? Why get stuck with just one? Here you can be treated like a queen."

Although Lizzie tried to halt it, the sound of laughter spilled from her lips to splash like droplets of sunshine in the dark room. Rising, she leaned on the rounded back of the chair.

"No, thank you, Delilah. I know how I will be treated if I am forced to share my bed with Sam Winchester and his cronies. I think I will take my chances back east."

Delilah cursed angrily. "You fool, no man will marry you when you have those two brats. Do you think any man would want to give you his name when he learned you have been traveling with Cliff Hollister alone through the mountains and across the desert?"

"I will take that chance," Lizzie reiterated calmly.

Delilah stood and pounded on the table, which shivered under the force of her blow. "You are stupid! Do you know how much money is being gambled on whether Cliff will take you with him or simply take your virginity from you and abandon you here?"

"That is no one's business!" Lizzie snapped.

"Don't waste your money betting against me, Delilah, because when we leave, it will be together."

She whirled to go out the door. Seeing the rain had returned to swamp the street in ankle-deep mire, she changed direction and climbed the stairs. Although she heard the woman's command to think again about her offer, she did not pause to acknowledge it in any way.

Locking the door, which reverberated from her vicious slam, she slid down to the floor. With her head on her drawn-up knees, she began to cry. All her life she had idolized her older sister. Whitney was the one touted as the beauty of the family. Lizzie had found it easier to remain in the background, accepting bits of praise for her brains. From her earliest memories, she knew her family felt that being intelligent was not as important for a woman as being pretty.

Maybe they had been wrong. She was wise enough to know that selecting the life Delilah offered would be the most idiotic thing she could do. With clearer vision, she could now see how Whitney's experiences at Delilah's had changed her radically. After that summer, Whitney no longer sang while she worked. When one of the miners came to the cabin, she would not speak to him unless absolutely necessary.

What Lizzie had thought was shyness was in truth shame. Although she had done what she thought was right, Whitney had compromised everything in which she believed. Instead of using her often admired assets to pay for her husband's dream, she should have come to Zach and Lizzie for help. Together they could have found a way to survive, or they could have admitted defeat.

Lizzie cried for her sister's broken soul, destroyed long before a fault brought down rocks to seal her into the mountain. More than ever, Lizzie was determined to take the boys and leave. She did not want them to have to choose between eating and doing what they knew was wrong.

Even after the tears ceased falling, she did not move until her body grew cramped against the carved surface of the door. Her palms were pitted by the rough texture of the worn rug. Standing up, she rubbed the lower region of her back.

Her brow wrinkled as she felt something in her pocket. She stared at the pack of cards she withdrew. At least she would have some way of entertaining the boys. All of them enjoyed playing cards, for it had been one of the few pastimes they could afford in the hut on the ridge.

She went to the bag that held all she owned. She put the playing cards inside and started to close it. Then she undid the latch. She slowly withdrew the miniature of her sister.

Whitney resembled an angel. Her white lace dress was the one she had worn to the church social the day Zach asked her to marry him. That was the way Lizzie wanted to think of her sister, not as one of the overworked, haunted women taking the miners to her bed in exchange for gold as cold and loveless as what they shared there.

"I will take care of them, Whitney," she vowed as if for the first time. "Tommy and Pete will never know how you sacrificed to let us live.

But, Whitney, why didn't you ask me to help?"

There was no answer for that or any of the other questions haunting her. She dropped stomach first onto the covers and watched the rain drizzling along the window. Its patterns never changed as the drops followed the same paths along the uneven, hand-blown glass.

As it grew dark, she lit the pair of candles and put one in the window. The light was reflected from the glass to brighten the room. When the food tray arrived from the kitchen, she was somewhat surprised. She had half expected to be asked to leave.

She picked at the food, not interested in eating. A knock on the door and the sound of a familiar voice calling her name caused her to leap from the bed to the door in a single step. Flinging it open, she held out her hands. She gathered the boys close to her, smothering their words as she hugged them tightly. Their own happy adventures went untold as she began to weep again.

"Lizzie, honey, don't cry. We're not that late. The road mired us a bit." A damp hand on her hair tilted her head back to meet Cliff's eyes, as dark as the clouded night sky. "You weren't worried about the boys while they were with me, were you?"

Biting her lip to keep it from trembling, she murmured, "No, of course not, Cliff." She stood up and turned to wipe her eyes on her sleeve. "Forgive me."

"What's wrong?"

"Not now." She gave the boys a watery smile. "Too many ears."

Instantly he understood. Downstairs, Delilah had hinted to him that he might be traveling alone and to enjoy Miss Buchanan while he could. He guessed exactly what had happened during the time he and the youngsters were away at Mud Hollow. If Delilah had asked him, he would have told her not to waste her time. Despite Lizzie Buchanan's rustic clothes, she was not the type to work in Delilah's Den.

Walking into the room, he dropped his wet hat and cloak on the floor. From beneath his coat, he pulled a wrapped packet. "For you, Lizzie."

"For me?"

He untied the dark stock at his collar. "I told you I was going to buy you some clothes for the trail. Try them on."

"Now?"

"Sure. Put them on over your denims. That is how you'll wear them once we get to the higher altitudes. It gets cold there early in the season." He sat down in the chair, disregarding the water dripping from him. "Go ahead."

"Come on, Lizzie," urged Tommy. He was stripping off his wet clothes and climbing under the covers as she had ordered.

As she finished undressing his younger brother, she smiled. "Very well. When you have been so generous, Cliff, the least I can do is try them on."

He mumbled something through a mouthful of roast chicken, but she paid him no mind. She wanted to be happy, not think of his barbed retorts. Unwrapping the brown paper, she lifted out buckskin pants and a fringed shirt like the ones she had seen mountain men wear when they came into the settlement.

The shirt went easily over her clothes. She tied the thongs that laced the front. It fit well, which did not astonish her. She would have guessed Cliff a good judge of women's forms. The sleeves were too long, but she knew they could be cut to the proper length with a well-honed knife. Kicking off her boots, she pulled on the leggings. She tucked in the shirt, but the waist was far too wide.

For a moment she frowned. Inspiration came as she noted the string that had closed the packet. Threading it through the belt slits at the top of the trousers, she tightened the girth to fit her.

"Well?" she asked as she spun to face Cliff.

His smile faded as he became as motionless as a statue. Then he slowly rose to his feet. Disquiet overwhelmed her as she stared at him. She could feel his eyes moving along her but was not sure what was wrong. Her hands smoothed the soft material over her hips. She didn't think she had dressed incorrectly.

Cliff swallowed the half-chewed meat in his mouth with difficulty. He could not take his eyes from her. In her baggy clothes, it had been easy to think of her as an urchin. The buckskins cinched at her narrow waist accented the feminine curves of her body, which told him she was definitely no child.

How he had laughed when he thought of Lizzie working for Delilah, sure that few men would choose this child over the more voluptuous women available. He was the one who was mistaken, not the madam. With her experienced eye, she had seen what he had missed.

Lizzie Buchanan was a beautiful woman, as delicate as a spring blossom and as elusive as the first star in the evening sky. When he heard her speak his name in the breathy voice that reached inside him and stirred up his gut, he forced his eyes back to hers.

"Is something wrong?" she asked.

"No, you look fine, Lizzie." He dropped the remains of his chicken on the tray. "I'll see you in the morning."

"You're leaving?" Her smile disappeared, to be replaced by the stern expression he was more accustomed to seeing on her face.

With his hand on the doorknob, he shrugged eloquently. "I thought I would go downstairs. Leave the door unlocked. I won't be back until after you are in bed."

In confusion, she asked, "You're coming back here to sleep?"

"It's my room. You've reminded me of that more than once!" he snapped with sudden venom. "Just leave me the damned settee, woman, and I will come back when I please."

"Cliff—?"

The crash of the door as it closed cut off her words. She stared at it in complete shock. Despite his orders, she pushed the bolt on the door. With all the depraved men frequenting Delilah's, she did not intend to leave it unlocked as an open invitation to trouble.

"Lizzie, what's wrong with Cliff?"

She shook her head as she turned to look at the children's unhappy faces. "I don't know, Tommy. Did he say anything about any problem to you?"

"No," Tommy replied, not having to take time to think about it. During their journey of four miles in each direction, Cliff had joked with them and entertained them with more stories of his exploits on the road west.

"Eat your supper," she said absently as she untied the makeshift belt at her waist.

Taking off the new clothes, she folded them carefully and put them on the chair. She listened silently as the boys told her of their day. She made the right comments in all the appropriate places, but she was paying little attention to their often confusing stories of the day's events.

What *was* wrong with Cliff?

One minute he had been delightfully friendly as he urged her to try on the lovely clothing he had purchased for her. The next he was as cold to her as a mountain morning. She wondered if he thought she was ungrateful for the fine outfit, for he had not given her time to tell him how happy she was with it. That could not be the problem. What was, she had no idea.

After she had tucked the boys into bed and put the tray outside the door, she sat on the settee and stared into the darkness. When the noise of the festivities below drifted up the stairs, it was a siren song, urging her to join the others. She resisted, wallowing in her own unhappiness.

She did not understand Cliff, and she did not know what would happen when they were on the way east together. Although she tried to discount them, Delilah's words remained in her head. The owner of the saloon was better acquainted with Cliff. Yet Lizzie remained sure he would not abandon them on the trail.

Or would he even take them when he left?

To herself, she had to admit she had been afraid he would not return that evening. He had made it clear he was fond of the youngsters but was only tolerating her presence. In the back of her mind had been the horror that he would take the boys and just keep on going east, leaving her in Hopeless with the choice of accepting either Sam or Delilah's offer.

She wrapped her arms around herself as she stood up. Tiptoeing across the room in her stocking feet, she climbed into the huge bed. Its squeak was ear shattering in the darkness, but the children only murmured before nestling down into the feather bed again.

Time passed with infinite slowness as she stared at the invisible ceiling above her. When in the hours past midnight there was a knock on the door, she rose and opened it to allow a whiskey-pungent Cliff into the room.

"Thank you," he whispered.

"You're welcome. Good night." She turned to go back to bed, although she doubted if she would sleep."

He took her arm and drew her back toward him. Her hissed protest sounded loud in the quiet room, but he ignored it. Other than his grip on her elbow, he did not touch her. When he placed his face close to hers, she coughed as she was swept by the conflicting odors of drink and the heavy perfume favored by Delilah's women.

"Don't stay here, Lizzie. Delilah will allow the men to use you up until there is nothing left of your luscious beauty."

"Cliff, let me go," she ordered quietly. "You are drunk. You don't know what you are saying!"

Insulted, he demanded, "I don't know—? Oh, all right. I know the boys are sleeping." There was irritation in his lowered voice. "I have had a few drinks with friends I won't see until next season, but I'm not drunk. This is free advice for you, honey. No matter what Delilah has offered you, don't accept it."

"I don't intend to, even though she offered me half of all I could coerce from the miners. Will you let me go to sleep?"

"Half?" His profanity was choked by his outrage. "Most of the women get to keep two-thirds of what they earn. She was going to cheat you—"

A soft laugh interrupted him. "Cliff, I told her no, so it doesn't matter if she was going to take advantage of my innocence. Now go to sleep. Don't worry about something that will not happen."

He did not release her as he stared down into her face, barely visible in the twilight created by the glow that crept from the hall past his large form. Innocence was exactly the right word for this child-woman. When Delilah had bragged to him that night that he would be traveling alone, he learned why Lizzie had cried earlier when she saw the children.

He remembered the Greenway woman from the trip west. Her blond, faerylike beauty had not appealed to him. What Lizzie's sister had suffered, he would be sure Lizzie was spared.

Lizzie stiffened as she felt the gentle stroke of his fingers on her arm. Reaching across her body, she put her hand over his to peel his fingers from her elbow. She could not read his expression, but some inner sense warned her of danger.

"Good night, Cliff," she said pointedly.

"Lizzie . . ."

"Don't say anything except good night. I have had a horrible day, and I don't want to start the new one by arguing with you."

He smiled at her candid words. "All right, honey. Go back to bed. Sunrise is plenty early for us to begin snapping at one another again." He rumpled her hair as he would the youngsters'. "I think you and I are going to have a fun and loud trip east, Lizzie."

"Loud, anyway." She laughed as she crossed the room.

Climbing beneath the covers, she drew them up to her chin. She heard his footsteps on the other side of the room, and she could identify Cliff's actions without looking at him. He placed his gun belt on the chair and drew off his boots. Only when she knew he was sitting on the settee did she close her eyes.

For the first time she was anxious to start the journey with Cliff. As he had said, it would be fun and undoubtedly very stormy as both of them vied for control. Smiling into the musty pillow, she decided those arguments would just be another part of the fun.

CHAPTER FOUR

WITH ALL THE WORK THEY HAD TO DO BEFORE they left Hopeless, the day sped by far more quickly than had the two previous ones. Despite their dark predictions in the middle of the night, both Cliff and Lizzie made an effort to be congenial. More than once she bit back sharp words when he gave her an order. She was sure some of her comments irritated him just as much.

Cliff volunteered to ride out to the mine so the boys could say a final good-bye to the only home they had known until a month ago. Thanking him, she refused to go along. She had said her farewells when she sold the claim to another miner who possessed dreams of gold.

Once she had returned there. At the wind-battered cabin, she found the other miner already had taken up residence. He was not there when she arrived, but his personal possessions littered the

once-clean floor. That sight made it easier to close
the door on the past. She did not need to go back
and see the imposing cliffs of the ridge where two
people had died on a fog-gray spring morning.

She did take the boys for a walk along the
creek, so they could play once more in their
favorite spots. When they walked back into
Hopeless, Lizzie regarded the town with objective
eyes. The buildings appeared to be held together by
patchwork and prayer and leaned in the direction
of the prevalent wind. Their built-up facades made
them appear taller than the two stories they
actually boasted. A group of men lounged in front
of the assayer's office hoping to be the first to hear
of a new strike. Few of the stakes in this area
proved to be worth the effort required to wrest the
gold from the earth, but that did not deter the
dreamers.

She tightened her grip on the boys' hands as
they entered Delilah's. She looked directly in front
of her as she heard the buzz of conversation from
the saloon. The owner's strident voice drowned out
the others.

"Well, if it isn't *Miss* Buchanan."

"Tommy, Pete, go on upstairs. Quickly," she
urged. She did not want them to hear any poisoned
words Delilah might say. There was no need for
them ever to know the truth. Remembering not to
put too much weight on the cracked staircase
railing, she stopped halfway up and turned to
speak to Delilah. "Good afternoon. If you will
excuse me, we have a few tasks to complete before
our departure from your fine business emporium."

Delilah laughed, although the other women were shocked into silence by the aura of mutual dislike that seemed to hang in the air. "Mighty uppity, aren't you, dearie? So was your sister until we taught her a few things."

"I am glad I will not be required to attend the same lessons," Lizzie said, although she winced internally at the crass words.

"So you're really going east?" Delilah crossed the room to stand at the foot of the staircase. Today she was wearing a revealing gown bedecked with ruffles and bows, and she appeared every bit the madam of the brothel. "Dearie, you'll be sorry. Didn't anyone ever tell you the truth about Cliff Hollister? He has made love to enough women to stretch from here to St. Louis. You'll just be another."

Rigidly, Lizzie stated, "I will remind you that Mr. Hollister and I have a business relationship. I have no interest in his personal affairs." She blanched at her own unfortunate choice of words.

Hoots of disbelief echoed in the room as the women at the bar nudged one another with their elbows. Delilah's feline grin broadened as she said, "Believe that if you wish, dearie, but don't forget my warning when you and he are alone midway up a mountain. You're the kind to lose your heart to any man you take to your bed. Beware, dearie. He will make you sorry you ever left Hopeless."

"I doubt that."

"We shall see who is the wiser when spring arrives. Just remember that my offer is good only until you walk out that door with him. If you want to stay and work, you have to decide now."

Lizzie had regained her composure and smiled coldly. "I cannot tell you how much that breaks my heart, Delilah. If you will excuse me, I must speak with Cliff about—"

"Yes, I've been wondering where you were," sounded a growl from the shadowy second-floor corridor.

Lizzie's smile became sincere as she looked up the stairs to see the tall man who appeared as lofty as the giant sequoias that grew in the countryside around Hopeless. From where he stood, none of the others could see him. He gave her a lazy wink. As he walked down the stairs, his gray eyes twinkled merrily over his scowl.

"I was coming, Cliff, but Delilah—"

Viciously he stated, "You know I told you to get back here right away! Woman, you had better learn now that I am the boss, or you will learn it the hard way on the trail."

"I am sorry. Really I am!" She shrieked in mock terror as he took her arm and pulled her up the stairs.

"You will be when I'm done with you."

The women in the saloon glanced at each other as they heard Lizzie cry out again just before the door slammed on the second floor. When they heard their employer give a satisfied chuckle, they began to giggle.

The too-proper Lizzie Buchanan would get her comeuppance from Cliff Hollister. As they began to imagine aloud what he would do to her, they grew weak with laughter. Seeing the young woman dragged up the stairs put Delilah in such a good mood, she ordered a serving of whiskey for everyone.

In the room above, much softer laughter was being shared by the four partners. Lizzie shook her head when Cliff asked her if he had really hurt her.

"No, and thank you yet again. I owe you more than I can repay."

"I thought Delilah would be much happier thinking I was abusing you." His hand was on her arm, and he slid it upward to drape it over her shoulders. As she laughed, glad to be away from Delilah's vicious glare, she leaned her head unselfconsciously against his chest. His finger under her chin tilted her face up to look at his.

In the middle of a word she had been saying to Tommy, her voice vanished. As she beheld Cliff's wolf-pelt gray eyes, she became aware of the lean line of his body so close to hers. She knew she should step away, but as she put her hand up to push against his chest, he turned her into his embrace.

His gaze drifted across her face as he examined each inch of it intimately. When he put his hand on her cheek, she closed her eyes to savor the tender touch. A single finger traced the high bones of her cheeks and the narrow surface of her nose. As it moved to her lips, she looked at him once more. The feather-soft stroke of his fingertip along the fullness of her bottom lip created a warmth that spread from her center to weaken all her limbs.

Continuing to outline the pink moistness of her mouth, he whispered huskily, "Honey, I cannot

understand why anyone would want to hurt you
when there would be so much more pleasure in—"

"No, Cliff, I—I—"

"I know, the boys." He looked over her head.
The youngsters were more interested in the pieces
of candy he had purchased for them at the store in
Mud Hollow than in what the adults were doing.

She shook her head. "It's not just the boys."

"You believe what Delilah said," he said
sorrowfully.

"How much did you hear?"

He released her. His lighthearted grin surprised her. "Enough to know that my reputation
remains as outrageous as ever."

"Is it only reputation? Delilah seems unduly
concerned about my physical well-being on this
trip."

"She's trying to scare you." He stepped over
the boys on the floor as he went toward the bed.
On it were the last of the unpacked items. As he
spoke, he finished placing the things in his canvas
saddlebag. "You know she wants you here working
for her."

Putting her fists on her hips, Lizzie spat,
"Never! I would starve first. I would sleep with
Sam Winchester first."

"Or me?"

"Cliff!" She colored as she went to sit on the
settee. It was impossible to explain the difference to
him without revealing the undeveloped feeling
roiling within her. "Will you stop it? It is not
funny."

He sighed and sat on the bed. "You must be

tired, Lizzie, if you can't come back with a sharp answer to my jokes. I suggest you get a good night's sleep later. You hardly closed your eyes at all last night."

"H-how did you know?" She wondered if he could read her thoughts as easily as her feelings. The idea made her feel naked before him.

"You get used to being aware of every noise when you're on watch on the trail. This bed squeaks like a woman screaming in the night. I heard each time you or the boys moved." He grinned roguishly as he motioned with his hand. "Come here."

"Come there?" she gasped in horror.

With a grimace, he said, "Look, honey, it's going to be you and me and those youngsters alone for a very long time. If you can't trust me here when there are many women more desirable than a little girl dressed in oversized men's clothing, then we might as well forget about this journey right now."

Lizzie blinked rapidly as she fought to hold in the tears that filled her eyes at his callous words. If only he could know how she pined to wear a gown again, to feel the gentle swell of calico billowing about her ankles, to wear satin slippers instead of these heavy boots. "But just a moment ago over there by the door—"

"You made your feelings very clear," he finished. "We are partners, Lizzie. I think we should leave it at that. You want nothing else, and you are right. You're a nice girl, and you don't need someone like me to mess up your life."

"Cliff, don't say things like that."

He smiled sadly. "It's the truth though, isn't it? You are going home to make a life for yourself. This is my life. Hard work half the year leading tenderfeet across the prairie, and the other half going from one drinking binge to the next. Playing cards and consorting with the kind of woman you will never be." He shrugged. "Not that I'm complaining, mind you. I like my life, and I don't want to change it, especially not for you, honey. So we'll be partners on the trail and keep it like that. Now come over here and sit down."

She would not let him know how much he had hurt her. With her head high, she crossed the room and sat next to him. Perhaps it was better that he thought of her simply as his companion on the trail. As he had said, she must trust him, or there would be problems while they were far from any settlements.

"Good girl," he said. He grinned at her, but it was nothing like the expression he had worn when she was in his arms by the door and he had caressed her with his eyes.

She tried not to feel insulted, but she did. Three years before, she had longed to have him notice her as she watched him walk past their wagon. A pat on the head then was her reward, and nothing had changed.

While she listened to him telling her about their route and what would be expected of her, she sternly told herself she was acting like a fool. Cliff Hollister clearly was determined to treat her and the boys well. She should be grateful. Now she did not have to worry about fighting off his unwanted advances on the trail. She had had enough of wrestling with Sam Winchester. She should have been happy, but she was not.

After dinner that night, Lizzie and the boys sat silently watching Cliff finish shaving. He grimaced as he splashed his face with bay rum. Unable to watch the masculine ritual because of the uncomfortable yet pleasant sensations it aroused, she aimlessly crossed the room. A smile tilted her lips when she saw the saddlebags. Opening hers, she pulled out the deck of cards.

The boys let out a whoop of excitement when she called to them and urged them to join her. Let Cliff go play his games downstairs. They didn't need him to enjoy themselves. She listened to the children chatter as she delt out the cards for one of the games they knew. Whitney had been insistent that they not gamble, so Lizzie chose a simple game for them.

"What are you doing?" Cliff leaned on the bed and glanced over to where the three sat on the floor. His dark eyebrows formed a line across his forehead. "Lizzie, you are very good at handling cards."

She lifted her hand of cards and regarded him coolly. "I've had practice. We enjoyed playing cards at the Whitney's Dream. Go ahead, Pete. You start."

Although he knew she was angry at him for going out again that evening, he watched them for a few minutes. Lizzie's slender fingers cupped the cards easily. His eyes were held by the flashing laugher in hers as she helped the younger boy play his cards.

Love like this made him envious and extremely uncomfortable. Bits of it splashed over onto him when he spoke to the boys, but most of it was reserved for their tightly closed family circle. With a silent groan of frustration, he whirled to finish dressing for the evening's festivities downstairs.

When he was ready, he walked around the bed. He tweaked both of the boys' noses, and they giggled. His hand paused in midair as he was about to touch Lizzie's hair. With an odd expression, he turned away to check his stock. He adjusted it with a flair before the mirror.

"Lock the door when I leave. I'll knock twice when I come back. Don't open it unless you know it's me." He glared at her. "Don't be as foolish as you were last night, when you opened it without asking who was there."

"You told me not to lock it last night. Now you scold me?"

He smiled superiorly. "I knew you would bolt it. One thing I like about you, Lizzie. You have plenty of common sense. It will help us while we travel."

"I know." She pouted; she was becoming exasperated by his continual insistence on treating her like one of the boys.

He turned to leave, then paused. "Lizzie, how about an advance?"

"What?"

"A bit of the gold. I could turn it into a fortune tonight."

She scowled, her brown eyes forbidding. "Or you could lose it all. No, Cliff. I said you'd get it when you deliver us to the Mississippi safely. Not before."

Grasping her shoulders, he drew her to her feet. "I've spent all my remaining money providing for you. You can give me a small piece of gold."

Fearfully she stared up into his eyes. She did not like him when he was like this, for he frightened her. Cautiously she drew away from him. She could not let him know why she was afraid. Reaching into the pocket of her denim trousers, she withdrew a precious coin. It was her last.

"Thanks, Lizzie. I knew I could count on you."

"This is it. No more until we reach our destination."

He grinned, amused by her unbending stance. If she knew how much he delighted in teasing her, he thought, she would quickly see through him. Every time he caught himself thinking of her too much, his best defense was to taunt her until she pushed him away from her. The only way he could deal with her was to keep her off guard, since he didn't know of any other way to handle the odd feelings she generated inside him.

He had never met a woman like her—she was one of a kind. He was finding himself too fascinated by her rag-doll winsomeness and steely strength.

"Go to sleep, honey. We have a long trip tomorrow. I want you to be fresh for the journey."

Lizzie sat on the floor again and picked up her cards. "And you?"

He laughed lustily. "I've never missed a wagon call, Lizzie. I won't be late in the morning." With a wink at the boys he was gone.

Her feet felt heavy as, standing up again, she crossed the room to the door and threw the bolt. Clapping her hands, she said to the boys with false gaiety, "You heard Cliff. Into bed. Let's get to sleep."

"Do you think we'll see some real Indians tomorrow? Do you think we'll see a bear. Do you think—?"

Smiling, she nodded. "Tommy, I am sure we will see all that and more, but only if you go to sleep now. You know Cliff won't take you if you aren't wide awake in the morning."

She kissed each boy and blew out the candles on the windowsill. As she sat on the settee, she could hear their muffled whispers from beneath the covers. The sound recalled the nights when, as children, she and Whitney were safely ensconced in their bed in the loft of the house in Louisville. That seemed a century ago. Who would have thought things would turn out as they had?

She wondered if she would ever be able to rid herself of the image of Whitney dressed like one of those women downstairs, serving the needs of any man who could afford to pay her price. Her sister had been so lovely, Lizzie was sure that price had been high.

It had all ended with a crash echoing on the mountainside. Again she could hear her own screams as she clawed at the rocks until blood flowed down her arms. Only when the sun set behind the western hills did she realize there was no reason to continue. In all that time, she had not moved more than a small pile of rubble.

She shook her head to clear it of these horrible thoughts. It would be better to think of the hours they'd spent racing through the thick grass of the Kentucky hills and playing among the trees in the fields behind their parents' house. Finding a comforting memory, she drew it around her like a warm coat to protect her from the coldness of the present.

When the double knock resounded on the door, she was startled awake. She didn't realize she had fallen asleep on the uncomfortable settee as she reminisced. Stumbling to the door, she rubbed the sleep from her eyes and yawned.

"Is that you, Cliff? Have you lost it all already?" she asked as she reached for the bolt. When she heard a mumbled assent from the other side, she pushed the bolt aside and opened the door.

Light from the lanterns in the hall blinded her. Her sleep-slowed reflexes kept her from evading the hands that reached for her. The scream erupting from her throat was cut off by a palm over her mouth. Several forms crowded into the room. From the bed came the cries of the two youngsters as they were routed awake.

"Shut those brats up, will you?" spat a too

familiar voice loud in her ears.

Twisting her head, she looked up to see Sam Winchester holding her. Her panic metamorphosed instantaneously into rage. Although she should have expected such antics from this idiot, she was tired of fighting him off all the time.

"Get the kids. I'll need them to keep her in line at the Dry Gulch." He bent to whisper in her ear. "You will be good, won't you, Lizzie, to keep your boys from getting hurt by a very lonesome man?"

She looked across the room and saw the children being held as securely as she was. Her curses were mumbled against his hand. As Sam spoke softly to his compatriots, she moved her mouth slightly.

When she bit him, he shrieked in pain. He lifted his hand high and she cringed, closing her eyes. The battering she anticipated never came. Instead she was released quickly and pushed against someone. Together they tumbled to the floor as, amid confused shouts, the room cleared.

"Damn! Woman, can't you ever—"

"Be quiet!" she snapped as she tried to control her dizzy head. Cliff's body was as rock hard as it appeared, and her head ached where it had impacted against him. She scowled as she smelled the odor of liquor. "If you were interested in something other than drinking Delilah's cheap whiskey, you could have made him pay for this."

"Next time I'll let you deal with your heartsick lovers alone."

She snarled, "Cliff Hollister, will you please just shut up?"

"Look, honey, let's get one thing straight—"

Ignoring his comments, she pushed against his chest to help herself rise to her feet as she heard a sob from across the room. His complaint did not reach her ears as she ran to the bed.

Holding out her arms, she felt a small form nestle close to her. "It's all right, Pete. Sam won't bully us anymore. It's over, darling. Shh! It's all right." She held him close as she called out to his brother. When she received no answer, she repeated his name more loudly.

Fear cut into her like a heated brand. For a moment she froze, afraid even to think that what was in her mind could be true. Then she screamed hysterically. Scooping up the child, she raced toward the door.

Cliff steadied her as she nearly fell over him, blinded by her panic. He leapt to his feet as he fought her to keep her from streaking out of the room. In her condition, she was sure to injure herself and whoever stood in her way.

"Let me go!"

"Whoa, honey. You can't go after Winchester. He'll be halfway to his mine by now."

Her voice broke as she sagged against him. Tears running down her cheeks seeped through his thin shirt. "Cliff, Tommy is gone!"

"Gone?" He released her so rapidly she rocked on her feet. As she had done, he ran to the bed.

Instantly he discovered what she had. He lit the candle and searched the room. It took only seconds to learn the truth.

"Sam took him," Lizzie moaned. "Oh, he'll hurt him just to hurt me."

Cliff swallowed the curse on his lips as he saw her pale face. Reaching for the pistol in his gun belt, he checked it to be sure it was loaded. With a grim expression, he placed it carefully back in the holster. He picked his hat up from the floor and dusted it off on his sleeve before placing it on his head.

"Wait here! I—"

"No!" she cried. Putting the three-year-old down, she crossed the room to stand next to the enraged man. "Don't you see? This is what Sam hopes you'll do. He'll send Tommy out to the Dry Gulch with one of his men. When you chase after him, he'll come back here for Pete and me."

"Let him come" shouted the little boy. "I will—"

Cliff reached out his arms for the child, picked him up, and tapped his nose. "Hush, Pete. We'll need you to be quiet if we're going to outsmart this weasel. Lizzie, is there more than one way to this Dry Gulch place?"

"Yes. We can go over Blackman's Ridge to reach it. It won't be easy in the dark, but . . ." She didn't finish as she thought of how frightened Tommy would be. More than ever, she despised Sam. She was determined he would pay for making Tommy suffer.

"Get your things. It's close enough to daylight. We're leaving Hopeless by way of the Dry Gulch Mine."

"How will we get Tommy back? There were at

least five of them."

Cliff smiled with a ferocity that made every other emotion she had seen on his face pale by comparison. "We'll have to make up our plan as we go, Lizzie. Until I know what Winchester has up his sleeve, we have to pretend we are falling into his trap. Go down the back stairs and wait by the door for me. Don't go outside. I'll settle up with Delilah and then meet you there." He started out the door with the boy in his arms. Turning, he said sternly, "Don't go outside, Lizzie! Only together can we rescue him."

"I know." She wanted to say more, but her mind was too numb to form the words.

Picking up her two saddlebags as well as the one Cliff had packed for himself, she slung them over her shoulders. As she went out of the room, they banged into her shoulder blades in tempo with her steps.

Glad of the freedom of movement afforded by her denims, she moved cautiously along the passageway. She lurked in the shadows to avoid being seen. Not knowing how far Sam might have carried his evil plan, she couldn't guess whether he had left someone behind at Delilah's to snare her. She did not want anyone to remember that she had come this way. When she saw an open door, she peered in to be sure nobody was lying in wait for her.

The room was empty, but she saw a gun belt, complete with pistol, on a chest. Scooping it up, she hitched it around her. Her waist was too small even for the tightest cinch, but it rested comfortably on her hips. With her shirt over it, no one would guess she was now armed.

Her thievery didn't bother her; she was contemplating murder. She wouldn't be afraid to use the gun at the Dry Gulch Mine. All she could think of now was rescuing Tommy from Sam Winchester. The knowledge that he expected her to run headlong into any trap he set, using her nephew as bait, did not deter her from doing what she felt she must to rescue Tommy.

Although it seemed an eternity, in reality she did not have long to wait for Cliff. He still held Pete securely. Nodding toward the door, he signaled for her to open it. She noted he held his gun ready. It was comforting to know this strong, intelligent man was on her side.

Silently they skulked across the back of the saloon to the stables. She held Pete's hand while she watched Cliff saddle their horses and secure their bags behind the saddles.

When she was about to put the child on her horse, he whispered, "No, Lizzie, I'll take Pete. You lead the other horse. I know Shadow well, and he knows me. We can handle the extra burden of the boy."

She didn't argue but simply mounted as he sat Pete before him in the saddle. Reaching behind her, she took the lead of the other horse. Without waiting to see if she was ready, Cliff ordered his horse to a gallop out of the stable yard.

Once they were past the small settlement, he slowed to let Lizzie draw even with him. She pointed the way along the moonlit hills. The Dry

Gulch Mine was about five miles north of the Greenways' claim.

"We can drop Pete off at Marta Seeckt's house. She and her husband Elbert hate Sam because he tried to cheat Elbert out of his stake when they first arrived."

"Good," Cliff said grimly. "I want to have both hands free when we meet up with Winchester."

She didn't say anything as she urged her steed along the path toward the small cabin where her friends lived. When she knew Pete was safe, she would be able to concentrate on rescuing Tommy and forcing Sam to pay for the awful things he had done. As she bounced along on the back of the horse, the pistol slapped against her thigh harshly. Each time it hit her leg, the bruises it caused got worse and her fury increased.

At the Seeckts', Cliff did not dismount as she went to pound on the door. A bleary-eyed Elbert came to the door. He was a squat man, not much taller than Lizzie, but his rage was towering as he heard her rapid explanation.

"Hollister ist going vid ye?" he asked in his thick German accent. "Good man. *Ja*, ve vill take Pete. Do ye vant me to go vid ye?"

"We'll manage. Just take care of Pete, please."

He nodded as she ran to the horse to take the child. She whispered into Pete's ear that she wanted him to stay with the Seeckts and guard them. She was sure if he thought he was helping, he would be more cooperative.

Cliff said nothing until she remounted after kissing Pete farewell and tying the extra horse to a tree in the yard. Then he said, "Ready, honey? You can stay here too, if you like."

"No. I want to see Sam squirm when we force him to give Tommy back to us."

"This is no game." He twisted in the saddle to look at her. "If Winchester decides to fight, it could be very nasty."

She frowned. "You aren't going to talk me out of riding up to the Dry Gulch with you, Cliff Hollister. Tommy is my nephew, and I want to—"

With a laugh, he put up his hands in a gesture of defeat. "All right, honey. Let's go."

Lizzie did not smile as she set her horse on the shortest route to the Dry Gulch Mine. Her easy nature would not reassert itself until she was sure her nephew was safe. Grimly she wondered what the price of his freedom would be. In spite of the dangers and the fears, there was a warm feeling inside her as she realized she and the boys were no longer alone. Cliff's unquestioning assistance strengthened her to do what she must.

Her fingers lingered over the hard butt of the gun on her hip. She prayed she wouldn't hesitate to use it if it became necessary.

An hour later, a bush overlooking a nondescript clearing moved slightly. Two faces peered out to view the ravaged area. What once had been a pristine forest glade was littered with rusting tools and trash. A cabin whose roof sagged dangerously in the center stood to one side, next to a creek that glittered intermittently in the dim light.

"There," Lizzie whispered as she crawled forward slightly to point out the landmarks to her companion. "See that bit of light there? That's Sam's cabin. To the north and about halfway up the ridge is the Dry Gulch Mine. I doubt if he took Tommy there. There would be too much chance of Tommy escaping in the dark."

Cliff murmured, "Wait here." Then he said quietly, "This shouldn't take too long."

She put her hand on his arm to keep him from rising. "No, Cliff. I won't let us be separated. We're partners in this as well."

"Honey, you're safe up here on the ridge. You don't have anything to worry about here."

"I am not worried!" she spat out. "I want to see that snake pay for scaring my nephew!"

He drew away from her to look at her face in the pale light of the setting moon. As if she were a chameleon, her visage had changed from that of a sweet child to one of a feline hunter anxious to pounce on its prey. He knew it was useless to argue with her. If he told her to stay behind, she would follow and create havoc, totally upsetting his plans. There was nothing to do but take her with him.

"Be quiet then." He took her shoulders and brought her close to him. "Lizzie, no heroics. If you go bursting in there, that idiot Winchester may do something stupid. Just follow me and we'll get Tommy out of here. Then we can pick up Pete at the Seeckts' and be on our way. We've delayed too long as it is."

"I will not risk Tommy." When she started to rise, he tightened his grip on her shoulders and pressed her back against the ground. "Let me go!"

"Promise me," he repeated stubbornly, "that you'll obey me while we get Tommy back."

"Cliff, you know I will do nothing to harm him." With a grimace, she stated, "All right, I promise I'll do nothing to pay back Sam for this."

He smiled. "That's what I wanted to hear, honey. Now let's go get your nephew back from that slow-water scum."

"Then let me up!" she hissed through her teeth. Her eyes widened as she saw his face over hers, moving closer to her. "Cliff! What are you doing?"

"For luck, honey."

She was so shocked she did not resist as he tilted her mouth beneath his. The quick caress of his lips on hers was over quickly. Her hands striking his cheek was loud in the predawn silence.

"You're lucky I don't have a knife!" she spat. "I would have slit your throat, Cliff Hollister. You keep your hands off me. I don't want to be another in your vast parade of lovers."

She jumped to her feet but couldn't move swiftly enough to avoid his hand, which reached out and grasped her leg. She tried to shake off his grip, but he refused to release her.

"Don't go off half-cocked, woman. You'll ruin everything."

"You have no right to offer me the advice you should keep for yourself." With a twisting motion, she broke away from him.

His irritation changed to anger, but Cliff swallowed it as she started down into the valley. If he let her go alone, she would simply infuriate Winchester until he did something else foolish. She seemed to have that effect on men. Already he had seen how she could drive both him and Winchester to distraction. Once they rescued the child, he would have to teach her a lesson or two about the proper respect she ought to have for a man.

But that was for later. He concentrated on following her lithe form down the hillside. He had to admit she was not headstrong enough to become reckless. Knowing they must have the element of surprise on their side if Winchester's cronies were in the cabin with him, she zigzagged along the hillside, crouching behind the trunks of the trees.

It took Cliff only a few seconds to catch up with Lizzie as she ran from tree to tree. She flinched when he put his hand on her arm, but nodded as he signaled that she should follow him. Only when they reached the sentinel trees did he motion for her to wait in their protection.

Lizzie nodded again. As much as she hated to admit it, she knew she would not be an asset in a confrontation like this. Her role would be to act as Cliff's ace in the hole. She watched as he sneaked across the open area. There was no challenge to him from the cabin.

For a fearful second, she was afraid she had guessed wrong. If she had, then Sam had Tommy somewhere else. Where, she did not know. Thinking of what he would demand for the child's safe return, her stomach knotted. More than ever, she was determined he would not become a part of her life.

Her eyes were riveted on Cliff's back as he kicked the cabin door open. Even from across the clearing she could hear Tommy's exultant shout as he recognized an ally. Cliff's chocolate rich voice resonated through the clearing as he ordered the child released. Lizzie began to relax with relief until she saw a shadow near the side of the cabin.

Treachery should be part of Sam's name, she decided viciously, but she had no time for such useless recriminations. She had to act. Reaching under her shirt, she drew out the pistol. She held it carefully so it would not discharge by accident and harm her. She had fired a pistol many times when she used it to signal Zach that she had reached safety before he detonated explosives in the mine.

The situation she was facing was just as unstable and eruptive as those at the mine. This had to be Sam's final play. He couldn't afford to lose now—it would destroy his last bit of pride before his cronies, who were as loathsome as Sam. She had to show no sign of fear as they faced him together.

Crawling through the underbrush in a line parallel with the cabin, she reached a point closest to the man inching along the wall. She heard the man call, "Drop it, Hollister!"

Her heart froze in midbeat, although she had been expecting something like that at any moment. She watched unmoving as Cliff glanced over his shoulder. Silhouetted against the comparatively bright glow visible through the open door, his every motion was clear to her.

His muttered curse was swallowed by triumphant laughter from within the hut. The heavy sound of Cliff's gun hitting the wooden floor of the rickety porch was like a fist in her middle. Wetting her lips, she crept from the safety of the trees. As the man had done before her, she clung to the shadows of the wall of the cabin.

From inside she could hear Sam's victorious gloating. "Hollister, you fool, what are you doing here? I expected Lizzie Buchanan. Don't you have anything better to do than to play the hero for that little gal?"

"I'm sorry to disappoint you. Now, let's pretend the joke is over. I'll take the Greenway boy and go back to town. You've had your laugh."

"But I don't have Lizzie."

"And you won't have her. She's leaving with me in the morning."

Again came the chuckle. "Not without the boy, she won't."

"So what's the point? You have the kid, ⟨ she won't give in to you easily. This is no way to woo a lady, Winchester."

She could almost see Cliff's easy smile while he chatted with Sam as if this was a purely social call. He was at his most charming, and she was sure he had Sam and his friends puzzled. His calm voice made it almost impossible to believe that another man was pressing a gun in the middle of his back.

"I want Lizzie. You don't need her, Hollister. Go back to St. Louis and find yourself some lacy-dressed lady. I want her. She worked well for Greenway, and she'll keep me from getting lonely up here alone. Her sister was a decent whore. With the fire in hotheaded Lizzie, think how fine she'll be. Or do you know that already?"

Rage blinded her to all good sense as she heard him insult Whitney. Spinning out from the darkness, she pressed her weapon into the side of the man holding his gun against Cliff. "Drop it to the ground, sir, unless you want to feel the breeze of this bullet passing through you."

"Good girl," Cliff crowed; then laughed with relief.

Again the sound of a metal object hitting the floor was loud in her ears. Cliff scooped up the man's gun as well as his own and raised an eyebrow in Sam's direction. "I think it's time for you to send Tommy Greenway out to us, Winchester."

Knowing he had lost in his attempt to keep Lizzie in Hopeless, Sam nodded. He wanted her, but he was not going to risk three pistols firing at him. With a shove, he pushed the child toward Lizzie.

She stepped past Cliff. With her gun steady in her hand, she raised it to center on Sam's chest. His bravado failed him as he stared at the fury in her nugget-hard eyes.

"Put the gun down, Lizzie," Sam ordered, but his voice trembled.

"I am tired of you, Sam Winchester! I am tired of your sausage fingers touching me, and I am tired of hearing you speaking about Whitney like that. If I pull this trigger, I will be doing the world a big favor."

He shrieked and cowered as he saw her draw the trigger slowly back. At the sound, she smiled coldly and lowered the weapon, cautiously returning the hammer to its place. When she felt Cliff's hand on her arm, drawing her out of the cabin, she went willingly. She had proven what she wanted to prove—Sam Winchester was a coward and a fool.

Winchester, sweating profusely, realized she was not going to kill him for kidnapping her nephew. His eyes swept the room and noted the disgust on the faces of his one-time allies. Desperately he fought to salvage what he could from the situation.

"I'll bring you back, woman!" he snarled. "You owe me!"

"I owe you nothing!" Placing her pistol back under her shirt, she took Tommy in her arms. His long legs dangled down hers as he clung to her neck. "Touch my nephews again, Sam Winchester, and I will show you exactly what is due you. I will aim my gun so that you won't have any use for me or any other woman again."

"Enough, honey," came the whisper in her ear. "Come on, before you get him mad enough to carry out his threats."

She glanced over her shoulder and saw Cliff struggling not to laugh at their adversary. A smile drifted across her lips and settled in her eyes. He ordered her to step behind him, and they backed off the porch. He held his pistol ready in case one of Sam's men decided to attack them even at this late stage of the confrontation.

Slowly Lizzie and Cliff moved toward the first cluster of trees. There they would find their horses, stop at the Seeckts' to collect Pete, and soon leave Hopeless far to the west. Halfway up the hill, Cliff took the terrified child from her. She was not sure that Tommy would leave the haven of her arms, but he went to the man willingly.

"Thank you, Cliff. Thank you again."

He grinned in the lightening gray of the hour before sunrise. "You do owe me for quite a few favors, don't you, Lizzie?"

"And you plan to collect?"

"Yep!" He laughed. "All that gold dust at the end of our journey."

She started to speak but paused. It was both far too early and far too late to talk of the truth. The journey along the trail of deception had begun the moment she had approached him as he lay in the mud. As far as she had traveled, she could not turn back now. So instead of the truth, she spoke of how silly Sam had looked with his mouth gaping open as she held the gun up to scare him.

As he was setting Tommy on the saddle, Cliff turned to her. "Where did you get that pistol?"

"From here." She pointed to her hip. Lifting her shirt slightly, she revealed the gun belt, which was steadily slipping toward her knees.

"I realize that!" he retorted. "But you didn't have it earlier—I repeat: where did you get the gun?"

"I stole it from Delilah's." She mounted her horse easily and picked up the reins. "I figure she owed my family something. I bet she took half of Whitney's money also."

"You took that gun from Delilah's?"

She smiled. "I saw the holster in an empty room, so I took it. If you insist, Cliff, I can return it. I just thought I might need it, and I did."

Taking the reins of his horse, he stepped closer to her. He rested his arm on the neck of her steed as he asked, "Did you check to see if it was loaded?"

"Loaded?"

"You little fool, don't you realize no one would leave a pistol lying around with bullets in it?"

With a gasp, she drew the weapon from its holster and placed it in his hand. He flipped it open. Snapping it shut, he then held it over his head. When he depressed his finger against the trigger, there was only a small click. With a laugh he handed it to her.

"Next time, honey, check first. Your bluff might have been called. Winchester would have been even more mortified to think he was terrorized by an empty gun, and you would have paid the price."

His amusement with her mistake rekindled her rage. Stuffing the weapon back into its holster, she demanded, "Are you always right?"

"Yes," he replied quietly as he swung into his saddle. "I am always right. You have to be, on the trail, or you're dead. You were lucky, Lizzie. Don't expect to be so lucky next time. Let's go."

Thoroughly dressed down, she tried to regain her composure as she urged her horse to follow his through the trees. She wished she would have a chance to prove his superior words wrong, but her life was too high a price to offer to see him put in his place.

"By the way, Lizzie, I wanted to let you know I won tonight. Around one hundred dollars." He pressed something warm into her hand. "Here's your coin back with interest."

"You are disgusting," she snapped.

"I know." He laughed and she joined in, although she didn't understand why she liked him so much when he was so overbearing and despicable. She would have months on the trail to discover that.

CHAPTER FIVE

BEFORE THE DAY WAS HALF OVER, LIZZIE WAS grateful for the thick buckskins that helped protect her from the uneven motion of the saddle beneath her. She and Cliff rode side by side amid the trees, each with a boy sitting in front, sharing the saddles. The surefooted pack horse followed complacently.

Among the tall pines, the aroma of the sun-warmed pine needles was intoxicating. It was as if they were the first to discover this unpopulated land. The sound of their horses' hoofs on the thick carpet of golden grass clinging to the hills and the childrens' voices were often the only noises to be heard.

Their pace remained an easy one. With a journey of many weeks ahead of them, they had no need to hurry. It was early in the season yet, so Cliff did not rush them. No one waited anxiously for them in the east. Lizzie's family was complete here, and Cliff's life was his own, with no ties.

As she listened to the tales he spun for the boys, she hid her smile. Such outrageous stories entertained them as the hours passed, and she marveled at his storytelling ability, and enjoyed listening to the adventures in spite of herself. When she heard the boys' enthusiasm, she even forgave Cliff for making himself the hero of each saga.

Tommy told and retold his version of the kidnapping until they all wanted to cry they had heard enough. But both Cliff and Lizzie knew this was his way of dealing with the fright of his abduction. His brother was less compassionate.

"Don't want to hear any more!" snapped Pete with every ounce of his three-year-old annoyance and envy. "Lizzie, next time can I be the one Sam steals?"

She swallowed her gasp of horror as she looked at Pete, mounted in front of Cliff. Her eyes rose to meet the man's amused smile. With an effort she fought back the remembered panic that still threatened to overcome her.

Quietly she replied, "We won't be seeing Sam Winchester again, but I'm sure you will have many exciting things happening to you on this trip, Pete. Don't you think so, Cliff?"

"Of course," he seconded quickly. "This long trail will provide even you, Pete Greenway, with all the excitement any lad could want."

Cliff looked back at Lizzie. He was concerned about her. She remained tight-lipped about what had happened during the night. As Tommy told his tale, her face had become more and more pale. She appeared as taut as a bowstring. Cliff knew that if she did not let her outrage escape, she would snap.

When he called a rest for them and their horses, he cornered her. She tried to avoid him until he physically backed her against a tree trunk. With his hands on either side of her head, he imprisoned her there.

"Say it," he urged.

"Say what? Will you let me go? Is that what you want to hear?" When he grinned, she stated coldly, "All right. Let me go! I want to keep track of the boys."

"They'll be fine," he said with an indifferent shrug of his shoulders. "There is nothing to hurt them here, and they gave me their word they would stay within sight. It's their aunt I'm worried about."

"I'm fine." She scowled up at his bewhiskered smile. "Will you let me go? They're just children. Promises are something they forget when it's convenient." She put her hands against the sun-heated warmth of his flannel shirt. When one of his hands covered hers to keep them against him, she gasped. "Cliff, please!"

He released her slender fingers but did not move away from her. "I told you I was the boss on this trip, but each member of this crew affects the others. We can't have you flinching like a startled rabbit every time Tommy mentions what happened last night."

"I have a right to be upset."

"Well, be upset! You haven't been anything

but courageous, Lizzie."

Putting her hands on her hips, she glared at him belligerently. "If you expect vapors, I will not oblige you."

He knew his smile would infuriate her even more, but he couldn't keep from grinning at her. "That's the last thing I expect, but dammit, Lizzie, let your anger go. You don't have to cry. Swear, if it helps. Slug someone. Just do something."

"I am fine," she repeated coldly. "And if I was going to hit someone, I guarantee you would not like it!" Ducking beneath his arm, she ran to where the boys were busy investigating the nooks and crannies of one of the trees.

Dammit!

Cliff wondered how much longer he would be able to keep from treating Lizzie like the spoiled child her behavior made her seem. He suspected if he spanked her, as she so richly deserved, he would waken to find himself facing a gun pointed at him and Lizzie behind it, just as she had confronted Winchester. She was so capable of handling everything—everything but her own volatile emotions.

With a malicious smile, he trotted across the clearing. He grasped her by the shoulders, interrupting her in midword. Twisting her into his arms, he leaned forward to place his lips on hers.

She screeched her outrage while the boys laughed at what they saw as a game. As she had the night before, she raised her hand to slap his face. He easily blocked it, holding her wrist while his other hand around her waist kept her close.

"Let me go!"

"No," he said in his most reasonable tone.

"Stop it. You don't need good luck today."

"I needed it last night!"

Lizzie shook her head. She did not want to think of those long minutes of scrambling along the ridge, fearing she had guessed wrong about Sam's actions and would cause more trouble than good. In a softer voice she said, "You had it last night."

"Because of you. Both Tommy and I were saved by you. A foolish woman who used bravado to convince an idiot she would shoot him."

"I would have!"

"I don't doubt that." His smile grew cold. "You would have killed him in cold blood. With the bullet from your gun, you would have ended that man's life. He would be dead, and you would have saved Tommy."

"Don't!" she whispered, trying to pull her hand from his grip. She wanted to cover her ears and keep out his horrible words. He would not release her, so she pressed the right side of her head against his chest while her other hand covered her left ear.

Shivers wracked her as she recalled the fear she had known the previous night, first when she had confronted Sam and then when Cliff had shown her the empty gun. She had been frightened and angry frustrated by her inability to solve the problem with simple bargaining. That she had done all she could but was overwhelmed by Sam's brute strength had enraged her.

Suddenly she shrieked, "Shut up! Shut up, Cliff Hollister! I don't want to hear any more of this! What did you expect me to do? Just sit there and wait for Sam to do something awful to Tommy?"

Instead of the sharp answer she expected, he grinned. "Good. You can be angry."

"Angry? I'm outraged!" Her eyes snapped. "I know what you're trying to prove, but I'm fine. I just don't want to be pawed by a moronic wagon master who cannot find his way out of the mud by himself."

Slowly his hands dropped to his sides. His face lost all expression. "You're right, Lizzie. I'm wrong to try to help you. You don't need my help, do you?"

"I don't need you or anyone else. I can manage all alone."

"That sounds simply wonderful," he snapped with sudden sarcasm. "Come on. Let's go. The quicker I can be rid of you, the happier I'll be."

"Me too!"

He did not look back at her as he went to his horse and remounted. Once again he had tried to help her only to have his kindness tossed back in his face. It would not happen again. Instead he would press them on as quickly as he could until he could leave her at the Mississippi. Then he would have that fistful of gold and enjoy women who appreciated him.

Lizzie despised the circumstances that forced her to follow his lead silently. If there had been any other alternative she could accept, she would have turned around and gone back to Hopeless to find someone else to help her.

There was no choice but to go with Cliff.

At the day's end, they camped near a lake. The boys ran beneath the trees, joyful at their freedom from the cramped saddles. Lizzie shouted a warning to them as they raced toward the lake, which reflected the scarlet splash of the sunset. When they turned to wave to her, she knew they had heard her.

Wincing, she sat on the ground and leaned back against the luxuriously golden grass of the slope. With her arms folded beneath her head, she gazed up at the darkening sky. Satisfaction settled on her. Hopeless was miles behind them, and she could finally believe that she would see Louisville again.

A shadow blocked her view, and she turned to see Cliff digging a pit in the dirt for their fire. Involuntarily, she groaned as she moved tender muscles.

"Stiff?" he asked as he grinned at her.

"You don't have to look so pleased." She grimaced as she rose. "It's been a long time since I was on a horse."

"Don't worry. You'll have plenty of time to become accustomed to the ride." He withdrew a packet of food from his saddlebag. Calling to the boys, he asked them to bring some water from the lake.

"Be careful you don't fall in!" added Lizzie as their shadows flitted among the trees.

As he placed a skillet on the fire, Cliff glanced up at her. "Do you always nag those boys so much?"

She bristled. "I don't think it is your place to tell me how to raise them. What do you know about it?"

"I was a boy once." He shrugged. "I guess that gives me some experience. Grant them a little room to explore. You're going to suffocate them by trying to protect them from things that don't even exist."

"Cliff, don't start that again."

When he heard the fatigue in her voice, he bit back the words. He had noted that for most of the day, tears clung to her eyelashes. Sometimes he had to force himself to remember that no matter what else Lizzie might pretend to be, she could not hide how easily she was hurt. Her scars were hidden, but the wounds continued to fester. He hoped she would find what she was seeking in Louisville, although he suspected she was in for a surprise when she became aware of how much she had changed from that young girl who had left there in the spring of 1849.

He stared at the tattered figure sitting on the far side of the fire and recalled the first time he had seen her. Even then, her pretty smile stood out among the crowd of strangers, drawing his eyes to it again and again. In many ways she had been far more innocent than her nephews were now. Kind and generous, she had done more than was necessary to ease the way west for her family and the others in the train.

The soft curls that had flowed beneath a feminine bonnet were hidden now under the floppy hat. Her smile was tinged with sadness, bitterness, reflecting the burdens California had inflicted on her. In the last few days she had learned more about herself and her family than she ever wanted to know.

Nodding his head he replied, "A truce, honey. At least through supper. All right?"

"All right," she said seriously. "Oh, no! He's going to fall in and be soaked."

She was racing away before he could answer. When he heard her voice lilting back to him on the breeze from the lake, he smiled. With her nephews, Lizzie Buchanan could still feel joy. Perhaps she would be able to build on that to make the life she wanted for them in the east.

He concentrated on making them a meal of the side meat and already stale bread. He fried them together in the pan and then drew four tin plates from the bags that had been packed on the extra horse. He took the pail of water Tommy brought from the lake and put it over the fire. Into it he threw a handful of coffee. His cooking wasn't fancy, but they would be able to live adequately on his meals as they crossed the Sierras.

During the meal, the boys carried on most of the conversation. If they noticed the silence of the adults, they did not pause to mention it. Instead they chatted about the fish they had seen swimming in the lake and all the squirrels in the trees.

When Lizzie ordered them to go to sleep beneath their blankets, it did not surprise her that they went without protest. Their feverish conversation was a sign of their exhaustion. Within minutes they were lost in dreams of their eastward journey.

By the time Lizzie had finished tucking in the boys, Cliff had cleaned the dishes and stored them back in the bags. She offered to pour a second cup of coffee for him, and he nodded. With a soft thank you, he took the cup. Sitting on the ground beside her, he waited for her to speak. What she said startled him.

"I'm sorry for being so cross today. You were right. I was upset about Sam's attempt to hurt Tommy."

"This is quiet unexpected. I didn't think you would apologize."

"I apologize when I am wrong, but I don't back down when I'm right!" she retorted tartly.

"That I have noticed." He put his half-filled cup on a stone by the fire to keep it warm. "Partners again?"

"Always, although perhaps not always on speaking terms." When he laughed, she asked with an expression of pure innocence, "Would you like to play cards?"

"Cards?"

She smiled. "I assume that is what you did at Delilah's to amass a hundred dollars. Or—?"

"Enough of that, Lizzie." He laughed. "I don't like hearing you suggest that!"

"What? That you spent your time drinking instead of playing cards?" She smiled at him coquettishly. "I wouldn't stoop to suggesting that you earned it another way."

Cliff muted his laughter as he noted the boys stirring on the far side of the campfire. "All right, Lizzie. I'll play cards with you, just to prove to you that you can't make comments like that without paying the price."

"Price?" she repeated. As she drew the cards from her bag, she asked, "Does that mean you wish to gamble?"

"Why else would I want to play cards? You have the coin I gave you this morning. If you'd like, I'll advance you two more. It shouldn't take too long for you to lose them."

As she shuffled the cards and dealt them easily for the game favored by the miners around Hopeless, she smiled. "We'll see how long."

"I'll wager it won't take more than a half hour."

"All right." She placed her sole coin by the stack of cards remaining. "Match it, and if you take my last coin within a half hour, this one is yours as well."

He smiled confidently. Withdrawing his pouch from the pocket of his shirt, he spilled a pile of gold onto the ground. Lizzie's eyes widened involuntarily. She had not seen that much money in one place for longer than she could remember.

"There's more than a hundred dollars there," she whispered.

"I didn't want to brag."

"You didn't, did you?" she retorted sharply. "That is a change for you. All right. Give me two coins, and we can start."

If Cliff thought he would beat her quickly, his

complacency was soon shattered. She played with easy confidence and was not afraid to be bold. As the pile of coins by her knee grew, he began to think it could not be Lizzie sitting in the shadows winning every hand. He wondered if the urchin-woman he'd led away from Hopeless was the same person who now regarded him with the cool assurance of a veteran cardsharp.

He finally tossed his hand down in disgust when he saw she had not been bluffing this last hand. "That's it. You've cleaned me out. I haven't won more than three or four hands tonight."

"Five," she said with a smile. Picking up the cards, she stowed them away. Then she scooped up the pile of coins in front of her and deposited them before him. "Here."

"You won it, Lizzie."

She shook her head. "No. I don't want to take your money. This was just for fun."

Grudgingly he put the money back in his pocket. He did not want to admit to being bested by a pint-sized lass, but he could not afford his pride. That money would get them east, if no disaster waited ahead.

As she wrapped her blanket around her shoulders and prepared for sleep, he said, "I have to ask you one thing, Lizzie. It had to be more than luck. How did you get so good with cards?"

"I cheat." He could hear the smile in her voice. "Good night."

Strong hands gripped her shoulders and brought her upright. She gasped as she saw Cliff's face close to hers. In the flickering light of the dying fire, she couldn't guess what emotion was etched across his shadowed features.

Softly he demanded, "You were cheating?"

"I gave back your money." She tried to shrug, but his tight clasp on her arms blocked the motion. "It doesn't matter, Cliff. It was just a joke to show you that I can take care of myself."

"A joke? Honey, you could find yourself in deep trouble if you pulled that at a real game. If . . ." His voice faded away as he looked over her head.

"If what?"

Slowly he released her. She rubbed her upper arms where his fingers had bitten into her skin. His finger under her chin brought her eyes up to meet his.

"What games do you know so well?"

"The one I know best is faro, but it doesn't work so well with just two players. It—"

"I know how to play faro," he stated tersely. The intensity returned to his voice as he asked, "Can you win all the time?"

"It works better with a partner. Zach taught me a lot of tricks during the winter storms when he couldn't get up to the mine. We used to laugh about it and try to best each other. Whitney wouldn't play with either of us; she'd accuse us of cheating even when it was only good fortune."

He took her fingers and sandwiched them between his. A lazy smile played across his lips. "I think you've given me a wonderful idea, honey. There are plenty of mining camps between here and where we cross the Sierras. All those miners like to play cards, and many of them have money."

"No!"

"No?" he repeated in shock.

"I won't do it! I won't cheat to line your pockets with gold dust."

Lizzie jerked her hands away from him and leapt to her feet. She ran down to the edge of the lake and crouched on the pebbled beach. Staring at the path of moonlight rippling on the water, she wished she had never suggested they play cards. Teasing Cliff was not the same as intentionally duping miners to strip them of their hard-earned gold.

When she heard footsteps pause behind her, she knew Cliff had followed her to the lake. She did not turn; she had nothing to say to him. Even when he sat next to her, she continued to look only at the water that lapped softly at her feet.

The minutes crawled by while neither spoke. Finally she could stand the uncomfortable silence no longer. Rising to her feet, she turned to go back to their campsite. A long arm snaking around her waist stopped her.

"Let me go!" she ordered. "When are you going to stop grabbing me all the time?"

"Wait a minute, Lizzie."

She shook her head. "I have nothing to add to what I said before."

"I have something to say, and you are going to listen." When she didn't answer, he continued, "If you can play so well that you can cheat me without me knowing it, you must be pretty wise to the ways of cards. I want you to be my partner while we clean the pockets of the miners legitimately."

"No," she whispered.

"Honey, I said legitimately."

When she tried to break his hold on her, he stood up towering over her. She told herself not to be intimidated by his strength, although it was something else entirely that weakened her knees. So few times had they been close like this. Each time she was overwhelmed by the aroma of damp buckskins and his pure male essence.

Softly she said, "I can't, Cliff! If that was the life I wanted my boys to have, I could have stayed in Hopeless. Delilah didn't always have a monopoly on entertainment there."

The anger faded from his face as he saw, in the weak light of the moon, the honesty in her face. Seldom had she been this open with him. Now that she was, he knew it was useless to try to change her mind. His fingers rose to brush her tangled hair away from her face.

"Lizzie, I didn't mean we were to do this for the rest of our lives—only during the part of our trip that takes us through the mining camps. Look at it this way. If we win, and we should, you'll have a bit of gold to buy your dreams."

"Buy my dreams?" She laughed harshly. "That's exactly what Zach used to say. I don't want to make my dreams come true with bloodstained gold."

"And how to do you plan to buy them otherwise?" he demanded sharply. Frustration deepened his voice as he glared at her. "Have you thought of that? Look at you, dressed in a man's cast-off clothes. Will you be welcomed in Louisville like that?"

In a muffled voice, she repeated what she had told herself and others so often: "I will manage."

"How?"

Furiously she spat, "I don't know. Why do you care? It's not as if you are going to worry about us after you cross the Mississippi. You only want me to do this so you can get rich easily."

"Partially true," he admitted with an openness that further fueled her ire.

"You are disgusting! Good night."

He easily blocked her way. When he reached out to grasp her arms, she stepped away from him. He demanded, "Don't you want to know the rest of my reason for playing cards with the miners?"

"Not particularly." She tried to step around him; she didn't feel like sparring with him that night. Her body ached from the ride, and her eyes burned from reading the cards in the wavering light of the fire. "I'm tired. Good night," she repeated.

Again he kept her from leaving the pebbled beach by stepping between her and the path. "Woman, I am tired of you already, and we are barely on our way."

"That makes two of us." She put her hands on her hips, presenting a threatening silhouette. "I did not come along on this trip simply to make you rich. I would not have come with you at all if I had any other choice."

"You had plenty of other choices, honey." He laughed when she did not snarl a reply. His voice softened from its harsh tone as he added, "Look, I know how much it means to you to give those boys a good life. How else are you going to do it?"

She stared up at his face. For once the two-facile smile was missing. Uncertainty tugged at her. She didn't want to trust him. If she did, he would simply hurt her again. The words he spoke were true, no matter how much she wanted to deny them. Without money to buy them a home and some clothes, she and the boys would never be welcomed back into the society she wanted for them.

"I don't know," she whispered. Wrapping her arms around herself, she gazed across the moon-swept water. The gentle waves lapped at her boots.

When she felt his broad hands on her shoulders, she flinched. He bent down to whisper near her right ear. "Lizzie, we'll divide the winnings four ways. One for each of us."

Whirling to face him, she gasped, "You would give us three shares?"

"If you'll give me one." He tilted her hat back so he could see her face. "Without you, it won't work."

"It doesn't always work anyhow," she cautioned.

"It brings the odds more in our favor. The way you play, honey, we could beat them legitimately. But I think we should use your tricks. They'll guarantee that we'll have something at the end of the trail."

"We may end up with nothing."

"We don't have much more than that now."

"Cliff, it's dishonest," she argued, aware that her own resistance to the idea was fading.

He laughed and slipped his arm around her shoulders. As he walked with her back toward the dim light of the fire, he said, "You were going to kill Winchester this morning, but you balk at taking a bit of gold from some men who would risk playing with us."

She sighed resignedly. "All right, Cliff, but only until we each have a thousand dollars. That will give you plenty, and the boys and I can live well on three thousand dollars until we decide what we want to do back east."

Squeezing her shoulders companionably, he said, "I knew you would be sensible, Lizzie." He whistled a light tune until they reached the place where the boys slept. There, with a whispered good-night, he released her.

She watched as he sauntered over to where his blanket waited for him. Pulling her own covers over herself, she wondered what else she could have done. Once she had been foolish enough to let him see the skills she had been taught, there was no turning back. Guiltily she wondered if she had wanted him to suggest just such a scheme so she could have funds to start anew.

It was easier not to think about it. She burrowed under her blanket and let her dreams erase her guilt over cheating hardworking miners.

Lizzie's first feeling in the morning was regret. As she saw the smiling faces of her nephews, she wondered why she had agreed to Cliff's proposition. She told herself she was lucky that playing cards was the only offer he had made to her by the lake.

He himself seemed to have no second thoughts about the new aspect of their partnership. The tune he had whistled in the middle of the night he now sang in the sunshine. His singing voice had the same rough texture as his calloused hands.

Shaking her head at that thought, Lizzie rose and folded her blanket so it could be packed behind her saddle. Then she sent the children to wash in the icy waters of the lake. When Cliff offered her a cup of the bitter coffee, she drank it gratefully. That and a piece of the hard bread was their breakfast.

During the day all was as it had been before. Cliff made no mention of their agreement. She suspected he knew how distressed she would be if the boys guessed their plan to cheat the miners. Just as she hoped they would never know the secret of their mother's occupation two years before, she wanted to keep them from learning that their aunt meant to play cards in gambling halls to gain the money they needed to enter the genteel society of Louisville.

The day passed as the previous one had. They climbed higher into the mountains, but the pattern of the trees and scrub brush was never changing. They made camp for the night in a sheltered glen. After allowing the boys to play, Lizzie gave them a quick supper and sent them to bed.

"All right," Cliff said when the children were sleeping and they were sitting near the fire, "teach me what I need to know to play faro with you."

"Just like that?"

"Why not?"

Her eyes twinkled as brightly as the stars overhead as she put her hands over her mouth to stifle an explosion of laughter. She untied the twine holding her hat on her head and dropped the misshapen felt material on the ground. With a shake of her head, she loosened her hair so it fell free to her shoulders.

"Did you see what I did?" she asked serenely.

"Sure. You took off your hat. . . ." He frowned as he saw her smile broaden. Then, noting with surprise two cards dealt face up on the ground before him, he growled, "You're tricking me again."

"At least you figured that much out." Her voice grew serious. "This, as you told me, Cliff, is no game. It takes every bit of your concentration. You cannot be flirting with one of the women in the saloon while we work. If there's a fight going on over in a corner of the room, you cannot spare a moment to watch, even if the cards are not on the table."

He stretched out and rested on one elbow. "It doesn't sound like much fun."

"It isn't. This is work. I know you dont' relish having to do any work unless you are leading a wagon train, but . . ." She shrugged eloquently. If he was starting their venture with the expectation they would make easy money, she had to show him the idiocy of his illusions.

"If we are going to be partners, Lizzie," he said in the soft tone that was a sure sign he was angry, "we have to get one thing straight. I am not going to accept any more of your snide remarks for the rest of this trip."

She stared into the dusky pools of his eyes. In the shadows she could not read any expression there. Despite that, an invisible thread seemed to bind her gaze with his. The too familiar flush that crept up her cheeks disconcerted her; he wasn't touching her sweetly or complimenting her. Just the opposite was true, but she still couldn't stop the heated thrill spiraling along her skin.

Moistening her lips with the tip of her tongue, she broke the enchantment. Her voice wobbled like that of a toddler, but as she continued to explain what tricks Zach had taught her, it became steadier.

Cliff watched her facile fingers manipulating the cards. When his eyes felt as if they were going

to remain permanently strained, he raised his
hands and asked for a break.

"Lizzie, I'll never learn all that. Not if we were
to take a year to get east. Where did your brother-
in-law learn those tricks?"

With a sad smile as she reminisced, she said,
"Zach picked them up while he was working the
Mississippi on a keelboat before he settled down in
Louisville with Whitney. After they met, he gave
up his wandering life for a short while. When
stories of gold in California reached us, he would
talk of nothing else. So west we came. During the
long nights we had to wait by the fords or sit out a
prairie storm, he taught me all he knew about
cards."

"You're a better student than I am, then." He
sighed and reclined to rest in the grass. "How long
do you think it will take?"

"Two or three more nights and you should
understand enough so you can see what I'm doing.
All I need is that you be an observant partner."

Grumbling, he complained, "I don't like the
idea of you being in charge of this scheme, half-
pint."

"Why not?" Then, as an afterthought, she
snapped, "Don't call me that!"

"Why not?" he echoed. "That's what you are.
You aren't much bigger than Tommy."

Defensively she said, "He's tall like his father.
I'm sorry if you don't like my plans for the card
games. You can't learn all you must know so

quickly, so I guess you are going to have to depend on a 'half-pint' female."

"Dammit!" His fist pounded the ground. "Are you always so nasty? Winchester must have been mad to want you up there at his mine."

She shivered as she dropped the cards on the ground. Drawing up her knees, she wrapped her arms around them. The soft texture of buckskin was comforting beneath her cheek. She felt Cliff's hand on her arm, but she didn't look at him.

"Lizzie, I'm sorry."

His breath stroked her face as he put his arm around her. She closed her eyes and leaned her head against his chest. As she rested there, she realized she didn't want to move out of his arms. He was exasperating, but when he touched her, she discovered another Cliff Hollister. He caressed her trembling shoulders gently, and it comforted her as no words could.

In a whisper she said, "Don't worry. You needn't apologize. It's just that I never want to hear that man's name again."

"I'll remember that."

"Thank you."

When he felt her move in his arms, he tightened his grip. He didn't want her to reerect the barrier between them again so quickly. His fingers slipped along her tangled hair and reached her night-cooled cheek.

She watched his face as he touched her. She closed her eyes as she was swallowed by the tumultuous emotions gaining control of her. Savoring the liquid fire blazing through her body, she raised her hands to encircle his neck, and buried her fingers in the thick jungle of his collar-length hair. At the sound of her name, she opened her eyes.

"What is it?" she murmured.

Her words faded into a gasp of astonishment as his lips covered hers. Then her momentary confusion was banished as she settled more securely in his arms. Never had any kiss melted her into such a succulent pool of longing. As his mouth tested the textures of her face, she felt his fingers teasing the velvet-soft skin behind her ear.

Sensations of exquisite pleasure exploded inside her, making every inch of her skin tingle, as his lips warmed the length of her neck. With her hands on his back, she pressed him closer to her. His broad chest seemed to engulf her slender form. Her smiled disappeared beneath his hungry mouth.

Suddenly he pulled away and gazed at her as if he didn't understand how she had come to be in his arms. In a strained voice, he commanded, "Go get your blanket, Lizzie, and go to sleep."

"Cliff, what's wrong?" She put her hand on his muscular arm.

Roughly he shook it off. Grasping her by her shoulders, he put his nose close to hers. His words were as vehement as his actions. "I said to go to sleep, Lizzie. I meant it as an order. If you're going to question everything I say to you, we'll have trouble."

"Not everything! But, Cliff—"

"Shut up!" he snapped. Releasing her, he leapt to his feet and lurched to the far side of the fire. As she watched in bafflement, he wrapped his blanket around his hunched shoulders.

Lizzie twisted the fringe on her buckskin shirt. She tried to determine what had spoiled their brief kiss. Her mouth straightened into a hard line as she decided she knew the truth. A man like Cliff Hollister was unaccustomed to sleeping alone when there was a woman nearby. He had been overcome by his own desire until he remembered it was "half-pint" Lizzie Buchanan in his arms.

Putting the playing cards in her saddlebag, she pulled her blanket up to her chin. Silent tears rolled along her cheeks. He could have pretended, at least. He did not have to show so blatantly how disgusted he was to have only her to caress.

She pressed her hand against her mouth to contain her moan of anguish as she recalled how fantastically alive his fingers had made her feel. She learned nothing from each new heartache.

"I hate you," she whispered into the rough wool of the blanket. She vowed to help him win his money quickly so she and the boys would be rid of him as soon as possible. When she had enough gold to buy passage for the boys and herself on a ship in San Francisco, she would tell him their partnership was dissolved.

"I hate you." Although she repeated the words again and again, she wondered why she ached for his lips on hers. For the past three years she had waited for that kiss. Once more he had cheated her as he showed how little he cared for her.

Several hours after she had wound the blanket around her, she heard her name whispered softly in the voice that made her heart leap with joy. Clamping her eyes closed, she pretended to be asleep. She did not want to be forced to listen to Cliff's apology; it would complete her humiliation.

When she did not respond, the grass rustled as he moved back to the other side of the boys. Listening to the sounds of their sleep, she suffered the hot tears welling from her eyes until she found her own pallid, useless dreams.

CHAPTER SIX

THE ROAD INTO THE MINING SETTLEMENT WAS thick with mud. Lizzie had thought Hopeless, California, had a monopoly on filth, but she realized it was lovely in comparison with this crowded tent and hut town. As she maneuvered her horse around a hole left by an earlier prospector, she wished she could hold her breath the whole time they would spend there.

Offal reeked in the air. Each step of the horses raised more odors from the sludge beneath them. A crudely written sign tacked to a tree stated, "Welcome to Sparkler's Drift." Someone had painted across it, "Get out."

"Friendly place," Cliff remarked dryly.

"Let's go on. We don't want to stop here. They've made it very clear they don't want outsiders."

Finally the days of silence were behind him.

The youngsters couldn't understand why the two
adults didn't speak to each other that third day on
the trail. Lizzie could not forgive Cliff for his
coldhearted rejection. For the rest of the first
week, she spoke to him only when necessary or
during the lessons she gave him each night in how
to cheat without getting caught.

Slowly she allowed the icy front she presented
to thaw. For his part, he made no effort to heal the
rift, whether because he knew she would not
forgive him or because he simply didn't care she
couldn't guess. She pretended she felt the same,
but in truth she was miserable. As she glanced
around them now, she knew she would be even
more unhappy in this desolate, dirty town.

"There must be another place where we can
find shelter," she continued, "even if we have to
sleep under the trees again."

He smiled over his shoulder. "But trees don't
have one of those." He hooked his thumb toward
the only painted building in the valley.

Lizzie did not have to read the sign to know it
was Sparkler's Drift's version of Delilah's saloon.
She bit her lip as she heard the excited voices of the
youngsters. This was what she had hoped to escape
from, but Cliff was determined to steer her into
this horrible life. Her sole hope of escape was to let
him earn his share of the money as soon as she
could.

They stopped in front of the wooden porch,
where there was space at the rail to tie their horses.
Cliff leapt down and turned to take Pete from his
saddle. By that time Lizzie and Tommy had

dismounted.

"Listen to me," Cliff said quietly. "Don't say a word unless necessary, especially you, Lizzie. I think it would be best if you didn't let it be known you're not a boy."

"What?" she gasped. "Cliff, are you insane?"

He put his hands on her shoulders. His broad palms nearly covered them and he could feel the nervousness she was trying to hide. When she struggled to escape his grasp, his fingers drilled into her sensitive bones.

"Stop it!" he ordered sharply.

"You stop! You're hurting me."

He loosened his grip but did not let her go. "Listen, half-pint—"

"Don't call me that!" She snapped at the boys, "Stop laughing at his insults."

All of them ignored her. The children continued to giggle and Cliff went on. "Half-pint, you've been warning me for the last week how dangerous what we are attempting will be. Do something stupid and I'll leave you to face the consequences alone."

Her mouth opened, but no sound emerged. She felt a surge of pain as she listened to what amounted to his betrayal of her. Searching his stiff face, she saw he meant exactly what he said. She wondered how the same mouth that had so delighted her could be turned down in such a forbidding manner.

"I understand," she managed to say with some semblance of serenity. "Yes, Cliff, I understand you completely."

A tic raised his right eyebrow, but that was the only motion on his granite-stern face. "Good." He turned to the boys who, growing bored with the argument between their aunt and their new friend, had been pointing out sights to one another. "You two understand too? Lizzie is going to pretend to be your brother."

Pete's face screwed up in concentration. "Lizzie is not my brother. Tommy is my brother."

"Make believe," said the older boy with impatience. He grinned at Cliff. "Don't worry. Nobody listens to him anyhow because he's just a baby."

"Am not a baby. I'm a big boy."

"Hush," ordered Lizzie as she saw some of the miners on the street looking curiously at them. "Behave, boys."

While Pete glared at his brother, Cliff turned his attention to their aunt. Looking into her anger-brightened eyes, he asked quietly, "Will you give me a chance to explain?"

"Go ahead. I am sure you have some wondrous plan that calls for me to be the boys' brother."

Ignoring her sarcasm, he stated, in a more heated tone, "To tell you the truth, I do. I think you will be more readily accepted at the card tables if the miners see you as a lad. They aren't as likely to sit down with you if they think you're some strange type of woman in men's clothing. . . . Hmm . . . perhaps we should cut your hair."

"No!" she cried. "I won't do that!"

"Good." He smiled, confusing her more. "I

really like to see you brush it out so it crackles in the morning sunshine. Just keep your hat low over your ears and be quiet."

Telling the boys to hold their aunt's hands, he walked toward the saloon's door. Lizzie stared after him, baffled by the unexpected compliment in the midst of their argument. When he turned to ask if they were coming along, she hurried to follow. He led the way into the dim recesses of the so-called boardinghouse. Walking to the bar, he dropped their saddlebags on its grimy top. When no one appeared, he banged his fist on it.

Uttering a string of obscenities that brought a flush of embarrassment to Lizzie's cheeks, a small man appeared from the darkest shadows. "Yeah, what is it? I sawd you, I did. Jes' because I don't come right away, don't be a-thinking I ain't here."

"You Marcy?"

"Marcy? Who the hell—?" His laugh grated in their ears. "The sign out in front. Marcy be gone for nigh onto two, three years. The sign is good, so why get a new one, right? I be Stevens. R. B. Stevens."

"R. B., are you the proprietor of this place?"

The man leaned on the bar, enjoying the verbal jousting as each man felt out the other to see if there was a good bargain to be made. "Could be. What you and the young 'uns want?"

"You got rooms?" Cliff asked with studied nonchalance while Lizzie chafed at the delay. The boys were restive, and this was not the time for him to play games as he usually did.

R. B. rubbed the top of his balding head, then

pointed to a tattered and nearly illegible sign. "Says so here. Have to charge five dollars, seeing as how there is so many of you."

"Five dollars?" Cliff turned and motioned to Lizzie and the boys to head for the door.

Lizzie breathed a sigh of relief. This place was filthy; she would prefer sleeping under the stars. Although she had practiced card games with Cliff for the past week, she was not ready to test their prowess in a real game. She was glad the exorbitant rate for the room had brought Cliff to his senses. When the owner of the building called to them, she turned reluctantly.

"How about three dollars?"

"One," retorted Cliff.

"With so many of you? One dollar and four bits."

"Does that include hot water and breakfast for all of us?"

With a smile, the man nodded. "Aye, it does. You sure drive a hard bargain, Mr.—"

"Hollister."

"Cliff Hollister?"

Cliff bowed his head like a king acknowledging his lowest subject. "I'm afraid so."

The shorter man bounded around the counter and held out his hand. "Why, I heared of you from most of the boys 'round these parts. You got yourself quite a reputation, Mr. Hollister."

"Cliff," Mr. Hollister said magnanimously.

" 'Tis a true honor to have you here . . . Cliff." The little man's head bobbed up and down like a bird looking for food in the spring grass.

In disgust, Lizzie turned to look at the rest of the room while the two men shared reminiscences of common friends and tall tales of the trail. Now they were stuck in this horrible place. She would never be able to convince Cliff to leave while their host fawned over him like this. R. B. was sure to spread word of his guest, which would bring in others who knew him. Cliff would not depart from Sparkler's Drift as long as there was a loose bit of glitter to be won.

The saloon boasted a half dozen tables and less than twenty chairs. In the dim recesses of the ceiling rafters, she could see no more than one or two lanterns. As expensive as kerosene was that didn't surprise her, but the room had no windows to allow even the dim light of the moon to penetrate.

Across the back of the bar stood an assortment of half-filled bottles. None were labeled, and she suspected all held the same acidic whiskey that numbed the agony left by the hard work in the mines. It was a depressing place, and she wanted nothing more than to flee.

Cliff called to her, and she reluctantly went back to join the conversation. He was introducing them to the barkeeper.

"The little one is Pete. Middle one is Tommy. The big one is—Izzy." The hesitation was noticeable only to her.

She scowled. "Izzy?" What a horrible corruption of her name! When she saw Cliff's grin, she

wanted to shout her outrage at him. Instead she
heard herself greeting R. B. pleasantly.

Lowering her voice slightly, she asked, "Cliff,
are you going to stand here jawing all day? We're
paying for this room. Least we can do is see it."

"Sassy kid you have there, Cliff!" said R. B.
with a snort of disgust.

"He's not so bad once you get used to him.
Right, Izzy?"

She snarled some answer he took for an
affirmative. R. B. went toward the stairs, and they
all followed. Lizzie fought the nausea in her
stomach as she saw stains that could only be blood
left from some battle in the saloon. More than ever
she regretted leaving Hopeless. As horrible as it
had been, at least it had been familiar. This was far
worse, and she suspected she had not seen the
depths of depravation Sparkler's Drift had to offer.

A nasal voice called from the dim recesses at
the top of the stairs. "R. B.? Where are you?" A
string of oaths followed that matched the ones the
man had used when they first came into the main
room.

"Don't pay her no mind," the barkeeper said
with an absent wave of his hand. "Jes' Peg
chattering away."

Peg refused to be ignored. Glaring down at
them with her hands on her cinched waist, she
blocked the top of the stairs.

Lizzie felt her traitorous blush seeping along
her skin as she saw how little the dark-haired

woman wore. Peg's chemise dipped deeply across her full breasts, which were pushed upward by her corset. A generous vista of bare skin was visible nearly anywhere Lizzie looked. When Peg pointed at her and laughed, Lizzie's embarrassment turned to horror.

"Well, look at that! I do declare that young 'un has never seen a woman in her unmentionables before." The slow slur of her southern accent flowed over them like heated honey. Stepping toward Lizzie, she leaned down, offering an unrestricted view of her lush body. Grasping her hand, Peg lifted it. "Don't be scared, my lad. You can touch for free now. I wouldn't mind teaching you a few things. It's been a long time since I was anyone's first."

In disgust, Lizzie pulled back her hand. "No, thanks," she mumbled.

"Have it your way, laddie." Peg's midnight eyes began to glow with pleasure as she turned to the man standing behind the shy boy. This was the one she had been interested in since she saw the quartet ride along the street. "How about you, sir? Shall I be seeing you tonight . . . in the saloon?"

Cliff smiled. As Lizzie fumed silently, he lavished his charm on the prostitute. Lizzie's rage tripled as she was forced to listen to him flatter the coarse-featured woman. Finally, when she could tolerate his hypocrisy no longer, she turned to R. B.

"He may be a while with her," she stated with a nonchalance she didn't feel. "How about showing us the room? We'll be using it tonight."

"R. B. cracked with easy humor. "No saying where Cliff will be, huh? How did you hitch up with him, boy?"

"Me and my brothers, we had to go home to our grandparents. Our folks died, so they want us now to work on their farm. Figure anyone who could blast rock can plow."

"That is a surprise. A boy like you don't need no looking after. Except maybe by someone like Peg, eh?" He poked Lizzie in the ribs with a conspiratorial elbow. "California needs lads like you. What do you want to be going back east for? It's just filled with tenderfeet, bellyaching 'bout everything. Here there's room for a man to stretch out. If you don't like yer neighbors, you find a spot where there ain't any."

Truthfully she answered, "I have to look out for the boys."

He shrugged as he opened a well-scarred door. "It's yer life, Izzy. Cain't say I agree, but it's yer life. Well, here you be. Hot water comes up when the gals are gettin' ready for the miners."

"All right." She stepped in the dingy room to hide her reddened cheeks.

Her shoulder sagged with exhaustion as she dropped into a hard chair. As they had before, the youngsters raced about to explore every inch of their new room. It didn't take them long. A wide bed and the chair filled the small room nearly to capacity. If there was a washstand, she couldn't see it.

She didn't look up when the door opened. From the children's reaction, she knew it was Cliff. At the moment she didn't feel especially interested in speaking to him. He spent a few minutes playing with the boys, then turned to speak to her.

"All set, half-pint?"

"Cliff, is there anything I can do to make you stop calling me that horrible name?"

He sat on the floor next to her chair. Leaning against the wall, he looked up at her with his easy grin. "I doubt it. Look at it this way. If I call you half-pint downstairs, no one will think anything of it. Can you imagine what would happen if I called Izzy honey?"

"That's horrid!"

"Izzy? It is, but it's close to the way Pete lisps your name. I thought it would be easier for the boys." He yawned as he pulled off his hat and slapped it against the wall to beat out some of the dust. "After you put them to sleep tonight, come downstairs, and we'll see if we can't make a few ounces of gold."

When she rose to wander about the narrow room, he watched her openly. Since he had been idiotic enough to kiss her, she had treated him with unadulterated contempt. His eyes moved slowly along the curves of her body, nearly hidden beneath her layers of clothes. Each time he touched her, it startled him to discover how birdlike her fine bones were.

How difficult it had been to draw away from her when she was so compliant in his arms! She affected him like no other woman he had met. Not that she was the type of women he normally chose. Peg epitomized those pillow-soft, black-haired women, yet today he did not want the whore. All the time he had been speaking to her, he had been thinking of delicately sculptured Lizzie.

He did not want to force Lizzie to be more than his trail partner, and he suspected that she would not sleep in his arms willingly. Although he had been allowed to sample the untutored passion on her lips, he was sure she would push him away if he touched her as he longed to do. Now that she was worth a fortune to him, he did not want to scare her into fleeing from him. He suspected she would not continue all the way east with him, but even a shorter trip could be profitable for them both.

"If we put the boys in the middle with their heads at the bottom of the bed, we should all fit," he mused as he saw her staring at the iron bed.

"All of us in that bed?"

"You slept with the boys at Delilah's."

"But not—" She turned away to hide her scarlet face.

Rising, he went to her and put his hands on her shoulders. As he had done so often, he turned her so he could see her delicate features. When he put his hand on her cheek, she flinched. As if she had struck him, he pulled away.

"Lizzie," he said tightly, "I know what you're

thinking, but I have yet to make love to any woman with two kids in the middle of the bed. You will be as untouched as if you were sleeping in a nunnery."

"Thank you. I appreciate your concern for my feeling." Her voice was as hard as her glittering eyes. "It's nice to learn everything will happen at least once in my lifetime."

"And what is that supposed to mean?"

With a sigh, she sank down on the edge of the bed. She shook her head as she said, "It means nothing. I'm nervous. Not only do we have to play cards tonight, but—"

"You don't like being considered a boy."

"No, I don't." Her sudden laugh brightened the dark room. "I don't like having to convince an overworked prostitute I am not interested in her charms. This is not how I thought it would be on our trip."

He sat beside her. The boys began to clamber all over them, but Cliff held them off easily. "Don't worry, half-pint. Peg will be too busy tonight to worry about your initiation into love-making."

"Cliff, remember what I told you—" she began, concerned by the expression on his face as she spoke.

"You have my vow, Lizzie. While we're at the table, I'll look at no other woman but you."

"I am honored."

His eyes glowed with a strange light as he said with complete seriousness, "You should be, honey.

You should be."

She had no chance to ask him what he meant as he began to tickle the boys. Soon all semblance of order disappeared as the three rolled on the bed like a litter of puppies. When she tried to stand up to avoid Pete's boot, which was aimed at her head, Cliff grasped her arm and drew her into the melee.

They soon were breathless from laughing. Tommy and Pete leapt off the bed as Lizzie announced it was time for supper. She started to follow. Instead Cliff pinned her beneath him on the lumpy mattress. Her eyes widened as she saw the amusement on his face.

"Don't worry tonight," he ordered. "You'll do wonderfully well, half-pint."

"I hope so. I have never played for real stakes before."

When his hands framed her face, she did not try to move away. Every inch of her body was aware of the movement of his body against hers as he lowered his mouth to hers. The kiss was luxuriously luscious, and her arms rose to his shoulders. When she felt the tip of his tongue caressing her lips, she parted them eagerly and welcomed his exploration of her mouth's shadowy interior. At the same time, his hands slipped along the slender curves of her body. Too soon he drew away from her.

"For luck?" she whispered, her breath as short as if she had run a mile.

"For luck. Somehow I knew from the first

that you would be lucky for me, half-pint." He tweaked her nose and rose. Offering her a hand, he drew her to her feet. "I'm going to see what's happening downstairs. Wish me luck in finding some fools to join our table."

In a soft voice, she murmured, "Good luck, Cliff." She stood on tiptoe. With her hand against the back of his head, she brought his lips over hers again.

His hands gripped her arms and drew her away from him. He knew if there was much more of this, he wouldn't be able to leave her alone in this room, which was meant for loving women who were nowhere as soft as Lizzie. When he saw the pain in her eyes, he knew she had misunderstood again. And again he would let her think exactly what she wished. She could not be allowed to guess his true thoughts.

Perhaps he would take Peg up on her offer tonight. He grimaced. He had never thought he would take a whore to bed simply to forget another woman. Then again, he had never thought he would meet anyone like Lizzie Buchanan.

"Be downstairs by nine, half-pint," he ordered.

Her voice was tart as she retorted, "And don't be drunk!"

He didn't answer her as he smiled at the boys. The way she could read his mind was uncanny. He had been thinking that a few shots of whiskey might erase the harsh edges of his longing for her.

Once more he repeated the vow he could not seem to keep. He would not touch her again. He could not have her and also the wealth she could bring him. If it had to be a choice between the two, he knew he should select the gold. He did not need a half-pint and two children complicating his life. The gold would make him happy.

If that is so, why are you so miserable? he asked himself. To that there was no answer. He shut the door behind him and went down the hall to escape what he did not want to face.

Later, when Lizzie was sure the boys were asleep and wouldn't wander out of the room, she, too, left the room, closing the door silently. She walked along the unlit hallway. Her fingers slipped along the wall to guide her. In disgust she pulled them away. The wallpaper was hanging in tatters and was caked with dirt and grease that clung to her skin. Grimacing, she wiped her hands on her stained denims.

She nearly stumbled over a prone figure, but she managed to swallow the scream that rose in her throat. Looking closer, she could just make out the face of an intoxicated miner sleeping off his whiskey. She straightened up and looked around but saw no one else in the corridor.

She smiled tightly. One of R. B.'s women had probably taken the man's money and left him there without fulfilling their agreement. It was the perfect solution. The woman was free to return to the main part of the saloon and search for another customer. This one would never admit in daylight that he had fallen victim to drink before he could sample the delights of his chosen whore.

The false gaiety in the saloon reached out to suck her in. She sought through the crowded room for Cliff. A man growled at her as she bumped into him. She ducked automatically as he swung his fist in her direction. With a hasty apology, she fled toward the bar.

That was one thing Cliff had not considered in asking her to be part of his charade. The drink-befuddled miners would have no patience with what they saw as an undersized lad. In a brawl she would be hurt easily, for she had not been raised to indulge in rough horseplay with the men at the local tavern.

With a sigh of relief, she saw Cliff talking to a blond man. She longed to rush to him and urge him to take them far from Sparkler's Drift, but she remembered his promise to give her most of the money they won together. That gold would be a great asset when she and the boys reached Louisville.

"What are you doing here, boy?"

She whirled to see a man bearing down on her. He was scowling and appeared intent on causing trouble for her. With her back against the bar, she lifted her chin high. In the deepest voice she could manage, she said, "I am here for the same reason any come here, mister."

The darkly bearded face stared at her as his frown deepened. "We don't like sass here in Sparkler's Drift, boy. Why don't you get the hell out of here before I teach you what happens to naughty brats?"

"I don't have to leave." His words were not loud enough to carry over the general hubbub. She had no one to help her, so she would have to deal with this bully herself. Motioning to the bar, she started to step aside. "You can have my spot, mister."

Lizzie cried out in shock as the man grabbed two handfuls of the front of her loose shirt. When he whirled her to toss her across the room, her reaction was instinctive. The pain of the concussion of her fist against his chin reverberated up her arm and settled in her aching shoulder.

He staggered back, bumping against a table. The men sitting there shouted and shoved him away, even as they grabbed for their drinks and the cards scattered on the tabletop. Others noticed the battle and turned to watch the amusing scene of a large man lurching toward a slight lad balanced on the balls of his feet. Catcalls accompanied the big man's progress as he bore down on the ashen-faced child.

"Dammit!" muttered Cliff under his breath as he looked over his shoulder to determine the cause of the excitement. What he saw did not surprise him. That Lizzie was in the middle of this latest mess somehow seemed to be normal.

She was thinking of nothing but how to avoid those ham-sized fists that seemed determined to beat her into the floor. Although she had known instantly how stupid it was to hit the stranger like that, she couldn't let him hurt her without protesting. Now, with the bar behind her, there was no escaping the man.

He stepped closer to her. His red-rimmed eyes glowed like a cat's in the dim light. When he grinned evilly at her, his broken teeth created a mask of horror. "I'll teach you to hit me, boy," he snarled.

As his arm swung, she ducked. She looked up to gauge his next action. Astonishment froze her against the sharp edge of the bar.

Cliff was holding the man's arm almost casually behind his back. He smiled at Lizzie and motioned with his head for her to stand up. When the man began to struggle, Cliff merely tightened his grip on the arm. Pain seared across the bully's face and echoed in his shout.

"You all right, Izzy?"

"Except for my fist," she said with a sudden grin. She shook her hand to relieve the cramping of her bruised knuckles. "I think I hurt it on his rock-hard head."

He grimaced at her as he heard the laughter around them. The man he held prisoner growled. Would Lizzie never learn to control her sharp tongue? Even an incident like this only whetted it. After this insulting her assailant, there would be no way to smooth the ruffled feelings of the angry man.

Releasing the man, Cliff shoved him toward the door. "Get out of here," he ordered without rancor. "Leave the kid alone."

The man glared once more at Lizzie but obligingly stamped out the door. Chairs scraped on the floor and conversation started up again as the other men realized the brief excitement was over.

Cliff reached out a long arm and grasped Lizzie. Pulling her away from the center of the bar, he spat at her, "Don't you have any brains?"

"What was I supposed to do? He started it."

"Avoid trouble."

"I can't when it comes after me," she stated reasonably.

Forcing his rage back inside him, he nodded. They would discuss this later. Now he wanted to play cards. He had heard that some of the men had hit a small vein up the valley and were eager to lose that gold tonight.

As if it was a casual meeting, he stopped at the table where the lucky miners sat. Two empty bottles lay on their sides in the center of the table, and two more were in the process of being emptied. The four men laughed loudly as they celebrated their fortune. Cliff had been watching them all evening and had decided they would be the first to test Lizzie's skills. With their minds befuddled by drink, they wouldn't notice the still-crude signals passing between the newly arrived man and boy.

"Good evening, gentlemen. I hear congratulations are in order."

One of the men stood up. Fighting for his balance, he held out his hand. "Cliff Hollister! I heared you was in Sparkler's Drift. I didn't believe ole R. B., but I sees he was right this time."

"Just passing through on my way east."

"Sit yerself down and join us. We're drinking to that purty yellow glint in the rocks in the St. Louis Mine." He leaned forward as if to whisper a confidential secret. "Me and the boys are going to be rich. Real rich!"

Lizzie struggled to swallow her disquiet. She didn't want to cheat these hardworking men. The miner's words echoed those Zach had uttered so often in a wistful voice. That was everyone's dream here. To strike it rich fast. Few thought beyond that golden moment.

Despite her misgivings, she found herself sitting between Cliff and a man who was introduced as Allard. Whether that was his first or last name she had no idea, since that was all he was called. A taciturn man, he glowered into his drink and grunted if anyone spoke to him.

She was unsure who suggested they play cards, but she guessed it was Cliff. Sprague, the mining boss who had greeted them, agreed enthusiastically. From his pocket he drew a bagful of gold, which he placed in front of him.

"I don't think I have enough to cover that,"

said Cliff slowly. "I have to give the boy a few coins to play with and . . ."

"Naw, let the kid be the banker. We'll give him enough money to cover a few bets; that should keep him going. He can pay back what we lend him at the end of the game." Sprague had no idea he was doing exactly as Cliff wanted. "That'll keep him out of trouble, and we can each give him a coin when we're finished if he wins nothing. How's that, boy?"

"Fine," she whispered, sure her face was betraying her. She did not want to continue the charade. It was madness to think they could get away with cheating these men so blatantly.

A pack of cards was pressed into her hands. She looked up to see Cliff smiling at her. Competently she shuffled the cards. She offered them to Sprague to cut. He did not pause in his conversation with Cliff as he waved his hand over them. His faith in her honesty bothered her even more.

She placed the cards on the table. No dealing box was visible, so she turned the first card up. The men placed their bets on the crudely drawn cards on the tabletop. They bet on the cards they thought would be drawn as winners. She glanced at the table. Cliff had his money on three, the others on six, eight, nine, and the queen.

Taking a deep breath, she turned up the next card. It was the losing card, a nine of hearts. She took the coin from that spot on the table and added it to the small pile next to her. She watched as the men rearranged their bets as they wished. She flipped the next card, which would be a winning card.

It was a three.

As she handed Cliff a coin to match the one he had placed on the table, he smiled roguishly at her. This turn of the cards had been pure luck, and it boded well for the night to come. As she reached for the next card, she wished she could share his confidence.

The night rushed by as the pile of coins and gold dust next to Cliff grew steadily. The other men won enough so they did not become suspicious. The whiskey pressed on them by the exuberant winner eased any suspicion of cheating they might have had.

Again and again they went through the pack of cards. None of the miners noticed when Lizzie switched to the deck she had prepared. Except during the first and the last games, that was the pack she used. When Cliff signaled to her that the next would be the last game, she went back to using the deck Sprague had given her.

Rising after the last play, Cliff stretched broadly. He smiled at Allard, who was sleeping noisily next to Lizzie. The melancholy man was out of the game early on, so he had comforted himself with Cliff's free whiskey.

"Thanks for the game, friends." Cliff scooped up his winnings.

"I cain't say it's been exactly a pleasure,

Hollister," remarked Sprague. He shrugged as he smiled. " 'Course, what does it matter? Lots more gold where that come from." He swayed as he stood up. Then he slapped Lizzie on the back so hard she fell forward on the table. With a laugh, he said, "Yer a good lad, Izzy. See ya around."

His friends aided the sleepy Allard to his feet, and the quartet staggered out of the saloon. Lizzie did not watch to see if they made it through the door. Fighting the aching muscles of her tense body, she pushed against the tabletop in an effort to get to her feet. The table tilted, but she managed not to fall. All the winnings were secured in Cliff's saddlebag, so there was no danger of losing them.

"Let's go, Izzy."

"Don't call me that!" she hissed under her breath. When she heard his laugh, she wondered if "Izzy" would replace "half-pint" as his despicable nickname for her. If she had a choice, she would opt for the latter.

With feet that felt heavier at each step, she climbed the stairs. Opening the door to their room, she lurched into the darkness. Cliff jauntily followed.

"Six hundred dollars," he said with satisfaction as he removed his boots and placed them by the door. "Not bad for the first night. You're so good, Lizzie, it's hard to tell when you're playing honestly."

"I don't like any of this," she lamented.

"I know." He patted her shoulder. "But at this

rate, honey, it won't be long before you're rid of me."

"How did you know?" Her eyes followed him in the dim room as he moved to sit on the far side of the bed. He motioned that he couldn't answer because he didn't want to wake the sleeping children. She went to her own side of the crowded bed. "How did you know?" she repeated in a whisper.

He shrugged. "You've made it clear you don't want them infected by my free-and-easy way of life. Go to sleep. We may stay here a few more days. I want you to be sharp again tomorrow night." He leaned across the bed and caressed her cheek. "You're a good partner, Lizzie. Good night."

"Good night." Her words were barely audible as she forced them through her constricted throat.

As she lay back on the paper-thin pillow, she felt Tommy's feet poking her in the small of her back. That was the least discomfort she had felt all night.

CHAPTER SEVEN

PEG SAUNTERED OUT THE BACK DOOR OF THE saloon. The afternoon sun blinded her, but she crossed the stable yard with easy familiarity. She smiled broadly as she noted the boy standing by the watering trough. The kid was tucking his shirt into his buckskin pants. The last time she had seduced a youngster like that, she had enjoyed it as much as he had. She was tired of the miners panting over her. With her regulars, she knew exactly what to do to please them and get rid of them quickly. It would be fun to take the time to teach this lad to please her.

She swaggered over to him. The first time she would give him a tumble for free. When she had him enticed by her charms, she would lure him back and get a share of the wealth the lad was accumulating at Cliff Hollister's card table.

Slapping the lad on the buttocks, she asked

with a husky laugh, "How are you doing, honey?"

Lizzie whirled. When she heard footsteps and felt the hand on her backside, she expected to see Cliff in his habitually jovial mood. Startled, she took a step backward to avoid the overflowing body of the whore.

"Good afternoon, Peg. It is a nice day, isn't it?"

"It could be nicer . . . for you and for me," Peg murmured.

Shaking her head, Lizzie backed away. She could feel the heat of her flushed face. "No. No, thank you, Peg. Not today."

"Ah, honey, don't be scared. Everyone has to have a first time. Just trust me, and I'll treat you really well." Her pudgy fingers settled on Lizzie's shoulder. For a second, a frown flitted across her face. The lad was as slight as a girl.

"No!" Lizzie skipped away to avoid the woman's touch. She had not thought Peg would renew her attempt to seduce "Izzy." Then comprehension dawned—the whore wanted to gain a share of the money Lizzie and Cliff had won last night. "I don't have anything to pay you," she said truthfully. "I gave it all to Cliff. If I asked him for it, he would want to know why I wanted it."

"You don't need no money, Izzy. I would be glad to teach a handsome lad like you for nothing." She moved forward to cut off Lizzie's escape. "Don't be so shy, honey."

Lizzie felt the wall of the stable against her back and knew she was trapped. Her eyes widened in horror as the whore closed the distance between them. Peg grasped her face and pressed her lips on Lizzie's.

With a shriek, the young woman pulled away. Desperation gave her the strength to push Peg back a step. Racing from the yard, she fled up the outside stairs to the second floor of the saloon. She did not pause as she ran to her room and barred the door.

She rubbed her mouth against her sleeve. She wanted to remove the feeling of another woman's lips against hers. Nausea welled in her stomach. Scooping up a handful of tepid water from the bowl and reaching for the harsh soap, she scrubbed her face until her skin felt raw. Even that could not erase the sickness inside her.

With her arms wrapped around herself, she stared at the bare walls of the room. The furniture wavered as tears rushed into her eyes. She was desperate to escape this hell. She didn't want to stay. She couldn't stay.

Flinging the saddlebags on the bed, she scooped up clothing the boys had left on the floor. She stuffed the garments into one of the saddlebags and rebuckled the pockets. As soon as Tommy and Pete returned from wherever they had gone with Cliff, she would inform them that they were leaving.

She paced the floor, feeling more like a prisoner than ever before. She was afraid that if she stepped through the door, she would find Peg there, ready to renew her attempt to woo "Izzy" to her bed. Then a hint of a smile touched Lizzie's lips, as she thought how funny it would be to pretend to acquiesce and have Peg discover the truth.

A shiver put an end to her amusement. Peg would not react kindly to such a trick. If it became known the whore could not tell the difference between a woman and a slender lad, she would lose whatever standing she had in the town.

A heavy fist hammered on the door of the room, but Lizzie did not open it immediately. Only when she heard Cliff's voice did she slide the bolt out of the lock. She was overwhelmed with greetings by the boys but listened with only half an ear as they chattered on about riding out to see the St. Louis Mine. Her lips tightened as she looked at Cliff.

He was tossing his hat on the wrinkled bed. Dust from the ride covered his beard and clung to his eyebrows. He slapped his hand against his pants. A cloud of dirt slowly settled to the floor.

"I think I like it better when it's muddy," he said with a smile. "We had a fine time with Sprague and his crew, but I don't think they're going to get much more out of that vein."

"Then there's no reason to cheat them out of any more, is there?" she asked tartly.

Cliff's forehead wrinkled in confusion as he heard the anger in her voice. "What's wrong, half-pint?"

"Everything. I'm leaving."

"You are *what*?"

"You heard me," she said sharply. "I'm leaving. I will not stay another day in this hellhole. You promised to take me east, Cliff. If we delay much longer, we'll be snowbound in the mountains."

He saw the desperation in her eyes. "What is it, honey? Has one of the men here done something to hurt you?" He was no longer startled by the rage that rose within him when he thought of a miner touching Lizzie.

"No," she whispered. She continued to gaze at the ripped blanket as she said, "No man has done anything to me. They all think I'm a boy. Don't you remember?" Swinging her saddlebags over her shoulders, she repeated, "I'm leaving."

She stamped to the door. He didn't move, and she hesitated as she reached for the latch. Again she announced, "I am leaving."

"Fine." He sat down on the messed-up bedclothes. "Have a pleasant trip."

"What—?"

He laughed at the expression of rage on her face. "What do I intend to do? Is that what you wanted to ask? I intend to take a nap. Then I plan to go downstairs and win a few more games of faro playing with those fools."

"I can't go across the mountains alone, Cliff! I need your help."

"I know." He leaned back on the pillows and folded his hands under his head. His casual grin did not match the intensity in his eyes. "It seems to me, Lizzie, that you have a real problem. You can't go east because you're afraid of the mountains, and you can't return to Hopeless because you don't want to end up sleeping with Winchester."

She tossed the saddlebags across the foot-

board of the bed as she dropped to a chair in
defeat. Negotiation would prove useless. He held
all the winning cards in this game. Somehow she
had allowed him to corner her. He could force her
to do as he wished.

Her eyes went to him as he reclined on the bed
with that superior smile just visible beneath his
scraggly moustache. One thing she knew about
Cliff Hollister: he would be sure to take care of
himself first. She and the boys would come in a
distant second.

Quietly she asked, "How much longer?"

"It all depends on what it is that's scaring
you."

"Nothing!"

"Then why are you running like a prairie dog
before a wildfire?" His casual attitude dropped
away as he stood up and came to stand in front of
her. "Tell me, Lizzie!"

She shrugged with false nonchalance. "I don't
like Sparkler's Drift. I don't like California. I want
to get out of here. Isn't that enough?"

"No," he said reasonably. He started to add
more, but the door opened without the courtesy of
a knock.

They looked up to see Peg sashay into the
room. She started, and they realized she had not
expected to see both of them. Unintentionally she
announced her foiled plan by saying, "Cliff, I
thought you were going out to visit the boys at the
St. Louis this afternoon."

"We did. Had a grand time too." He kept his
voice light, but his eyes narrowed as he saw Lizzie

draw back into herself when the whore entered the room. Comprehension dawned on him.

Lizzie had not been bothered by a man; it was Peg, who was obviously still determined to seduce the young boy who had ignored her blatant offers. The more Lizzie showed her indifference to and abhorrence of the prostitute, the more Peg vowed to bring "Izzy" to her bed.

"I heard you won big," purred Peg as she moved closer to Cliff. "Izzy here tells me you're keeping it all for yourself."

He grinned. Her words confirmed his suspicions. Sneaking a glance at his partner, he was not surprised to see her face twisted with loathing. But curiosity teased him. He wanted to learn what Peg had done to cause Lizzie to react that way.

"The kid doesn't need to squander his gold on something he can live without. I promised to deliver him to his family." He leaned on the back of the chair and exerted his charm on her. "What does a kid like Izzy need money for anyhow? It's not as if he was a man with a man's needs."

Lizzie watched in disgust as the other woman slithered over to Cliff and put her hands on his broad arm. He certainly seemed to attract a certain class of woman, Lizzie decided. Delilah had fawned over him the same way.

Her feeling of self-righteousness was replaced by a stab of jealousy when she saw him put his hand on Peg's bare shoulder and stroke it gently. Those same fingers had touched her and teased her to the brink of insanity with their fiery caress. She did not want him touching another woman while he had that glow in his gray eyes. Fiercely she submerged such dangerous emotions, which could betray her too easily. Cliff had no interest in her. That had been proven again and again. It was time for her to stop longing for the impossible.

His smile never wavered as he removed Peg's fingers from the buttons of his shirt. He doubted she would be bothered by the presence of others in the room, but he had succeeded in drawing her attention from Lizzie for long enough. Turning her toward the door, he gave her a small shove.

"Get out for now, Peg." When he saw her smile at his suggestion of a later rendezvous, he added, "Next time knock before you come in. We might be busy."

"You and the kids?" She laughed gustily as she went out as he ordered. The idea of virile Cliff Hollister being interested in boys delighted her sense of humor. She would enjoy retelling the jest to the other girls.

When the door closed, Cliff said, "Boys, go over to the store and buy me some bay rum."

"Bay rum?" Tommy wrinkled his nose. "That stinks."

"Run along. Here." He tossed the youngster a coin. Tommy caught it easily. "There's enough for a bottle and two peppermints for you and Pete. Scat!"

Chattering, the boys swarmed around their aunt to give her a quick kiss before racing down the stairs. They made enough noise to rouse the prostitutes from their late sleep. Behind them, Cliff shut the door quietly. He leaned on it and asked,

"What did Peg do to you, Lizzie?"

She started to snap a response. When her angry eyes met him, she saw he was not teasing her. She swallowed her outraged words as she realized he cared enough to want to know what had happened. As she spoke, she trembled. "She's trying to convince me to buy her favors."

"She has been doing that since you met her. I don't think she can be any other way with a man. What else?"

"Not much," she mumbled.

He tipped her chin up so he could see her troubled face. "Tell me, Lizzie." When he saw the stubborn tightening of her lips, he added more quietly, "Please."

A heated blush touched her skin. "She kissed me."

He fought to keep his laughter in. Stepping forward, he placed his lips against her forehead. "Did she kiss you like this?"

"No." Her voice was so hushed he could barely hear the single word.

"Like this?" He mouth touched the scarlet warmth of her cheek.

"No." She jerked her head away from him. In a more normal tone, she spat, "She kissed me like you kissed me!"

Moving so rapidly she could not react, he drew her lips beneath his. As he tasted the honeyed softness of her mouth, he longed to put his arms around her and bring her close. He had not been able to forget her warmth against him when he had stolen those few kisses from her their second night on the trail.

When he felt her outrage, he reluctantly released her. "Like that?"

"Exactly like that!" she snapped. "With exactly the same amount of sincerity."

"Lizzie, I like kissing you." He was surprised to find her words hurt.

She sniffed in derision. "I am sure you do. I don't think Peg detested it either. She came here for more, didn't she? I just don't want her touching me." She moved away far enough to place the small space of the room between them before she added, "I don't want you touching me either."

"You seem to have a difficult time remembering that when I hold you, half-pint."

"I trust you will remember, then, and stay away from me." She untied the twine under her chin. Pulling off her hat, she dropped it to the floor.

He watched as she stepped before the cracked mirror he had insisted R. B. find him to use when he shaved. Slowly she loosened her braids. From one of the saddlebags, she withdrew a sharp knife. Before he could say anything, she had hacked off a large portion of her thick hair.

"Lizzie!"

Without turning, she said softly, "I'm tired of wearing that hat all the time. The hair will grow back by the time I get to Louisville." Methodically she went on cutting her hair until a thick pile of shorn strands surrounded her. She took greater care as she trimmed it around her face.

Cliff's eyes widened as she turned to face him.

Wisps of soft golden brown curls clung to her cheeks. As if his fingers could form their own thoughts, they reached out to touch the aurora they made to outline her features. She jerked her head away, breaking the spell her beauty had caste over him.

"There," she said with satisfaction. "Now I can be your Izzy without wearing that hat all the time."

Taking her shoulders, he turned her so she could look into the mirror. The broken line of glass gave them a distorted reflection. His face was close to hers as he whispered in her ear, "Honey, look at yourself. Do you think anyone will believe you're a boy?" His palm stroked her cheek, and her eyes closed in guilty joy.

She fought the thrill that flowed through her like a river cascading down from a mountainside, brilliantly aglow in the sun. Her hands pushed his away as she stated, "They must. The rest of me is much harder to alter than my hair."

"You didn't have to do such a drastic thing." He looked with regret at the hair he had longed to feel along his skin.

"No? Would you take no for an answer tonight if I told you I didn't want to continue playing faro with you and the miners?"

He did not answer. Every effort he made to charm Lizzie was thrown back into his face. What worked so easily with other women failed miserably with her. She demanded total honesty from him. Too many years had passed since he'd been truthful with any woman. It appeared she intended to teach him that skill again whether he wanted to learn it or not.

"I'm going across the street to the store to make sure the boys buy what I wanted. Do you need anything?"

She shook her head, angry at herself for caring about what he thought. Bitterly she asked, "What could I possibly want? Don't I have everything a woman could ask for?"

The resounding crash of the door was the only reply. All the weight of her new life dropped onto her shoulders, making her back ache with the burden. She sat on the edge of the bed and stared at the wall. No answer awaited her there.

As if she had vowed love and fidelity to Cliff, she had entwined her life with him. He was correct. She couldn't go back to Hopeless. She couldn't find her way across the mountains alone. Somehow she had enslaved her life to this overbearing man without even realizing it. She wondered if she would ever escape.

"Lizzie, look!"

She spun around to see the boys race through the door. Her eyes widened as she reached out to touch the new clothes they were wearing. The smartness of their store-bought trousers and shirts matched the snappy rims of their hats. Shining boots had replaced the scuffed ones they normally wore.

"You look wonderful!" She had to fake her enthusiasm as she computed how much the two new outfits must have cost Cliff. Her false smile faded into a scowl as she saw him come into the room.

If Pete and Tommy looked crisp, Cliff had assumed the image of the dashing rogue he portrayed so well in the saloons. His black alpaca coat was open to showcase his gold satin vest. His tall stock collar was closed with a silk tie. Plaid trousers with loops worn beneath his brilliantly polished boots completed his stylish outfit.

Despite herself, as the trio came into the room, she pulled at the filthy buckskins she wore. She was overwhelmed by a sense of betrayal. Because of her, they had made a fabulous start on their way to a fortune, and every sparkle of the gold they had won she had entrusted to Cliff's care. Yet this was the way he thanked her—by spending the money on everyone but her.

"So what do you think, Lizzie?"

Her pain showed in her voice as she said shortly, "Wonderful, Cliff. Just wonderful! What a pair we'll make in the saloons. Dapper Cliff Hollister and his urchin partner."

With his eyes on her, he said softly, "Boys, go downstairs and have R. B. give you each a sarsparilla. Tell him I'll pay him later." Their shouts of excitement were muffled as Cliff closed the door. "Lizzie, I spent only half of our money. There is more if—"

"You spent half?" She could barely speak past the rage that clogged her throat. "Half of your share or half of everything?" When she saw the answer in his face, she stuffed her hands in her pockets and fought to keep from saying the words she wanted to shout at him.

Softly he said, "I bought you something too."

"Oh, Cliff," she moaned. "Why did you waste our money like that? We were well on our way to accumulating what we needed. . . ." Her voice faded as she saw what he pulled from the wrapped package he had been holding under his arm.

Despite herself, she could not help stretching out her fingers to touch the lace of the camisole. The sleeveless garment bore a single pale pink rose embroidered in the center of the bodice. In the sunlight, the silk glistened as if it possessed a life of its own.

"How beautiful!" She shook her head to break the enchantment. Stepping back, she said forcefully, "I don't want it!"

He laughed and placed it against her. With a half sob, she spun away from him. His smile faded as he tossed the pretty garment and its matching calf-length drawers on the bed. Taking off his coat, he hung it on the hook on the door instead of tossing it on the floor as he normally did with his buckskin jacket.

"You mean you don't want it because it's from me," he said as he sat down on the bed near where she stood.

"It is inappropriate to receive such personal gifts from a man." She did not look at him or the clothes, which teased her to caress their softness.

"Since when have you cared about proprieties?" he taunted. "You're just angry because I spent some of our money on new clothes."

Tears sparkled in her eyes as she whirled to face him. "Half! You spent half of our money. Without asking me! I thought we were partners, Cliff, but we aren't. I'm just a quick and easy way for you to live well until you have to hurry across the mountains to be back in Missouri in time to meet your next train."

Hurt by her words, he grasped her shoulders and pulled her close to him. His mouth over hers silenced her outrage. He held her tightly until she softened against him. Then his fingers slid along her back to feel the buoyancy of her short hair.

Lizzie fought her own yearning to be in his arms. She did not understand why she believed his lying lips when they were pressed to hers. Over and over he had proved her to be a fool, and she compounded it by coming back to his arms again. The tears overflowed as she pushed herself out of his embrace.

"Honey," he whispered as he put his hands on her shoulders, "I didn't mean to hurt you. I wanted you to be pleased with this gift. With you wearing 'Izzy's' clothes, I couldn't buy you the dress you should have. I thought you would like these things to wear underneath your denims."

She gathered up the dainty undergarments and shoved them into his hands. "Did you? Well, you were wrong. I am very happy with what I am wearing. If I want something different, I can get my own clothes. I do not need you buying me unmentionables, Cliff Hollister."

"All right." He threw the garments back on the bed. "Maybe you're right. You should wear these boy's clothes. You aren't what a woman should be."

Her eyes sparkled with rage. She pointed her finger at him to emphasize her words. "That is why you don't understand me, Cliff. You think women are good for one thing and one thing only. I can be your partner at playing cards. I can ride in buckskins across the mountains. I can do all that and more, and I still will be what I am. A woman! Just because I don't fall all over you with eager desire, don't think I can't feel that for some other man." She laughed coldly. "You aren't as irresistable as you seem to think you are."

"Be downstairs later!" he snapped. Then he walked out of the room, slamming the door. Her words rang in his ears. As he had so often, he wondered why he had bothered to shackle himself with such an impossible woman. If only he could keep her out of his mind.

When he saw those pretty lacy things in the store, he immediately thought of Lizzie and how alluring she would look in such feminine gewgaws. Her complaint that he considered women good only for the entertainment they could offer him stung. Too many of his fantasies revolved around seeing her face beneath him as he taught her of love in a bed they would share without her nephews.

Damn!

He strode into the barroom and pounded his fist on the counter. R. B., who was talking to Tommy and Pete as they drank their sarsparillas, looked up in surprise. Motioning to the two youngsters that he would be back in a moment, he moved along the bar to where Cliff stood glaring at the mirrored wall behind the liquor bottles.

"Whiskey," Cliff snapped as if there were a choice of drinks. "Leave the bottle."

Gingerly R. B. set a dirty bottle in front of him, then wiped a glass on his filthy shirt and placed it on the bar. His fingers barely had released it when Cliff grabbed it and filled it to the brim with the golden liquid. He tilted the glass and swallowed more than half of its contents. Without reacting to the bitter taste, he refilled it to the top and lifted it again.

"Whoa, Cliff," urged R. B. "Yer going to be soused afore the night begins."

"Good!" Cliff said. "Then I won't have to look into that ungrateful wretch's eyes and listen to her snarling words. I buy her presents, and she throws them back in my face."

Although the bartender had no idea what the other man was talking about, he commiserated with him. "Women be a nasty lot. They want promises and love when all a man needs is a bit of warmth. Don't know where they get all them ideas. Look at Peg. She knows what a man wants and gives it to him."

Cliff lowered the glass to the scarred top of the bar. A bit of the whiskey sloshed onto the uneven counter as he said softly, "That is exactly what she said. She said I wanted her only for an easy life."

Shrugging his shoulders, R. B. said, "Sounds good to me. Don't need no woman tying me down."

"I guess you're right."

R. B. glanced at his customer, but Cliff acted as if he were alone in the room. He stared again at the cracked surface of the reflecting glass. When he fell silent, the bartender shrugged and wandered back to exchange tales with the boys.

Cliff did not move after that, except to send Tommy and Pete upstairs for their supper and bed. The bottle remained by his arm, but he did not lift it to replenish the glass that sat on the bar top. The room filled with boisterous miners, but he didn't notice anything or anyone. The other men noted his withdrawal and respected it.

The hours passed, and the fun was well underway. When Lizzie descended the stairs, her eyes went instantly to Cliff, who still stood at the bar. She did not have to search for him. Even before this, when he'd been dressed the same as the tattered miners, she had always found him quickly. Some instinct drew her eyes to him in any crowd.

As she walked among the men, many of them called a greeting to her. Her surprising resistance to the bully the night before had earned her their respect. She waved to them without being aware of who was speaking to her.

Sliding past the full satin skirt of one of the women whose job was to lighten the miners' pockets, she stepped up to the bar. She had no trouble standing next to Cliff. The others were leaving a wide space around him as if he carried some contagious disease.

"I'm here," she said quietly. "Are you ready to play?"

"Huh?" He turned to look at her as if he were waking from a dream. "Oh, hello, half-pint." His eyes swept along her figure. Once again he wondered why she had to be so beautiful. From the soft curls around her rose-tinted cheeks to the curves hidden so adroitly beneath the rags she wore, unconsciously she beckoned to him to sweep her into his arms and love her as even though she had told him so clearly that was precisely what she did not want.

"Cliff, is something wrong?"

Her voice sounded as far away as if it were coming from across the continent. Shaking his head, he broke through the cloying web of desire that seemed to surround him. Fantasy was a worthless exercise. Lizzie never would allow him to hold her.

"Nothing is wrong." He picked up the bottle and glass. Pointing with it, he said, "Over there, half-pint. We certainly won't lack for victims tonight. Let them come to us."

Cliff's prediction proved correct. Within seconds after they had chosen a table, several of the miners wandered over. Their comments about Cliff's fine new clothes suddenly made it apparent to Lizzie that he had not bought them purely for vanity. His fancy outfit reflected his status as the big winner. Everyone was eager to relieve him of his newfound wealth.

No one mentioned Izzy's silence. The men were too busy concentrating on their gambling. So closely did they watch her hands that Lizzie found it difficult to substitute her cards for the ones provided by the other men. Only when she could signal Cliff she had made the switch did he gamble very much.

As the evening wore on, miners left the table as their money vanished. Others quickly replaced them. She carefully gauged the winnings Cliff accumulated. If he won too much too fast, the rest of the players might accuse them of cheating. Camaraderie and many drinks for the miners paid for by Cliff helped ease that concern.

"How about one for Izzy?" suggested a miner whose slurred voice came to them from the sour, alcohol-laden haze that seemed to surround him. He leaned forward and put a companionable arm around Lizzie, smiling as she averted her face from his foul breath. "The boy looks thirsty to me."

Peg turned from accepting payment from a miner for the five minutes they had spent in her room. Smiling, she said, "Rabbit Tyler, you are a generous man."

"Me?" The man grinned, revealing the two remaining front teeth that had earned him his nickname.

"Yes, you, darling." She slid her fingers along the tattered sleeve of his flannel shirt. "I do love generous men. Buy the kid a drink and come with me."

Nearly tripping over his chair in his eagerness to share the time of the saloon's madam, he dropped a coin on the tabletop. "Let the boy order his own."

Her sultry voice stroked him as gently as her fingers had moments ago. "I'll get it for him,

Rabbit." Then she asked offhandedly, "What do you want, Izzy? Sarsaparilla, I assume?"

"That would be fine." Lizzie threw Cliff a concerned glance. She didn't trust Peg. The whore did nothing out of kindness.

Cliff winked at Lizzie. With just a few words, Peg had the crusty miner obeying her every command. Cliff suspected Rabbit's pockets would be much lighter by the time he came back downstairs. Peg had charmed him by playing on his yearning to be noticed.

Peg placed the drink on the table by Lizzie. Some of it splashed onto Lizzie's hand, and she raised it to her mouth to clean off the stickiness. She met the prostitute's eyes as she said tersely, "Thanks."

"Nothing to it, kid. Nothing like what I would like to do for you. Just remember that later. I always have time for you."

All the men laughed as Lizzie fought the blush betraying her. Peg's caustic chortle resounded through the saloon as she led Rabbit to her private room.

Lizzie lowered her eyes to look at the cards in her hands. She picked up the glass and took a large sip. Grimacing at its too-sweet flavor, she continued to drink it to hide her shaking hands. The aftertaste lingered in her mouth, but she did not want to ask for anything else to drink. Unless she had more of the sickish sarsaparilla, she would be forced to drink whiskey. They were the only drinks R. B. served.

Just as the night before, when the time came

to end the game, a large pile of coins and nuggets sat in front of both Cliff and Lizzie. Cliff bought a last drink for everyone as Lizzie went to their room with their winnings. Laughter billowed up the stairs.

Feeling guilty but thinking there was little choice, she took two of the largest gold coins and placed them in a small pocket of her saddlebag. The rest she put with their previous winnings in Cliff's bag. She feared he would continue to spend all their fortune as soon as it came into his hands.

She readied herself for bed, being careful not to wake the boys. Easing into the bed, she withdrew Tommy's knee from the middle of her spine. A flush of heat rolled over her, and she shoved the thin blanket aside. Instantly she was cold. With a muted groan, she reached for the covers as the door opened to let Cliff enter. His whispered good-night received no answer. She did not feel like arguing with him again.

Another swelling of heat washed across her skin. She hoped she was not going to be sick. Having the ague now would be disastrous. She wanted to be done with Sparkler's Drift, not be stuck here while she recuperated from some sickness.

Sleep swept her away from her concerns. She did not feel Cliff get into bed on the other side or hear him murmuring her name. Sinking into her dreams, she tried to escape the horrors of her life.

Cliff wondered at her obstinacy in not answering him, for normally she started at the least sound. He sighed. She was making it clear she had no intention of forgiving him for his buying spree that afternoon. Tomorrow, he promised himself, he would find a way to make her accept his apology. Reclining on his pillow, he closed his eyes and smiled.

Things were going far better than he had expected. Lizzie's system would net them all they needed before they crossed to the far side of the mountains. He dismissed the twinge he felt at the thought of them parting and tried to concentrate on the fun he would have before the spring. It was much more difficult to create those fantasies now than it had been at the beginning of their trek.

Cliff woke to the sound of Lizzie moaning. He groped across two pairs of short legs to find her writhing on her side of the bed. When he called her name, she seemed unable to hear him. Hampered by the boys lying in the middle of the bed, he tried to wake her from whatever nightmare was haunting her.

Lizzie felt the movement of the bed. She grasped Cliff's shirt and pulled him to her. All she wanted was to feel his lips against hers, to have his hands soothe the fire scorching her skin, to ease the emptiness deep within her. A compelling desire she did not recognize stripped her of all sense. She could feel nothing but this need he must satisfy.

"Love me, Cliff," she whispered.

In shock, he gasped, "Lizzie, what did you say?"

"Love me." Her hand lifted from the covers and placed it on the softness of her breast. A heartfelt moan emerged from her lips as his touch only increased the fervor of her desperate craving. Unable to control her yearning, she reached up to undo the buttons of his shirt.

A flash of the fire searing her erupted within him as he felt her fingers play lightly along the skin of his chest. He pressed her to the bed, forgetting the children sleeping and oblivious to passions they could not understand. He reached for the few buttons holding her tattered shirt in place. He smiled when he felt the soft silk of the chemise he had bought for her beneath the flannel.

Lizzie had not been able to resist the sweet temptation of the feminine clothes. He longed to have a light to see her body highlighted beneath the sheer material.

He pressed his lips to hers as he slid the lacy strap down her arm to reveal her soft skin. Her eager breaths of pleasure wafted around him as he bent to place his mouth against the curve of her breast. As his tongue traced the gentle swell to its tip, he could feel the steadily increasing heat of her body as she moved sensuously beneath him.

"Love me," she commanded again. "I need you now!"

"Lizzie, my love," he whispered with a soft chuckle, "there's no need to hurry. Come, I'll take you where we can have more privacy."

She shook her head as her hand reached for his belt. "Now! Here! I can't wait! Please, Cliff!"

His fingers closed over hers as he glanced down at her face, so distorted by desire. This was not his Lizzie. She would never beg any man for anything. Just hours ago she had fought with him because he thought he could have some say in her life. That Lizzie would not grovel before him like this.

With a vicious epithet, he ripped himself from her arms as he rose from the bed. She gave a soft cry and followed him. In the moonlight he gazed at her pale skin, unabashedly displayed for his touch. He swallowed the longing exploding within him. It would be so easy to hold her against the floor and explore that body hungry for his loving.

He put his hands on her arms and felt hers go around him. The enticing caress of her body warmed his bare skin. An answering reaction from deep within him weakened his intentions; he could not deny the voracious need to sample her offered delights. For a brief moment, his mouth captured hers to feel the unfettered lust that possessed her.

Again he cursed as he pushed her away. Her cry of protest rang out. He saw Tommy peeking through the iron rails of the bed, and he quietly told the boy to go back to sleep. Knowing he could not deal with Lizzie's strange behavior in front of the boys, he scooped her up and tossed her over his shoulder.

Into the darkness of the unlit hall and out into the deserted stable yard he carried the thrashing woman. He knew she was not trying to escape him. When he set her on her feet, she pulled him into her arms. It took all his strength to break her obsessive hold.

"No, Cliff," she moaned. "Love me. I'll do whatever you want if you touch me."

He shook her. "Lizzie, stop it! Don't you understand?"

"I want you, Cliff. Why don't you want me?"

"Dammit, half-pint!" He placed his hands on her cheeks and tilted her face up to look at his. In the moonlight he could see the glitter of her glazed eyes. That, as much as her behavior, explained to him what had happened. "Peg must have slipped something into your drink tonight. Something to make you act like this."

Her fingers moved along the skin bared by his open shirt. As if she had done many times before, they teased his skin, urging him to give her what she wanted. He released her to grasp her wrists as she reached for his belt again. Had he not been so worried about whether the effects of the drug would linger into the next day, he would have laughed at his own actions. As often as he had thought of loving her, it was ironic that he would push her away now.

"Lizzie, listen to me."

"Will you—?"

"Yes!" he lied glibly. He would promise her anything if it would allow him to reach beyond the drug's power and force her to understand what it was doing to her. The night would be so sweet if he were to love her as she asked, but it would complete the destruction of Lizzie Buchanan. If only her dark eyes were not so filled with longing. . . .

When she answered, her voice was weak. "I am listening. I don't know how long I can."

"Good girl." Although every instinct urged him to hold her as he explained, he knew that would be disastrous. "Lizzie Buchanan, you have been drugged. Peg put something in your drink to make you so crazy with desire that you would go to her and demand she take you to her bed."

"I don't want her. I want you, Cliff," she pleaded painfully.

He smiled ruefully. "That's where she miscalculated. She has no idea 'Izzy' would be longing not for a whore but for a man. Honey, you have to fight this." Regret tinged his voice. "If I knew you would forgive me, I wouldn't hesitate to love you, for you are the most desirable woman I have seen in all my travels."

"I've listened to you. I'll forgive you anything if you help me. Cliff, I want—"

"I know what you want, honey." He hesitated before saying resignedly, "Not here. This is too public. Come with me."

Her feet followed his command as he walked toward the stable. What the rest of her body did mattered little to her brain. It remained under the influence of the drug, knowing only the anguish of unsated desire.

When he ordered her to sit on the floor of an empty stall, she did so eagerly. As he leaned over her, she welcomed his lips on hers. Then he raised his head to gaze down into her soft, vulnerable face.

"I don't know if you'll like the games I enjoy playing," he said as he brushed her hair from her eyes.

"Anything, Cliff. Anything you want."

He grinned. "Remember, you agreed to this,

honey."

Lost in the power of the drug and the anticipation of relief from the burning inside her, she complied docilely as he lifted her arms over her head and bound her wrists together with a piece of twine from the floor. He tied the other end to a ring on the wall designed to hold a horse's reins. Then he quickly but gently wrapped his handkerchief around her head and gagged her.

He sat back and looked at her. Rage rushed through him as he saw her so humiliated by Peg's cruel machinations. Leaning against the plank wall of the stall and outwardly cool, he regarded Lizzie.

"No," he said in answer to her unuttered question, "I am not going to do as you wish. You will stay like that until the drug wears off. I'm sorry, half-pint, but that is how it must be."

Her scream emerged as a high-pitched squeal around the cloth gagging her. Even in the darkness, he could see her dark eyes fill with fury at his betrayal, at the thought that he would deny her surcease from her suffering. She pulled at the ropes desperately, but he had secured her well.

Through the remaining hours of the night, he watched silently as she raved. He ached for her agony, knowing how delightful it would be to relieve her pain. As he listened to Lizzie's muffled demands that he make love to her, he wondered what it was Peg had used. Many exotic drugs came from the Far East ports of China. It seemed likely that one of them had been used in an attempt to corrupt Lizzie, force into begging for what she had resisted so vehemently until now.

When her voice began to sound like a croak, he untied the gag. At his touch, her eyes met his. The words she could not force through her parched throat, she said with her eyes. He wondered whether she could guess, under the bewitchment of the drug, how much he longed to moisten her chapped lips with his own.

His fingers swept the untangled curls from her face, and he saw her eyes close in eager yearning. ''I'm sorry, honey,'' he whispered as he moved to sit beyond her reach by the door of the stall. He tried to ignore the tears rolling down her cheeks.

He fought to stay awake as the sun rose in the sky. In the saloon, no one would be stirring until past midday. He hoped by that time that whatever was controlling her would wear off and release her from its cruel thrall.

Despite his best efforts, he had just begun to doze off when he heard a soft voice query, "Cliff?"

The difference in her voice alerted him. He crawled toward her and met her sorrowful gaze. "Half-pint? How are you?"

"What are we doing here in the stable?" She winced as she moved her arms. "Why am I tied up like this?"

He moved to undo the ropes. Her straining on them had tightened the knots. Impatiently, he pulled out his knife and sliced the thin twine into two parts. Warning her not to move, he cut the bonds on her arms.

"Don't you remember anything?"

She shook her head. "I remember going to sleep last night. That's all. I had some strange dreams, but that's all. Oh, my!" The last words came out in a gasp of distress as she glanced down at her open shirt. She pulled it closed as she stared at him accusingly.

Stretching his cramped muscles, he asked, in a deceptively calm voice, "What did you dream about?"

"I don't think that is any of your business!" she snapped.

"If you won't tell me, let me tell you. You dreamed that you seduced me."

Lizzie paused as she was about to snarl a retort at him. Slowly her mouth closed as she attempted to redo her shirt. Her numb fingers shook as she struggled with each button. Cliff pushed her hands aside and competently secured her shirt. She did not look at him, ashamed of what she feared was true.

He put his finger under her chin and tried to raise her face so that she would look at him, but she resisted. He touched her shoulder. She flinched and uttered a soft cry.

"Don't do that!"

Happiness rang out in his laughter. When she regarded him as if he had lost his mind, he wrapped his arms around her. "I'm glad you're back to normal, half-pint."

"It was all true then? I—I—I did that?"

"You tried to seduce me, if that's what you mean." He couldn't keep from smiling as he looked down into her shocked face. "Peg drugged your sarsaparilla with an aphrodisiac last night to bring 'Izzy' panting to her bed. She never considered that 'Izzy' might find someone closer to relieve the needs exaggerated by the drug."

She hid her burning face in her hands. In all her life she had never been so embarrassed. She fought the images that formed in her mind and wondered which were real and which fantasy. She recalled the ecstasy that overwhelmed her when his mouth moved along her body. Folding her arms over her breasts, she wondered how much he had seen of her body. She wished she could ask Cliff to tell her the truth, but she didn't dare. She was afraid to learn what had taken place.

As if he could read her mind, he bent close to her ear and whispered, "Honey, nothing happened."

"You didn't—?" She couldn't bring herself to say the words aloud.

He shook his head. "And don't ask me why I didn't take advantage of your tempting offer." He chuckled as her cheeks turned a deeper crimson. "I don't understand it myself. I guess I felt I owed you something after spending part of your share of our winnings yesterday. You sure do look lovely in that lace, honey."

"Don't!" Leaping to her feet, she tried to flee. Instead her vision blurred and her weakened knees threatened to betray her. Gentle arms caught her as she fell on the slippery hay. Cliff carefully lowered her onto the floor and leaned over her.

"Stop running from me when all I want to do is help. Why can't you trust me? If seducing you was the only thing on my mind, don't you think I would have accepted one of your many offers last night?"

"I don't know," she murmured.

He used a single finger to wipe the tearstains from her face. "Admit it, half-pint, as much as you hate to. I do not want to be with you simply to sleep with you. I will admit to something I hate to say and never thought I would to a member of your fair sex. I like you, Lizzie Buchanan. You're brave and a good partner."

She closed her eyes and willed the world to stop spinning crazily around her. Just now she didn't care what he thought of her. All she knew was that she wanted to leave Sparkler's Drift. She wanted to be far away from a place where a woman would slip a powder into a youngster's drink to bring him to her bed.

"I don't want to stay here," she whispered.

He nodded. Nothing more would he get from her now. Kissing her lightly on the forehead, he rose and offered her his hand. Cautiously he brought her to her feet. He put his arm around her slender waist to help steady her. Together they walked out of the stall and into the stable yard.

Lizzie froze as she saw someone standing in the middle of the muddy area. Her fingers clutched Cliff's shirt more tightly as she battled the terror inside her.

Peg's eyes went directly to the colorless face of the person she knew as Izzy. She stated accusingly, "I thought to see you last night, youngster."

"Izzy was busy," answered Cliff.

"Busy? How do you . . .?" Her voice faded away as she gasped in horror. She had never suspected virile Cliff Hollister would be the type interested in boys. That explained the closeness between him and Izzy. "You're disgusting! I hope you enjoyed it!"

He grinned tiredly. "To tell the truth, Peg, I've never had a night quite like it. Thanks. Come on, half-pint. I'll help you upstairs."

Peg quivered with outrage as she watched him gently lead the "boy" up the staircase. To think her efforts to seduce the kid would end like this. Shrugging her shoulders indifferently, she decided there was no way to explain people.

She turned to the trough to clean up from her night's work. Already the incident had faded from her mind; all that was left was a reminder to herself that the next time she used her special potion, she would first make sure its recipient wanted to sleep with a woman.

CHAPTER EIGHT

BY THE TIME THE SUN HAD REACHED ITS ZENITH, the quartet had put Sparkler's Drift behind them. After that, Cliff did not attempt to spend more than one night in any of the towns they visited. After two weeks, the small mining settlements blended into one another. McClellan's Cut, Golden Valley, El Dorado, nameless towns known only as "here"—all were the same. All had the tumble-down shacks, the canvas tends burdened by water that had formed greenish pools on their roofs, the mud, the dirty men sitting around tables losing their money.

The miners' faces melted together. Lizzie became more and more proficient in helping Cliff win at cards. They took gold from men with white faces, with black faces, with Indian faces tattooed with strange symbols. Cliff bought drinks for men who spoke with odd accents or could not understand a word of English other than "whiskey" and "gold." The fever that at first pulled men and their families from the eastern United States had reached out its lures to entice men from all over the world.

Each saloon resembled the one before. Some of the bartenders were as friendly and talkative as R. B. Stevens had been. Others barely grunted. Both men and women saloon owners had women working for them to satisfy the men numbed by whiskey and hard labor.

Nothing ever changed, and Lizzie began to wonder if it would. The collection of gold in her hidden cache grew more slowly than the one that filled Cliff's saddlebags. She had taken some of his money to buy some fabric that she kept in the bag with their special possessions. What she was making from it, she showed to no one. She would work on it only when the others were out of the room.

A heavy storm greeted them as they rode into Joplinville. Needles of sleet sliced into them, but no one spoke of it as they dismounted before the golden glow of the lanterns on the saloon porch. The sounds from within were even louder than the noise of the horses' hoofs on the plank road. Half-frozen mud oozed between the boards as Lizzie dismounted.

"All set?" asked Cliff from behind his turned-up collar.

She wanted to retort that she had little choice, but she was too tired. Since the episode with the drugged drink, she'd been having a difficult time regaining her normal vitality. With a sigh, she simply nodded.

He glanced at her worriedly. He knew about how much was in his saddlebag. Tonight, if they did as well as they had in the past, there would be over four thousand dollars in it. That was the amount they had agreed on at the beginning of their partnership. He hesitated to count it. To acknowledge they had reached their goal would mean the time had come for them to separate.

That he did not want. He could not imagine leaving the three weary travelers to find their way home alone. By delaying, he hoped Lizzie would mention something about continuing their partnership as they had originally planned. She said nothing, and he could not.

They entered the saloon as they had so many others. The boys had learned to fade into the background and not rile any of the miners. Lizzie walked slightly behind Cliff, holding her nephews' hands.

Cliff smiled at every woman they passed. With the ease of much practice, they reacted to his charm. Each continued to watch him as he passed, even if she was sitting on the lap of another man. He walked on as if his grin was spontaneous, not a well-calculated ploy to gauge the temper of the barroom.

Despite herself, Lizzie paused in midstep and gasped as she saw what was happening on the raised stage at the back of the saloon. Cliff heard the laughter behind him and turned to see his partner frozen by the obscene performance being enjoyed by the miners. Sounds of amusement came from the men sitting close to where Lizzie stood. Her shock titillated their faded senses. Too many times had they seen the whores displaying their talents on the stage for them to be shocked any longer.

"Come on, Izzy," he growled. He took her arm to break her catatonia. "Stupid kid!" His words brought more chuckles from the miners before they returned their attention to the show.

"Cliff," she managed to choke out, "they—they—are—"

"I know, half-pint." Sympathy for her innocent outrage shone in his eyes. "Keep the boys busy over there by the stairs, and I'll get us a room for the night. Maybe they haven't seen enough yet to know what is going on."

Lizzie urged Tommy and Pete to follow her by promising to get them each a sarsaparilla before bed if they cooperated. She had them stand in the shadows with their backs to the stage. Whenever the cheers of the miners made the boys want to look at the perverted entertainment, she diverted their attention by a comment on a funny riddle. She breathed a sigh of relief when Cliff finally walked over to them.

"I've rented a room."

"What's wrong?" she asked as they climbed the stairs. She and Cliff were careful to keep one adult between each boy and the stage.

"I don't like this place," he answered as quietly. "Not just the goings-on on stage. The whole place reeks of trouble."

She bit her lip as he opened the door of the room he had rented for them at a much higher rate than he normally paid. He had not bothered to bargain, wanting only to get the children away from the perversions being displayed for the miners.

"Maybe we shouldn't play cards tonight," she suggested.

He looked around the room. Like all the rest they had shared in the past two weeks, it stank of its recent use. He threw their bags on the bed. It was the only piece of furniture in the room and barely wide enough for them.

We'll play. Just be cautious. Bring the saddlebags down with you. I don't want anyone to come up and discover this loot here with only the boys to guard it." He shook his head as he evaluated their quarters again. Three dollars and two bits seemed far too much even for a chiseling saloon keeper to charge.

"Do you think it's safe to leave them here alone?"

He patted her shoulder as he drew his frock coat from the saddlebag. He shook out the wrinkles before he pulled it on to complete his image of an easy mark for the miners. "The boys will be fine. Just treat the saddlebags as if they're unimportant. Drop them on the floor by your feet and keep one foot on them, so no one can steal them. We'll do fine."

Until she had the boys in bed, he remained in the room. When they protested that they hadn't gotten their reward for good behavior, he placated them by promising to take them to the general store the next day for a peppermint. Gleefully they dove under the covers. He avoided Lizzie's worried eyes as he joked about how crowded they would be in the narrow room. Telling her he would see her in half an hour, he went downstairs.

Hushing the boys, Lizzie turned down the lantern and sat in the twilight. Her hands stroked the soft leather of the saddlebags. Joplinville was no different from all the other places where they had stopped. Since the beginning of their journey, she had seen things she never would have guessed existed. Men deprived of civilization reverted to basic, animalistic drives, which were only sharpened by necessity.

Soon she and Cliff would reach the point where they would have to choose whether they wanted to continue on together or separately. She tried not to think of that disturbing moment. She did not want to say good-bye to him again. This time it would be forever. She was learning too many things about him that she wanted to explore further.

He had not kissed her since the morning she awoke in the stable. Instead they had become better friends, chuckling together over half-spoken jokes, sharing stories with the boys. Pete and Tommy openly showed their adoration of Cliff. She could imagine their loud reactions if she were to tell them to bid Cliff farewell.

The time passed far too quickly as she sat there musing; Cliff would be expecting her downstairs very soon. She forced herself to rise and pushed her reluctant feet into the hall, closing the door behind her. Her gaze swept the corridor. A second staircase could be seen at the opposite end. She did not bother to see where it led. The cool air blowing from that direction suggested that it opened onto the outdoors.

The cheering had not diminished when she came into the saloon. She didn't look toward the stage with its single quilted curtain hung on rope. The glow from a lantern cast shadows of the action on the opposite wall, but she kept her eyes on the floor in front of her. The odor of spilled whiskey, unwashed bodies, and kerosene fumes nearly overwhelmed her. Sure that Cliff would have found a table as far from the "entertainment" as possible, she turned away from the stage.

"Izzy!"

She glanced up to see Cliff waving to her. She hurried toward him, ignoring the men grabbing for the well-exposed bodies of the women working among the tables. When she sat down in the chair next to him, she was overcome by a desire to press her face against his chest and demand that he take her away from this unspeakable place.

That hope died when Cliff said graciously to the half-dozen men also seated at the table, "Izzy is my young charge. I'm taking him and his brothers back to their grandparents. I thought I would show him a bit of the life he is passing up to go live in Kentucky."

Lizzie had heard the story too many times to show her discomfort with his easy lies. She smiled absently as the men teased her, using the same jokes she'd heard from town to town. All too soon the cards were pulled out, and she found herself caught up in the fever of gambling once more.

She was overcome by fatigue before the men decided they had traded enough gold for the night. Despite the fancy card table, with its green felt cloth displaying the suit of spades from ace to king and the abacus-style board to keep track of the cards played, there was little difference between the game here and those they had encountered in other towns under more primitive conditions.

Cliff gave her the winnings to place in her bag, but he reserved enough to buy a round of drinks for his new friends. They sat and reminisced about common experiences in California while she walked toward the stairs. She had her foot on the first step when she looked up and saw that one of the miners had obviously decided he couldn't wait until he and his chosen harlot got upstairs before commencing their activities.

In disgust, Lizzie spun around to seek the other staircase that led to the second floor. She began to be convinced that no other place could be as horrid as Joplinville. Even stories about San Francisco and the disreputable establishments there paled beside what she was seeing here.

A door to the left of the bar led her out into the night. She shivered in the cold. The weather was turning more frigid as they rode higher into the mountains. She wondered how much longer they could afford to delay. Hefting the saddlebags on her shoulders, she hoped Cliff would be satisfied with what they had won so far and would agree to take them east now.

After the hubbub in the saloon, the quiet back of the building was blissful. She took a deep breath of fresh air to cleanse the stench of the barroom from her nose and lungs. The rain and sleet had ceased, and the stars were admiring their cool reflections in the puddles.

Her satisfaction at escaping from the saloon abruptly vanished. Something was wrong. The feeling overrode her pleasure in being outdoors. Lizzie glanced over her shoulder but saw no one. She began to have the feeling of being followed. Forcefully she told herself to stop being foolish. The boys were asleep upstairs, and that was where she wanted to be also. Whether Cliff decided to come up or not was his decision. As deep in conversation with the miners as he had been, she doubted that she would see him before they rose at midday.

A board creaked as loudly as a shriek in the early morning darkness. She whirled to see two men on the wooden walk. Fear set her to running before her mind had time to create a thought. The sound of their feet behind her urged her to her top speed. Her fingers reached desperately for the stair railing. Once she reached her room, she could barricade the door and wait for them to leave.

Out of the darkness in front of her appeared a shadowy figure. Its hands grasped her before she could elude them. She opened her mouth to scream, but a fist slammed against her temple, knocking her down. The saddlebags dropped from her shoulder and crashed next to her on the boardwalk. Her sight blurred. She moaned as she put her hands to her aching head.

Jerked to her feet, she saw the three men had become a dozen, but she couldn't trust her eyes to tell her the truth. Where each wavy form ended and the next began she could not tell. Someone grasped her arms and held them behind her. She didn't see the fist until it emerged from the darkness to strike her again.

The salty flavor of blood filled her mouth, but she had no time to react as she was hit again and again. She heard exultant laughter. Their taunting words didn't pierce the pain.

Suddenly she was dropped, landing jarringly on the wood again. The fleeing footsteps vanished into the night as she tried to breathe without causing more pain. Her fingers clawed for the saddlebags, but she couldn't find them. Each motion exacerbated her agony.

"Lizzie! Oh, no!"

The words bounced through her head, but she could find none to use in reply. She tried to lift her hand. It dropped back into the dirt, which was damp with her own blood.

She screamed as gentle hands rolled her onto her back. They moved along her in a torturous route. Curses spoken in a familiar voice drifted over her, but she could think of nothing but the anguish of her battered body.

"Lizzie? Lizzie, honey, can you hear me?"

Whatever she mumbled did not match the thoughts in her head. She seemed disconnected, afloat in a seat of pain, her body no longer hers.

"Honey, I have to get you upstairs. You can't stay here. It's going to hurt, because I think you have at least one broken rib." Cliff's voice came closer to her ear. "Can you hear me? Honey, I'm sorry. This is going to hurt."

Her world exploded into red-hot torment as she was overpowered by the pain of her injuries. As the murmur of his comforting words surrounded her, she faded into senselessness, secure in knowing that Cliff would tend to her.

"Damn!"

It was the last word she could remember hearing as she fainted. The same word brought her back to full consciousness. Water dripped onto her face. She reached out her hand to brush it aside and moaned.

Cliff's face came into view. He smiled, but she could tell it was false. His lips were pulled too tightly across his teeth. A fake jocularity was in his voice. "Hello, half-pint. I thought you would be back with us quickly. You're a tough gal."

"Lizzie! Lizzie!" She winced as the childish voices cut through her head.

"Go back to your room, boys," commanded the man softly. "You can see her again in a little while. Cliff had had to rent the room next door for the boys so that he could give Lizzie the space and care she needed.

Through her swollen lips, she mumbled, "They stole the saddlebags. All our money . . ."

"Hush, honey. It doesn't matter." He dabbed at the cuts on her face with a damp cloth. When she groaned, he swore silently.

This was his fault. He had flaunted their good luck. Blithely he had handed the gold to Lizzie in plain view of all the others. Sending her out like a sacrificial lamb, he had guaranteed she would be attacked by men who would do anything for the shiny metal hidden in the bags.

He glanced down at her face, which no longer resembled the lovely one he was accustomed to seeing. One of her eyes had turned black already. Her mouth was encrusted with dried blood. Although he hadn't looked, he suspected other marks would be visible on her body.

That thought made him rigid. He had to bind her broken ribs. Looking into her pain-glazed eyes, he said slowly, "Honey, can you sit up?"

"Sit?" The idea seemed absurd. The very thought of moving sent spirals of anguish through her.

"It's your ribs. If I have to, I can wrap them while you're in this position, but I thought—" He didn't know what else to say. From the start of their journey, Lizzie had guarded her modesty obsessively. The only time he had caught a glimpse of her slender figure was the night she had begged him to love her.

"Will you help me?" she breathed. Her face contorted as she lifted her hand to him. The simple motion sent a knife of pain slicing through her.

Despite his best efforts to be gentle, she screamed as he brought her up into a sitting position. Weakly she waved aside his apologies as her bleary eyes went to the pale faces of her nephews. From their shocked expressions, she could tell she looked as horrid as she felt.

Her fingers shook so hard she didn't think she could unbutton her shirt. Cliff did not hurry her. Softly he said, "You don't have to undo your shirt. It's big enough so you can just lift it out of the way. Then I can wrap this binding around you to ease the pain."

"All right," she whispered. She would have done anything at that point to lessen the mind-shattering agony of her body.

Carefully keeping his eyes on the wall, Cliff wound the material around her middle, completely covering the silk chemise that clung to her body. He tied the makeshift bandage beneath her breasts and drew his fingers away. When she didn't move, he took the hem of the shirt from her hands and lowered it to cover the garish fabric he had purchased from the saloon keeper to serve as a bandage.

"While you're sitting up, drink this."

Her shaking hands closed around the mug. She didn't have to ask what he had poured into it. Although the whiskey burned through her, she knew it would ease her pain. Trying to keep from tasting it, she swallowed as quickly as she could. When she had finished, he refilled the mug and motioned for her to drink it as well. Praying her stomach would not embarrass her, she gamely followed his order. Within minutes, a warm haze blossomed around her.

When Cliff leaned back against the pillows, she giggled in the midst of her moans. The laughter made the pain worse, but she simply held out her mug.

"That doesn't taste so bad once you get used to it," she murmured. "May I have some more? It makes me feel as if I'm flying." She flung out her arms, then groaned as the motion triggered more waves of pain. The dregs of whiskey splattered on the wall over the bed, leaving a pattern of abstract dots.

"I think you've had enough." He plucked the mug from her fingers, which remained raised as if they still held an invisible glass. "You should rest."

"All right." She couldn't stop giggling.

To satisfy Cliff, she closed her eyes and was soon drifting on whiskey-laden clouds. The door opened and closed several times, but she couldn't force her eyes open to see what was happening. Voices spoke unintelligibly. The passing of time had no meaning.

When she regained her senses, leaving the cotton puffs of her intoxication behind, she had no idea where she was or what the time—or day—it might be. The room was hidden in the darkness, giving her no clue to her location. She tried to sit up, but pain flared through her, and she abandoned the effort.

"Cliff?" she whispered.

"Here I am, honey." A shadow moved against the deeper blackness of the room. "How are you doing?"

"I feel as if I wandered too close to an erupting volcano."

A smile could be heard in his words, although

in the dimness she couldn't see his face. "It was something like that. You're not as badly hurt as I thought you were. I checked your ribs a while ago. They may simply be bruised. Your face looks terrible, what with your two black eyes and all the cuts and bruises, but it'll all heal."

"Thank you for the compliment." She added more softly, "And thank you for saving me."

"It was the least I could do."

She nodded. Even that simple motion hurt. "Yes. When I begin feeling better, I'm going to—"

Taking her hand in his, he raised it to his lips. "You are going to get on the back of your horse and we are going east. You'll have the whole trip to lambast me for my idiocy in giving you that money in plain view of all those men."

"East? You're taking us east?" She couldn't hide the relief in her voice. Weak tears burned in her eyes.

"It's about time. We can't delay any longer. We've wasted too much time in trying to profit from the stupidity of these miners."

"The money—"

Again he interrupted her. "—is gone. I know. We'll manage somehow. Isn't that what you always say?"

"But how?"

"Don't worry," he soothed her. "I have nearly fifty dollars left. You still have the gold dust in your bag. That'll get us east. Once we're back there, we'll find someone to help get you and the boys settled. I have friends who'll tide me over until spring."

The tears began to spill over. They beaded at the corners of her eyes before rolling down her face to dampen the pillow. "Don't!" she whispered.

Bafflement replaced his hearty tone. "Don't what?"

She shook her head mutely and turned away from him. The motion was difficult, but listening to the easy way he announced that soon their lives would part ached far worse. The pang in her heart gave rise to the anguish that eclipsed the pain of the bruises on her skin.

She loved Cliff Hollister. In her weakened condition, she could no longer hide from the truth she had been fleeing for more than three years. She loved his irreverent wit and his charming smile. Once she had adored him with a childish infatuation not so different from the way Tommy and Pete worshipped him. When he returned to her life, she found that the flicker of adoration had become love. Each day she had fought it, urging her heart to be sensible, telling herself it was insane to love a man who could not hide his eagerness to be rid of her. More than gambling, more than whiskey, more than enjoying the company of any woman, Cliff loved his freedom, loved the joy of holding his face up to the wind as he led another group of dreamers west. That life he wanted to share with no one.

"Honey?"

"Cliff, please!" she moaned. "Leave me alone."

Leaning over her, he put his lips against her forehead. With a sigh, he stood upright and moved across the dark room. He placed his bent arm against the wall and leaned his head on it, closing his eyes. The image of her lying battered in the dirt burst into his memory. So many times had he been involved in such battles. Even Lizzie had dealt with a fracas or two in the rough towns along the mountains' spine.

This was different.

Somehow, in the past two weeks, he had convinced himself that he had to think of her in the same way he thought of the boys. He had forced himself to deny the sweet, feminine appeal that brightened his days and gave stregnth to her nephews. Wanting the money she could bring them at the faro tables, determined not to hurt her by showing her how easy it would be to hold her in their bed without the boys between them, he had tried to consider her no differently from any of the men who frequented the saloons.

He had been wrong.

Over his shoulder, he could see her on the narrow bed. The sound of her soft sobs resonated queerly through the room. Only because she was suffering from the abuse of her assaulters' fists did she allow him to see her tears.

He went to the ewer and poured some of the tepid water into a bowl on the floor. Taking one of the tattered pieces of cloth that had cost so much, he dipped it into the water. He wrung it out and walked to the bed.

"Here."

Lizzie took the dripping cloth and dabbed her eyes. "Ouch! Damn!" she cried as she touched the swelling near her left eye.

"You sound like me," he teased. He couldn't recall her ever using his favorite curse before. "You're learning my bad habits."

"Bad habits are the only kind you have." She reached out her hand to grasp his arm as he turned away. "I'm sorry, Cliff. I shouldn't have said that. You make it difficult to be nice to you."

He guffawed, unable to stop the laughter that burst from his lips. "Me? Honey, I've been made to feel more welcome by a nest of rattlesnakes than by you."

"I just don't want to—" She put the cloth over her face. From beneath it, she mumbled. "Forget it!"

"Believe me, I've tried. You're not easy to forget, Lizzie Buchanan."

She peered from under the cloth and saw him smile in the moonlight. Without saying a word, she held her hand out to him. He placed his in it and sat on the edge of the bed next to her. Quietly he talked of anything he could think of until he saw her eyes close.

As tenderly as he had tucked the boys in next door, he now pulled the well-patched blanket over her. He bent to kiss her forehead, covered with damply twisted curls. The next day he would have to bring the boys back here to sleep with them. He couldn't afford to pay Racine, the owner of the saloon, for two rooms for the time it would take Lizzie to recuperate enough to leave Joplinville.

With a grimace, he drew off his frock coat. As soon as the store opened in the morning, he would pawn his fine clothes to gain a few dollars. He would get only a fraction of their worth, but he couldn't afford to quibble when they needed money so desperately. They had too little now to risk using it as an ante at the faro tables. Without Lizzie, he had no guarantee of winning.

Without Lizzie.

He paused at that thought and looked at her again. Tomorrow night Tommy and Pete would rejoin them. Tonight he had their beautiful aunt to himself. She was so bruised she would be less willing than usual to let him show how much he yearned to love her.

Sitting on the bed again, he reclined on the thin mattress. Gently he slipped his arm under her shoulders and brought her to rest close to him.

Her eyes opened slightly. He touched her discolored cheek with his lips and whispered, "Sleep, Lizzie."

"Stay with me, Cliff," she murmured.

"Yes, half-pint, I'll stay with you tonight and as long as you wish." He wondered if she had heard him, but it didn't matter. It was a promise he intended to keep.

The days passed slowly. With the two boys imprisoned in the room with them, they all soon grew short-tempered. Lizzie's aches and bruises faded a little more each day, but she left Cliff to handle their needs. He soon became proficient at entertaining the boys with cards and stories.

One dreary afternoon she was sitting on the bed sewing a rip in Pete's new shirt as she half listened to the tale Cliff was telling them. Her needle paused in midstroke as she looked up in surprise.

"That's me you're talking about!" she gasped.

"Of course. I thought the boys should know how brave their aunt is, rescuing her family's wagon from destruction."

She shrugged off both his praise and the fervency in his expressive eyes. As she pushed the needle through the material, she said coolly, "It's nice for them to hear a true story for once."

"All my stories are true," he retorted.

"All?" She lowered the cloth to her lap. "The ones about the Indians, the ones about the prairie schooners—they're all true?"

In mock sorrow, he asked, "Did I ever give you cause to doubt anything I've said?"

Lizzie laughed as she had not since the attack on her. His face assumed a distressed expression that didn't match his twinkling eyes. She only laughed harder. The boys joined her, although they had no idea what she found so amusing.

He stood up and walked toward the bed. Sitting on its edge, he reached out his fingers to the greenish tint of one of her fading bruises. As he touched her skin, her giggles faded into a smile.

She placed her fingers over his. Her eyes met his steadily as she said, "I feel well enough to travel, so we can leave any time now."

"It's been only a week."

"We can't delay any longer, Cliff."

Reluctantly he nodded. This brief interlude could not have lasted much longer in any case, even if they did not have to make their way to the other side of the mountains before the early snows overtook them. Racine demanded ten dollars each day for the room and the sparse meals they ate. The barkeeper knew they had no other choice but to pay him while Lizzie was recovering.

They had to leave Joplinville. Cliff didn't want to think about the other reason they had to seek the trail east. Her suspected he knew which men had attacked Lizzie. He had overheard rumors that more money was hidden in their room. If he didn't get Lizzie and the boys out of this collection of derelict huts, the same men, still hungry for gold, might injure her again.

Softly he said, "Tomorrow at sunrise."

As the two boys whooped in delight, he brought her head to rest against the comfort of his flannel shirt. They had a harder road ahead of them than anything they had attempted so far, but together they would find the stamina to overcome any obstacle to their goal.

CHAPTER NINE

LIZZIE TOOK GREAT DELIGHT IN REDISCOVERING the pleasures of their life on the trail. At first she found she could not go far without being overcome with exhaustion. The beating she had undergone had taken more out of her than she had realized. Cliff allowed her to gauge the distance they traveled each day. If she did not call for a stop when she grew fatigued, he would stop them himself and berate her soundly before setting up camp.

His concern eased some of her deepest fears. She knew how little gold he must have left after buying, at vastly inflated prices, the supplies they needed for this part of their journey. That his fine clothes had disappeared from among their limited possessions, she noted but did not mention. She didn't want to think about what else he might have sold to finance their trip. She wondered how they would manage to reach the Mississippi on the little that remained of what they had worked so hard to gain.

Whenever he could, he had them stop early. Then he would hunt among the trees for fresh meat. Squirrel and rabbit became the staples of their diet. Lizzie learned to skin them quickly so they were ready for cooking by the time the fire was blazing. The sizzling of grease tantalized them as they waited with appetites whetted by a long day of riding.

Sometimes Cliff would take Tommy with him when he hunted. Lizzie was properly enthusiastic and Pete jealous when the boy came running back to her one night with the rabbit he had shot himself. When she thanked Cliff for treating the boys so well, he brushed it off as unnecessary. He couldn't hide the strength of his feelings for the boys any more than they could conceal their adoration of him. He promised her he would be especially cautious with the gun when the boy was with him. To assuage Pete's envy, he promised to take him fishing when they reached lower altitudes.

Between the two adults existed an unspoken truce. Any hints of yearning were disguised as they struggled to restrain their feelings. Instead they spent the evening playing cards and chatting. Cliff taught her to play the game called poker, which was becoming increasingly popular in the gaming halls.

"I don't think I could trust you in a game you already know," he teased.

"How do I know you aren't cheating me?"

He laughed. "Because I have an honest face."

"Is that so?" she retorted tartly. "I must admit

I've never noticed that. I'll see your bet and raise you two pebbles."

It was easier to continue that kind of light-hearted joking than to open the door to the stronger emotions lurking within each of them. Whenever Lizzie looked up from her cards to see his eyes on her, burning with unsated desire, she would pretend she hadn't noticed. If his hand lingered against hers as she gathered the cards to deal them again, she acted as if her heart was not pounding, its beat echoing throughout her body, which so longed to be against his.

The weather remained pleasant. With cool days and pleasant nights, they slept easily in the open. Rolled in their blankets, they nestled together like a litter of puppies. Each night Lizzie was careful to insure that the boys slept between them. No longer did she fear Cliff. Now she was frightened of her own compelling yearning to feel his arms around her and the caress of his lips on hers.

All that came to an end about a week after they left Joplinville. They were well into the mountains that formed the backbone of the California Territory. As they reached ever-higher elevations, the soft rain that had started at daybreak slowly changed to sleet.

Lizzie pulled her felt hat down over her eyes and concentrated on holding a blanket around Pete. The ice cut into her face like a hundred tiny insects. When Cliff called to her, she brought her horse to a stop.

"We're going to get out of this," he announced. "There are caves all along this ridge. We can sit out the storm and start again when it passes."

"There is no town nearby?"

He shook his head. "None that I know of. Of course, that means nothing with the way these towns sprout like spring shoots around here. But I don't want to waste time wandering through the storm looking for something that may not exist. A cave may not be as comfortable, but it should be dry and warmer than this wind."

"I think it's an excellent idea. I don't want the boys to become ill."

His eyes were the only part of his face visible. Like her, he had drawn his hat down low over his forehead and pulled the high collar of his buckskin shirt up past his chin. In front of him, hidden by his coat, sat Tommy.

"How are you doing, half-pint?"

"Fine, Cliff. We can go on as long as we must."

"We'll be out of this soon. Follow close behind me. This sleet can easily turn to snow. Watch the trail; it's slippery for the horses."

She felt the first twinges of fear as she heard the worry in his voice. In the past seven days, she had again come to acknowledge that Cliff's statement about being the best wagon master on the westward trail was not a boast. He could see trouble ahead and anticipate their needs in a way she would never be able to do. This world of tall trees and empty silences belonged to him like a second soul.

Now he knew they were being threatened by the very forces of nature he loved.

Keeping her horse directly behind his, she bent her head to protect herself from the biting wind that numbed her still tender cheeks. Considering the force of the storm, she began to fear they might be stranded for awhile. That could become months if the snows arrived early in the high passes.

Don't worry, she thought, attempting to reassure herself. There was little she and Cliff could not handle together on this journey. Already they had proven that. Even the boys were trailwise now. The four of them had become a team. They would survive.

Cold drops slipped between the back of her hat and the collar of her shirt. She shivered as they made an icy path along her spine.

"Lizzie?"

She smiled at the little boy cuddled against her. It wasn't easy for an active child to sit for hours each day in the saddle while they rode through the stands of white birch and pine. Not once had either boy complained to her. She was sure they had said nothing to Cliff. They wanted to be as strong and independent as he was.

"I'm fine, Pete. Just some raindrops dripping down my back." She ran her finger between his slender shoulder blades. "Just like that." As he giggled, she laughed also.

No matter what trials they had to face on the journey, she was happy to put the horrors of California behind her. Never would the boys have to learn the truth of what their mother had suffered there. They could grow to be what Whitney and Zach had wanted them to be. The guilt that had ripped her apart each time she sat down at a card table would attack her no more. Although they had drifted from their eastward direction to try to win what was not meant to be theirs, now they would reach the golden goal of the sun sparkling on the Mississippi.

Only when her horse halted abruptly did she notice the animal in front of them had already stopped. She saw Cliff dismounting. Waiting patiently in the cold, she watched as he walked up a nearly invisible path overgrown by brush. What his keen eyes had seen was hidden from her.

He came back quickly. Standing on the lee side of her horse, he took her hand and drew her down closer so she could hear him through the muffling thickness of his clothes.

"I recognize this road. There's an abandoned miner's cabin up this way. I think that's our best bet. It's not far. Can you go on?"

"Yes." She winced as the wind swirled higher to attack them even more viciously. "Will there be shelter for the horses?"

"There was. If not, we may be crowded in the cabin, honey. I don't want to leave them without a roof. The sleet is already turning to snow."

"Oh, no!"

In the deepening twilight, she noted the way his eyes twinkled and guessed that, beneath his turned-up collar, his mouth was curved upward in a smile. "Don't worry. We have plenty of food. This early in the fall the storms are heavy and short. Even if we get any amount of snow, it'll melt away soon."

She gripped the reins tighter. When Pete complained, she loosened her hold on him. She wished she could share Cliff's lighthearted optimism. She had heard too many tales of frozen corpses discovered during spring thaw. These mountains did not allow the unwary to make mistakes and survive.

As she turned her horse onto the path, she checked to see that the packhorse followed. From the beginning of their journey, she had the extra horse made her responsibility. That left Cliff free to act in case of attack. They had to worry not only about hostile Indians but also starving miners who barely scratched out an existence in the mountains and would covet such a horse and what it carried. The fading discolorations on Lizzie's face were reminders of how desperate such men could become.

The road was thick with slimy mud that threatened to bring the horses to their knees. As it sloped uphill more steeply, Cliff dismounted. Lizzle quickly did the same, leaving Pete on the back of her horse clutching the saddle horn.

"That wasn't necessary. I'm far heavier than you," Cliff called. The wind sucked his words from his mouth and tossed them like flotsam in the sea of snow. In spite of the roar of the storm, she was able to guess what he was saying.

"We can't have one of the horses going lame," she called back. She grimaced as she lifted her foot from the mire. The deep mud flowed over the top of her boots and oozed through her holey socks. "Let's go. It's getting colder."

When he held out his hand to her, she was glad to put hers in it. He looked at her reddened fingers with concern. "Honey, why haven't you put on your gloves?"

She looked up at him; his beard was encrusted with pellets of ice and wet snow. "I don't have any. Last spring I traded them for food. I thought you realized I have only what I'm wearing."

"Why didn't you tell me that before? Never mind."

He berated himself for not noticing that when she did laundry for them, she continued to wear the same shirt and denims, but it didn't surprise him that she made sure the boys had a change of clothes while she wore these threadbare things. Now was not the time to tell her he finally understood her rage when he had bought new clothes for everyone but her.

He pulled off his right glove. "Here. Take it. Your fingers are going to freeze if you don't cover them."

"Cliff, no. I'm fine," she protested, although she longed to reach for the leather glove.

"Take it, honey. We need to have your fingers in good shape. I can't have them freezing until they turn black and fall off."

His words had the desired effect: she took the glove. Cliff's concern was not exaggerated. Too many people had lost fingers and toes to the cold of the high mountain winters. Tales of the temperate mountain summers had deceived some miners into believing that the high-altitude winters would be as mild. Sometimes they learned the deadly lesson too late.

It was not easy to pull the glove over her stiff fingers. She smiled as she felt the residual warmth of his hand. In the too-large glove, the sting of feeling returned to her hand. She kept flexing her fingers to regain motion and warm them up.

Following his orders, she took the reins of her horse in her gloved hand. He grasped the leads of the other two horses. Finally he turned and held out his right hand to her. She placed her icy fingers in it, and he wrapped his much warmer ones around them. Then he carefully inserted both their hands in his coat pocket. The snow that also sifted in melted as their fingers touched it.

"Awkward, I know," he said with a laugh, "but I think we can manage."

She nodded, her eyes sparkling as brightly as the ice that coated the nearly bare branches of the trees and emphasized the needs of each fir. No matter the reason, she enjoyed life far more when she was close to Cliff. She could forget for a short time how stupid it was to savor dreams of a future that had them all together.

"We'll manage." She smiled as she repeated the words that had become a hallmark of their struggle.

Hearing the softness in her voice, he glanced at her and then quickly away. Mumbling a command to the horse, he started along the road, adjusting his long steps to her shorter stride. He couldn't allow himself to think now of the slender line of her body, so near him. Each movement of her leg caused it to brush against his. During the week it had not been easy to watch her sleep on the other side of the boys and not show her how much sweeter the nights could be if she shared them with him.

Any closeness seemed to drive her farther from him unless it was absolutely necessary, as this was. She was frightened of him, of her past, of life. Her whole being was centered on her nephews. She was sacrificing everything she could be for them. It was a noble purpose, and he couldn't blame her for choosing it, but he wished she could see there was more to life than striving to find happiness in the past.

They remained silent as they struggled along the path. Perched on the backs of the horses, the children bent forward and swayed with the wind. The crash of the trees over their heads sounded sharply. Ominous creaks were a warning that some might fall before the end of the storm.

Lizzie's legs ached with the effort required to pull her boots from the solidifying mud. Whenever she slipped, an iron-strong arm went around her to keep her from sprawling in the road. She smiled her thanks to Cliff but said nothing. She needed every bit of her strength to make the upward journey.

When she finally saw a break in the trees, she almost cried out in joy. Even through the capricious, spiraling dance of the storm, she could see the outline of a small cabin. To one side appeared another shadowy shape that she hoped would be a shelter for the animals.

She did not bother to lift her feet but simply sloshed through the freezing puddles and sculptured mud. When Cliff released her hand, she slipped it into the glove he had given her, along with her other hand. His hands were so large, she could fit both of hers in the single glove.

Although she could not hear the sound of Cliff's bare knuckles as he pounded on the wooden door, his shout drifted through the woods. "Hello? Is anyone in there?"

She lifted the boys from their horses when he motioned for her to come to the door. Swinging it open on its rusty hinges, Cliff led the way into the deserted cabin. While the boys explored the hut in the twilight, he knelt in front of the fireplace and made sure the flue in the chimney was clear.

"I'll bring in some wood," he said. Standing up, he wiped his sooty hands on his mud-streaked trousers. "You can start a fire while I tend to the horses."

"Here." She held out his glove. "You'll need this."

With a smile he put his hand up to push her battered hat back from her eyes. He stroked her damp hair with his broad fingers. "Thanks, half-pint. I'm glad you're along on this trip. You can be the most difficult woman I have ever met, but I can't think of anyone else I could depend on as I have you. Lizzie, don't let anyone tell you that you aren't special. You certainly are."

She stared at him as he went out into the storm. This was neither the moment nor the circumstances during which she would have expected such a comment from him. As the door closed, muting the howl of the wind, she tried to remember when she had thought he might say something like that to her.

The answer was easy.

Never.

"I like Cliff," stated Pete with all the assurance of a three-year-old. He wrapped his arms around Lizzie's left leg and leaned his head against her hip.

Putting her hand on his soft blond hair, she said softly, "I like him too, Pete." She looked toward the door and smiled. "Yes. I like him very, very much." Only in her mind did she change the word to "love." To no one else could she admit the truth hiding in her heart.

Lizzie turned as Tommy called to her. She went to see what he had discovered beneath a bed frame. It and a table with a wobbly bench nearly filled the small room. The state of deterioration of the furniture told her that at least a year had passed since its owner had left. Empty shelves hung at strange angles on the wall. Although the house was filthy, the wood floor beneath their feet and glass in the windows made it seem luxurious. They would be snug in it during the storm.

Soon she and the boys were all laughing as they collected the assorted remains of nutshells and other debris and tossed them into the fireplace. Cliff brought in wood from outside. While he tended to their horses, she lit a fire to warm the interior of the cabin.

That night, while they ate precious food from
their dwindling supplies, they celebrated their good
fortune in finding the cabin. The boys crowed with
delight when Cliff took two candy sticks from a
secret pouch in his remaining saddlebags. He had
saved the sweets for a time like this. Despite their
enthusiasm for camping they had felt at the
beginning of their journey, the youngsters were as
pleased as the adults to be sleeping with a real roof
over their heads and real walls to enclose them,
warmly and safely, in their snow-covered lair.

Cliff unrolled the two smallest blankets onto
the bed platform after they had cleared it of the
rotting remains of what must have been a feather
bed. Only some scraps of ticking and bits of fluff
remained in the corners.

When the two children were finally asleep, he
leaned back against the bench with his stockinged
feet toward the fire. He watched as Lizzie competently finished cleaning the remains of their meal
from the dishes. He could think of no other
woman who would be so stalwart and uncomplaining on the road east. Few men could tolerate the
rigors she accepted as inevitable.

She wiped her hands on her denim pants after
she poured the dishwater back into the bucket by
the door. They might need the water later. She did
not want to send anyone on unnecessary errands
into the storm screeching at the eaves. Her
buckskins were draped over a bench with the
others to dry before they were donned again in the
morning. She felt Cliff's eyes on her and glanced
questioningly across the small room at him.

"Why don't you sit down for a few minutes?" he asked. He patted the floor beside him. "You're tiring me out just by watching you scurry around."

"Because if I stop, I don't think I'll get started again." She put the tin cups and plates into the saddlebag. "I want to be ready for an early start."

"We won't be going anywhere for a few days."

She sank to the floor next to him by the hearth. The flickering light of the fire created an abstract pattern of shadows across his face, giving it an almost diabolical appearance. His narrow nose became hawklike, and each whisker was individually highlighted. The line of his square jaw was visible through his dark beard.

"A few days?" she breathed as if she had been struck by an unforeseen blow.

With a soft laugh that would not wake the children, he asked, "Is it so horrible, Lizzie? It was snowing pretty hard when I came in with the wood, so I guess we're in for an early blizzard."

"Snow? It's been so long since I've seen much snow." Her memory supplied scenes of frosty mornings that too often turned into slushy afternoons.

"I think you'll be seeing more than you ever wanted to over the next few days. There's no sense trying to get through it when we're safe and warm here. You deserve a few days of rest. I know how poorly you've slept since we left Joplinville. This will give you some time to recuperate. I'll watch the boys, and you can hibernate."

Carefully she put her most dire forbodings into words. "Hibernate? You don't think that this is an early winter?"

"No, honey." He reached out and took her hands in his. There was a hint of amusement in his words. "This is only October. We don't have to worry about having to endure each other's company in this tiny hut all winter."

"That's not what I meant," she said hastily. "I meant that I was concerned about—"

He tugged at her hands sharply. With a laugh at her gasp of astonishment, he wrapped his arms around her body, which by that time he held against his chest. Gently, persuasively, he placed his mouth over hers. She tensed against him, but he didn't release her.

Instead he lifted his lips from hers slightly so that he could speak. "Lizzie, don't be so afraid of me. I'll do nothing to hurt you again."

"Again?" Her eyes tried to rearrange his face into its normal laughing lines, but it was too close to hers.

"I've hurt your more times than I wish to think about, haven't I? And not only on this trip. Do you think I didn't see the wistful expression on a young girl's face when she came west with her family? You were such a pretty little thing in your calico gown with all the petticoats beneath it."

"You never let me know that. You barely said hello to me twice the whole time we traveled west."

He smiled sadly. "Your brother-in-law made it quite clear to me from the outset that you were to arrive in California in the same untouched condition as when you left Missouri."

Pushing herself away from him slightly so she

could see his face more clearly, she frowned in bafflement. "You do remember me. But it's been three years, with so many faces in between."

"You remembered me. Isn't that why you waited six months before you picked a trailwise traveler up out of the mud?"

She fought to find words, but there were none to mask the truth. Deciding there was no reason not to be honest, she whispered, "I remembered you, Cliff, because I have never met anyone like you."

"The same reason a little girl named Lizzie has been hidden in the back of my mind since that trip." He touched her hair, smoothing it back from her face before entwining his fingers in its gentle curls. At the same time, his mouth found hers once more. It tasted delicately sweet, despite her many tart words to him. He noted with pleasure that she did not stiffen in his arms.

Awash with emotions she could control no more than she had the night she had begged him to hold her, she welcomed his lips on hers. When the tip of his tongue traced their circumference, they softened to grant him entrance to the hidden treasures of her mouth. Her hands clenched on his shoulders as she dissolved into the glowing embers of their mutual desire. The caress of his tongue against hers matched the slow stroking of his fingers on her skin beneath her thin flannel shirt. He was careful not to touch the sensitive spot on her left side where her assailant's fist had struck her.

A cry of rapture came from her mouth as he

explored the length of her neck. Each touch of his lips on her skin aroused her. With her head cradled on his arm, she swayed to the tides overtaking her. The roughness of his beard did not distract her from the fire of his kisses.

When his lips returned to hers, all gentleness had left. Before he had been awakening her to the passion they had sampled so briefly. Now his mouth demanded she share that newfound emotion with him. Feeling her breath warm and rapid in his mouth, he felt he had never wanted a woman as much as he wanted this one. Without removing his mouth from hers, he leaned her back toward the floor.

Instantly, Lizzie's eyes popped open. She pressed her hands against his shoulders. "No, Cliff, please."

He chuckled against the warm corner of her throat where she had reacted so strongly to his kisses. The movement of her slim body beneath his told him she could not restrain her own passions. "I would be very happy to please you, honey."

"No," she whispered. The word was tinged with desperation as she closed her eyes.

Seeing the frightened expression freeze her face into hard lines, he sat up. He drew her up to rest in his arms. When she tried to pull away from him, he said, "No, Lizzie. Stay here with me."

Tears glittered in her eyes as she wrenched herself away from him. "Why? So you can make me another on your long list of conquests?"

"You shouldn't listen to all everyone tells you." He grinned. "Delilah! She must have had quite a talk with you the day she asked you to work for her. Did she fill your head full of lies?"

"You always have all the answers, don't you?" Lizzie demanded bitterly. "You're so glib, Cliff Hollister. Don't think you can use your tales to charm me into your arms."

He took her arms and pressed her back onto the uneven boards. When she opened her mouth to protest, he smiled without humor. "Go ahead and scream!" he said darkly. "All you'll do is wake Tommy and Pete. I don't have any intention of raping you, but you will listen to me."

"Why?"

"Because it's time you listened to someone sometime." When she stubbornly refused to answer, he sighed. "All right, pout if you wish, but you will hear what I have to say. I do remember you. How could anyone forget someone as full of life as you? Do you need an example?"

She shook her head. "Never mind. Just let me get up. I'm tired. I want to go to sleep."

Gritting his teeth, he fought the desire to turn her over his knee and spank her like the sassy child she resembled. That would solve nothing and ruin their partnership, if it had not already been destroyed tonight by his inability to curb his longing to hold her.

"Lizzie Buchanan, do you remember the night we were delayed because one of the wagons busted a wheel crossing the first ford on the Humboldt River?"

"Yes," she said grudgingly. She relaxed against the unsanded boards.

"The people in the wagon train panicked when the Indians came to check out the campfires."

"I remember."

"And I asked you . . .?" His hands loosened their painful grip on her as he slipped one of his arms beneath her shoulders. He leaned forward so his mouth was only inches from hers.

She dampened her lips as she stared up at his face. Fiercely she fought back the desire to caress it. In a small voice, she finished his sentence. "You asked me why I wasn't hysterical like all the others in the train."

"And you told me it was because you wouldn't waste your fear. You would save it for the time the wagon master—me—showed he was scared."

"You remembered that?" she whispered. "That was such a little thing. I barely remember it myself."

Sitting up, he released her. "I remember a lot about you, honey, and I've forgotten things I would like to relearn."

She stood up and gazed down at him. "I'm sorry, Cliff. I recall many things about you too."

"Such as?"

"Remember Lynn Birley?"

His forehead furrowed as he concentrated. He knew that must have been the name of one of the women traveling with the wagons when Lizzie had come west, but he couldn't remember it. When he said as much to her, she laughed coldly.

"I'm sure she remembers you. Did you ever

see your son? I did, shortly after he was born. He has gray eyes like yours, although he had his mother's red hair."

"Red hair?" That triggered a dim memory. His eyes narrowed as he stood up to tower over her. "I remember her now. She was a strumpet, pretending to be a wide-eyed maiden looking for a husband. I don't know who fathered her bastard, but it wasn't me." He grasped her shoulders and drew her against him once more. "When I hold a woman in my arms, I don't like to think there are men standing in line beyond the door waiting their turn to enjoy what I have."

Lizzie couldn't avoid his mouth as it retook hers. Regretfully, she pushed against his chest. He loosened his embrace to allow her to escape. Without meeting his eyes, she whispered, "Good night." She did not dare stay in his arms; that might lead her to do something she did not want to do in this small cabin.

Silently he watched as she went to her blanket, which she had placed by the bed in which the boys were sleeping. He dropped back to the floor and heard something beneath him crunch. Without saying aloud the curses that ran through his mind, he picked up the half-eaten nut and threw it into the snapping flames.

Damn woman! She got under his skin. She let him sample her sweet lips, then she pushed him away.

His eyes involuntarily went to her figure curled up beneath the paper-thin blanket. From the moment he saw her in Winchester's arms, struggling against impossible odds to have her way, he had known he wanted her to share more than the trail hardships with him during their journey east.

Reaching for his own blanket, he stretched out before the fire. Sleep was elusive as he fought his longing to make her his. Never again would he try to seduce her! She had made it clear too often she did not want him. Then that was the way it would have to be. At the end of the road, he would take her gold and spend it to find a woman who would erase the memories of her bright brown eyes and her lithe body, which felt so warm beneath him.

He smiled. There was some sense of justice in using her money to forget her.

The morning dawned with no change in the weather. The white world remained misty beneath heavy clouds. Beyond the window could be seen nothing but grayness. Often it was impossible to see where the mountainside ended and the sky began.

When Cliff came back from feeding the horses, a Lizzie as cold as the wintery wind screeching through the treetops greeted him. She was politely correct with him but no more. Not that he expected her to be any other way. He suspected her thoughts during the night had resembled his.

"Good morning, Cliff." She placed his plate with rewarmed rabbit meat on it before him. "I thought you would want something hot after facing the storm."

"Yes, thank you."

Her eyebrows rose slightly in an unspoken taunt. That his attitude mirrored hers did not surprise her. Let him play his games. She had been forewarned not to trust him. Never again would she forget those warnings.

The youngsters didn't notice the wall between the two adults as they chatted excitedly about the storm, which was throwing its full force against the building. More than once a crash would signal that a tree had been vanquished by the load of snow and ice on its branches.

Even the boys' enthusiasm dimmed as the day became night, then day again, and the storm showed no signs of diminishing. Sitting on the floor and staring at the ever changing dance of the fire no longer entertained them. Tommy began to race madly around the room until Lizzie had to banish him to sit in a corner. His younger brother whined whenever he thought anyone would listen to his complaints.

"Can't you do something with these kids?" Cliff demanded as the third day of their captivity in the cabin dawned.

"And what do you suggest?" She pulled the wet blanket away from the door and replaced it with a dry one. The wind-driven snow used the poorly hung door to invade their shelter. Blocking the door with a blanket had worked, but once the blanket became soaked, a cold wave would billow from it. Every few hours, she switched the one against the door for the other that was drying by the fire.

He lifted his shoulders and grimaced as one of

the boys shrieked in outrage at his brother's antics. "I don't know. Think of something."

"All right. *You* tell them a story while I try to figure out how we're going to eat a full meal with the short supply of food we have left." When he started to protest, she placed her fists on her hips and stared at him squarely. "Don't tell me that you don't know how to tend to kids! You've had to mollycoddle greenhorns across the plains for years. I think you should be able to handle two small boys."

Lizzie spread the wet blanket on the bench and returned to her depressing task. As far as she was concerned, the conversation was over. She had more important things to do than to argue with Cliff yet again. She felt his hands on her shoulders and looked up at him. Her sharp words died unspoken when she saw the expression on his face.

In a low voice, he stated, "Lizzie, I told you there could be but one boss on this trip."

"Fine! Be the boss! Order them to behave." She jerked her shoulder away from him."

Regarding the top of her head, he wanted to snarl a retort. He paused. That she proved to be right so often irritated him. She did not remove her eyes from her chore, but the stiffness of her back told him she was quite aware of him standing directly behind her.

Then a slow smile drifted across his lips. He went across the room and herded the boys into a corner. He placed a hand on the back of each head and tilted them so the boys would pay attention to his whispered plan. When one giggled, he put his finger to his lips.

Lizzie appreciated the silence. As she suspected, once Cliff overcame his stubborn insistence, he would do the better job of keeping the youngsters well behaved. They respected his orders as they did no one else's.

While she divided the small quantities of food into piles, each of which was a tentative meal, her thoughts settled on her secret happiness. Her love for Cliff demanded to be recognized, but she held its precious joy close to her heart. Until she could hide the truth no longer, she would pretend he loved her too. She feared announcing the state of her rebellious heart, which seemed determined to have its way, would bring her only sorrow, since she was sure he would tell her he did not feel the same.

Not that he would be averse to sleeping with her. She chuckled silently. *That* was no secret. But for her, simply, love was given totally and eternally. That was the way she loved her family—the way she doted on her nephews. For that reason she had been unable to accept Sam Winchester's invitation even when she had thought she had no other recourse but starvation.

Her thoughts were abruptly interrupted as she felt a strong forearm slip around her waist. Hands covered her eyes as someone lifted her off the bench. Her feet hit it, knocking over on the floor with a crash.

"Cliff!" she warned with a laugh. "Stop it! I have to—"

"Now!"

She had no chance to respond to his strange answer. Tiny fingers easily found the most ticklish spots along her sides. She dissolved into uncontrollable giggles. Twisting violently to escape the torment, she broke Cliff's hold on her. With a mock growl, she made a horrid face at her nephews.

They squealed with delight and fled across the room to hide under the bed platform. Her eyes twinkled with the malicious desire for revenge as she whirled to confront Cliff.

"Are you ticklish?" she demanded.

He chuckled as he held up his hands to fend her off. "Do you think I would tell you if I was?"

"Then I'll have to find out!" She leapt at him like a mountain lion pouncing on its prey.

He easily held her at a distance with one hand. Her shorter arms couldn't reach him. When, with a victorious laugh, he used his other hand to tickle her where the boys had told him she would react most, she collapsed into involuntary mirth.

"E-e-e-enough!" she gasped through her laughter.

"Never, half-pint." The tone of his voice sobered her instantly.

She opened her teary eyes to see his face close to hers. Her breathy whisper of his name vanished into his lips. Careful not to press her too tightly to the uneven boards of the floor, he sought deep within her fragrant mouth for his pleasure.

Her fingers clutched his arms. As the power of their passion crashed over her, she slid her hands along his hard muscles to caress his broad back.

The whole world seemed centered on the rapture that possessed them. She surrendered herself to it and sighed with escalating desire as he sampled the skin revealed above the collar of her flannel shirt.

"Hey!" he shouted suddenly.

She froze and clasped her hand to her ringing ear. Throwing off the lassitude that her passion had brought on and that weighted down her limbs, she sat up to find that her nephews were determined not to let their fun be interrupted by the strange behaviors of the adults. From a running start, they had propelled themselves across the room and landed foursquare on top of Cliff.

Cliff rolled over on his back as the two youngsters scrambled over him. He laughed as she had moments before. Tommy called, "Lizzie, come and help us! On his side by his belt!"

She leapt into the melee and tickled Cliff as unmercifully as he had tormented her. At the same time, Cliff attempted to stave off all three of them by threatening the same gentle mayhem. Soon they all fell into a pile of laughter-sapped bodies on the floor.

With her hand on his heaving chest and his arm around her, Lizzie managed to murmur through her rapid breathing, "You sure know how to entertain the boys."

"And you?" He rose slightly to gaze down into her bright eyes. His fingers stroked her satin cheek until she held up her lips to him in a succulent invitation.

"Don't ask silly questions!"

He kissed her lightly before turning to the

children. Standing up, she went back to her task. Her eyes returned again and again to his strong profile as he regaled the youngsters with another of his tales. For the first time she wished the snow would never end. Here in the small hut, she had found a sweet serenity she had not known existed. She didn't want to lose it.

CHAPTER TEN

LIZZIE GASPED AS SHE PEERED FROM THE CABIN doorway in the aftermath of the blizzard. The snow had drifted against the walls and lay as high as her waist. She grabbed Tommy before he could run past her.

"No, you can't go out into that. You could get lost in a snowbank and we would never find you."

"Ah, Lizzie," he moaned. "We're tired of being inside."

"I'll take them outside," Cliff offered. "It'll only be for a few minutes. I want to gauge the condition of the road and see how much longer we'll be stuck here."

She turned to face him. Slowly she nodded. Making herself heard over the whoops of happiness from the boys, who ran to put on their warm buckskins again, she said, "Don't let them out of your sight, especially Pete. He's so little."

"I'll take care of them."

"I know you will, Cliff." Although she often doubted the validity of his feelings toward her, she knew he loved the boys. She enjoyed watching the three together.

Their open love made her yearn to share it, but she forced herself to remain somewhat distant, afraid of being drawn into the magic snare of Cliff's charm again. Only when she was in his arms did she cease questioning her foolish longing for his love. So close to him, with his lips against hers, she could not deny the love that longed to burst from her heart.

She finished her chores in the cabin. None of them had complained about the short rations, but their food wouldn't last much longer in the snowbound cabin. As soon as possible, they must find a settlement and replenish their depleted supplies. How they would pay for them, she didn't know.

Involuntarily her hand went to the string that held the small bag against her stomach. So often she had wanted to open it and show Cliff what it contained, but she always found a reason to postpone the revelation. He had some gold, and she had a few coins she had secreted from their cache of winnings. That must tide them over until they reached Missouri and civilization.

From the window she regarded the three frolicking in the snow. She sighed. If she had fewer tasks to complete, she could be out there with them, delighting in the escape from the four walls of this cabin. Suddenly she reached for her buckskin shirt. She was not going to be denied her happy times with her nephews. Or with Cliff.

In a few minutes she had readied herself for the winter weather. The cold reached deep within her chest to snatch her breath from her. She tightened her shirt around her awkwardly. With her hands wrapped in rags, she could do little but stand on a snowbank and watch the others. The boys were playing in the snow, scooping up great armfuls of the white powder and tossing it at each other. Cliff was walking around obviously exploring the area, but she had no idea what he was looking for.

Tommy saw her first and struggled through the snow to reach her. Taking her cloth-covered hands, he called, "Look who's here!"

Like a young snow creature, Pete jumped toward her. She laughed as she went down, pretending his assault had dropped her into the snow. Soon she was wrestling with the boys as if she were as young as they. Leaping to her feet, she spun around, calling to them to catch her.

When she knew they were close to her, she let herself fall again into the fluffy blanket of snow. The dry flakes puffed into the sky, blinding her. She giggled as Tommy bounced into the snow beside her. She held up her hands in defeat as more of the crystal particles floated over her.

"Stop!" she begged.

Only laughter met her words as she squeezed her eyes shut. As she wiped the cold particles from her face, she, too, laughed. "I surrender!" she gasped. "Enough!"

"Really, Lizzie? I never thought I would hear surrender on your lips."

Looking up at Cliff, her smile changed to a scowl. The boys continued laughing as Cliff bent down and picked up handfuls of snow and began dumping snow on Lizzie. They thought it was hilarious that their friend had taken their place as her tormentor.

She put her hands down to push herself to her feet, determined to repay Cliff for his prank. Instead, her hands sank deeper into the drift. Frustrated, she fought the snow, only to become more deeply mired in it. "You *could* help me!" she snapped at the man who was watching with open amusement.

With an insolent shrug, he laughed. "Why? I think you look fine like that, half-pint. What do you think?" he added to the boys, who crowed with delight.

"Oh, stop jawing and help me."

"No."

"No?" She gasped in disbelief. She had ceased to struggle against the quicksand effect of the snow drift.

"You heard me, honey."

Her eyes sparkled with rage. It was obvious he wanted her to beg him to help her. Never would she do that. She recalled the horrifying time when she had pleaded with him to ease the pain burning through her dreams. A twinge of longing raced through her as she remembered the half-formed sensations they had shared that night, but she squelched it.

Concentrating, she began to move slowly. As when she had extracted her boots from the thick mud they'd encountered on the way to the hut, she found she could pull her arms out of the gentle vise of the snow if she did not make any sudden motions. When she finally stood upright, she shot Cliff a victorious glance before holding out her hands to the boys.

"Let's go inside. No," she said quickly to hush their complaints. "If it is nice, you may come out again tomorrow."

Lizzie did not look back to see whether Cliff was following. The door opened and closed again after they entered the cabin, announcing he had come in also. She was not surprised to see him pull some candy from his saddlebag and handed a piece to each of the youngsters. He seemed to have an endless supply of the striped sticks in there.

"Is there any more coffee, Lizzie?" he asked quietly when the children were busy enjoying their treat.

"Check the pot."

He did not move as she went to hang their wet clothes on a bench by the hearth. With an incoherent growl, he took her arm and spun her to face him. He started to speak but paused as she opened her mouth. Then he said, "Go ahead, honey. Say it. I haven't heard you say it in days."

"Very well. Let me go!" Her eyes narrowed as she let them rove over her. Fighting to hide her laughter, she asked, "Has anyone ever told you that you have the manners of a pig, Mr. Hollister?"

"I am sure you're not the first, Miss Buchanan." He grinned. "You may be the first to say it to my face."

"But certainly not the first to think it." When he released her, she draped the rest of the clothes over the bench. She thanked him when he offered her a cup of thick coffee. Anything warm was bound to taste heavenly after their romp in the snow. Carefully she asked, "What did you find outside?"

He smiled at her over the rim of his cup. "Not bad. All signs point to clear weather for a few days. I think we should go back to lower altitudes and head south. The northern passes fill first. As the snow grows deeper and heavier, there's the chance of an avalanche bottling us up in a pass. But if we go fifty miles south, we should have no trouble crossing."

"We need food."

"I know. That's why I don't want to risk waiting for the snow to melt. An early storm makes the game skittish. I have a friend who lives not much more than a day's journey from here. Two days, possibly, in this weather. He'll have shelter for us and advice on the best route."

She nodded, not asking the questions trying to escape her lips. What one of Cliff's acquaintances in these mountains might be like concerned her, but she had to trust him. She had gambled on him helping them. She couldn't quit the game when it had just begun.

"What is his name?"

A smile teased the corners of his mustache, wet with melting snow. "Cal Feathersong."

"Feathersong? That sounds like an Indian name."

"It is. He's half of some kind of Indian. Sometimes he claims to be Comanche. Sometimes Cherokee. I've heard him answer to any tribe suggested. I doubt if he knows. His mother worked the Spanish settlements along the coast. She died of some disease common to her trade when he was just a baby. He was raised by the missionary fathers but left as soon as he could. Ten or twelve, he was at the time. You'll like him, half-pint. He's a survivor like you."

She did not reply immediately. The idea of liking some half-breed bastard child of a whore did not come easily to her. To be compared with him bothered her. She struggled to find an answer until she saw Cliff's grin.

"You're joking!" she exclaimed.

Cliff's expression did not change as he replied, " 'Fraid not, honey. Cal is what he is. Unmoving as these mountains but able to bend with the winds of change. Determined to make his way in this world, even if it is against common sense. Fiercely loyal to his friends and family." He slipped his arm around her shoulders. "Does that description remind you of anyone else you might know? You'll like him, half-pint."

"Are you sure?"

"I'm sure." He squeezed her, refusing to let her dour face ruin his good humor. It was two years since he'd last seen Cal Feathersong. They would have many tales to share and good times to recall. Lizzie would enjoy their visit with Cal also, once she overcame her prejudice against his origins. Cliff was determined about that.

Lizzie said nothing as they entered the clearing where Cal Feathersong lived. Since they had left the cabin higher in the mountains two days before, she had been extraordinarily reticent about Cliff's plan. She did not want to state outright that she had no desire to meet Cliff's strange friend.

The open area resembled many along the forested ridges. A half-frozen creek tumbled across one side of the clearing. Opposite stood a cabin and several battered outbuildings. Smoke drifted from three chimneys to hover over them in a thick fog.

She shivered. Her mouth was dry from more than the cold wind. She was terrified of the Indians who frequently attacked the outposts of white settlements. Although she had come to trust Cliff's judgment, she wondered if he had made a horrible mistake this time.

Faces, unfriendly and unfamiliar, turned to gaze at the small party invading their home. Her eyes tried not to stare at the weapons piled on the ground in front of the plank-covered cabin. When Cliff stopped his horse before it, she drew back on the reins of her mount.

"Wait here," he ordered quietly. "Stay on your horse, and don't speak to anyone."

Her throat tight, she nodded. She was afraid that if she opened her mouth, the scream that was clamoring against her clenched teeth would break loose. As she watched Cliff vanish into the house, she hushed the questions of the little boy in front of her. She tightened her grip on Pete and held out her hand to Tommy when she saw him showing interest in the children who clustered around them. If he decided to clamber down from his horse to join them, she couldn't begin to guess what the result might be.

Seconds lasted an eternity as she waited stiffly for Cliff to return. She was afraid to do or say anything. Stories she had heard of the mountain savages warned her that they could be set off by the slightest miscalculation.

She felt eyes on her and turned. A flash of fear cut through her as she met the steady stare of a strange creature. Whether it was male or female she couldn't tell. Its collection of clothes appeared stranger than anything Lizzie had ever worn. Patches covered almost every square inch of the denim trousers. The buckskin shirt was decorated with odd symbols that matched those on the felt hat that was pulled low over the enigmatic figure's brow.

It stared at her for a long minute, then scurried off toward the door through which Cliff had entered the cabin. The children who surrounded the horses were careful to keep their distance from the silent person. But Lizzie doubted that they were afraid of it, for they were giggling among themselves.

"Here, give me the boy."

Glancing down, she realized she had been so immersed in her observations, she had not noticed Cliff return to the horses. She picked up Pete so he could be placed next to his brother on the wooden porch but froze as she saw the man who was emerging from the cabin.

His bare, sun-burnished skin glistened with perspiration, although a brisk wind chilled her. His loose sable hair was held back by a beaded band. His eyes were as dark as his hair and clearly curious as they regarded the strangers. He made a sharp comment in words she could not understand. When Cliff laughed lightly, she knew he was able to speak this language.

A heat far more intense than that of the feeble sun overhead brightened her cheeks. That the two men were talking of her she could not doubt. It scared her not to know what they were saying.

She put her hands on Cliff's shoulders and let him help her to the ground. As she held the awed Pete's hand tightly in hers, she was glad of Cliff's arm around her. Tommy clutched Cliff's other hand as he gazed openmouthed at the man standing in the doorway. She was aware of the other children gathering to watch this meeting.

"Lizzie, this is my friend and brother Cal Feathersong. Cal, my—my woman, Lizzie. The smaller boy is Lizzie's nephew, Pete Greenway; the larger is his brother Tommy."

Noticing that slight hesitation in his words, she glanced up at Cliff in shock. She was not his woman. When he turned to her for the briefest second, she saw his eye close in an easy wink. Instead of being consoled she felt even more disquieted. If this was Cliff's idea of a joke, she did not appreciate it.

Cliff went on, his smile broadening, "These I give to you."

"Cliff!" she cried in horror. When his arm tightened around her shoulders, she wondered if he was mad. He had brought them through disasters and had been their ally in their darkest moments. Now he was offering them to this savage.

As if she had not spoken, the other man answered, in nearly accent-free English, "Such a gift, brother of my heart. It grieves me deeply that I cannot accept such. My wives would not share the fruits of the hunt with another. Forgive me, for I must refuse." His hand swept out to encompass the clearing. "To repay you for such an insult, I offer you all I own."

"My heart regrets that I, too, cannot accept your generous gift," Cliff answered in the same ceremonious manner. "The roads from the sunrise to the sunset are mine. I cannot take all you offer me when I seek the sleeping place of the sun. It seems we should keep exactly what we have."

With a laugh, the dark man stepped forward and embraced Cliff. Because Lizzie could not move quickly enough, she was included in the hug. She found it disconcerting to have her nose in direct contact with such a wide expanse of bare male skin. Happily for her, the man moved away and laughed again.

"One of these days, Cliff," he said in a more normal, thunder-deep tone, "I'm going to accept your gift. Then I'll own that magnificent horse of yours."

"And I'll find myself with a trapper's cabin,

two wives, and all these children." Cliff chuckled. "I think both of us are smart enough to avoid that."

"Come in. Come in. Your woman is breathless from the fear that she would belong to me."

Lizzie considered denying that, but it was the truth. She had never thought of any Indian as having a sense of humor. When Cliff pushed her in the small of her back, she followed the half-clothed man into the cabin. As soon as she passed through the door, she understood why he was dressed so skimpily. The heat of the fires on the three hearths nearly suffocated her. Beads of sweat formed on skin that had been covered with gooseflesh just moments before.

The children made no attempt to hide their excitement as they entered the cluttered interior. On every surface, shelves had been built. They were loaded with supplies of every kind. Even the table in the middle of the room struggled to hold its burden of miscellaneous items. Little light sifted through the filthy windows. A movement in the shadows became the strange creature they had seen outside.

Cliff greeted it with the charm he normal bestowed on the women in saloons. "How are you doing, Andy?"

"Well, Cliff Hollister. I'll be damned!" The person waddled out of the dimness and approached him eagerly. "I didn't think you would be stupid enough to show your face here again."

The creature's fist swung powerfully, but Cliff's arm stopped it. Without losing his smile, he grasped Andy's wrist and twisted the powerful figure into his grip. Cliff's other forearm went around his shorter adversary's throat. Although the goblin creature fought to escape, Cliff held on easily.

"Cal," he asked in a light tone, "if I break Andy's neck, can you manage alone?"

"Probably. It would make my wives happy to be rid of her."

Despite herself, Lizzie squeaked, "Her?"

Malevolent, red-lined eyes glared in her direction while the men burst into laughter. Cliff released the bulbous character. Andy turned to the astounded Lizzie. Standing face-to-face, Lizzie could see that "Andy" was, indeed, a woman, but one scarred by the rough life of the mountains and not ashamed to show it.

"Where did you find this bit of fluff, Hollister?" demanded the deep voice. What seemed to be a laugh crackled at Lizzie. The open mouth revealed few remaining teeth. "And young 'uns! Never thought I would see you playing pa to some woman's kids." Andy crackled again.

Cliff answered, "Don't be deceived by her looks, Andy. Lizzie is about as tough as they come."

"She must be, if she can put up with you!" Her little blue eyes roved over Lizzie once more before she sniffed, "Looks like fluff to me."

Infuriated by the other woman's dismissal, Lizzie said coldly, "And you look as if you crawled out from under a rock!"

Cal's roar of laughter drowned out everything

else. He slapped Andy companionably on the back. "Cliff warned you not to be fooled."

"Hmph!" snorted Andy. "He don't care nothing 'bout her, except she's pretty and soft. Girl like that couldn't last ten minutes alone in these mountains."

"Jealousy doesn't become you." Cliff drew off his heavy shirt and draped it over a bench. "Is there a chance you might have been pining for me, Andy?"

She snorted again. "Keep you city lady, Hollister! I know better than to listen to your shams."

Cal interrupted the conversation by calling to one of the shadows clustered in a corner of the shanty. It moved to reveal itself as a slender woman of Indian descent. She wore buckskins not much different from Lizzie's. Two dark braids hung down her back. She kept her head bowed as she listened to what were clearly Cal's orders. When he finished, she nodded and moved out of the room as quietly as she had been standing earlier.

A hand on Lizzie's arm kept her from speaking. She glanced at Cliff and saw him shake his head slightly. She was surprised that he had sensed her fury at the subservience of Cal's younger wife. On his part, he tried to imagine Lizzie reacting with such humility and found it impossible. How Cal would act if he heard her outrage Cliff knew all too well. His friend did not answer to any authority but his own.

When Cliff suggested Lizzie take off her buckskin shirt, she nodded. She moved away to place it on the bench over his and help the children remove theirs. He began to frown as he realized he was not the only one watching Lizzie's lithe movements. Cal's eyes glittered avidly as he appraised her. Only the fact that she had arrived with Cliff kept him from acting on his impulses. Until then, Andy might have been the sole woman to come to this cabin and leave without sharing Cal's bed. He valued Cliff's friendship too much to risk it over a matter he would consider as insignificant as having his meal served on time.

Cliff motioned to his friend to join him at one of the hearths. The lust vanished from Cal's eyes as he shoved a scrawny dog out of the chair he wanted and lowered his long, lean form into it. He accepted a glass of whiskey from the tray his wife carried without acknowledging her.

Sending the boys off to play with the other children, Lizzie smiled and refused the woman's offer of whiskey. The woman did not return the smile as she scuttled away like a frightened rabbit heading for its hole in a hedgerow.

"Don't drink, girl?"

She turned to see Andy viewing her with the same malevolent glare that had greeted Lizzie. They were standing close to one another, and Lizzie was startled to see that the odd woman actually was several inches shorter than she. Andy's presence so filled the room, she seemed huge.

"It makes me giggle. That can be very embarrassing."

Andy smiled at her. "So you know your limits?" She drained her glass. "I do too, but I ignore 'em. Hell, who wants to spend her whole life being as perfect as a puritan? Where you going?"

"East." After a second of silence, Lizzie added, "Home."

"Why d'ya want to be going back there?"

For some reason, Andy's question did not irritate her as others' had, perhaps because she knew the woman had no ulterior motive for asking it. Quietly she said, "I want to take my nephews home."

"Why? So they can grow up to be lily-livered tenderfeet?" Andy's smile faded. "And to think I believed Hollister when he said you were more than fluff! Go on back and leave California to us who love it."

"You're welcome to it!" Lizzie snapped. "You can have the mud, the gold lust, and all the perversions it has encouraged. I have dug and drilled and slaved and starved for this state. I won't do it any longer. All I want is a peaceful place to raise my boys without them having to worry about being accosted by a drunken miner or trapper!" She added the last as she glared at the shorter woman.

If she thought she might intimidate Andy, she failed miserably. For her outspoken words, she received a friendly slap on the back that nearly knocked her off her feet. Andy put her arm around Lizzie's shoulders and steered her toward where the men sat.

"You got yourself quite a gal here, Hollister," pronounced the odd woman. She shoved Lizzie onto his lap. "She don't take no humbug."

Cliff grinned as he wondered whether Lizzie recognized what a great compliment she had received. Andy did not like many men, and fewer women. That was why she had chosen a life in the mountains with Cal as her partner in their trapping business. Cliff put his arm around Lizzie as he felt her move to rise.

"Cliff!" she hissed quietly.

He simply tightened his hold on her to keep her close. It felt too fine for him to let her leave so soon. He ignored the fingernails biting into his wrists as he turned back to his conversation with his friend as if there had been no interruption.

When she discovered she could not escape, Lizzie relaxed against him. She truly did not know where she would go in this strange house. From where she sat, she could see the two women Cal considered his wives huddling in their corner. Their silence unnerved her, and she wondered what life was like in the cabin when there were no strangers visiting.

Nearer the door, the children played in the manner of children everywhere. That the youngest offspring of Cal's household spoke no English did not hinder the youngsters' enjoyment of the Greenway boys. They made themselves under-stood without words as they created their own world from bits of wood shavings and bark.

Lizzie's smile wavered as she looked at their host. He made no effort to hide the fact that he was watching everything she did. She felt his eyes slide along her in an intimate caress and recoiled. Her movement made her bump against the tin cup in

Cliff's hand. The whiskey spilled onto her denims.

"Get the girl a wet cloth, Cal," ordered Andy presumptuously. "She don't like whiskey. Don't want her to smell like a distillery."

Cal snapped his fingers. The other wraith in the corner emerged to answer his call. Quick orders set her into action. Lizzie accepted the cold cloth with whispered gratitude and dabbed at the stain.

Cliff bent over ostensibly to watch. In her ear, he whispered. "How are you doing, half-pint?"

"How long do we have to stay in this insane asylum?"

He chuckled. "Not long."

"I'm glad you find this amusing," she said tersely. She added nothing more as she rose and moved to a stool near him.

When Cal's wives began to prepare dinner, no one paid them any attention. Lizzie felt odd sitting idle while they worked, but she understood now their desire to blend into the shadows. She longed to do the same as she listened to the conversation. While Cliff, Andy, and Cal reminisced about people and times she did not know, she hugged her knees to her chest and tried to remain inconspicious.

The fragrant aromas of their meal wafted through the room, luring the children closer to the cooking hearth. From there came the quiet sounds of a loving family. It was as if a wall stood between them and the people gathered by the other fireplace. Neither group acknowledged the presence of the other.

Feeling stifled by conversation she could not

share, Lizzie rose to cross the room. She smiled at the younger wife. "May I help?" she asked.

The woman's blank stare wiped Lizzie's friendly expression from her face. She quickly headed back toward the group occupying the chairs. She knew that Cal's wife had understood her. The blinking of the Indian woman's eyes and the tightening on her lips were clear evidence of the woman's comprehension. The younger wife wanted nothing to do with her husband's guest. Lizzie could not guess why, for the boys had been accepted gleefully by the other children.

Lizzie stopped to take a ladleful of water from the bucket by the door to make it look as if she had left her seat primarily for that reason. She didn't want everyone to know how disconcerted she was by these queer people.

When she sat down next to Cliff again, he reached out to take her hand. He made his motion seem perfectly natural. Glancing at him out of the corner of her eyes, she saw he was also watching her surreptitiously. His eyes met hers for the shortest moment, and he smiled reassuringly. His hand tightened around her slightly to signal that he understood her disorientation.

Cal graciously allowed Lizzie to sit at the table with them. She realized what an honor that was when his wives and all the children were relegated to the floor. The only time the other women approached the table was to serve food to those sitting there. Sharing Cliff's bench, she found herself across from Cal. While Andy and Cliff bantered some long-dormant joke back and forth, she tried to think of something to say. Finally she fell back on the inane.

"It is very kind of you to welcome us under your roof."

"Cliff is my friend. He is my brother. You are his woman," Cal stated gruffly. "I do not turn my brother and his family from my door." He leaned forward and pointed at her with the tip of the hunting knife he was using at the table. "Do you tire of this man?"

Unsure of how to reply, she kept her eyes on Cal. She prayed Cliff was not listening to their conversation. Deciding the truth would be best, she answered, "We have been together a very short time, Cal."

"Long enough, it would seem." He chortled with delight as he stabbed at a chunk of venison on his plate.

"Long enough? What do you mean?"

Cliff interrupted, thus warning her that he had been listening; "Cal is teasing you, half-pint."

She wanted to demand an explanation but decided ignorance might be best in this strange game which seemed to have no comprehensible rules. Forcing a false smile to her lips, she bent her head to her dinner. She continued as she had, letting the others talk around her.

Only when Cliff began to ask about the weather in the mountains did she listen closely. Surprisingly, Andy answered his questions.

"Hell, Hollister, you picked a poor time to go gallivanting through the Sierras. Whether winter is going to be early this year is anyone's guess. Winter

comes when it wants to. No one's gonna stop it."
She picked up the bottle of whiskey and splashed
some of it into her cup. "But furs are growing thick
real fast. Sure sign of a dandy of a winter."

Reaching behind her, she grasped something
and tossed it to Cliff. He ran his fingers along the
pelt before handing it back. "Yes, it is thick. But I
still think we can beat the weather if we hurry south
and over."

She shrugged with little concern. "Your life,
Hollister. I ain't planning to wager mine so
foolishly. What if you get snowbound? What good
will Lizzie here be if you have to spend the winter in
the high snows? Don't forget her condition."

"Condition? Cliff—"

He waved her to silence. To Andy he said,
"Lizzie is good on the trail. I told you we were
snowed in north of here. She didn't panic once."

"If you take the trail east within the next
week," intoned Cal after deep reflection, "you
should have little trouble. The migration of the
animals and birds has not been early. The high
passes should be open for another few weeks.

"That was my opinion." Cliff raised his cup.
"To good friends. May we be together more often."

The other man did not lift his tin mug. "We
will not be here when you come back this way next
year. Too many people cluttering up California. We
are going to Canada or even on to Alaska."

Cliff nodded. This was not a surprise. Although the closest neighbor to Cal's desolate cabin
was more than a dozen miles away in any direction,
for Cal Feathersong that was too crowded. He

wanted to be the only man within a week's walk of his home. All his life he had fled from the encroaching edges of civilization and would spend the rest of his days trying to find what he never had.

In spite of her efforts to stifle it, Lizzie yawned. Cliff had pushed them to a faster pace than normal to reach his friend's house. She noted that her nephews were asleep alongside some of the younger children on the floor in front of the cooking hearth.

Cal chuckled at her unintentional display of fatigue. "You should get a second woman, my friend," he said to Cliff. "That way one is always fresh."

Knowing that Lizzie was blushing at the crude words, Cliff placed his arm around her waist and drew her closer. "I am happy with things the way they are now. However, we have had some long days of traveling and have more ahead of us. I think we should rest."

"You and Lizzie have my room, Cliff."

When Lizzie politely started to refuse their host's kind offer, she felt Cliff's arm tighten around her. That second of hesitation allowed him to say, "Thanks. It will be good to sleep on a bed after so many nights on the cold ground."

"Not so cold as your previous trips, when you traveled alone, eh?" Andy reached for her tin cup of whiskey and emptied it easily.

The heat along her cheeks warned Lizzie of her deepening blush. It was confirmed when the odd woman and Cal chuckled loudly. Wanting nothing more than to run away, Lizzie mumbled her good-nights as Cliff took her hand and led her to a door that opened into another room, obviously Cal's. He closed it behind them to shut out the sound of laughter that followed them.

Leaning against the door he looked across the room at Lizzie as she stood by the hearth. The stiffness of her back warned him of her unexpressed rage. He said softly, "They're good friends, Lizzie."

"I'm sure they are. After all, you've received the royal treatment, haven't you? This lovely room, a fabulous meal that your 'woman' was so graciously allowed to attend—everything but the offer of sharing Cal's harem!" When he grinned, she snapped, "He would have offered you that if I weren't here!"

"Cal refuses to be bound by the standards of other men. He would see nothing wrong with me sleeping with one of his wives or him sharing your bed." He crossed the room and sat on the bed to remove his boots. "In fact, he suggested exactly that."

Lizzie blanched. Instantly she knew why Cal's younger wife wanted nothing to do with her. The young woman expected his guest to be sleeping with her husband tonight. Somehow, around her anger, Lizzie managed to squeeze out, "He— What did you tell him?"

"Don't get angry, half-pint. I said you were pregnant. Cal has an aversion to pregnant women —even his own wives, when they're expecting."

Her pale cheeks became rosy. "Why didn't

you tell him I was infected with some dreadful disease?" Cliff's confession explained Cal's somewhat solicitous behavior and Andy's amusement.

"That wouldn't have kept him from being interested in you. Few women as pretty as you come this way. He wouldn't have wanted to miss the chance to sleep with you." He reached out a long arm to take her hand. When she tried to pull away, he simply smiled and drew her to stand between his knees. He put his hands on her elbows to bring her toward him until her face was on the same level as his. Softly he said, "Instead you'll be sleeping with me again, honey."

"Cliff—"

"No, don't say it," he commanded softly. "Don't tell me again what you have said so many times already. I know you don't want to waste your virginity on a man like me."

She shook her head. "Don't make me sound so calculating."

He released her and began to pull off his boots. When he didn't say anything else, she sat down next to him and did the same. Then she removed the rest of her buckskins and set them to dry before the fire. She wondered if they would ever lose their dampness.

A shiver raced along her back. It was as if the same coldness had seeped inside her, freezing her heart so that she was unable to accept what she desi' wanted. She glanced at Cliff as he sat on the bed next to her, staring at the opposite wall. She was sure his thoughts matched her own.

Her eyes followed the strong line of his face,

muted slightly by his bushy beard. Since she was attacked in Joplinville, he hadn't trimmed it. Biting her lower lip, she glanced at his hands as they rested on the blanket. So powerful, yet their touch was as gentle as a spring breeze.

All evening in this strange house, he had defended and protected her and still had managed not to alienate his strange friends. And not just this evening; he had been safeguarding her since he had reentered her life, first from Sam, then from others during their journey. Never had he asked for anything in return.

She smiled softly. He *had* asked but had accepted her refusal each time he thought she might come willingly into his arms. For a man like Cliff Holllister, such patience had to be a most exquisite torture.

She looked at the fire before she closed her eyes, seeking in it the thing she could hide from herself no longer—what he wanted was also the longing of her soul. Her fingers reached for the buttons of her flannel shirt. Not moving from the hearth, she undid each one slowly. The material fell in folds down her back as she slipped her arms from the sleeves. Loosening the cloth belt at her waist, she unbuttoned her denims. They slid down the silken line of the calf-length drawers.

Slowly she turned and said in a soft voice, "Cliff?"

"Lizzie!" He stood up regarding her in open wonder.

His look of surprise brought a loving smile to her lips. She walked to him and drew his arms around her. "If I tell you that I am cold, will you hold me tonight and warm me?"

"Half-pint, you know I can't hold you close like this and not love you." His husky voice deepened as his eyes slid along her, searing her skin with their fire.

"You're finally beginning to understand me," she murmured with a soft laugh as she raised her hands to stroke the fullness of his beard.

He shook his head. "No, half-pint, I don't understand you at all, but I'm not going to try to figure you out now."

Although she had seen the yearning in his eyes and felt the need in his lips, she was unprepared for his fervor as he grasped her and pressed his mouth to hers. The hard line of his body molded along her curves to fit her perfectly. All thought vanished from her mind as she was overwhelmed by the explosion of his desire.

With a laugh, he lifted her into his arms. Cradling her in his arms, as unyielding as tree trunks, he held her to him. His lips moved along her skin, touching, teasing, urging her to surrender to him.

The bed screeched as he set one knee on it. She looked up into his disgusted face and giggled. "Very kind of Cal to offer you this room," she teased. "Now he'll know it every time you roll over in bed."

"Let him satisfy his baser drives another way, honey." He grimaced as he moved away from the

bed and heard it squeak again. "This is ridiculous."
His eyes swept the room; then he smiled.

She said nothing as he placed her on her feet.
With her hands folded in front of her, she watched
as he went to the wall opposite the fireplace. A
massive bear pelt hung there. Bracing his foot
against the wall, he put both hands on the top of
the skin and yanked. The brads holding it to the
wall popped out, falling in a metallic shower to the
floor. He swept them aside with his foot.

Dropping the black skin on the floor, he
spread it out. Then he sat down and reached up to
take her hand. Her bare feet made no sound on the
floor as she moved to sit next to him. A smile
drifted across her lips as she ran her fingers across
the thick fur.

"This is wondrously soft," she murmured.

"It doesn't feel as lovely as you do, honey."

She turned to look at him and saw the naked
yearning in his charcoal gray eyes. The raw
emotion awed her. She watched, unable to move,
as his mouth descended toward hers. Captured by
the blending of his desire with hers, she placed her
arms around his shoulders. When he leaned her
back into the plush surface, she smiled against his
mouth.

He traced the textures of her face with eager
lips. His fingers stroked the length of her side from
thigh to waist. She moved sinuously beneath him,
introducing him to every inch of her lithe form.
When a single finger roamed across her to explore

the valley between her breasts, she sighed in breathless longing for his touch, with not even the thin silk of her camisole to separate them. His finger slid feverishly along the delicate garment until he hooked it in the lace at her shoulder.

His beard brushed the hollow of her throat luxuriously as he bent to place his mouth against the sensitive area that was revealed when he lowered the strap along her arm. With surprising lack of haste, his tongue sought an unchartered trail across her bared skin. The way she whispered his name breathlessly and the tingle of her fingers as they slipped along his back stripped him of any emotion but the fierce desire that consumed him.

He pushed her camisole lower to expose the smooth curve of her breast. His tongue blazed a heated path along its slope to tempt its rosy tip to cede its delights to him. Her fingers entangled themselves in his hair as she nibbled at the crescent of his ear. She moaned soft words of longing as a lightning-hot bolt of desire cut through her. She tightened her arms around him as his lips ensnared her in a web of rapture.

With a throaty laugh, he rolled onto his back and brought her to lie on him. Her glazed eyes met his before she encircled his face with her hands. He groaned as he hungrily reached for her mouth and she lowered her lips to his. She savored the taste of his skin as ardently as he had hers. Her fingers quickly undid the buttons of his shirt. With his arms holding her close to him, he watched her face as she worked to loosen the garment.

"Do you need help?" he teased as he pulled her face against his lips.

"I can manage alone!" she retorted pertly.

"Well, I can't! I need you, honey."

Sitting up, he motioned her to move aside as he pulled off his flannel shirt. He tossed it on the floor next to the bearskin. His eyes widened in delight as he turned to her. Lightly he caressed her pliant skin, now glowing in the flickering light of the embers. He put his hands on her shoulders, gently urging her to lie back on the black fur.

She closed her eyes and savored his touch as he tenderly removed the bits of silk and lace he had given her. When he ran a gentle hand along her bared skin, she reached up her hands to draw him close.

"Just one moment," he whispered.

Her eyes followed his hands as he slid his denims down the coiled strength of his body. The very maleness of him thrilled and awed her. Her fingers itched to touch him. When he entered her arms, she enfolded him, and his lips settled over hers.

The strong passion that had been born more than three years before raged through them, blinding them to everything else. The fur caressed her as she moved with the force of his kisses. His mouth discovered parts of her she had not suspected could feel such glory. As her fingers clenched on the thick hide, she felt his lips teasing the flat surface of her stomach.

A cry exploded from her, uncontrollable, as he sought her most feminine secrets. His touch awoke sensations she could not restrain. Whispering his name, she grasped his shoulders and brought his mouth to hers.

"Love me," she murmured.

"Smiling, he wondered if she could know the memories her words brought of the night he first discovered the sweetness of her body. Then he forgot it as well as he drew her beneath him. In the warm aura surrounding them, he brought them together to share a joy too long denied.

She felt his rapid breath in her mouth, matching her racing pulse. Everything became that pulse, that tempo, that power that came from within her to spiral through both of them and release them to float free in a world apart from reality. In one golden moment of ecstasy, she lost herself in the perfection of a love that lifted her beyond herself to the heat of the sun. Two souls merged in that fire to be alone no more.

Lizzie opened her eyes to the morning light spilling through the window. A heavy arm rested on her side. She turned to look at the man sleeping beside her. In repose, Cliff's face gained a boyishness only suggested by his normal wry grin. Never again would she disbelieve her heart. This man with a day's stubble darkening his cheeks had reached inside her to release a rapture that had waited only for him.

Nestling back against him, she wondered if anyone since the beginning of time had ever been this happy. The dream she had treasured seemingly forever had come true last night in his arms.

She felt his lips against the top of her head. Tilting it back, she smiled up at him. "Did I wake you?"

"No," he said gently. "I've been awake since dawn. Old habits are hard to break. I so enjoyed watching you sleep in my arms, honey, that I didn't want to deny the pleasure I saw on your face just now."

"I didn't know you were awake." She reached for her scattered clothes, but his hand caught her wrist and drew it back to him.

"Not yet, half-pint."

She grimaced. "Half-pint? Is that an appropriate name for . . ." She did not know if Cliff loved her in the same heart-strong manner she adored him. Not once during the times he had made love to her during the night had he mentioned the word.

His laughter covered her hesitation. "I could call you sweetheart or darling, but other women are called that by other men. I doubt if there are many 'half-pints' like my Lizzie."

Her heart swelled with happiness at his gentle teasing, and she welcomed his kiss. Her lips felt tender from the voracious kisses of the night. Other parts of her recalled his loving also, but she longed to have him hold her close once again. The desire she had known seemed tepid in retrospect.

A knock sounded on the door as they cuddled close and spoke of the simple, mundane things made perfect by the sharing of their lives. "Hollister, are you going to stay in there all day? I thought you were going to shoot a few targets with me!"

"Andy!" he muttered in resignation. Louder, he shouted, "Ten minutes! Give me a chance to get a cup of coffee."

She mumbled something that was indistinct through the door, but the sound of her heavy boots indicated she was willing to wait in the main room. Cliff turned to apologize to Lizzie and saw she had lept to her feet and was scurrying to her clothes before Andy could invade the room.

Rising, he took her hand and brought her back to him. "Half-pint, you were worth waiting for, but I don't think I can wait three years to hold you again."

"I don't think you'll have to." Her eyes searched his face, willing him to say the words pounding in her heart. She wanted to hear them on his lips.

When he smiled before kissing her lightly, she turned to finish dressing. She told herself she was being foolish for wanting the impossible when she had been offered her heart's desire. A teasing kiss on the nape of her neck dispelled the sorrow within her.

She turned to face him. "Andy is waiting for you," she reminded him when he tugged her against him.

With a laugh, he released her only enough so that he could redo the buttons on her shirt. "I don't want to think of her or anyone else but you." He framed her face with his broad hands. In a far more serious voice, he asked tenderly, "Do you have any regrets about what happened?"

Instantly she understood what he could not say. Cliff could make no promises to her. For too long he had been alone, so alone he could not reach past the barrier of that loneliness to allow in the one who would have relieved it. She wanted to break down the wall, but she knew she must patiently dismantle it stone by stone.

"Cliff, I have no regrets," she whispered. Her hands stroked the firm skin of his chest, revealed by his open shirt. "What we had last night and will have again tonight is so wondrous I feel like shouting praises to the sky. I waited too, you know. Three long years I waited before my dreams came true last night."

He crushed her to him, feeling the passion erupt within him again at her soft words. Discovering her love whetted his appetite for her gentle sweetness. He knew it had been wrong to lure this lithe sprite into his arms, but he'd been unable to resist her.

Lifting his lips from hers, he started to speak, but the crash of a fist made the door shiver. "Hollister! Haven't you had enough of that? Get out here!"

"You had better go." Lizzie laughed and snapped his suspenders. "You don't want to disappoint Andy."

"Later, half-pint."

She smiled and put her hand on his arm. "Later." She watched as he walked out of the room. His roar of mock anger at the goblin-like woman brought a smile to her lips. Slowly she turned to look around her. The nondescript room would linger forever in her mind as the place in which she found the deepest meaning of love.

CHAPTER ELEVEN

LIZZIE COULD NOT BE SORRY TO BE SAYING FAREwell to Cal Feathersong. Although she had found paradise in his home, her distrust of him never tempered. She politely thanked him for his generosity. To Andy, she made an equally trite remark.

"Say what you mean, fluff," commanded the diminutive elf. She grinned, still pleased she had bested Cliff in the shooting match.

"All right." Lizzie leaned forward to put her face near the battered one under the droopy hat. "Andy, you are the most despicable excuse for a woman I have ever met, and I'm sorry we can't have a chance to know each other better. Cliff is still stinging from your display of marksmanship, but I think I could beat you in my sport."

"Sport, fluff?" Andy rumbled a laugh. "Is that what you city gals call it? Ruined Cliff's eye, you have, with keeping him awake all night."

Grateful her blush did not blossom forth to betray her, Lizzie answered, " 'Twas a different sport I was thinking of. If you ever want to risk playing cards with me, Andy, just let me know. I'd be glad to take whatever you wish to wager."

Andy shook her head, disturbing her mass of tangled gray hair. "Naw—don't play cards. Too tame. I like wrestlin' with things that can bite back." She held out her hand. "Good luck, gal. You'll need it with that man."

Lizzie shook the proffered hand seriously. "Thank you, Andy. Good luck to you when you reach your new home in the north."

Cliff called to her, and she went outside where the others were waiting. His eyebrow quirked at her as he handed her the reins of the packhorse that carried their supplies newly replenished from Cal's vast storehouse. She smiled to let Cliff know she had parted amicably with the irascible Andy. He lifted her into the saddle, his fingers lingering on her waist. Looking down into his face, she saw the longing that mirrored the hunger within her.

With an effort, he turned away from her. He smiled as he said, "Cal, as always, my stay with you has been an adventure."

Andy will not forget soon that she outshot you." Cal grimaced, his stern face contorted with unusual angles. "She may prove to be as impossible as my wives. Journey with the wisdom you have learned, my brother, and you will find the wind clears the trail ahead of you."

"We will do well."

Cal added offhandedly as Cliff prepared to

mount, "You do know your enemy precedes you?"

Cliff dropped back to the ground with a thump. Exchanging a shocked glance with Lizzie, he heard her hushing the boys. His eyebrows underlined his furrowed brow. "Enemy? Who?"

"A man with hair the color of the western sky at sunset stopped here. He knew of our friendship. He wanted to learn if I had see you."

Lizzie gasped, "Sam Winchester!"

Choking back a strangled oath, Cliff wondered how he could have been so stupid. While he had been drinking with Winchester, much of their pasts had been shared in a whiskey haze. Then that last night on the ridge overlooking Hopeless, Winchester had vowed to make them pay for foiling his plans. Naively, they had forgotten him. Only their zigzag journey from mining town to mining town had kept them from meeting up with him.

Cliff quickly realized Winchester had to be far ahead of them by now. If they were careful, they would avoid encountering him on the trail. Cliff had allies all along the route east. Forewarned, they wouldn't let Winchester catch them off-guard.

"What did you tell him, Cal?" he asked quietly.

Cal gave them a ferocious smile. "I spun him a tale that would have delighted you, my friend. He is sure I betrayed you. It is not difficult to fool fools."

Cliff nodded with less enthusiasm. Winchester might be a fool, but he had proven he was a determined one. Such men could be very dangerous. He swung into the saddle easily. With a wave of farewell, he led the way from the clearing to the road south.

As the sound of the voices behind them faded into the distance, Lizzie urged her horse forward to draw even with his. She did not have a chance to ask any questions before he spoke.

"What Winchester wants is obvious, halfpint. Revenge. Why he is chasing us across the mountains to get even for such a small slight is something I can't figure out. Can you?"

"No," she said quietly. Since Cal had described Sam, she had been puzzling over that same dilemma.

She had known Sam since shortly after their arrival in Hopeless. He scratched a passable living from the rocks. Never a big strike, but enough to keep him in supplies while he waited for that dream to come true. He worked when he had to, but no harder than necessary. It didn't seem like Sam to embark on this difficult journey simply for revenge.

She added, "What shall we do, Cliff?"

He smiled grimly as he studied the road intently. "We'll do what we have to do. Winchester won't keep us from going east." His grin became predatory. "I almost hope we do run into him. I wouldn't mind a little revenge of my own."

"Can I help you?" asked Tommy, barely able to sit still as he listened to the exciting prospect of another run-in with Winchester.

Cliff tweaked his nose. "Sure partner. As

good as you've become with the rifle, you can have dibs on the coward."

"Me too?" piped up Pete.

Looking past him to his aunt, Cliff's expression softened. He wrenched his eyes from her loving gaze; it made him unable to think of anything else. "Of course, Petey, my boy. We're all a team. No one will come between us. Ever!" While the boys cheered, he continued, "Right, half-pint?"

Disquiet taunted her, urging her to look for Sam behind each huge tree they passed. Instead of saying what she thought, she smiled with the joy she felt. "No one will come between us ever, Cliff," she answered fervently. She hoped it was a vow they both would keep.

After they had left Cal's clearing, the silence of the mountains closed around them. If they had not been in such a hurry to be free of the mountains before winter settled on the lower slopes, they would have liked to pause and enjoy the incredible landscapes. There were vistas of mountains piercing the clouds to seek the sky, and rivers dropping countless feet in ear-shattering cascades. The pines rivaled the peaks as they stretched their green spires toward the clear blue heavens.

Fatigue at the end of the day left them little time to sightsee. Often Lizzie fell asleep in Cliff's arms with no more than a gentle kiss to take with her into her dreams. After a day on the trail, finding and preparing meals, and keeping an eye on the rambunctious youngsters, they were happy just to be with one another.

The nights they shared more than proved to them that the love they had discovered in the rustic cabin only grew with the passing of the days. Passion so intense she was sure the stars must be dimmed by its brilliance overcame Lizzie as she sampled again the ecstasy Cliff brought to her.

A precious peace settled over them, although they could not forget that Sam Winchester was seeking them intent on causing trouble. But they ceased to worry about it. He had been chasing them since they had left Hopeless. The chances of him finding them now were minute.

After a week of following the trail heading south, Cliff decided it was time to turn east again. That decision was greeted with enthusiasm by everyone. Even the children understood the need to put the mountains behind them as quickly as possible. They were cooperative and uncomplaining about the long hours in the saddle, learning to entertain themselves while the adults spoke over their heads.

The first night on the eastbound journey, they paused in a clearing more beautiful than any they had stayed in so far. Lizzie gazed at the waterfall glowing in the sunset. Its sibilant song lilted through the trees, whose leaves rustled in the breeze. The raw aroma of mud, enhanced by the scent of sun-heated pine and sparkling water created a potpourri of scent.

Without waiting for the others, she walked to the massive boulders overlooking the precipice. The roar of the cataract deafened her as she regarded the wind-sculptured monuments standing their silent vigil on the far side of the water. Spray dampened her face and spotted her filthy clothes, but she only laughed and shook her short curls to free her delight at this natural beauty. She held out her hand to watch as it became encased in diamond sparkles.

When an arm slipped around her waist and drew her back against a figure as hard as the granite domes surrounding them, she leaned her head against Cliff's chest. "It's so beautiful!" she whispered. To speak louder seemed as outrageous as shouting in church.

In the same low tone, he teased, "I thought you hated everything about California."

"This isn't like the other. Around the mining towns, the miners have changed the course of the rivers and invaded the sanctity of the mountains. Everything that was once lovely has gone. Here it's different."

"And Kentucky? Will you like it when you return there, honey, or have you been infected by the wilderness as Cal has?"

"And you?" She placed her hands over his in front of her.

"And me. This is what keeps me on the road, traveling through the hell-hot desert and the treeless plains. To see these mountains again and to savor the sight as much as I did the first time nearly ten years ago."

Her gaze rose to watch a golden eagle soaring in seemingly effortless flight. "Ten years? You first came to California a decade ago?"

"Nearly." He laughed, realizing how much longer the time seemed to her. "I came with my family to seek a western utopia of free land and perfect climate. That was before the scent of gold rolled across the plains to lure too many." His voice softened with memory as he mused, "I remember my first sight of the Sierras. Their beauty was unbroken by any human settlement. I thought I had found heaven."

"But you didn't stay."

He shook his head as he looked into the foam at the bottom of the falls. "No, and I'm not sure why. Perhaps I am not so hateful of my fellow man as Cal Feathersong is. I need people to share my life, but I can't turn my back on this wilderness." With a laugh, he turned her to face him. "Why the interrogation, half-pint?"

"I don't know that much about you."

"There isn't that much to know. I'm a simple man; I get my joy from the simple things of life. This scarlet-tinted mountainside, a freshly caught supper sizzling over the fire, and your lips against mine."

He drew her into his arms. With the power of the water beating against the rocks below them, they vanished into the glory of their passion. His fingers drew her thick shirt from her buckskin trousers so he could caress her without its bulkiness in the way. Her breath of yearning was swallowed by the thunder of the cascade.

"Don't be too tired tonight," he teased.

"And who fell asleep last night before I had finished the dishes?"

He laughed. "I promise you that will not happen tonight. I'm going to take Tommy and get some fresh meat for supper. We might be a little longer than normal. Game is getting scarcer with the coming of winter."

A screech negated his words. She glanced up to see that the eagle had ceased its patient circling and had found its prey. He chuckled and squeezed her hand.

"Be careful, Cliff," she urged. "Don't forget he's still just a little boy."

"How can I, half-pint, when you always remind me of that before you let us leave your sight?" He kissed her lightly on the forehead before returning to where the horses were tethered.

Lizzie ignored the sounds behind her as she glanced once more at the scene stretching beyond the horizon. So desolate, so beautiful. She had not answered Cliff's question by changing the subject. Yet it remained in her head to haunt her.

The young girl who had left Louisville three years ago to come west had disappeared. What she was now might never fit into the life she had enjoyed then. "Infected by the wilderness," had been Cliff's words. Perhaps he was right. A love of these untamed Sierras had sunk into her and was urging her to reconsider her goal.

She sighed. No life existed for them here. If they chose to stay, she doubted that Cliff would remain with them long. The call of the road would urge him to journey on alone.

Walking back to the clearing, she was greeted by an enthusiastic Pete. The child's task each night was to gather kindling for their fire. He had collected a pile that would have been sufficient for a dozen. She praised him and promised to play a card game with him as soon as the fire was burning steadily. This ritual eased his envy of Tommy's leaving with Cliff to hunt.

Contentedly she sat with the youngster. In the flickering light of the fire, the deepening of the twilight was less noticeable. The animals of the night called to one another but otherwise did not intrude on their private haven. She shuffled the cards, dog-eared from use, and dealt them out.

Pete chattered on about any subject that entertained him. Although she listened to him at first, as time passed she found herself paying little attention. She concentrated on hearing another sound, one that would signal the return of the hunters.

"Play this card," urged Lizzie, trying to keep her mind on the game.

"Why?" Perversely Pete chose another card. When he realized it would not help him, he cried, "I don't want this one!"

She threw the pack to the ground. "Why don't you ever just do as I suggest instead of questioning everything? You could have won!" As his eyes filled with hot tears and his lower lip trembled, she was instantly contrite. "I'm sorry, Pete. I shouldn't yell at you. It's just—"

Her eyes went again to the spot where Cliff and Tommy had entered the shadows beneath the trees too long ago. Normally it took them less than half an hour to find something for their evening meal. Cliff had said they might be delayed, but she hadn't thought it would take four times as long.

"Here," she said in a calmer tone. "Put away the cards, then run down to the river away from the falls and get some water. I think we'll have hot chocolate tonight with our supper."

"Hot chocolate?" His eyes brightened at the thought of the treat.

"Just don't fall in," she cautioned as she handed him the bucket. "If you get wet, you'll have to roll up in your blanket, and you can't drink chocolate then."

"All right. I know." He gave her a three-year-old expression of disgust at her often-repeated warnings.

She watched as he raced down the bank to the pool of water just beyond the light of the fire. From where she was, she could hear the splash if he slipped into the water. She suspected there would be no problem. Without his older brother, Pete was far less adventuresome and more content to do as he was told.

Walking to ease the tense muscles of her body, she went from one edge of the clearing to the other. Every few seconds she would pause to listen for the sound of returning footsteps. She glanced up in expectation when she heard the brush parting but sighed when she saw it was only Pete coming back from the river.

She relieved him of his burden and poured the water into the coffeepot. Placing it over the fire, she left the rest in the bucket. The boys would use it to clean up after supper.

"Here they come!" called Pete. The exultation in his voice told her he had sensed her disquiet.

Fleeting relief was superseded by rage because Cliff had worried her needlessly. "Where in heaven's name have you been?" she cried as she saw him push through the undergrowth.

"Lizzie?" A strange, tight sound had replaced his normal tone.

She leapt to her feet as he struggled awkwardly to tote something into the clearing. "What is—?" Running to him, she choked on her question. As she came closer, she could see what he was carrying.

"Tommy!" she screamed. "Tommy!" Frozen to the ground in horror, she pressed her hands over her mouth.

Cliff said nothing as he continued toward the fire. The child's slim limbs hung over his arms, but he had the boy's head cradled against his chest. In the uneven light, she could see the dark stain on Cliff's shirt. When he placed the limp body on the ground next to the fire, he turned to look at her.

"Lizzie, I—"

She ignored his words as she brushed past him. Her voice was a soft moan, "Tommy, oh, Tommy." She dropped to her knees by the motionless form. Her eyes stayed fixed on his colorless face, which seemed only to be smooth by sleep. She could not bring herself to look at the rest of him to determine the severity of his injury.

A shiver raced through her, and she stood up. She had to do something to help the child. He could not lie there untended. Cliff's hand on her arm halted her headlong flight toward the horses.

"Let me go!" she cried. "I have to get my supplies. I have to . . ." Her voice faded as he shook his head in slow negation. In horror, she spun to gaze at the child. Forced by Cliff's mute sorrow to see what she had denied, she riveted her eyes on the dark, oozing hole in the center of the child's shirt.

"Oh, Tommy. No, not my Tommy!" Sobs wrenched her voice as she moaned, "Whitney, I'm so sorry. Oh, Whitney, forgive me."

"It's not your fault, Lizzie," came Cliff's consoling words from too far away. She could not listen to them.

She sat on the ground again and picked up the small hand from the dirt. Death was not something that should happen to this youngster so full of life. Just hours ago, she had been reprimanding him for being silly. Now she would never hear his childish laughter again.

A pair of small arms wrapped themselves around her neck, and she drew Pete onto her lap. He did not ask what had happened. He remembered Lizzie's face looking like that the day Pa and Ma were killed. Without asking, he knew the same fate had come to take his brother from them.

Their sobs mingled as they mourned anew for the ones they had lost. Pete clung to her as the only thing that was keeping him from being drawn into the maw of darkness. With one arm around him and the other holding Tommy's hand, she wept as she had not been able to when Whitney and Zach died.

Cliff could not intrude on their private grief, although he shared it. He sat on a hillock several yards from them, not bothering to wipe his damp face. With his head in his hands, he tried to erase the sound of the child's voice and the explosion of the gun.

It was not Lizzie's fault the boy had had the accident. It was his. The first day they had gone hunting, Tommy had badgered Cliff to let him carry the rifle. Although Lizzie had specifically asked him not to let the lad do as he wanted, Cliff had acquiesced after extracting a joking promise from Tommy not to tell his aunt. For the past five days, Tommy had walked proudly by his side with the gun. Nothing had happened.

Until today.

Cliff was not sure exactly what happened. One minute they were walking and laughing together. The next, the boy had tripped and the gun had fired. Before Cliff could react, it was too late. The angle of the barrel had been fatally perfect. Within minutes, the child was dead. He never reopened his eyes as his lifeblood seeped out to stain the autumn leaves.

Denied from sharing their mourning, unable to allow the pain in him to show, Cliff rose to wander toward the fire. He swore softly under his breath as he pulled the coffeepot off the coals. Sticking his burned finger in his mouth, he could not bring himself to look at the small group. Lizzie's sobbing had eased to a raindrop-soft sound.

He glanced down as he felt an impatient hand

on his trousers. Masking his shock, he asked in a husky voice, "What is it, Pete?"

"I'm hungry."

Astonishment stripped him of speech. The reprimand he wanted to shout disappeared as he saw the innocent inquiry in the large eyes. Pete did not mean to be insensitive. With the self-centeredness of a three-year-old, he did not comprehend that his brother was dead. He had cried only because he saw that Lizzie was so upset.

Nodding, Cliff threw some food in the pan and fried it quickly. As soon as it sizzled, he spooned it onto a plate. He never noticed what he cooked. He gave it to the child and started to move toward Lizzie. Another tug on his trousers halted him.

"What's wrong now?" he demanded too sharply.

Pete's lip quivered as his luminous eyes glowed with unshed tears. The sight broke Cliff's heart. Kneeling, he held out his arms to the child. Pete, with a half sob, propelled himself into Cliff's embrace. The food struck Cliff's shirt before settling back in the center of the tin plate.

"I'm sorry, Petey," he whispered. What he felt the most regret about he could not say aloud.

"It's all right. I just need a spoon. Don't squeeze me so hard." Pete wiggled out of the embrace.

Cliff fished a small spoon out of the saddle-bags by the fire. He handed it to Pete. Blinking rapidly, he watched as the child sat and began to wolf down the food. He wished he could be so ignorant of the tragedy.

His eyes moved involuntarily to the one who was grieving the most. Lizzie's head remained bent over her older nephew's body. He wanted to comfort her, to take her pain into himself and store it with his. Without quite realizing what he was doing, he walked around the small fire to where she sat.

Kneeling, he put his hand on her shoulder. "Lizzie?"

"Cliff, please, just leave us alone," she said without looking at him.

He nodded. Her request was a reasonable one. Blindly he rose and went back to sit by Pete. That the child spoke to him he guessed by the movement of Pete's mouth, but the sounds made no sense in his head. He did not want to look at Peter Greenway. The towhead reminded him of one who would never grow to be a man.

Somehow Cliff managed to help the child ready himself for bed. He made up some reason as to why Pete should wait until the morning to kiss Lizzie good-night. It was harder to devise a lie about why Tommy was not cuddling up with his brother. Cliff did not have the heart to explain the truth.

When Pete was finally asleep, Cliff knew he could not delay the inevitable confrontation. He went silently to Lizzie. Her hand still held Tommy's. In a grief-laden voice, he said, "Honey, we have to bury him."

"Here?" Her ashen face, streaked with the salt trails of her tears, gazed at him in horror. "Here, all alone? Oh, no, Cliff! I can't leave him here all alone."

Knowing his words were cruel, he used them to shock her out of her grief. An angry Lizzie he could deal with. This pitiful wraith he could not. "What do you suggest? That we take him back to the Whitney's Dream? Shall we open it and leave him in that mountainside mausoleum with his parents?"

"How dare you! You are not welcome here, Cliff Hollister. Why don't you just leave?"

"And what will you do?" His heart contracted at the sight of the naked emotions she could not hide.

"I'll take care of my nephew. We don't need your help. I think you've done enough for him already."

Lizzie was wrenched from her own pain as Cliff's outward calm shattered before her eyes. She had been sunk so deeply in her grief, she hadn't noticed his mourning. His mouth worked, but no sounds emerged. She saw the tears in his eyes and understood he was hurting as terribly as she was.

Knowing no words to ease the pain they shared, she held out her arms to him. He drew her to her feet. Leading her to the spot where he had sat before, he settled her on his lap. As she had with Pete, he simply held her.

"I'm sorry," she whispered. "I don't mean to

take out my anger on you. I don't know who I'm angry at. It just doesn't seem fair."

"Be angry at me. I let him carry the rifle."

"I know."

He looked into her eyes, so lustrous in the moonlight. "You knew that?"

"Yes, he told me." A weak grin tipped the corners of her lips. "Six-year-olds can't keep a secret. It's so precious, they can't wait to share it." A sob ripped the smile from her face. "I knew you would take care of him."

Swallowing harshly past the lump of sorrow in his throat, he answered, "I did a hell of a job of it."

"It was an accident, Cliff. That's why I can't be angry at anyone. There was no reason it should be Tommy, but it happened." She leaned her head on his shoulder. "At first I wanted to kill you too, but nothing will bring him back. He wanted to stay in California. Now he will."

The quaking of her slender body in his arms belied her calm words. She had accepted what he had forced her to see. She must leave her nephew here in the mountains. They could not take him on to the next real town, where there would be a church cemetery.

His eyes rose to the snow-topped peaks of the highest mountains. Tommy Greenway loved this land. When Cliff was hunting with the child, the little boy had told him how he planned to return to California when he was old enough. He wanted to prove to everyone that his father was right about gold in the Whitney's Dream mine. Now that would never happen.

Lizzie clung to Cliff's strength, wishing she could awaken from what she felt must be a horrid nightmare. It couldn't be real. She closed her eyes. Each breath she took required a conscious effort to move the lump of lead sitting on her chest. It seemed as if all her involuntary movements needed her to direct them.

Beat, heart. Breathe, lungs. Think, brain. Nothing would work correctly or automatically. Only the pain continued to swell overwhelming her in its intensity.

It all seemed impossible. Each time she fought to tell herself that what had happened was real, she suffered an overwhelming resurgence of grief.

"Lizzie, do you want to stay here?"

She shook her head vehemently. He did not need to explain. "I want to help. I must be with him. Let me check on Pete first."

"That's a good idea." Their minds worked in unison. He could sense what she thought even before she spoke.

"Get Tommy's blanket. I don't want him to be cold." Tears balanced on her eyelashes as her voice caught on her words. "Cliff?"

He rose and lifted her to her feet. His broad palm covered her cheek as he tipped her head back to see her face. "See to Pete," he whispered. "I'll take care of—of everything else."

"Thank you."

He nodded, his guilt biting into him like a bullwhip. She might justly have chosen to blame him for his refusal to listen to her common sense, but she had already forgiven him. He wondered if he ever could forgive himself.

Pete proved to be awake, but he was cooperative about going to sleep once he received his kiss from her. Whether he was truly exhausted or realized his aunt was in no condition to argue, he drew his blanket up to his chin and folded his hands under his cheek. Lizzie patted the wool cover gently and rose.

A pang went through her like a knife when she saw that the clearing was empty except for herself and Pete. When Cliff emerged from the night and held out his hand to her, she walked stiffly to where he stood. He took her fingers and led the way through the trees.

"We can't go far. We can't leave Pete." Panic sharpened her voice.

"Hush, honey. We aren't going far. He'll be fine for a few minutes."

They emerged from the trees into a moonlit glen. If they had not been on such a horrible errand, she would have admired the lovely greenery barely visible beneath the trees. The river whispered its many secrets to accent the distant roar of the water falling into the ravine.

He tugged at her hand. Reluctantly she dragged her feet forward. Anguish closed her throat until she was sure she would never swallow again. She clenched her fingers, not realizing that she was squeezing his hand painfully. With her eyes on the small, blanket-wrapped figure lying next to a dark void dug in the earth, she was aware only of her own heartache.

"I didn't cover his face. I thought you might want to tell him . . . something." For once, words did not come easily to Cliff.

She nodded without looking at him. Then she walked across the clearing. Her body was so stiff with misery it seemed to creak as she knelt. Tentatively she reached out a trembling finger to push Tommy's always recalcitrant hair from his closed eyes. She bent and kissed his too-cold cheek.

When she felt a hand on her shoulder, she drew the cloth over the child's face. She tried to remind herself he was safe with his parents now. That offered little comfort; a hollow feeling of desolation swept through her.

"All right, Cliff." She stood up and watched as he carefully lowered the small form into the grave.

He glanced at her. "Do you want to say anything?"

"I don't know what to say."

"Neither do I." He had seen too many buried on the trip west, but none had been as important to him as this child he had grown to love. Even on the trail, he had found it easier to be elsewhere during such rites. As wagon master, he had many tasks he would use as excuses to avoid being one of the mourners.

Picking up a small spade, he scooped up some of the loosened earth. Lizzie bit her lower lip as Cliff shoveled the dirt back into the grave. The impulse to reach past him and lift out Tommy's small figure was very strong. She wanted to have someone wake her from this nightmare so she could see Tommy's smile again.

When Cliff placed a marker in the ground, she held her hands folded before her lips. She tried to contain the tears his kindness might release. As he piled rocks on the cairn to keep away scavengers, she knelt to look at the words he had carved into the primitive marker:

Thomas Zachary Greenway, Dreamer
b. 1846 d. 1852

Lizzie could not halt the soul-wrenching sobs that exploded from her body. Over the harsh sound of the rocks grating against one another as Cliff worked with seemingly emotionless efficiency, her weeping filled the night. When he had finished, he came to her and helped her to her feet. With him leading her, she took several steps, then stumbled against him.

He lifted her into his arms. Her arms went around him as she hid her face against his neck. The heat of her tears burned his skin, matching the pain he felt inside. He carried her back to the campsite and placed her gently on the ground near

Pete, who slumbered on, oblivious to everything.

"Honey, can I do anything? Are you hungry?"

"No," she murmured. "I want to sleep. Hold me, Cliff. Hold me and never let me go."

"Forever, honey." At that moment, he sincerely meant what he said.

He handed her a blanket and watched as she curled up under it. Although he doubted that either of them would rest that night, he lay down next to her and closed his eyes. They popped open immediately as the awful scene he longed to erase from his memory played itself out again in his mind.

Lizzie struggled to control her ravaged emotions. Tomorrow they would be on the trail again. She had to rest tonight. She could not allow herself to forget in her grief that Pete was depending on her as much as ever. California had claimed too much from her family. She did not intend for any others to be sacrificed on the golden altar of false dreams.

Cliff woke to the vivid pulse of sunshine. As soon as he moved, Pete leapt on him. He chuckled while he tickled the child as he did each morning when they awoke.

"Howdy, kid!"

"Get me some breakfast, Cliff?"

"Breakfast? Didn't Lizzie—?"

"She went for a walk. She told me to stay here with you."

Memory broke over him. He shivered as he

recalled the terrible events of the past day. Somehow he had convinced himself that when he awoke that morning, he would discover that Tommy's death had been nothing but part of his imagination.

He fried some food over the nearly dead coals. He didn't feel like stirring the fire higher. Although Pete ate ravenously, Cliff had no desire for food. He doubted that Lizzie had eaten either. With a sigh, he realized he probably would have to force her to take care of herself. She would argue with him, even though he would be thinking only of her welfare.

After the child was finished with his breakfast, Cliff washed the dishes and stored them in the saddlebags. With Pete's help, he packed all they had used last night. Pete prattled on, but what the child said made little impression on Cliff. All his thoughts were centered on the woman.

He knew exactly where Lizzie would be. He took the reins of the three horses. Leading them through the trees, he warned Pete to silence. The little boy clutched his hand fearfully and glanced up at the man beside him. Cliff suspected the child had little concept of what had happened but accepted it as he had his parents' deaths.

When they reached the second clearing, they paused. The sight of the woman on her knees with her hand on the rocks over the freshly turned earth renewed the grief for Cliff. He watched as she patted the soil-stained stones as lovingly as she did the children's heads.

She must have felt their eyes on her, for she

rose without her usual grace and came toward them. Red-ringed eyes stared from her alabaster face. "I had to say good-bye," she whispered. "He is so little to be alone."

"I know," he said as he held out his hand. She placed her own hand in it, and he led the way toward the horses. They did not look back.

CHAPTER TWELVE

TEARS BLURRED LIZZIE'S VISION AS THEY RODE deeper into the mountains. She recalled Tommy's questions the night before they had left on this awful journey. He had seen his Indian and had his adventures, but it had come to an end. She turned in her saddle to gaze at the wavering landscape to the west. Behind them remained the lonely grave. Only she and Pete would escape from the mountains that had claimed the lives of the rest of their family.

Nothing of this did she say to Cliff. Their mutual sorrow expressed itself in irritability as they snapped at each other about the smallest detail. When, after they broke camp the next day, Cliff offered Pete the chance to ride with him, Lizzie protested. She needed the youngster next to her to ease the emptiness within her each time she thought about Tommy.

"You're just being selfish!" she exclaimed.

"Selfish? If you weren't so damned overprotective of those boys, he would have known how to use a gun safely."

Her dark eyes widened in disbelief. "Don't try to make this all my fault, Cliff Hollister! I told you to be careful with him. I trusted you, but you betrayed that trust again."

"Me?" he exploded as he did so seldom. His voice resounded across the mountainside. He grasped her upper arms in his painful grip and drew her away from the horses. Shaking her, he tried to force some sense into her stubborn head. "You speak of trust so easily, Lizzie, but you're the one who hid some of our winnings away every night."

"I admit it! And why not? If I had left all the money in your hands, you would have spent it for foolish luxuries. Now we have something with which to buy supplies."

He put his finger directly in front of her eyes. "You know what your problem is?"

"I assume you are about to tell me," she retorted snidely.

"You're damned right! You don't know how to live!"

She grimaced and turned to walk away. When he reached out a hand to pull her back, she slapped it away from her. "Don't touch me!"

Ignoring her words, he caught her and brought her back to him. "Stop it, honey. You know you like it when I hold you."

"You're wrong, Cliff." She calmly peeled his

hands from her arms. Her voice remained devoid of emotion as she stated, "You're wrong. I did, I must admit, but you have made it clear that loving you is a stupid thing to do. I'm tired of your childish refusals to see the least bit of common sense!"

"Childish?" he roared.

She smiled coldly. "Yes, very childish. When are you going to stop playing boys' games and start being a man?"

A wordless growl erupted from his throat as he viciously pushed her against a broad tree trunk. He pressed his mouth over hers, forcing her head back against the rough bark while he held her hands away from her squirming body. Staring down into her snapping dark eyes, he threatened, "I can show you I'm a man!"

"How? By raping me?" She hid her aching heart behind bravado. "That doesn't prove you're a man, Cliff! It proves only that you're stronger than I."

He snorted in derision. "Rape? Who would want you? A man wants a woman who can feel something other than hatred." He released her and stepped away as if her proximity was distasteful. "Why don't you go back to Hopeless and take up at Delilah's where your sister left off? You would make a fine whore, with your stone heart!"

Her hand rose of its own volition and struck his face. Then she cringed, frightened by her own rage, as he glared at her. His clenched fist remained tight at his side. With his lips set in a straight line, he snapped, "Go and get on your horse! Now!"

Lizzie ran to the horses. She mounted and hushed Pete's questions by refusing to acknowledge them. She kept her eyes focused directly in front of her horse's nose as Cliff eased himself into his saddle. Lizzie longed to dissolve into tearful recriminations as he continued in morose silence. Pete watched, unsure and lost without his older brother to guide him.

To Pete, as the days passed, the adults remained pleasant. But they treated each other with a cold politeness that frightened him. He didn't like being without Tommy, and he hated having the two most important people in his life angry at each other.

When he slept at the end of each day, silence would descend between Cliff and Lizzie. She made no effort to break through the wall of her sorrow. Any statement he made to her brought him only a terse response. Almost as soon as the echo of the heated words they'd exchanged the morning after the tragedy had vanished into the autumn sky, Cliff regretted them. He refused to apologize when every attempt to speak to her brought a baleful glare.

When they came upon a small village surprisingly nestled in the lee side of a wide valley, they paused by mutual, silent consent. The dingy room over the saloon was only too familiar, but now only one boy explored its corners.

"I think I'll go downstairs," Cliff murmured as they finished supper.

"All right."

"Do you want to come?"

"Not now." She sighed. "I won't cheat at cards anymore."

He nodded. During the past week he had become accustomed to her short replies and long silences. He understood. He could not speak without mentioning something about the dead child. It was better to be mute.

"I'll see you later then."

"All right," she answered in the same lifeless tone.

Picking up his gunbelt and his hat, he went to the door. He did not look back to see the shattered expression on her face. Closing the door, he wondered if he would be forced to pay for his error the rest of his life. He found it impossible to forgive himself, but he thought she would sense his pain and try to ease it just as he wanted to lessen hers.

Lizzie squeezed her eyes shut to dam the ever-present tears when she heard the latch drop back into place. Whenever Cliff had threatened to leave her before, he had taken his hat and pistols with him. Now she was afraid he wasn't planning to come back to her that night.

Not that she could blame him.

She had treated him abominably, but each time she wanted to tell him how she felt, he snarled something at her. The truth she concealed within her had become an ulcer, burning unremittingly. Nights brought no relief, for the brief love they had shared had vanished in the aftermath of the accident. Once again, they slept with Pete between them.

As if he could read her thoughts, the child

crawled into her lap. She wrapped her arms around him and placed her cheek against the softness of his hair. The love she wanted to give to so many found its only outlet with Pete.

Determined to fight off her feelings of dejection, she lifted him to his feet. She said with false lightness, "You, young man, are going to have a bath. Who knows when we'll be in a civilized place again?"

"Lizzie," he whined, "I don't want to take a bath."

A true laugh drifted from her lips as she recalled many such fights with him and Tommy over the past six months. They both despised sitting in a galvanized tub having too-hot or too-cold water splashed over their heads. The rush of grief she felt at the thought of Pete's brother was diminished when she hugged Pete again.

Taking him by the hand, she went down to the stable yard in the back. She knocked on a door she thought would lead to the kitchen. A dour man peered out through the narrow slit he opened.

"What d'ya want?" he demanded shortly.

"Hot water."

"Cost you eight bits."

She frowned. "We already paid for it when we rented the room upstairs."

"So? You made a deal with the boss for that. If you want water from me, you bargain with me." He grinned as he eyed her up and down. "Eight bits, honey. In gold or in trade."

Her eyes narrowed as she glared at the homely man. His brow seemed to wide for his face.

Pockmarks indented his cheeks on either side of a
nose broken too many times in barroom brawls.
From him wafted an odor that spoke of his
disinterest in bathing.

"Sorry," she said in the softly seductive voice
she had heard Peg use to entice a customer. "I
don't think you're worth eight bits. I'm sorry I
don't have a single copper to offer you."

"Why, you—!" He lunged toward her and
tripped over her outstretched foot. A thick thump
sounded as he fell face first on the ground.

Grabbing Pete's hand, she leapt aside and
raced through the door. She slammed the kitchen
door shut and dropped the bar into place. As she
expected, a big pot of water was heating on the
cookstove. She ordered Pete to find a tub while she
bolted the door leading into the saloon. The single
window was warped shut and too small for the
man to crawl through should he want to make her
pay for fooling him.

She ignored the pounding on the door. The
child laughed as she stripped his clothes from him
and stood him in the tub. Quickly she poured a
mixture of the hot and cold water over him. She
handed him a bar of harsh soap which he used
under her close observation. Frequently she looked
over her shoulder at the door to the stable yard, but
the pounding brought the man no success. The
door was sturdy enough to withstand his assaults.

"This is fun, Lizzie!" Pete crowed.

She poured another bucket over him to rinse
him off. When she heard a crash from the saloon,
she glanced up expecting to see trouble. No one

appeared, and she realized the noise had not been caused by the cook. Normal rowdiness, she guessed.

"Do you think so? This may be the fastest bath you have ever had. Hair next."

Within minutes, she had him clean. He redressed while she found a long knife to put in her belt. She didn't know if the cook would be waiting outside in the yard. As angry as he must be, she wanted to be prepared.

A more hysterical sound came from the back door. "Lufkin! Lufkin! Man, open the door! It's Diehl. Let me—"

A scream followed an explosion beyond the door and raised the small hairs on the back of her neck. Her fear was mirrored by the look of terror on the boy's pale face. Motioning to Pete to follow her, she unbolted the back door. She left the pan of dirty water on the floor.

As the cook had done, she peeked around the door. The stable yard appeared deserted. She started to move forward when her boot struck something soft. A scream wrenched her throat as she saw the blood-soaked planks by the door. In the center of the crimson stain a man stared sightlessly at the roof. She leaned against the wall by the door and fought the revulsion that churned in her stomach. Her plan to stay inside the kitchen vanished when she heard a crash against the other door and the sound of more rifles firing.

She took Pete and lifted him over the corpse. The child clung to her as he regarded the dead man with uncharacteristic silence. Staying in the shadows of the small porch roof, she led the way to the stairs. She suspected they would be safest in their room. A movement on the opposite side of the yard caught her eyes.

"Run!" she commanded.

Holding the bare knife in her hand, she started to sprint across the open area. Pete's short legs flew along behind her. They were halfway up the stairs when she began to congratulate herself on getting them to safety.

Her scream was involuntary as she heard the explosion and the whir of a bullet not far from her head. She dropped to the shadows of the steps, keeping herself between Pete and the yard. Not daring to move, she let her eyes sweep the space. No one was visible. She had not thought any man would shoot at a woman and child. The one who had killed Diehl had to be very drunk.

She counted slowly to one hundred, cautioning the child to silence between numbers. When she heard nothing more from the stable yard, she began to wonder if the bullet had been only a random shot from the street. She could hear other guns. What might be taking place beyond her hiding place, she could not guess.

Cautiously she lifted her head to peer over the warped planks connecting the rail to the steps. She saw movement and ducked as another bullet sailed over her head. Another exploded through the boards not far from them.

"Climb!" she ordered the child. "On your hands and knees. Don't get up!" She pushed on his back to keep him low.

Another shot sounded. Hot pain cut through Lizzie's leg, but she didn't pause in her upward climb. She was alive. To stop for any reason might mean dying. Once in the hallway, she regained her feet and raced along with Pete to their room. Rushing in, she shoved Pete to the floor and told him not to move.

She grimaced as she put her hand to her thigh. Splinters were embedded in the buckskin. The heavy material had protected her from more than a few cuts. Withdrawing the splinters like pins from a pincushion, she slunk slowly along the wall to the window overlooking the street below.

"Oh, no!" she breathed. "No, Pete, stay down!" Out of the corner of her eye, she had seen him ready to bounce up to find out what had upset her.

With her back against the wall, she watched the deadly action on the street below. The twilight could not conceal the figures lying face down in the mud. Again and again came the staccato pop of gunfire matching the screeching beat of her heart. She didn't believe the horror could become more intense. How wrong she was she discovered when she saw the men moving with steady precision toward the saloon.

"Cliff!" she screamed.

He was downstairs where the carnage was centered. Ordering Pete to stay on the floor and wait for her, she ran to the door and flung it open. To let Cliff die thinking she hated him would be the final agony she could tolerate. She ran along the hall. Arms grabbed at her, but she shook them off.

One pair refused to release her.

"Don't go down there!"

"Cliff! Cliff is in the saloon!"

A hand struck her cheek and broke her hysteria. She cowered away from the person holding her. When she looked up, she recognized the woman by her clothing. The satin dress dipped deep across her nearly bare bosom. Strands of pale hair hung on both sides of her plain face. Lizzie noticed all that in the second before her eyes were caught by the recently wet splotch of red on her skirt.

The prostitute said, "You go down there, girl, and you'll be dead. Frenchie Jack and his men intend to make sure that what happened in Mokelumne Hill don't happen here. They don't want to lose their claims to no Americans anxious to see the French gone from here." When she saw Lizzie's blank expression, she stated, "Don't you know nothing, girl? The French miners in Mokelumne Hill done lost their claims to the Americans. Frenchie Jack's crew struck what might be a wide vein. They don't aim to lose it."

"So they're shooting up the town?"

The other women clustered in the hall laughed at her naivete. "Why not?" asked their spokeswoman. "Gold is gold. You can find new friends and enemies easily, but gold is hard to come by. Once you discover it, you hold on like a mud turtle."

A louder spurt of gunfire erupted up the staircase. Several of the women squealed and raced to their bare rooms to hide. A shouted order halted all of them in their tracks.

Lizzie whirled to see a dark-haired man, his eyes ablaze. Although his denims were spotted with blood, he seemed unharmed. He waved his gun wildly. When he spoke, she could not understand his words.

"English, Frenchie Jack," urged the blond prostitute. "We don't understand none of that Frenchie talk."

"Men! Jenny, you hiding any of those—how do you say—?"

The blond, whose name appeared to be Jenny, interrupted him. "No men up here, Frenchie Jack. Just the girls. You don't want to shoot us." She laughed lightly. "Shoot us, and what are you going to do for entertainment after you strip that vein of all its gold? Adder Hill and us girls are so convenient to you."

He lowered his gun and smiled at her seductive suggestion. His muscular, none-too-clean arm swept around her and pulled her close to him. She did not resist as he kissed her enthusiastically.

Lizzie closed her eyes as she saw his hand reach for the neckline of the whore's gown. She did not want to watch as they enjoyed themselves in the hallway. Afraid to move, she thought of Pete witnessing this from the doorway of their room.

"Who is that?" demanded the man in his thick accent.

She looked up to see the gun pointing at her. Fear stripped her voice from her. Jenny answered, "Oh, Frenchie Jack, leave the kid alone. She's just traveling through Adder Hill. She and her little brother."

"Brother? I thought you said no men."

Lizzie cried, "He's only three years old!"

The man walked toward her. He spoke as casually as if no shooting was resounding up the stairs. "You are—?"

"Lizzie—Lizzie Buchanan." Her eyes moved back and forth between his face and the gun he held with such easy confidence.

He reached forward and used the barrel to tilt her face first one way and then the other. A smile appeared on his lips. With the pistol pressed to her cheek and the end of the barrel against her temple, he assessed her coolly.

"Where do you go, Lizzie?"

Swallowing with difficulty past the lump of fear in her throat, she whispered, "Home to Kentucky."

"Alone?"

"My little brother is traveling with me." She continued the lie Jenny had begun and prayed no one would betray the truth.

He grinned, the narrow lines of his face wrinkling into grooves. Lowering the gun, he slapped her cheek softly. "Don't hurry away, Lizzie. Stay for the celebration later."

She muttered something which he took for an affirmative. He laughed, spun around, and, with a wave to the women, raced down the stairs. They heard his exultant shout and the echo of his gun firing from the staircase. The prostitute with blood on her dress shoved Lizzie toward her rented room.

"Get out of here, girl. You'll learn if your man

be alive or dead after this is over. Frenchie Jack
don't have more than a dozen men. They can't last
long with everyone shootin' at them. You'd best
take care of your young'un."

"Will you call me—"

"No!" she snapped. "I don't run no errands
for no one. Now get out of here!"

Lizzie knew the crudely spoken advice was
sound. She had to watch out for Pete. If she went
down into the melee and was killed, he would have
nobody left to take care of him.

Going into her room, she closed the door but
did not bolt it. She didn't want to deny Cliff an
escape route if he needed it. If he was still alive . . .

"I don't know," she answered her nephew
after praising him for staying in the room. "All
they said was that it's a war between the miners.
Why don't you get into bed?"

"I want to help Cliff, Lizzie!" He bounced
about, aiming an imaginary rifle at invisible
enemies.

She smiled weakly. "Good. Get some sleep.
Then if he needs you, you'll be all set to go." She
pulled the covers up to his chin and leaned over to
kiss him.

There was a crash as a bullet burst through the
window and glass shards rained down on them.
Lizzie pressed her face to the bed, her body
shielding the child. In the puff of cold air whirling
through the broken window, she could hear the
sound of rifles firing into the night.

Picking up the frightened, crying child, she
examined him to make sure he was unhurt. Except

for a few superficial cuts on his left arm, he showed
no signs of injury from the insanity surrounding
them. She pulled the blanket from the bed. A few
sharp shakes sent slivers of glass flying across the
room. Then she placed it on the floor close to the
hallway wall and lay down on it with Pete.

She soothed the child's tears with promises of
a treat in the morning. In spite of his tears and the
violence around him, he fell asleep with little more
trouble than normal. She did not move from his
side.

When silence dropped over the town, she
didn't believe her ears. Intermittent shots still
sounded, but they were far from the saloon and
seemed to be moving away from the settlement.
She was afraid to believe the battle was over.

A soft knock sounded on the door. She froze,
terrified of who might be on the other side.
Frenchie Jack had hinted he would come back and
the thought of what he might do petrified her.
When she didn't answer it, the knob turned slowly.
She groped for the knife still in her belt. Raising it
in wobbly fingers, she held it out in front of her.

It clattered to the floor as she recognized the
silhouette in the doorway. She leapt forward with a
cry.

"Cliff!"

He groaned involuntarily as she clutched his
arms. In shock, she pulled back her right hand to
see it wet with a dark fluid she feared was blood.

"I'm fine, half-pint. Just a flesh wound in my
left arm. I was lucky. There must be twenty dead
men downstairs, and I don't know how many

outside." Fatigue slowed his words.

She groped for her saddlebag. A splinter of glass on it sliced her finger, but she ignored the pain. Finding her small supply of medicine, she turned up the lantern slightly and moved back to Cliff. If the light woke Pete, she would have more help than she needed tending the injury.

Grimacing, she ripped Cliff's shirtsleeve open with one ferocious tug. A small hole in his upper arm oozed slowly. Gently she turned his arm and saw a matching hole on the other side. The bullet had ripped through the fleshy part above the elbow. She didn't look at him as she opened her tin of salve and spread some medicine on two small strips of cloth. Competently she tied them around his arm and bound them in place with more bandages.

"Thank you, honey." He flexed his arm slightly and smiled. "It'll heal quickly. How are you and Pete?"

Involuntarily she glanced over her shoulder. "They shot out our window, but we got only a few cuts here and in the yard out back."

"Out back?" Ignoring his wound, he grabbed her and pulled her close. "You weren't hurt?"

"We're fine." Her eyes searched his face. "How did this all start? Why tonight?"

He shook his head. "I'll be damned if I know. Some guy came racing into the bar shouting French gibberish and waving a gun. Within seconds, some fool had pulled out a rifle and shot him. Then all hell broke loose."

She leaned her head against his chest. Even as

he explained what had happened, she was wondering why she had forbidden herself this comfort for the past week. The gentle stroke of his fingers along her back loosened the last vestiges of grief within her. The undammed force dissolved all her anger at him.

"Cliff," she sobbed, "don't leave me again."

"I won't, honey. Don't cry." He felt the urge to join her, for he knew she was thinking of the single death last week instead of the carnage in the street below.

"All I could think of was you dying without knowing how much I love you, Cliff."

"I know, half-pint." He kissed the top of her head. "Believe me, I know." She would never know how he had feared for her as he fought for his life against the man whose gold-maddened fury had been unleashed in the taproom. Using the bar as a shield, he had fought next to men he didn't know but who shared his desire to emerge from the battle alive.

"Just hold me. Don't let me go."

"I would be glad to hold you anytime." He tilted her face back so his lips could taste the delicate flavor he had been denied too long.

"Cliff?" she asked before he could put his thoughts into action.

"What is it, honey?"

She swallowed her yearning once again to hear him tell her that he loved her. To have him here and safe would have to be enough. Perhaps someday he would say it. She did not want to waste this time by asking for the impossible. Looking into his shadowed eyes, her hands enclosed the outline of his face. She ached inside, and his kiss would cure the cramp twisting her stomach. She pressed her hand against the back of his head to bring his mouth to hers.

As her arms encircled his neck, he was captured again by her bewitching charm. Her soft hair teased his arm as he rediscovered the rapture she created within him. He entangled his hands in its short curls and held her mouth ever tighter to his.

Her fingers reached for the buttons of his flannel shirt. She fumbled in her hurry, so that the task took longer than she wished, but he did not mind as he felt her fingers against his skin, thrilling him as much as it had the first time. Beneath his mouth, her lips curved up in a smile as she caressed the hard muscles of his chest. When she heard his gasp of pleasure, she laughed softly.

The laughter faded into a sigh as he kissed the skin at the base of her neck. He breathed in the delicate perfume of her hair. With the hunger growing stronger each time she whetted it with her nearness, he lowered himself slowly to sit on the floor, bringing her to rest on his knees.

She did not have a chance to say anything as his lips delighted her. Her hands clutched the bare skin of his shoulders under his shirt as sensations she was powerless to stop took control of her. His fingers teased her skin through the thin fabric of her clothes. She became lost in their shared passion.

"You feel so wonderful," came the tickling

whisper of his breath in her ear.

"I do," she agreed.

The amused sound of his chuckle momentarily interrupted their steadily mounting desire. His gray eyes regarded the woman resting across his chest with her hand over the beat of his heart and her eyes closed as she savored the warmth of their kisses. For a long minute, he simply held her, feeling he would never know such powerful feelings for another. He did not want to do anything to disrupt this moment, with her nestled snugly against his skin and his arms holding her close to him.

Listening to the even rhythm of his breathing, she knew the same contentment. She could imagine nothing better than to be held so tenderly in his arms.

His hands tightened on her seconds before his lips covered hers again. A flare of passion disintegrated their tranquillity. When he placed lightning-hot kisses on the skin above her shirt, she moaned in pleasure. His fingers encircled the roundness of her breast, and she gasped aloud as the streak of heat from his touch ignited her passion. She could not stop the urging of her body as she pressed closer to his sinewy strength.

Greedily he kissed her heated mouth, forgetting everything but the delicious taste of it. He tilted her back gently so he could partake of her more deeply. Exulting in her rapid breath against his ear, he bent again to trace the pulse line along her throat. As she felt the heat of him on her skin, she whispered, "Love me, Cliff. I need you tonight."

He wanted nothing more than to comply, but the room suddenly began to spin around him, making it impossible for him to do as she asked. With blurred eyes, he gazed at her face, glistening with the streaks of her tears. Then a fresh wave of pain swept all vestiges of desire from him.

He shook his head. "Half-pint—"

Lizzie caught him and eased him to the floor next to her. Guilt smothered her passion. She should have realized the wound would sap his strength. Crawling to the bed, she brought back a musty-smelling pillow and placed it under his head.

"Rest, Cliff."

"Will you rest next to me?" He held out his unwounded arm and drew her close to him.

"I don't want to be alone. The dark scares me. Cliff, I need you." Her voice broke as new tears rolled down her cheeks. "I don't want to be alone."

"You aren't alone," he said soothingly.

"I need you!" she repeated.

"And I'm here for you as long as you want me to be. I'll hold you all night, every night, if that's what you want."

She leaned her head against the warmth of his bare skin. "How do you know me so well?"

Pondering her question, he gazed across the moonlit room. The glow moved as clouds wove their patterns on the floor. "I don't know," he finally answered. "You make every effort to be dishonest with me. But I know I need you too tonight, Lizzie."

"Hold me," she whispered.

He tightened his arm around her, bringing her more securely against him. "I won't let you go."

Slowly her tear-hot eyes closed. Her breathing grew less frantic as she relaxed against him. With the sound of his heartbeat like a sweet lullaby, she faded into sleep. Exhausted by the tragedies haunting them, Cliff soon followed, his head resting on the top of hers as they nestled together on the floor.

CHAPTER THIRTEEN

GARLAND CREEK PROUDLY BOASTED THE TRAP-
pings of civilization. Three disastrous fires in two
years had convinced the local merchants to rebuild
with brick and stone. Only the plank road and
sidewalk were constructed of wood. Two streets
ran through the settlement, one for trade and
honest boardinghouses, the other for the single
saloon and the businesses it attracted.

Cliff headed unerringly for the latter. They
could not afford to stay in the "better section." He
feared that in addition to the dozen coins Lizzie
had taken from her cache, they would have to dip
into the gold in the small bag around her neck.
More than once, as she slept next to him at night,
he had felt the temptation to determine exactly
how much awaited him at the end of the journey.
But he had resisted, aware of how betrayed she
would feel if he violated her trust again.

While he went into the bar to inquire about a room, Lizzie stiffly paced the boardwalk. After days in the saddle, she found it difficult to relieve the cramps in her legs. The cold contracted her muscles as the minutes became an hour.

The music of a piano rang tinnily through the night. She winced chuckling as the player hit one wrong note after another. Holding up her fingers, now covered by the gloves Cliff had obtained from Cal, she wondered if she could play the instrument she had not touched since she and her family had left for California.

She heard steps behind her and turned to see Cliff. He smiled as he held up a key. "No rooms, but I got us a house."

"A house! How are we going to pay for that?" Knowing the rates the saloonkeepers usually charged for a single room over their taprooms, she hated to imagine what a whole house would cost.

"It's costing us less than the room in Yankee City did last night." He grinned. "The owner recognized me, asked my name. Seems he came west with me a few years ago, although I don't recall him. Out of gratitude, he offered us this house that a miner lost in a big game." He put his arm around her waist. "Are you impressed, half-pint?"

She laughed. "That a man remembers you and offers you a shack to pay you back for allowing him to amass a fortune? Let me see this rat's nest before I make a decision."

When she moved toward the horse, he shook his head. "It's only a few steps from here." He took the reins and motioned to her to take Pete's hand.

Unable to hide her curiosity, she followed him. The bitterness of the night sliced into them each time they passed an occasional alley between the buildings. She lifted her collar and shrank into it to keep warm.

"This place?" she gasped when he paused.

Lantern light spilled from the windows to reveal a door situated between two glass panels. She could see little else of the house in the darkness at this end of the street. Cliff tied the horses to a post in front of the building before going to the door. Instead of using the the key, he knocked. Before she could ask why he was doing that, the door opened.

He urged them into the warmth billowing from the house. Lizzie pulled Pete after her. In awe, she looked around her. It was not what she expected.

Spanish-style stucco decorated the walls, built in the smooth curves favored by the earlier white settlers of the region. Beneath her feet, terra cotta tiles glowed in the red light from the hearth in the adjoining room. A staircase rose on the left, leading her gaze to the *vigas,* log rafters, supporting the roof. The massive timbers still wore their coating of bark.

Opposite the stairs beyond a low wall was what could only be a parlor. Artwork hung on the wall. In niches vases filled with dried flowers added a festive note to the room. Fine furniture was arranged around the beehive-style hearth built three feet off the floor. On the floor a woven rug

teased the eyes with its intricate pattern. Through a
door at the far side of the room, she could see a
hallway leading to other rooms.

This was far from the miner's shack she had
expected. She was sure this house had been there
before gold fever had lured fools into the once-
beautiful valley. At one time dominating a tree-
ringed clearing, the gracious house was now as out
of place as a crown on a burro.

When she heard Cliff talking to the person
who had admitted them, Lizzie halted her exploration of the foyer. Her eyes widened as she saw the
squat woman who was answering his questions in
heavily accented English. Lizzie didn't recognize
the language that colored the woman's English, but
she suspected it was Spanish.

"Lizzie Buchanan, this is Stella. She's the
housekeeper here." He grinned at the gray-haired
woman whose face bore the imprint of her years.
"Stella, my partner Lizzie. The lad it Pete."

The older woman did not respond to his
attempts to charm him. Instead she turned to
Lizzie and Pete. Her jet-black eyes softened as they
lit on Pete. A maternal smile transformed her face.
She reached out a hand to him.

"*Niño, que lindo y precioso,*" she murmured
as friendly Pete obligingly gave her a hug. She
looked over his head at Lizzie. "Your son is so
lovely."

"My nephew," Lizzie corrected gently. As she
had so many times, she explained that Pete's
parents had died and left him in her care.

"It is good of you to care for him." Stella's

voice was as dark and rich as molasses. It swirled around Lizzie, welcoming her.

"He is my nephew. I love him," she replied revealing the honest feelings she shared with so few.

"*Bueno.*" When Stella saw Lizzie's lack of comprehension, she added, "That is good. That is how families should be." She turned to gaze at the child holding her hand. "And to have a *niño* in the house again! How long do you stay?"

Lizzie looked at Cliff, who shrugged. The warmth she had felt upon entering this house vanished. She should have guessed as soon as he told her this house had been won in a wager. In Garland Creek, there was obviously much money to be won and lost. He wouldn't leave until he had acquired some of it for himself or lost all they possessed.

As Stella noted the strained expression on the señorita's face, she said nothing. Too few decent women came to Garland Creek. Too many of those who did wore the same sadness on their brows. The longing for gold proved hard on the ones who wanted only the security of a home in which to raise their children.

Cliff filled the uncomfortable silence by saying, "It's late. Pete should be going to bed. I was told this house has three bedrooms."

"*Si,* three. I have mine by the back door. There are two upstairs."

He smiled. "Perfect." Turning to Lizzie, he asked, "Will you settle us in, half-pint? I want to check out possible victims in the saloon."

She longed to savor the ease of this house, which teased her to stay, but all her joy disappeared as she listened to his plans. Her voice hardened. "Possible victims? I told you I wouldn't play cards again, Cliff. I cannot risk what happened before."

"I didn't ask you to play with me." He frowned. He had thought she would be grateful for a fine house like this and the chance to recuperate from the horrors of the past few weeks. They were nearly through the Sierras. Soon they would be suffering in the hot desolation of the desert. That he wanted to enjoy himself a bit before entering that hell was understandable, in his lights.

Lizzie put her hand on his arm as he moved toward the door. "Cliff, how long will you be?"

"Don't press me, half-pint."

She recoiled from the anger in his eyes. Biting her lip, she watched as he walked out into the night. The man she had come to love in the mountains had, before her eyes, changed back into the one obsessed with easy riches. Tears pricked her eyes. She thought he had put all that behind him. Again he had forced her to see the futility of her dreams.

When Stella asked if she wanted to go upstairs to see the bedrooms, Lizzie nodded. She said nothing as she examined the lovely room Pete would have for his own use. It was luxury unlike any they had known since they'd left Kentucky.

Pete jumped on the feather bed while Stella pointed out the armoire and the washstand. Draping his only other set of clothes on a peg inside the tall maple cupboard, Lizzie urged the child to ready himself for bed. But Pete was too excited to settle down. All her efforts met with resistance.

"Señorita Buchanan, let me help."

"Please, Stella, call me Lizzie." She smiled. "If you can slow that rascal down tonight, I would appreciate it."

"Kiss him good-night . . . Lizzie. I will rock him and put him to bed. That will give you time to visit the rest of the house." She smiled gently. "And it will give this old woman a chance to hold a *niño* again."

Pete seemed to have no hesitation about being left with Stella, so Lizzie did as the older woman suggested. Saying good-night, she wandered out into the hall. A lantern sat on a small shelf carved into the wall. Its glow turned the gray wall golden.

She went into the other bedroom and gasped in delight. Whoever had built and furnished this house had created a paradise in the wilderness. The massive canopied bed gleamed with the polished look that only loving care could give it. Its cherrywood surface matched the cabinet carved with a pattern she could not make out in the dim light. Chairs clustered around a table next to a window. She went to it and looked out at the outline of the mountains silhouetted dark against the night.

Removing her boots, she scuffed her toes in the rich nap of the Oriental rug covering the tiles. She opened one of several doors in the room to discover it concealed a hip bath. The second led to a private rooftop patio. She shivered as she closed it. The sunny hours of early afternoon would be the time to explore that.

Exhaustion weighed heavily on her. She took off her traveling clothes and padded across the room in her underwear to store them out of sight in the armoire. With a gasp of delight, she pulled out a silk nightgown that was neatly folded among other clothes on the shelf. Whirling, she held it in front of her as she peered into the oval looking glass set in a brass floor stand.

"How lovely you look!"

She whirled to see Stella in the open doorway. A heated flush betrayed her embarrassment. "I hope—I mean—"

"Wear it, senorita. Senor Blake bought it for his lady." The way the housekeeper spat out the word led Lizzie to believe that Mr. Blake's companion had not been a lady, in Stella's opinion. "*She* never wore it. When he lost the house to Senor Riggins at the Trail's End, she left him for a wealthier benefactor."

"What is the Trail's End?"

"The saloon down the street where your man must be now. Senor Riggins has put all the other saloons in Garland Creek out of business. Your man went there for excitement."

Lizzie lowered her eyes to avoid the fury in Stella's. Already the housekeeper liked her and did not want to see Lizzie suffer what Mr. Blake's "lady" would have, had she stayed. Stella's few words made Lizzie face the truth she had been trying to avoid.

Forcing such distasteful thoughts from her head, she said in a studiously casual voice, "This is a wondrous house. I never expected to see something like this out here."

Stella smiled with pride. "Would you like a cup of tea before you retire?"

"No. I'm fine. Thank you." Lizzie wanted only to be alone. She did not know how much longer she could maintain the charade that she had compliantly accepted Cliff's sudden metamorphosis into the easy-living gambler again.

"Good night. I will serve breakfast when you are ready in the morning."

"Cliff will probably not . . ." Lizzie's voice faded away at the same time as Stella's smile vanished.

Stiffly Stella said, "I understand." She closed the door before Lizzie could respond.

Lizzie stared at the plain portal. Stella did not like Cliff. Everyone they had met on their trip had been so charmed by him that the realization came as a shock. She grinned. If she knew Cliff at all, he would expend much effort in endeavoring to get the housekeeper to change her mind. It should be an entertaining experience.

At the bowl, Lizzie washed the filth of the day's travel from her skin. Slipping the elegant nightgown over her head, she spun about the room gaily. The swirl of translucent silk against her skin felt heavenly. To feel so feminine seemed to be the realization of a dream.

She went to the bed and drew back the covers to discover satin sheets beneath the thick blankets. Her hand stroked them as she wondered how anyone could risk such a wonderful house on the turn of a card.

All her joy vanished as she realized how useless all this beauty was without someone to share it. The siren song of the saloon had drawn Cliff away from her. As much as she wanted him with her, the only way she could woo him to her side would be to sit next to him at the faro table.

She drew the sheets up to her chin and clutched the thick pillow to her cheek. Tears spotted the satin surface of the pillowcase. As he had at Sparkler's Drift, Cliff was again showing her how much his prisoner she was. And how little he cared.

Lizzie wiped a yellow stain of egg from Pete's cheek with a fine linen napkin. Sending him off to play in the enclosed yard at the back of the house, she smiled at Stella. The housekeeper lowered her coffee cup to the table.

"I hope everything was satisfactory, Lizzie."

"Excellent. I can't remember when I've had such a wonderful breakfast. You're spoiling us."

Stella did not meet Lizzie's eyes as she said softly, "I think you and the child could use some spoiling. Especially you. From what you've told me, you have not had a good trip this far with him."

"It hasn't been that bad." She noted how Stella avoided calling Cliff by name. The housekeeper's dislike of the man leasing the house colored every word she spoke. To change the subject, Lizzie asked, "May I help you with some chores?"

"No, senorita." Stella laughed as she began to clear away the dirty dishes. "You rest today. If you wish me to do some laundry for you, I would be glad to do it."

Lizzie glanced down at her filthy flannel shirt and denims. If she could find something else in the armoire to wear, she would love to savor the feel of clean clothes. As it was, she had nothing else to put on while those she wore were being laundered.

Before she could answer, the front door blew open to allow a cool breeze to swirl through the house. Lizzie heard Cliff jauntily calling her name. She did not look at Stella as she rose. To see the recrimination there would hurt too much. She knew she was foolish to answer Cliff's call so readily, but her love for him overcame her common sense.

He was tossing his hat unsuccessfully at a hook on the wall when she entered the foyer. Picking it up, he tried again. It sailed into her hands. She placed it on the hook silently. He smiled broadly.

"Half-pint, you see before you a wealthy man." He took her hands and pulled her close.

She turned her face from the thick smell of whiskey and another odor that undeniably belonged to whores who worked the saloons. With her hands against his chest, she pushed herself out of his embrace. He rocked back on his feet. He put a hand on the wall to steady himself as he laughed.

"You're drunk!" she stated accusingly. "It's past daybreak, and you're just getting home."

His good humor disappeared as she touched a

sensitive chord. Although he knew he should have been back hours before, he had been unable to pull himself away from the Trail's End while luck sat on his shoulder. He scowled and gripped her arm.

"Listen here, Lizzie. You aren't my wife, to nag me about my habits. I had no intention of leaving while there was plenty of money to be won."

"You smell of cheap perfume and cheaper women!".

"So I celebrated a little. Dammit, Lizzie, don't be so grouchy." He laughed again suddenly. "One thousand dollars, half-pint. One thousand dollars, and I did it without you."

She recoiled as if he had struck her. Tears burned in her throat as she asked in a choked voice, "And that makes you happy? To do that without me?"

"Of course. It means I don't have to depend on you to win." He lurched toward the stairs, then paused. From a pocket he pulled a handful of coins. Lifting her right hand, he turned it palm up and dropped them in her hand. "What I owe you, half-pint."

With a snarl, she threw them back into his face. "Keep your money. You can't buy me with it!"

When she raced out of the foyer, he regarded her fleeing shadow with blurry eyes. He thought about following her. Then he shrugged. If Lizzie did not want to share in his winnings, that was her decision. Using infinite caution, he bent to pick up the gold coins. His fingers did not close easily on one of them. Only on the fourth attempt could he scoop it up and place it in his pocket.

His eyes met the unsmiling face of Stella as he straightened up. The housekeeper said nothing. Not even when he offered her his most charming smile did she react. She merely walked into the parlor.

Cursing, he slapped his hand against the newel post. Then he climbed the stairs to their room. Last night he had enjoyed good fortune unequalled by any he'd had except when he met Lizzie again. Only a fool would have turned his back on it. Lizzie would always be waiting for him, but he might never have a run like this again. He grinned as he recalled how he could make no bad decisions last night. Even Riggins, the saloon owner, could not beat him when the two of them played head-to-head for five hours.

He closed the door behind him and winced as the sound echoed in his head. Already he was beginning to pay the price for his intemperate celebration. He had not drunk that much since the night before he met Lizzie.

"Dammit!" he said aloud. Why did every thought bring him back to her and her urchin face that so clearly showed her sense of betrayal? He was doing as he had promised. He was taking her east. If they were delayed awhile, it shouldn't matter to her. She had no one waiting for her, after all.

Dropping his boot on the floor, he grasped his head as pain as wide as his streak of fortune seared across his brain. He placed the other boot far more carefully on the rug. Slowly he lowered himself onto the bed. He glanced at the netting on the canopy, but the pattern just danced before his unfocused eyes. He closed them with a groan.

His hand groped for the covers. The silken nightgown was lying there, and he inadvertently pulled it over him; he growled and threw it on the floor without noticing what it was. Then he jerked the blanket over him and was asleep within minutes.

Lizzie stared into the fire on the raised hearth in the parlor. She held a two-month-old newspaper in her lap but did not turn its yellowed pages. Forcing her mind to think of nothing was proving to be far harder than she expected. Cliff's face continued to invade her thoughts.

The truth had been thrown at her once more. Cliff had no interest in loving her. Everything everyone had told her had proved to be true. He enjoyed her because she was convenient. On the trail he could not do enough for her, knowing he would have her in his arms at the day's end. As soon as they reached a settlement, he ceased to think of her. He preferred the company of other gamblers and the women they attracted.

"Lizzie?"

She looked up to see Stella's concerned face.

Glibly she lied, "I'm fine. I just want to be alone now."

"I understand. I will keep Pete entertained. If you would like to talk . . ."

Lizzie shook her head. To talk to anyone would risk revealing the truth of her broken heart. The future had been shown to her. Cliff did not care enough about her to be concerned with her feelings. She had no choice but to determine a way to make her life alone in California until she could afford to take Pete east.

Rising, she smiled grimly. For the first time, she felt true empathy with Cal Feathersong. To be far from other people lessened the chance of being betrayed by those one trusted most. She would never be so foolish again.

On silent feet she climbed the stairs to the bedroom where Cliff slept. The sound of his snores rumbled along the hall. She doubted there was any need to be quiet. The day she had toted him to the cabin in Hopeless they had carried on their normal activities, and it had not disturbed him.

She paused as she entered the huge room. Her eyes went to the pale pink silk nightgown crumpled on the floor. It seemed the final perfidy. Instead of allowing the tears in her eyes to fall, she straightened her spine. Walking to the armoire, she quietly opened the door and reached in for her saddlebag. She pulled out the length of gold material she had kept secreted in the bag since Sparkler's Drift.

Folding the gold cloth over her arm, she

glanced at the man sprawled across the bed. She found herself wanting to tuck the covers around him. Only the knowledge of how little he cared about anything she did for him kept her from following the impulse. She walked to the door. Without another backward glance, she walked out, shutting it and him behind her.

CHAPTER FOURTEEN

CLIFF WOKE TO THE FIRE OF SUNSET BURNING through his eyelids. He groaned as he rolled over in bed. Threads snapped on his shirt as he stretched muscles unaccustomed to such a long period of sleep. Frowning, he stared at the white canopy. Memory came back slowly.

He sat up and then fell back against the carved headboard. Profanity spilled from his tight lips. Wanting nothing but to be rid of the pain hammering in his head, he staggered to the washbowl. He hung his head over it. His fingers grasped the pitcher and poured its tepid contents over his head.

The water blurred his eyes before flowing through the jungle of his beard. He rubbed his face with the heels of his palms and tried to bring feeling back into his numb skin. He didn't know what Riggins served in that bar, but it was far more

341

potent than anything he had been drinking. Four nights of gambling had left him richer than he ever expected to be and far weaker. Yet the streak continued unabated. . . .

His head jerked up as he heard the door open. Water sprayed in every direction creating rivers on the walls to match those running down his face. He reached for a towel but found nothing as he stared at the pain-filled face of the woman standing in the doorway.

"I didn't think you'd be awake," Lizzie said quietly. "I shall just be a minute. Then I'll be out of your way."

"Lizzie—"

She cut him off by turning her back and walking to the armoire. She placed whatever she was carrying inside it. Just as silently she returned to the door. When he realized she intended to leave without speaking further to him, he tried to move forward to stop her. His feet refused to obey him. He finally stumbled to the door only to have it close in his face.

"Dammit!" he growled.

In his fuzzy memory of the events of that morning, he recalled her anger when he had brought home for her one of the silk flowers the whores at the Trail's End wore on their bodices. Holding his head in his hands, he wondered how he could have been so stupid. There were few things that could have insulted her more. She clearly suspected the woman had given him the rose in private instead of, as was actually the case, as a trophy for an especially large win.

He had expected Lizzie to be over her rage by now. After all, she had forgiven him for everything else he had done so far. Pain twisted in him as he thought of how she had even excused him for his part in Tommy's death. If she could pardon him for that, he couldn't understand why she had slammed the door just now.

Determined to discover the answer, he hurried to dress himself. He pulled a clean shirt from his bag. Running his fingers through his hair, he decided against shaving. As tremulous as his hands were, he did not trust them to hold a straight-edge razor. He decided he would trim his beard before he left for the Trail's End saloon later.

He wandered through the house. Their first day there, he had been surprised to discover it was far bigger than he had thought. He wondered why Riggins had given it to them so cheaply. Even friendship did not warrant such luxurious quarters for so little. Besides the two bedrooms, he glanced into the sun-washed parlor and the small dining room. Signs of a recent meal did not entice him to eat. His stomach still burned with the residue of Riggins' gut-wrenching whiskey.

In the kitchen attached to the house by a short walkway, he found only Stella. She answered his questions tersely. No, Senor Hollister, she had not seen Lizzie. He quickly backed out of the room which seemed filled with her outrage. If Lizzie was truly angry at him, she had found an ally.

He saw Pete playing in the yard. Going out into the pale warmth of the late autumn sunset, Cliff called to the boy. The child leapt to his feet and raced to fling his arms around the man.

"Cliff! Cliff!"

"How you doing, Pete, my boy?" He glanced at the strange configuration of branches and leaves Pete had been working on. "What's that?"

"I'm building a house for me and Lizzie."

"A house?" He chuckled. "Don't you like this one?"

Pete frowned. "Sure, but Stella says you'll be just like Mr. Blake. You'll—"

"Blake?" Cliff interrupted. He recognized the name. Riggins had spoken of the man last night.

Blake had been one of the early settlers of Garland Creek. He had claimed much of the valley. When he discovered gold, he sold claims of no more than sixteen square feet each to those eager to work for the glitter. But all his business acumen vanished whenever he sat at the card table. In three years, he had gambled away more than most men could hope to earn in a lifetime.

"He threw away everything he loved," parroted the child. "Stella says you'll do the same. That's what she told Lizzie."

"Did she?" Cliff didn't say the harsh words he was really thinking. "What did Lizzie say?"

Pete considered the question seriously. The conversation had taken place only an hour before, so he could still remember how upset his aunt had been. He did not like to see Lizzie without a smile. Since they had arrived in Garland Creek, she seldom smiled. Even when she did, he could tell by the sadness in her eyes that she did so only to make him happy.

"Lizzie didn't say anything but that she and I would m-m—"

"Manage?" Cliff supplied.

The boy nodded, pleased to have gotten the message across so easily, although he did not understand what was bothering the two women. He already adored Stella. Every night she rocked him to sleep with Spanish lullabies sung in her rich alto voice.

Cliff patted him on the head and told him to go back to his project. Without another word, Cliff continued his search for Lizzie. He felt they had a few things to iron out before events exploded in a detonation that would destroy anything they had left between them.

He found Lizzie sitting on the porch at the end of the kitchen wing. In the private courtyard it faced, she was not bothered by street traffic. Only the sound of the wind playing in the bare branches of the trees intruded on her. He paused in the doorway. With her legs tucked under her and her chin resting on her hand, she presented an enticing outline of her profile.

From her curls, golden in the sunlight, his eyes followed the slim contour of her body. She sat deep in thought, unaware of him watching her. As if he was awakening from a deep dream, he realized how long it had been since he had held sweet Lizzie. They had never shared the bed upstairs. She slept there at night, he during the day. That was something he wanted to rectify immediately.

"Lizzie?" he called.

She glanced up but didn't smile. "Oh, hello,

Cliff. Supper is available in the dining room."

"I'm not hungry now. I can eat at the Trail's End later if I want to."

Her face froze at his words. "You're going out again tonight, Cliff?"

"I told you I had a streak going, half-pint. I can't stop until it runs out."

"Or until your money does?"

He grinned as he leaned forward to place his hands on the arms of her chair. With his face close to hers, he said, "No worry about that, honey."

"That's wonderful." She picked up the paper and began reading it again, effectively dismissing him.

Sudden rage ripped through him. He tore the pages from her hands and threw them across the courtyard. "Stop it!"

"Stop what?"

He snapped, "Stop acting as if you're a prisoner. You can go out anytime. Stella is here, and she can watch Pete."

"Me alone on these streets?" She laughed coldly.

"I don't think you'll run into any trouble you can't handle. You certainly did well enough in Hopeless." He bent and kissed her lightly on the cheek. "I have to get ready for tonight at the Trail's End. I think I'll be home early. It's been too long since you shared my bed, half-pint."

"No," she whispered. She pushed away his arms and stood up. Walking to where the paper lay on the ground, she picked it up and held it. "Don't plan on sleeping with me anymore, Cliff."

He smiled assuming what he considered his most winning expression. With his arms held out to her, he urged, "C'mon, half-pint, you've said that before."

"But this time I mean it." She watched the expectation fade from his face as he became aware of the burning sorrow in her eyes. "I loved you, Cliff Hollister. For three long years, I loved you, or what I thought you were. Even when everyone warned me that you would only use me and then cast me aside, I refused to listen. I would have done anything for you. I did. I lied. I cheated. I gave you myself and my love. I cannot give anything else to you."

When he took a half step toward her, she backed away. She did not want him to touch her. His magic would pull her into his enchantment again. He paused.

"Lizzie, it hasn't been only you who has sacrificed—"

"What have you given up?" she demanded bitterly. "What have you done to prove that you care about me? You know the answer as well as I do." She turned her back to him. "Don't come to me tonight or ever again, Cliff. Find somewhere else to sleep. Find someone else who wants only what you have to offer."

She heard nothing but his footsteps on the tile floor. The sound of the thick door closing was like a knife in her heart. She had said what was needed to be said, but that didn't ease the pain swelling in her. She had lied, for she continued to love him. She was sure she always would.

* * *

Cliff threw open the door of the saloon. It was far earlier than he usually arrived, but the entertainment always started before the sun headed for the horizon. Only for a few hours in the morning did Riggins close his business.

The room sparkled with the lanterns hung from the smoke-darkened rafters. To the left the stage remained dark. Later there would be a show for the patrons to watch or ignore as they wished. A broad spectrum of offerings, from a young dancer to a juggler and on to risqué acts would be displayed for their pleasure.

Dozens of tables filled the large room. Many were covered with the green felt cloths used to play faro. At some the chairs were taken already. Intense faces monitored each turn of the cards. Across the top of the wall opposite the door ran a balcony that led to the rooms reserved for men eager to share five minutes of a whore's time in exchange for a hefty portion of gold.

He did not pause to gossip as he headed directly for the bar. "Gilbert!" he called,.

The bartender turned and smiled. Throwing over his shoulder the cloth he used to clean glasses, he wandered along the twenty-foot-long bar toward Cliff. He plucked a bottle of whiskey from the group on a shelf beneath the portrait of a reclining nude.

There was much speculation over the painting. All the men enjoyed looking at the doe-eyed beauty. Whenever anyone asked who had posed for it, Riggins invariably answered that the woman had been one of the fine French whores imported for the bordellos in San Francisco. The answer always brought more questions about which prostitute in which house she was. That Riggins in reality had no idea who the woman was, for he had bought the painting from a man who was anxious to lighten his load before tackling the last series of mountains on his way west, the saloon keeper told no one.

"Howdy, Hollister. Early tonight, ain't ya?"

Cliff did not look at the perennial smile of the bartender. The short man loved his work, and it showed. He always had a tale to share or a moment to listen. Although he was a young man, the hair at his temples was streaked with gray. Few who came into the Trail's End saloon failed to become Gilbert Palmer's friend, although he acted as his boss' eyes in the large room.

"Just the whiskey," Cliff ordered sharply. "I don't need the chatter tonight."

Gilbert held up his hands in mock surrender. "Whoa! Only trying to strike up a conversation. I thought you would be home having supper with your kids."

With a frown, Cliff picked up the bottle and poured a generous serving of whiskey. Instantly the image of another glass of the liquor he'd taken to help him forget Lizzie and another barkeeper came into his mind. His eyes clouded as he recalled Tommy sitting by his brother at the end of that other bar.

Warm arms and thick perfume enveloped him. A soft body pressed against him. Cliff ignored the bartender's expression of disgust and turned to the over-painted face of the woman who hung over him.

"Did anyone ever tell you that you're wasting your time, Alice?"

Her dark eyes glittered with amusement. Slender fingers roved along the sleeves covering his hard muscles. She stood so close, his breath moved the strands of her black hair. Taking his hand, she held it beneath hers as she stroked the lines of her body beneath the worn satin gown. The emerald cloth covered only the bare minimum of her figure.

"Cliff," she murmured as she urged his fingers to caress the fullness of her breast, "You can't ignore me much longer. How long you going to go without a woman to warm your bed?" She giggled childishly. "I hear the only woman in your house is old Stella. She can't be what you want."

Without rancor, he shoved her away. "You don't make any secret of what you want, honey. Go and find yourself another sucker. I came here to play cards with your boss."

She smiled and rubbed her bare thigh against his leg. "He ain't here tonight. Business, so he says." She leaned against him so he had a fine view of her body beneath the skimpy satin dress. "Truth to tell, he goes to visit his mistress over on Churchy Street."

Cliff understood her reference immediately. The two streets of Garland Creek had gained the names of Churchy and Hellbound. The residents appreciated the humor of the titles and used them as if they were the original names of the streets.

Interested in learning anything he could about his adversary, Cliff put his arm around Alice to keep her close.

He murmured in her ear, "So Riggins has a mistress on Churchy? Who would sleep with him over there?"

Her giggles irritated him, but he did not allow it to show as she answered, "The widow Bannister. Her husband left her plenty of gold when he did her a favor and got himself killed. She's a young thing and very pretty. Blond. Jerry does like blonds."

"Shame for you, isn't it?" he said offhandedly as he batted away her caressing hand. He didn't intend to let her guess his thoughts. Now that he knew Riggins preferred that type, Cliff was determined to keep Lizzie away from Trail's End.

Anguish so strong he could taste its bitterness would be hard to conceal from Alice. Lizzie had made it clear he would meet no welcome in any part of her life in the future. Baring her soul to him, she had told him that she once had loved him and that now that love had died. His attempts to explain had been cut off before he could defend himself. If he hadn't been aching so much, he would have told her what he thought.

If only he knew.

"Scat, Alice," he urged. He brushed her hand off his leg and pushed her toward the other end of the bar. "I'm not interested now."

"Later?"

"I'll let you know."

With a pout, she said, "I may be busy later!"

He picked up his glass and raised it to her in a salute. "That is a chance I will have to take."

Although she longed to retort, she saw another man crooking his finger at her. She looked at him appraisingly. He might not be Cliff Hollister, but he would be worth gold to her. Smiling, she allowed her hips to sway alluringly as she walked toward the miner. She hoped Cliff was watching and would realize what he was missing.

Cliff forgot Alice as soon as she stepped away. He wished the other woman in his life was as easy to get out of his mind. Grasping the bottle, he pushed his way through the thickening crowd to an empty table. He began to shuffle the pack of cards waiting there. Without looking up, he knew several men had surrounded the table.

"Faro, gentlemen?"

Chairs scraped on the floor as the men sat down. Even before they had introduced themselves, gold appeared on the green cloth. Many had seen Hollister's luck the past four nights. Everyone wanted to be the one to bring that good fortune to an abrupt and costly end.

The hours passed easily and profitably for Cliff. He smiled as he raked pile after pile of coins toward him. The other men at the table grumbled at his continued good luck, but he ignored them. Gloating would cost him when this streak vanished. He had played long enough to know he could be the one losing soon. It was not as if he had Lizzie there to guarantee him a certain amount of winnings every night.

A frown crossed his face as he thought of

Lizzie. She knew he was planning to leave her to continue on alone, but he doubted if she understood why. He was not sure if he himself knew the truth. All he knew was that he could not go on hurting her as he was doing. When he left, he would give her some of his winnings. She would manage somehow. She always did.

"Will you look at that?" asked the man across the table from him.

"Well, well," came the reply of the man next to him.

Cliff saw the gleam in their eyes and knew a beautiful woman had entered the room. As they straightened their frock coats and rose, he realized she was coming toward them. He grimaced. Another woman was something he had no interest in now. Lizzie gave him enough problems without having Riggins' whores pushing themselves onto him.

Despite his thoughts, he automatically turned to see this paragon as he heard the continuing comments of the card players. His eyes widened.

As she walked toward the table, the woman's full skirt swayed with the gentle rhythm of her steps. Its adobe color highlighted the golden gleam of her hair which was tied back from her face with a single velvet ribbon. His gaze moved from the concealing width of her skirt to the lace-decorated pleated bodice that outlined her body. A rose-colored shawl draped around her shoulders accented the skin revealed by the stylishly round neckline of the gown.

"Lizzie?" he managed to choke out. Even in

his imagination, he had not thought her as beautiful as she was in a dress. He could see no sign of the urchin who had lurked in his shadow, dressed in pants that dragged on the floor behind her boot heels.

"Good evening, Cliff." Her sultry voice caressed his ears. She smiled as warmly at the other men. "Good evening, gentlemen. Excuse me if I have interrupted your game."

"No, miss. Not at all," gushed the balding man who first had noticed her. "Please, would you sit down with us?"

His kindness was rewarded by her brilliant smile. "How nice of you, sir! I do not want to—"

"Nonsense." He drew a chair from a nearby table, paying no attention to the angry comments of the miners sitting there. "There's plenty of room." As if he were a young lad in his first infatuation, he babbled, "Sit, miss. Please. We would be honored."

A second man who held a pack of cards in his hand said, "Yes, sit. Hollister has us nearly cleaned out as it is."

Lizzie's eyebrows rose serenely as she thanked the man holding her chair. "Cliff, it seems you have been lucky tonight."

"Not just tonight," said a third man, dressed in the most ornate silk waistcoat she had ever seen. "Hollister has been winning almost every bet for the past four nights."

Her smile tightened only slightly as she thought of how she had to watch every purchase she made for their odd household. Since that morning when he had showered gold on her, he had not offered her a single copper. If she had not known it before, she was sure now that Cliff intended to desert them.

"Hollister, you know this lady?" demanded a miner dressed in dusty denims. "Ain't you going to introduce us?"

"Gentlemen, this is my business partner, Lizzie Buchanan," Cliff said grudgingly. He had noted her reaction to Hemmes' announcement of his winning streak. Beneath her ladylike demeanor, he was sure Lizzie was seething with outrage.

He named each of the men at the table and watched uneasily as they bowed over her fingers. Her soft inviting laugh drove his blood to a fever pitch, and he longed to shove the other men aside. He wanted that sweet sound to belong to him alone.

Hemmes asked, "And what kind of business can such a lovely lady like you, Miss Buchanan, be involved in with this rogue Hollister?" Hemmes suspected it was of a highly personal nature, although that did not explain why Hollister haunted the saloon when he had such a beautiful woman waiting at home for him.

"Cliff promised to deliver a very special parcel to St. Louis for me." Her cool brown eyes met Cliff's squarely as she spoke. "Unfortunately, I was not wise enough to request that it arrive on a specific date."

"Would you care for a drink, Miss Buchanan?"

"She doesn't drink," stated Cliff tightly. "It makes her giggle like a six-year-old." He wished he could bite back the words as soon as he spoke them. He saw sorrow weaken her smile as she thought of Tommy. The cruelty of his open envy would not win her again. For the first time, he was afraid nothing would.

Turning to the man beside her, she said, "Thank you, Mr. Lyons. A glass of sarsaparilla would be welcome, if the Trail's End serves such tame drinks." She laughed lightly, and everyone but Cliff chimed in as if she had made the funniest joke.

A barmaid came over to the table; it was Alice. She smiled at the men, but when her eyes met Lizzie's, she started. "You sure do bring to mind someone I've seen around town. Do you have a brother about so high?" She lifted her hand to approximate Lizzie's height.

"No," Lizzie answered honestly as she listened to Mr. Lyons order for her. She glanced at Cliff and saw him slouched in his chair. If he did not like her as she was, that was his problem. She loved the feel of six cotton petticoats beneath the silk of her gown.

Her lips tightened as the serving woman slipped her hand around Cliff's neck and teased the skin revealed by his open collar. Bending so that her full body caressed him, she drawled, "Anything for you, Cliff? Is it later yet?"

He looked past her to see the pain on Lizzie's face. Suddenly he wondered why she had come to Trail's End. If she wanted him to come back into

her life, she didn't have to be involved in this
elaborate game. Then he realized she would never
ask him back outright. Perhaps she was wiser than
he. He had to admit that seeing her in that dress
was helping him determine what he wanted.

Without pulling his gaze from Lizzie's averted
eyes, he peeled Alice's hand off him. "Get the
drinks, woman. Do your job."

"I'm trying to!" she snapped. Her frustration
at being unable to woo this man into her bed
erupted. She shot a malevolent glare at the pretty
woman at the table. If this blond stole Cliff from
her as the widow had taken Jerry, she would find a
way to make her pay.

"Do it somewhere else then," Cliff retorted.

Flouncing her full skirt, Alice stamped back
to the bar to give Gilbert the drink orders. Then she
heard someone call to her. She paid no more
attention to the other woman for a while as she
negotiated with a young miner for a few minutes of
her time. Someone else took the drinks to the table,
but she did not notice as she walked arm-in-arm
with the lad up the stairs.

Lizzie thanked the girl who put a glass of
sarsaparilla in front of her. Taking a sip, she said,
"Gentlemen, I fear I have interrupted your game."

Hastily they assured her they appreciated her
charming company. When Cliff asked innocently if
she would enjoy playing with them, Hemmes
reprimanded him.

"Hollister, you forget what we are playing. I
am sure Miss Buchanan does not know how to play
poker. That is not a lady's game."

"On the contrary." He leaned his elbows on the table and held out a deck of cards to her. "She plays many games very, very well, don't you, Lizzie?"

Her false smile never wavered as she said, "I know several card games quite well. Poker is one that I am a novice at, I must admit." She treated each man to a gentle glance. "If you can bear with my clumsy attempts, I think I would enjoy playing with such charming gentlemen."

"In that case, we would be pleased to have you join us. First, deal out five cards to each of us," urged Hemmes. "Then I'll help you bet."

"Bet?" Her dark eyes widened in a winsome expression. "Oh, then I am afraid I can't play. I have no money."

Before anyone could comment, Cliff shoved a small share of his winnings in front of her. His icy smile did not become any warmer as she regarded him steadily. She thanked him briefly and turned away to talk to the others.

Although he knew she was acting that way only to infuriate him, her ploys were proving successful. As she chatted and laughed with the other men, he wondered that he could have been so insensitive to her and her need to be the lovely woman she was. Her dreams of returning to Kentucky were laced with reminiscences of church socials and family outings. Instead of belittling her longings for the stringent bounds of society, he should have listened to her and learned what she truly wanted.

He watched as his companions barely concealed their yearning to touch the body once given to him so freely in the greatest act of love he ever had known. Lizzie's words were true. She had done everything for him. All he had given her in return was heartbreak.

Now his heart ached for what he might have lost. Caring nothing for the opinions of the other men, he put his hand on her arm. "Lizzie?"

Beautiful eyes gleaming brighter than the gold turned to him. They could not hide what she felt. As his fingers stroked the bare skin below her elbow-length sleeves, she automatically placed her hand over his. The others at the table vanished as she stared into his earnest face.

"Yes, Cliff?"

"Let me take you home. It is late."

She nodded. Glancing down at the pile of gold before her, she was not surprised to see it was far more than Cliff had given her. Her assumed air of innocence had kept the men from suspecting that she had bluffed them on several hands. Despite her best efforts, she could not keep the yearning from her voice as she asked, "Are you coming home now?"

Lyons interrupted, "You can't leave yet, Hollister. You've got to give us a chance to win back some of this money."

"You had your opportunity," he said quickly, before the lure of gambling could wrench Lizzie away from him again. He waited for Lizzie to place her winnings in a satin reticule that matched her gown. Then he drew out her chair and helped her to her feet. His eyes swept over her as he savored her graceful figure. "Good night, gentlemen."

"Good night," echoed Lizzie. She smiled. "Thank you for being so patient with my clumsy attempts at the game."

Leaping to their feet as she rose, the men nearly knocked over the table in their eagerness to out do each other in gallant courtesy as they bid her farewell. To their subtle queries if they would see her again, she simply smiled. She had no plans of returning to the place. If she could convince Cliff to leave for good, she would never come here again.

Cliff settled her slim fingers on his sleeve as he led her across the saloon to the door. He noted every eye in the room followed the living fantasy next to him. Silence flowed in their wake leaving the miners wondering how such a lady could have come to Hellbound Street without them learning of it before that night.

As he opened the door to the street, Cliff noticed Alice standing on the balcony over the bar. Rage had transfigured her face from its chipmunk cuteness to a mask of feline ferocity. He shrugged off her display of possessiveness. He had certainly made no promises to her. He had repulsed every attempt she had made to coerce him. Perhaps now she would be convinced that she ought not waste her time with him.

The door closed, and normal conversation resumed in the barroom. Laughter bubbled up to the woman on the second floor. With a scowl, she accepted payment from the young miner whose whiskey-soured breath still offended her senses. He

two steps below her, his eyes level with hers. In the dim light of the single lantern, she could see the hunger in his eyes.

"Half-pint—" He laughed ruefully as he stepped up the risers to stand next to her. "You don't look like my half-pint any longer."

She smiled sadly. "You see, Cliff, that's where you made a mistake from the beginning. I was never your 'half-pint' or your anything else. Oh, there was a time when I would have died of joy if you had smiled in my direction. That time is past. Children grow up, or at least most of us do." Standing on tiptoe, she kissed him on the cheek. "Good night."

"Lizzie?" When she paused at the door of the room with her hand on the doorknob, he added hurriedly, "Honey, I love you."

Her poise broke as she shook her head in denial. "I'm sorry, Cliff, but I find that hard to believe. You've been planning to abandon Pete and me here in Garland Creek. And now you say you love me?"

"It's true." He took her hand away from the door. In the warm glow of the lantern reflecting the adobe walls, he said in an earnest voice, "Don't you understand? That's why I was going to leave you here. I love you, but I don't want to ruin your life. Dammit, Lizzie, I think I've love you from the first time I saw you."

"The first time you saw me I was surrounded by crying relatives of the others in our train." She yearned to believe him. More than leaving California, more than her longing to undo all the mistakes that had led to death and horror, more than anything else in her life, she wanted to believe his soft words. She wished she could see inside his heart to learn whether he was finally telling her the truth rather than merely trying to bend her to his will.

He stroked her cheek and felt her tremble. Or was it him? He felt as nervous as a young lad asking for his first kiss. In a way he was as untutored as that imaginary child. Although he had held many women, never had he loved any before Lizzie Buchanan.

Softly he reminisced: "In the middle of that confusion, you looked as serene as a summer dawn. The other women were lamenting what they were leaving behind. But you looked toward the west, and your eyes met mine." The loving tone of his voice warmed her as he whispered, "I know I have been less than honest with you, Lizzie, but believe me now. I love you."

"I believe you," she said. Somehow she knew it in the language his heart spoke to hers.

In his turn he reached for the knob of the door. His hand tugged at hers. "Stay with me tonight. Come back to my arms where you belong, my love."

"Do you mean it?" she asked, afraid to believe the sincerity in his voice.

He drew her into his arms. Putting his mouth close to her ear, he whispered, "I need you, half-pint. If I've been a fool, don't punish me for my stupidity by denying us what we both long for."

"I love you, Cliff," she murmured, feeling her resistance fade.

"I don't know why you do, but some miracle has kept you waiting for my stubborn heart to admit the truth. What made you so patient?"

Lizzie said nothing as he opened the door to the bedroom they finally would share. After all the nights of sleeping side by side, it had seemed odd to be separated. She dropped her bag on the shelf by the door.

Hands encircled her waist. The tingling breath of his whisper sent waves of delight through her. "You're so pretty tonight, half-pint." He laughed. "I have a hard time calling you that when you look so wonderful. Did you find that dress in the armoire?"

With her eyes closed and her body swaying with the power of his kisses along the back of her neck, she answered, "I made it. I bought the material in Sparkler's Drift. At the time, I hoped to wear it when we arrived back east." She turned to face him. The fullness of her skirt swirled around his legs. "I decided to wear it tonight."

"To lure me back to your arms?"

"To see if you wanted me." She placed her face against the soft nap of his shirt. "When you left, I knew you didn't want to come back."

He chuckled softly. "I never thought I would hear you admit to such a big mistake, Lizzie Buchanan." With his thumbs beneath her chin, he tilted her head back to meet his loving gaze. "Don't you know I never want to leave you?"

His lips over hers muted any answer she might have given. While his hands stroked her silken softness, he thought how much more wonderful her bare skin would feel next to him. He laughed as he lifted her into his arms.

"Tonight," he announced, "we'll share our love in a bed. No pelts or bare floors or blankets in a mountain clearing. Do you think you'll enjoy such tame wooing?"

As he placed her on the cool surface of the smooth silk sheets, she held her arms up to him. Obeying her, he leaned over her. She murmured, "How soft it is on this thick mattress, but I don't think it matters where we are when we are together like this."

While he undid the many hooks she had sewn with such care along the back of the gown, he teased her, between passionate kisses, about how much easier it was to undress her when she wore flannels and trousers. Soon the frock and its accompanying petticoats lay like slumbering butterflies on the floor. His clothes were dropped into a jumbled pile next to them.

A sigh of rapture too deep for words flowed from her lips as he pressed her bare skin to his. Lying side by side, eyes inches apart, they fought to control their longing until it became unbearable. Her fingers followed the lines of his body, delighting in the myriad textures of his skin and the sinews beneath it.

His mouth made a leisurely exploration of her. Each place it touched came to life with the gentle burnishing of his beard against her. She laughed as he tickled her with the tip of his tongue. With a half-spoken vow of vengeance, she sought the spot where he was most ticklish. They laughed in delight at and with each other; their enjoyment of each other added a sweetness to their lovemaking.

"As long as I can make you laugh, half-pint, I'll know you love me." He swept the curls from her forehead as she leaned over him.

"I will always love you!"

"Love me now."

With a giggle, she asked pertly, "Isn't that my line?"

He twisted to bring her back against the pillows. All laughter faded from her lips as he stole her breath from her with a fiery kiss. His fingers renewed their acquaintance with her soft skin. When she moaned deep into his mouth, he smiled.

She did not see his happiness as she became lost in the rapture he spun around them. All she knew was the caress of his lips and the alluring touch of his hands. As she moved to the melody coming from deep within her, she drew him to her.

In the second of perfection, she was sure she heard him whisper once more against the half circle of her ear that he loved her. His hushed voice was lost among the waves of ecstasy that crashed over her, carrying her far into the depths of love. She floated on the joy of knowing her dreams had come true.

The soft velvet of the afterglow of their love brought more laughter to their lips as they cuddled close beneath the thick covers of the bed. At that moment, as she clung to the man she loved, she could not imagine a time when the dream would die.

CHAPTER FIFTEEN

LIZZIE WATCHED WITH BARELY HIDDEN LAUGHTER as Stella's resistance faded before Cliff's determination to charm her. She was tempted to tell him that Stella was not impressed by his handsome smile or his perfect manners but by the fact that he was finally devoting all his time to the woman and child who loved him.

They spent three days enjoying the gentle peace they found within the house's adobe walls. While rain pelted on the roof and sang against the windows, they sat by the fire and talked. Pete exulted in having time with the man he idolized. He no longer spoke of building a house for himself and Lizzie but of the journey ahead of them. When Cliff promised that, when Pete was grown, he would hire the boy as an assistant wagon master, the child talked of nothing else.

Stella made sure the little boy spent hours

helping her so the adults could have time alone together. Sitting on the floor of the parlor, watching the flames pop into the chimney, Lizzie was sure she had found heaven.

"I don't want to leave," she whispered as she leaned back against Cliff. He sat with his back propped against a chair and had both arms around her waist. Her arms rested on his.

"You don't want to leave California?" He chuckled in her ear. "Isn't this quite a change?"

She grimaced at him. "I hate the California we left behind, but I could live in this luxury with you forever."

With a sigh, he looked at the fire. "It's tempting, especially when we've got to start facing the hardships of the trail tomorrow, but I think you'd soon tire of this tame life."

"No! Never!" She laughed at her own fervor. Her voice softened as she said, "I just don't want to end this wonderful time when I've had you to myself—"

"And to Pete and to Stella," he teased.

"To myself!" She nestled closer as she said, "I never thought the day would come when you loved me."

He twisted a strand of her hair around his finger. "Admit to it, is what you should have said. I can't remember a time when I haven't loved you, half-pint. It may be because I've dreamed of loving you all my life. And to think I nearly let you leave me."

"You just had to learn that you can trust me, Cliff!" she retorted.

Drawing her lips to his, he said, "That, for me, wasn't easy, but I'm glad I took the chance on you."

They savored the morning in front of the fire. After lunch, Cliff left for the general store to purchase the supplies they would need for the next leg of their long trip. Lizzie worked with a very teary Stella to pack the few belongings they had brought with them to Garland Creek. Over and over, she tried to comfort the older woman. It was useless. Stella did not want to lose her *niño* and the rest of her newfound family.

She urged them to stay. When Lizzie explained they could not afford to rent the house for any extended period of time, Stella suggested Cliff buy it.

"I don't think he'd stay in one place that long," Lizzie said regretfully. "His life is on the road. To pin him down in one location would be like clipping the wings of a bird."

"And you, Lizzie?"

She lifted her shoulders in a silent answer. What she would do, she did not know. Cliff spoke of love and the many nights they would share, but she could not ignore the knowledge that when the west winds blew in the spring, he would risk everything he loved to follow them to their source. For now, she would think only of today and the joy it contained. She did not want to anticipate the sorrow that might lie in wait for her.

Cliff was thinking much the same as he paid the astronomical prices charged in the general store. For him, the idea of worrying about a day beyond the present was a strange sensation. Never, in the years since he had first taken the westward trail, had he thought about anyone but himself. Two pairs of eyes, one vibrant and dark eyes, the other young and trusting, teased his mind and urged him to consider what days ago he would have thought madness.

He took the packages and walked out onto Churchy Street. Tipping his hat at a fashionably dressed lady walking by on the boardwalk, he wondered how this world and Hellbound Street could exist side by side and so seldom interact.

Pausing to talk to two men lazing on a bench by the store's entrance, he waved aside the offer of a slug of chewing tobacco. They spoke of the weather and the steady decline of gold coming from the claims closest to Garland Creek.

"Hear tell they've found a big lode up yonder near Broken Wagon. Picking it up off the ground in chunks bigger than yer fist," stated the grizzled man sitting closest to the door.

"Is that so?" His young companion asked before spitting indelicately at a crack in the boardwalk.

Cliff admired his precision but did not mention it. Men had been killed for less when contests to determine the most accurate spitter led to drunken brawls. Shifting his packages to his other hand, he asked conversationally, "Going up there? Sounds like easy money."

"Naw," grumbled the old man. "Could be the rumor was started by some ornery bastard who wants to get his hands on my claim."

"Who would want your claim, Rod? You ain't got a sparkle out of there in weeks."

With a smile, Cliff bid them farewell. They took no notice of his leaving as they continued their verbal battle. In lieu of other entertainment, the miners always enjoyed these verbal duels about their claims, someone else's, or simply the state of the world.

As he crossed from Churchy to Hellbound through an alley next to the store, a jaunty bounce entered Cliff's step. He would be glad to be on the way east the next day. Although the small house was a pleasant stopover, he longed for the adventure of the road. With Lizzie by his side, he would have everything he wanted.

A voice called to him, and he waved. Only when the man motioned to him did he cross the dust-covered street to the saloon.

"Howdy, Riggins. What's up?"

The massive man dwarfed the wide doors of his saloon. Black hair hung past his shoulders, but his wide-jowled face was clean shaven. A fortune in gold and silver jewelry hung around his neck and gleamed on his pudgy hands. He gestured toward the saloon.

"Come on in, Hollister. I hear you're leaving without giving me a chance to even up the score between us."

"Sorry. Busy getting ready for the road." Cliff smiled lightly. "Look for me next year. I'd be glad to take more of your money then."

"Hey, Hollister. Let me at least buy you a drink for the road."

Cliff started to refuse, then decided it wouldn't hurt to leave on good terms. He had promised Lizzie he wouldn't gamble away the money he had won, but a drink between friends would be the perfect ending to his exploits at the saloon in Garland Creek. But he cared little for the celebration. His farewell to the settlement would come later, with the lady he loved.

The saloon was preternaturally quiet in the feeble light seeping through the shuttered windows. A few shadows moved in the corners, but the men ignored them as they walked to the bar. Riggins grabbed a pair of bottles in his huge fist and pointed to a table.

"Sit down, Hollister. No need to hurry off before we lift a couple of glasses and share some lies."

Dropping his packages in a chair, Cliff sat at the table. He took the full glass and drained it easily. Riggins served a smoother whiskey than many of these mountainside bars, but it still burned all the way to his stomach. With a laugh, the other man sat down opposite him.

"So you're bound for Missouri?"

"That's where the wagons start from."

Riggins refilled their glasses and folded his sapling-sized arms on the table. "Hear you have a partner. A pretty one."

"That's probably no news here. You missed her when she came into the Trail's End." Cliff leaned back in his chair and smiled. "Lizzie is a treat, Riggins."

"Blond, they tell me."

"Sometimes sunrise gold, sometimes corn yellow. She's quite a woman." Cliff smiled. "By the way, she appreciates the use of Blake's house. It's a shame she won't have a chance to tell you in person, but we have to be on the road early tomorrow."

Riggins nodded. "I understand." His eyes narrowed as he glanced past Cliff's shoulder.

Cliff turned to see Alice sauntering across the floor. He smiled more broadly. She could not compare to his spectacular Lizzie, but Alice was a fine specimen of a woman nonetheless. She placed her hands on his shoulders and bent to whisper in his ear.

"Cliff, how could you leave without letting me show you a bit of fun?"

"Leave us alone, girl!" snapped Riggins. "Get back to your chores. If we want you, we'll call you."

She sniffed and took herself and her

wounded dignity to the bar. Busying herself with some of the many tasks necessary to get the saloon ready for the evening, she acted as if the two men did not exist.

"How about a single hand of cards, Hollister?" asked the saloon keeper.

Cliff looked at the cards he was shuffling and meant to say he was not interested. Instead he heard his voice enthusiastically agreeing. He took a swig of the whiskey to moisten his suddenly dry throat and coughed.

"You all right?" A strange, solicitous concern filled Riggins' voice.

He nodded slowly. "Just deal the cards." He splashed more whiskey into his glass and swallowed it almost desperately. Picking up his cards, he did not think of anything but the markings on them. He heard Riggins' opening bet and jumped into the game with a fervency he did not recognize in himself. Gold appeared on the table, eye scorching in the dim light. He closed his eyes against its brilliance.

Lizzie paced from the door to the dining room where supper waited, soggy and cold. Only Pete had been able to eat. Stella made sure he ate while she tried to comfort the young woman.

"Cliff is never late like this," lamented Lizzie. "He said he would be back before dinner. What if something has happened to him? Maybe I should go to the store or to the saloon and see whether anyone knows where he might be."

"The store if closed," Stella said reasonably, "and that saloon is no place for you. Riggins' women are different from you."

She shook her head. "That's unimportant. I'm not worried about my reputation. What is important is Cliff."

"Let me go, Lizzie. I know Garland Creek far better than you." Stella pulled her shawl from a peg by the front door. "I may be an hour. Probably Cliff will be back before I return." She took Lizzie by the shoulders and stared into her worry-darkened eyes. "Stay here. Either Cliff or I will be back soon. Stay calm."

"I'll try."

That had been nearly an hour ago, and nothing had changed. Lizzie was sure she would wear a path to the door as she walked back and forth incessantly. Opening it and peering down the street in both directions relieved her need to do something but brought her no comfort. Swirling snow obscured her view.

Her stomach knotted while her muscles ached from tension. She was aware that to relax the least bit would bring a cascade of tears she would be unable to stop. She tried to keep her hands from clenching into fists, but it was impossible.

Pete came to her and pulled at the wide skirt of her gown. "Lizzie, my tummy aches."

Although she wanted to tell him she was too

preoccupied with her worry about Cliff, she knelt to look at him. She tried to smile but failed miserably. "Go and lie down on the settee. You probably ate your supper too fast. I'll check you in a minute."

"But, Lizzie, it hurts real bad."

"I know, honey," she said soothingly. "Lie down. When you feel better later, I'll tell you a story."

He whined, "I want Cliff to tell me a story."

"All right," she promised. "As soon as he comes home, I'll send him to your room to see you."

Pete wandered away. She watched over the half wall as he climbed on the sofa and curled up into a ball. He wrapped his arms across his stomach. Promising herself she would look after him in a few minutes, she resumed her pacing.

Being late was uncharacteristic of Cliff. He might be absentminded and easily distracted by the promise of riches, but when he prepared for the trail, he was like a man obsessed. Before he left earlier, he told her there were chores he had to do in the house and the horses to tend.

The horses!

She whirled and ran to the stables behind the house. The wind-blown snow cut into her face and bare arms, but she ignored it. Throwing open the small door, she entered the warm mustiness of the stable. The scent of animal waste and moldering hay mixed with damp grain assaulted her, but she ignored it.

"Cliff? Are you here?"

The soft whoosh of a horse's breathing was the only answer. She climbed several rungs of the ladder to look into the hay mow. No response came to her second call. With a bitten-off curse, she swallowed the bitter bile of her disappointment. She had so hoped he would be there.

Her screech shattered the peace of the stable as her slipper missed a rung. She fell heavily to the stone floor. For a long minute, she did not move as she struggled to regain the breath that had been knocked out of her. Rolling over, she pushed her hands against the floor. With an expression of disgust, she glanced at the filth on them. She wiped them on a cloth used to clean the leather tack.

More slowly she fought the wind on her return to the house. It sneaked under her dress to swirl amid her petticoats. When she closed the door behind her, she felt as if she had won a major victory simply by traversing the yard. Even as she was regaining her stamina, she was calling, "Cliff? Stella? Are you home?"

A weak groan met her words. On ankles rubbery with fatigue she lurched toward the front of the house. "Pete?" she gasped with concern.

She paused in the doorway to the parlor as she stared at the child writhing in obvious agony. Instantly her concern refocused on him. She pressed her hand against his clammy forehead to feel the heat of fever. Noting the paleness of his skin, she picked him up. His head lolled against her shoulder.

Fear raced through her. These mining towns so often bred epidemics of the worst diseases. Cholera, typhoid, and others even more horrible would sweep through, killing more than survived their ravages. She climbed the stairs to Pete's bedroom, longing for someone to return so she could send for the doctor. She had never felt so alone as she did in that house in the middle of the settlement with no one to aid her with the ailing child.

Stripping off his shoes, she placed Pete on the bed. His breathing was labored as he struggled to contain the pain roiling through him. She pressed her hand to his distended abdomen and prayed that whatever was torturing him would not cause him more harm. She dipped a cloth in the water pitcher and placed it on his forehead. She wanted to ask if he had eaten or drunk anything different that day, but he only moaned when she spoke to him.

Not daring to leave him, she glanced continually toward the door of his room. Her ears strained for the sound of the door opening downstairs.

Cliff, she cried in her mind. We need you. Come home!

* * *

Cliff forced his eyes open, wondering if he was feeling so awful because he'd drunk too much whiskey too quickly. He started to speak to up the ante but realized he was not in the taproom. Dim light obscured his vision, but he discovered he was lying down. He frowned. Had he fallen out of his chair? He usually could hold his liquor far better than this.

"What the hell—?" he muttered as he started to rise.

"Oh, don't go yet, darling."

At the feminine whisper and hands roving across his bare skin, he turned and saw Alice reclining on the bed next to the pillow that still bore the imprint of his head. Immodestly, she let the sheet slip away to reveal the full curves of her body. She ran her hand knowledgeably along his.

Shoving the hand away, he stood up to find he was as naked as she was. He grasped his trousers and pulled them on in one smooth motion.

"Cliff?" she murmured. "Must you go so soon?"

"I don't know how the hell I got here, Alice, but I'm leaving. I have a woman waiting for me who means more to me than anything else in the world."

She smiled triumphantly. "That's not what you told me earlier." She giggled. "You told me I was the best lover you had ever had." Her hand ran along the width of his bare chest. "It was a compliment I returned. What a beast you are, Cliff Hollister! Sweeping me into your arms and racing with me up to this room. You ripped my gown to shreds in your eagerness."

He looked quickly at the tattered remains of the emerald gown and then away. Pushing her hand from him again, he snapped, "I don't know what you mean. Play your games elsewhere, honey. I'm going home."

She leapt to her feet. Pulling a silk robe from the foot of the bed, she tied it loosely around her. The neckline revealed most of her breasts as she stepped in front of him. She stuck her hand out. "Pay up first, Cliff!"

"Pay? For what?" He laughed as he buttoned his shirt. "I don't know what game you and Riggins have concocted, but I don't owe you anything, honey. There's only one woman I want to sleep with, and she's not you."

Fury burned in her eyes as she reached behind her for a bellpull. She tugged on it and folded her arms over her chest. "You won't pay? I never figured Cliff Hollister for a chisler."

"I pay for what I've used. I haven't used you!"

"Just because you were too drunk—" She leapt aside as the door opened.

Riggins stood in the doorway. His hooded eyes went to the woman who worked for him. "What's the problem, Alice?"

"He won't pay." She pouted as if she was

deeply insulted.

The saloon keeper laughed. "Pay? How could he pay? He doesn't own a gold coin. The only thing he has are the clothes he's wearing and the nag he rides."

Cliff demanded, "What are you talking about?" He reached for his coat and delved deep into the pockets. The bag of coins had disappeared. A ferocious frown disfigured his face. Pushing the whore aside, he advanced toward Riggins. "Where in hell is my money?"

"*My* money," Riggins corrected with a laugh. "You lost it to me this afternoon in a high stakes game. You even gambled away your two extra horses. Too bad your luck decided to turn on you now, Hollister."

With a growl, Cliff swung his fist at the taller man. Riggins blocked his surprisingly awkward movement with little effort. Just as easily, he slammed his own fist into the dark-haired man's face. Cliff reeled backward and banged into the wall. As if he were hung on a hook, he leaned against the wall for a moment. Slowly he slid to the floor.

Through the ringing in his ears, he heard Riggins laughing with Alice. The two snarled some insult at him, but he could not understand it. They went out, slamming the door behind them.

He rubbed the back of his hand against the blood dripping from his lip. Riggins had bamboozled him. His slowed reflexes and his lack of memory of anything since he'd sat down to play cards warned him that he had been set up by the two. He groaned. It was all his fault. He could have refused Riggins' invitation. Instead, fool that he was, he had entered the trap like a naive boy.

Gingerly he pushed himself to his feet. Even as he was walking to the door, it opened. Two burly men, who worked downstairs keeping the miners in line, grasped his arms. They half carried him down a set of stairs and outside. With a warning not to come back until he could pay his debts, they threw him into the frozen mud.

The sound of their amusement gave Cliff the strength to rise to his knees. He moaned; it seemed as if every bit of his body had been abused. He stood up and reeled two steps along the street in the direction of home. How he would explain the situation to Lizzie he had no idea.

The snow blinded him. He rubbed his eyes, but nothing helped clear his vision. Again and again he fell to his knees but fought to stand up. After an eternity spent traversing the short distance from the saloon to the house, he opened the door. His voice sounded strange in his ears as he called, "Lizzie?"

"Cliff? Come upstairs! Hurry!"

Hurrying was the last thing he wanted to do,

but the urgency in her voice gave him the impetus to climb the endless flight of stairs. He careened off the walls until he found the door more by feel than by sight.

Lizzie looked up from the bed. "It's Pete. He's—my God, Cliff, what happened to you?"

"Later, half-pint," he mumbled through his swelling lip. "What's wrong?"

"It's Pete. He's sick." She swallowed her curiosity as Cliff moved toward the single lantern on the table by the bed. A gasp of despair escaped her lips as she saw his abused condition.

He waved her questions aside. His own agony was instantly forgotten as he leaned over the child. The vivacious boy lay as still as death. His narrow chest rose and fell too slowly. A hand against his skin told Cliff that the child was consumed by fever.

"Honey, we must get a doctor for him."

Her haunted eyes turned from the delirious child to the distraught face of the man across the bed from her. "Fine. Go for him. Stella went out to look for you, so you're the only one left here to find him."

"Give me your gold dust!" he commanded.

"What?" She clutched the bag around her neck. "Use the money you won at the Trail's End."

"It's gone."

"It's gone?" she repeated in disbelief. "How?"

He stated tersely, "Riggins cheated me out of it."

Her mouth opened in a circle to match her wide eyes. When she tried to speak, no words emerged. She had not believed he would break his promises so quickly and so thoughtlessly. While she had worried about him, he had been throwing away everything they owned at a card table.

"Come on, half-pint. Give me the gold dust."

Again her fingers went to the string around her neck. "No, Cliff! I can't—"

"Dammit!" His mouth twisted with rage at her obstinacy. "I know you aren't supposed to give it to me until the end of our journey. I thought you trusted me! I won't run off and desert you here. This is for Pete! Do you want him dead too?"

Lizzie's eyes brightened with tears. More than once she started to speak, but her lies were coming back as phantoms to destroy her at the worst possible moment. Looking at Pete, she touched his forehead. It was still as overheated as it had been.

Dampening her lips, she whispered, "There is no gold dust, Cliff."

"No gold?" he repeated, sure he had misunderstood her.

"None." She shook her head as she reached for a cool cloth to put on Pete's head.

He twisted her to face him. Ignoring her cry, he ripped the bag from her neck. Far more rapidly than he thought he could, he undid the knots at the top and tipped the bag onto a tabletop. Lizzie clenched her hands together as she watched his face. Anger changed first to shock, then to sorrow, as he stared at the pile of dried California mud.

"You never had any gold?" he asked in sad disbelief.

She wished she could lie again, but it was impossible. "No. I'm sorry, Cliff. I—"

"I don't want to hear it!" he spat. "From the beginning you've been using me to reach your own ends." His smile was cruel and filled with pain. "You accused me so many times of trying to charm you into my arms simply so I could use you to satisfy myself. Now we see who is the true whoremonger. You used your versions of the truth to twist me to your will."

"No, Cliff! It wasn't like that! At least, not after the first few days." She put her damp fingers on his bare arm. The soft feeling of the hair along his strong forearm did not arouse her as it usually did. "Please believe me, Cliff. If there had been any other way, any other at all, I would not have tried to cheat you."

Grasping her shoulders, he brought her toward him so that her face was close to his. "No other way? You had another offer, Lizzie my love, and I think you would have been wise to choose it. I was wrong when I said you weren't the type to work for Delilah. With your lying ways you would have been perfect—you would let each miner think you loved him, even Winchester."

"I'm sorry," she whispered. She longed to touch him, to feel his arms holding her as they overcame this storm as they had so many others. "I can't say anything else but that."

"Try good-bye."

"Good-bye?" A sob ripped her throat. "No, Cliff, you can't leave us here! You can't leave Pete when he's so ill!"

He hesitated as he was striding toward the door. Involuntarily he glanced back at the bed. She was right, and they both knew it. His love for the child had not been tarnished.

"What do you own of value?"

"Me? All I have are the things in my saddlebag."

The armoire doors crashed against the wall as he ripped them open. He picked up her bag and unbuckled it. Roughly he tipped it upside down and shook it. The few articles rained down on the floor.

"No!" she cried when his hand reached for the miniatures of Whitney and Zach. "Those are for Pete! They are all he'll have to remember his parents."

Cruelly Cliff said, "If he doesn't get better, he won't need them." He relented a little as he saw her colorless cheeks. Pressing his hands against the small portraits, he popped them out of their carved ivory frames. Silently he handed them to her. "The frames are the only thing that have other than sentimental value. I hope I can convince the doctor that these are worth his coming out on a night like this. I'll be back with him as soon as I can."

He turned to leave. When she called his name, he did not look back. His head swam from the effects of Riggins' fist against it. More viciously his heart ached with the combined pain of worry for Pete and anger at Lizzie's betrayal. He had thought he knew the woman, but she had proved him wrong.

The ice of the storm could be no colder than the growing void within him. He had trusted her. He loved her, and she refused to be as honest with him. He snarled a curse into the gray night.

"Damn you, Lizzie Buchanan!" he shouted as he stumbled along the street.

Only the moan of the sick child broke Lizzie's trance as she stared at the door. When she heard the slamming of the door in the foyer, she feared she had lost the most important part of her life. She had meant to tell Cliff the truth early on. She had delayed. In the past few days, when she could have told him the truth, she simply forgot. It had seemed unimportant. She saw now how wrong she'd been.

With her face in her hands, she dropped

onto a chair by the bed. Her foolishness had guaranteed that Cliff would walk out of her life just when she thought it was possible he might stay. If he remained, it would be solely because he was worried about Pete. He had made it clear he wanted nothing more to do with her.

Her eyes settled on the mound of dirt on the table. Leaping to her feet, she swept it onto the floor with a swift motion of her arm. Tears rolled down her cheeks as she thought about how she had gambled so foolishly on the one thing she wanted and had lost.

Forcing back the pain, she looked at the child on the bed. More than ever, Pete was all that remained for her. If he died, she would truly be deserted by all she loved. She wrung another cloth from the bowl of cool water and placed it on his forehead to replace the one that had dried out.

She did not move from his side as she waited impatiently for the doctor to come. She heard the door open, and Stella came in. Lizzie motioned to her.

"Lizzie, what is wrong?"

"Pete is sick," Lizzie explained as if for the thousandth time.

"*El niño*?" She rushed to the bed and stared at the restless toddler. "Do you want me to go for Dr. Webb?"

Lizzie shook her head tiredly. "No. Cliff went."

"Cliff?" The loathing had returned to Stella's voice when she spoke his name. "So that rattlesnake has decided to seek his nest after his day of sunning himself on a rock?"

"What?" Lizzie was too exhausted emotionally to try to puzzle through Stella's strange statement.

The housekeeper hesitated. She knew it was not the best time for the truth, but she felt Lizzie should know before she let that man back into their house. As gently as she could, Stella said, "I discovered where he was all afternoon."

"He was playing cards with Riggins at the Trail's End." She brushed a loose lock of hair away from her eyes as she lifted her eyes from Pete's face. "I know. He told me. He lost everything we had."

"He had enough to pay Alice Seeger for her time."

Lizzie gasped, "Alice? The Alice at the saloon? No, Stella, you must be wrong! You must be!" She struggled to keep her voice low, although her emotions raged through her like a conflagration.

"Squeaky McGuire, a miner up at the Buckeye Mine, saw them together. He told me when I spoke to him on the street. After *he* lost all your money and your horses as well, he took that one upstairs to enjoy with his last coin."

Anguish choked Lizzie, but she said only, "Be that as it may, what is important now is getting Pete well." Her voice was so calm it surprised even herself. Later, when she had room for more pain, she would mourn for the love that had been lost even before the contents of the bag were revealed.

She continued to watch the child while Stella went to make some sweetened tea for the nurses and the patient. The cup at Lizzie's elbow remained untouched as she tended the boy with a desperate need to heal him with her love.

Footsteps announced the arrival of the men even before their shadows filled the doorway. Lizzie looked up quickly. She bit her lip as Cliff refused to meet her eyes. By his side was a man in unrelieved black. He was as round as a coin, and his head with its forest of limp brown hair did not reach Cliff's shoulder. His hand, too fine boned for the rough life in California patted her shoulder as she came to greet him.

"Miss Buchanan? I'm Dr. Webb. I hear the boy is sick."

"Yes, doctor. Please help him."

The short man bustled to the bed, ignoring her words and hopeful face. His coattails flared behind him as he opened his bag of mysterious potions and instruments. His bushy eyebrows were enough to frighten the child if he opened his eyes.

Cliff said nothing as he watched the doctor examine Pete. If he felt Lizzie's shattered gaze on him, he did not acknowledge it. With his arms folded across his chest, he stood like a rigid statue, determined to remain unyielding to her broken heart.

"What do you think is wrong, doctor?" she whispered, trying to pretend Cliff's coldness did not hurt her.

"Don't know. He's sick, though. That I can tell you."

Frustrated, she demanded in a more strident voice, "Dr. Webb, you cannot leave it at that. You must know something."

He adjusted his glasses on his nose. For the first time, she noticed the right lens was cracked. "Young lady, I said he was sick. That is what a doctor is supposed to do. Tell you when folks be sick and treat them."

"And?"

Dr. Webb's frown deepened as he stared at the man by the door. "He may live. He may not."

"Cliff, is this quack the best you could find?" Hysteria colored Lizzie's voice. "Get out of here, both of you. Get out of here, and don't bother to come back. I could tell as much myself."

With an outraged huff, the doctor whirled and strode out of the room. They could hear his complaints until the front door closed resoundingly to cut them off. Lizzie put her hands over her mouth as she realized what her frayed nerves had led her to do.

"I doubt if I can get him to come back," Cliff said quietly. "I don't think there is another doctor."

Stella said, "No, there is only Dr. Webb."

"Lizzie, I can—"

Her rage at him exploded. "Get out of here! Take your lying lips out of here!" she cried. "What do you care about us? Go back to your girlfriend. Maybe Alice isn't busy stealing gold from the miners and will give you another tumble."

He stared at her unbelievingly. One look at Stella's wrathful face told him how Lizzie had learned those lies, which were probably a source of amusement to nearly everyone in Garland Creek by that time. "Half-pint—"

She interrupted him again. "Don't you understand? I don't want to hear any more of your lies! Get out of my life! You berated me about trust when you came to me from another woman's bed." She turned away from him.

Silently he watched as she went to tend her nephew. Stella glared at him once more before going to assist her. Their rigid backs plainly told him he was not welcome in the sickroom. With heavy steps, he went downstairs to the parlor. He opened the cabinet where the liquor was stored. Taking down a bottle, he twisted the cork out of the top. Without bothering to get a glass, he tilted the bottle back.

He walked out of the door with the bottle in his hand. Where he would go, he was not sure, but he refused to beg Lizzie to forgive him after her lies. The storm wrapped him in its cold clutches and screened him from the house where two women battled for a child's life.

CHAPTER SIXTEEN

THE KNOCKING DID NOT CEASE AS LIZZIE dragged herself to the door. She was exhausted, but she did not want to wake Stella, who was asleep on the settee in the parlor. The long hours of caring for the child had brought no reward. Pete was slowly slipping away from them.

Lifting the latch was a monumental task she did not know if she could accomplish alone. She used both hands to push it upward and stepped aside as the door swung open to wash the floor with moonlight. She was surprised to see it had stopped snowing. Then she realized she didn't know what day it was.

"Half-pint, is he still alive?"

Her eyes rose slowly to the beloved face. With her voice breaking, she cried, "Cliff!" Forgetting his rage at her, she flung herself into his arms. "Oh, Cliff, I thought you had deserted us."

"No. I went for help." He lifted her arms from around his neck. "Here is Dr. Yee. He is a doctor in the next town over the ridge. Will you let him—?"

"Yes, please, sir." She did not wait for Cliff to continue as she noticed for the first time the man standing in the shadows. "Come in and help, if you can."

Cliff waved the bent man into the house. Once he must have stood proudly, but the years had twisted him like a tree in the wind. His head reached no higher than Lizzie's, but a power emanated from him that had nothing to do with physical size.

Involuntarily she gasped as she saw that the doctor was Chinese. She had heard of the Orientals who had come to California in large numbers, but most of them were said to be young girls sold to the miners as concubines and to the bordellos of the larger cities. The tales of a subservient, ignorant people did not match the intelligence in this man's ancient eyes, though his long queue emphasized his strangeness.

After a brief glance in her direction, Dr. Yee paid no more attention to Lizzie. He went directly to the stairs leading to the bedroom where the child lay as still as death. Cliff put his hand on her arm to steer her after the silent doctor.

"Cliff," she whispered, "do you think a

Chinese doctor—"

"Hush," he commanded. "Trust me, Lizzie." His anger cut through her as he repeated in a more vicious tone, "Trust me!"

Tears burned in her eyes as she nodded. His words warned her he had not forgiven her. What he was doing was done out of love for Pete and nothing more. She tried to hide the anguish in her heart as she watched the doctor examine the child.

In his heavily accented voice, Dr. Yee stated, "Child has bad spirit within him. How long?"

Lizzie calculated quickly. "Two days—no, it's been three."

"I see."

She wanted to say that she did not, but she kept silent as he opened his small paisley-patterned bag. From it, he pulled instruments she didn't recognize. The sharp objects and needles looked more alien than the doctor. Without realizing what she was doing, she slipped her hand into Cliff's. She needed his closeness as she never had.

Stella burst into the room, but she was simultaneously silenced by both Cliff and Lizzie. From the doorway, they all watched as the doctor bent over intently and went through the strange procedures he had brought with him from the Orient. Time meant nothing to them as they stood mutely, wondering if Doctor Yee could help Pete and fearing what would happen if he did not.

When Lizzie swayed, Cliff put his arm around her and drew her closer. She leaned her head on him and clutched his shirt. Her fear that Pete would die was stronger than her pain over Cliff's betrayal.

Finally Dr. Yee straightened up. He nodded and smiled. Packing his supplies back into his bag with the same precision with which he had placed them on the bed, he turned to the anxious faces of his audience. He pointed to Lizzie.

"He is yours?"

"Yes," she whispered.

"Please, come."

Releasing her grip on Cliff, she went to stand before the doctor. He placed a half dozen packets in her hand. Closing her fingers over them, he said, "Boy will live. These are for him. Put in tea or in broth, in morning, at night. Give until all gone. You understand?"

"Yes, but how do I get him to drink? He hasn't taken anything for more than a day."

"He wake at sunrise. I gave him powder for now. You give then. Understand?"

"I understand." Hastily she added, "Thank you, Dr. Yee. Thank you so much. I have nothing to pay you—"

He waved aside her words. "Paid already. Take care of boy. Good boy. Let him grow strong."

"Thank you," breathed Lizzie.

The wizened hand rested on her shoulder for a moment as he pulled himself straighter. Even then, his eyes were not far above hers. He spoke a phrase in a language she could understand no more than she had his chants by the bedside. She longed to look at Cliff to have him translate the words, but she was captured by the ancient wisdom in his eyes, which were nearly lost in the wrinkles of his face.

When he spoke, she nodded in response to what was clearly a question, although she did not know what he had asked. After the miraculous way he had cured Pete, she was ready to promise anything to Dr. Yee, even at the cost of everything she treasured.

He looked over her shoulder to speak to Cliff. Again he received the affirmative he expected. He nodded and exited without another word. Stella followed to offer him something to eat before his long ride back to his home.

Lizzie swayed again as she watched the door close. Feeling strong hands supporting her, she leaned gratefully against the man behind her. "Stay tonight, Cliff. I know you're leaving me, but stay tonight."

"I'll stay with you until Pete is better."

"And after that?"

He turned her in his arms to look at her face, lined with fatigue and fear. "I don't know, Lizzie. I truly don't know." Hesitating, he thought about not telling her the truth, but did not want to lie any longer. "Do you know what you promised Dr. Yee?"

"No." She rubbed her aching eyes. "I don't understand what he said to me. You know that."

"I know a little Chinese from meeting Orientals in San Francisco. He asked if you will always honor the love between us," he said quietly.

All exhaustion left Lizzie's body as she felt a surge of hope. She put her hand on his arm. "You answered as I did, Cliff. Does that mean—?"

"It means nothing!" he spat. "There is no love between us. Just continual distrust and lying. Oh, you whisper so sweetly of love when I hold you in the darkness, but you think nothing of cheating me during the day."

She closed her eyes as she listened to the words that revealed how deeply he had once loved her. She could not blame him for feeling betrayed. "If you'll listen to the truth, I'll explain."

"Truth?" He snorted in disgust. "Half-pint, you've never spoken the truth one day in your life."

"Yes!" she cried. "Yes, I have. Only once have I lied to you, Cliff, and that was when I made the bargain with you to bring us east." She reached out to touch his chest. His strength always revitalized her own. "I had forgotten all about that promise. So much has happened since then, it seems impossible that I could have wanted to buy my way east by lying to you."

"You've paid the price now."

She drew away from him. "Maybe you're right. I may have lied to you once. Once! How many times have you lied to me? Playing cards with Riggins!" She laughed harshly.

"They hoodwinked me. Riggins stole my money and arranged it so I would wake up in Alice's bed."

"And I'm supposed to believe that? Take your lies elsewhere, Mr. Hollister."

His hands clenched at his sides as she walked to the bed where Pete slept, oblivious to the pain around him. How easy it would be to wipe that snide smile from her face with his lips against her mouth!

Damn woman!

Lizzie tried to keep the tears from falling as she heard him walk out of the room. The door of the other bedroom on the second floor closed. He would want to sleep after his long ride, she knew. Staring at her hands folded on the blanket, she realized she had not told him how grateful she was. Nor had she discovered what Cliff had given Dr. Yee in payment for his services.

She leaned her forehead on her folded hands and prayed as she had since Cliff had disappeared. She did not ask for anything specific, simply that her heart be healed the wounds inflicted on it.

Pete recovered quickly. Within a day after he started taking the pungent-smelling herbs in the packets left by Dr. Yee, he was sitting up and regaining a bit of his normal energetic liveliness. He made no effort to hide the fact that Cliff was his favorite guest in the sickroom. The two spent hours together, visits from which Lizzie was excluded.

She could not stay in the same room with Cliff. It was not easy to avoid him within the walls of the house, but she found ways. Having him sit with Pete all day solved most of her problems. Once again, they each slept alone and at different times.

He was upstairs with the child when a knock came at the door. Lizzie went to answer it, for Stella was busy in the kitchen preparing their supper. After all they'd been through it seemed pure luxury to have regular meals at normal times.

The cold blasted her face. She pulled her shawl more tightly around her shoulders as she asked, "May I help you?"

"Lizzie Buchanan?"

She nodded. The man before her looked as if he could lift a mountain with his bare hands. Muscles bulged under his clothes. His thick neck seemed as wide as his massive shoulders. Awed by the huge man, she straightened her back to bring herself up to her full height, nearly a foot less than his. "I am Lizzie Buchanan. Who are you?"

"I'm here for Mr. Riggins. You haven't paid your rent. He wants you out."

Swept by a feeling of having lived this horror before, she said quietly, "Cliff paid him."

"Not lately."

"My nephew is very ill. He cannot be moved yet."

He shrugged, plainly unconcerned by her woes. "Mr. Riggins wants you out. If you have any disagreement with that, take it up with him."

"Where can I see him?"

His eyes glittered as they roved over her. Automatically she pulled her shawl even closer to conceal her body from his lascivious gaze. "Mr. Riggins does all his business at the Trail's End. He thought you might want to see him. He told me to tell you to come at nine o'clock."

"All right." She reached for the door to close it. "I will see him tomorrow morning at nine."

A ham-sized fist blocked the door from closing. "Tonight, Miss Buchanan. Come at nine tonight, or by this time tomorrow, you'll be sleeping in the snow."

She started to protest but knew it was useless. The one time she had gone into the Trail's End, she had known Cliff would be there to protect her. The thought of entering that palace of illicit pleasure daunted her. But there was no other choice. Stella had told her Cliff could not return there without risking severe injury. Considering how Riggins had already treated him, Cliff was in no position to ask the saloon keeper for a favor.

"Very well. You may convey to Mr. Riggins that Miss Buchanan will call on him at nine tonight at his business establishment."

With a grin at her stilted words, he tipped his hat. "Sure thing, Miss Buchanan." His tongue dampened his chapped lips. "See you then, huh?"

She slammed the door in his lecherous face. A shiver raced along her. That was a sample of what she would have to tolerate if she entered the Trail's End. To the miners who patronized the saloon, the women there served only one purpose. She hoped she could get in and out of there without losing more than her pride.

Faking fatigue, she did not join Stella for a late supper in the dining room. Cliff and Pete ate upstairs in the smaller bedroom. Going into the room she had shared so briefly with Cliff, Lizzie locked the door. She needed all her limited props for this role.

From the armoire she pulled a gown she had reworked from one of those she had found in the room with the hip bath. Its royal blue silk had a life of its own as it rustled over starched petticoats. The tiers of white lace that covered the bottom third of the wide skirt matched the lace on the sleeves that ended in a bell at the elbows. Dropping off her shoulders, the simple neckline was enhanced by a small bow at the center of the V-shaped bodice.

Brushing back her unruly curls, she tied them with a ribbon to match those woven through the lace. She had no jewelry to compliment her outfit, but her eyes glittered in anticipation of the ordeal that lay ahead more brightly than the most brightly polished gem. Slipping a black velvet mantilla over her shoulders, she slunk down the stairs and out the door before anyone could see her.

The scent of snow filled the crisp air. Low, dark gray clouds clung to the dark pyramids of the mountains. Gusts of wind twirled the dry flakes into miniature tornadoes before capriciously dispersing them. The only sound came from the harshly lit tavern.

Lizzie paused as she stood before the door. If she went into the place, she was sure something horrible would happen. Fiercely she told herself she had no choice. Not to meet with Mr. Riggins as he had ordered would mean eviction. For Pete, that could bring about a recurrence of the fever.

Ordering her stomach to cease its painful knotting, she stiffened her back and pushed the door open. As she entered the saloon, she felt the eyes of the men closest to the door settling on her. The rumble of conversation died, then started up again as she crossed the room to the bar.

The bartender hurried down his side of the bar to greet her. "Yes, miss?"

"I am Lizzie Buchanan. Mr. Riggins is expecting me."

His birdlike face bobbed up and down. "Yes, miss. Please wait. I'll let him know you're here."

She folded her hands on the top of the bar. By keeping her eyes lowered, she did not have to look in the mirror and see the men in the room watching her. She could feel each lustful stare between her shoulder blades. Sternly she kept her back straight.

"Lizzie? You're Lizzie Buchanan?"

Shocked by the sound of a feminine voice, she turned to see Alice leaning on the bar. Her gown dipped deep to reveal the skin that Lizzie was sure had known Cliff's caress. A tray was balanced against her hip. Not knowing what to say, Lizzie resumed gazing at her hands.

"Well, I'm sorry I spoke, your royal highness!" taunted the prostitute. "What's wrong? Ashamed you couldn't keep a man like Cliff Hollister satisfied? It's no great crime, you know." She put her head closer to Lizzie as she whispered, "He was wonderful, Lizzie. He told me a lot about you, but the one thing I remember best is that he said you could profit from learning the things I know."

"Be quiet!" Lizzie cried, unable to stay

silent.

"Not listening to the truth don't make it not so!" Alice grinned superiorly.

A sharp command came from behind Lizzie. "Get away from her, Alice! She don't want you bothering her."

Lizzie whirled to thank her protector. The expression on the whore's face warned her of who stood in back of her. Her eyes widened as they traveled up the dark shirt to the face of Jerry Riggins. She had never seen a man so tall. If his messenger looked as if he could move a mountain, this man appeared to be the towering alp.

Dark strands of his oily hair drifted over her arm as he bent to lift her fingers to his lips in a genteel greeting. "Miss Buchanan, I'm so glad you've come to discuss your problem with me."

"Mr. Riggins . . ."

"One moment, my dear." His voice rumbled through her head, although he spoke quietly. "Shall we go to my office?"

In horror, she shook her head. "I can't do business alone with a man behind a closed door. It isn't right."

"Of course," he assured her quickly. "Forgive me, Miss Buchanan. You must understand I am not accustomed to dealing with ladies of your caliber. Shall we sit here?"

He pointed to a table some distance from the others. Lizzie placed her fingers lightly on his arm as she walked with him to the empty table.

Congratulating herself mentally on her attempt to emulate the fine eastern lady she once had longed to be, she was glad she had chosen that image. If Jerry Riggins suspected what her life had been like for the past months, he would not be treating her so chivalrously.

Seating her graciously, he asked, "Is this appropriate?"

"This is fine, Mr. Riggins." She clenched her fingers in her lap, out of his view.

"Any lady as pretty as you should call me Jerry." He sat down, his bulk overflowing the chair. It creaked as he lowered himself into it, but he paid the sound no attention. "Can I offer you a drink?"

She shook her head. Determined to have their business done as quickly as possible, she said, "Mr. Rig—Jerry, I understand you want us to vacate your house."

"A drink first to keep this meeting friendly," he ordered. He signaled the bartender. Almost instantly two glasses and a bottle appeared on their table. He pushed the glass of sarsaparilla toward her. "I didn't think you were the type of lady to want anything stronger than this."

"Thank you." She took a careful sip of the dark fluid. Its pungent aroma wafted through her senses. Each time she tasted it, she thought of the night she had begged Cliff for his love. She forced that thought from her mind as she must push him from her life.

Pouring himself a healthy serving of the whiskey in the bottle, he drank it in one gulp. He refilled the glass and leaned back against the chair, which protested again. "Now, Miss Buchanan, shall we speak of this business between us?"

"I know you want us to leave your house. It's impossible. My nephew has been very ill. I don't think he would survive if we had to find another place tomorrow. I don't have any money, but I beg you—"

"Whoa there, little lady." He held up his hands and laughed. "Slow down. One thing at a time. You have a sick young 'un in the house?"

"Yes. He's only three, and if—"

He interrupted her again. "I wouldn't throw a sick child into the snow, Miss Buchanan." A pained expression settled on his craggy face. "What kind of man do you think I am?" He chuckled as she hesitated. "No, don't answer that. You might say the truth."

"Thank you for your kindness. We'll leave as soon as Pete is well." She started to stand up, but his hand settled on her wrist, imprisoning her in its huge manacle of flesh.

Fear flashed through Lizzie as he motioned with his head to her to sit down again. Aware that she could not escape from his powerful grip, she lowered herself into the chair. If he loosened his grip enough, she intended to break free and run.

He leaned forward but didn't lift the hand pinning her wrist to the table. "Don't look so frightened, Miss Buchanan. Lizzie, right?"

"Yes, that's right." Taking a deep breath, she gained the courage to say, "Please, sir, you're hurting me."

Instantly he loosened his grasp on her but didn't remove his fingers totally. "Forgive me, my dear. I just don't want you to run off before we complete our business agreement." He paused, then added, "Lizzie, are you interested in earning some easy money?"

With a smile, she ran her finger along the top of her glass. The motion hid her nervousness. "It depends on what would be required to earn that easy money."

"Very good." He smiled and released her hand. "I like women who think. Of course, women like that one over there don't need to think." He hooked a thumb toward Alice. The black-haired woman scowled at the two sitting at the table before she sauntered over to a man who was snapping his fingers at her. "But you're smart. I saw that from the moment you entered the door. You calculated the reaction of every man in the room."

"So?" she asked carefully.

"So I thought I would offer you a job as my hostess."

Her brow wrinkled in distress. "Hostess? That sounds entirely too much like—"

Hastily he reassured her. "No, Lizzie, don't think that. Madge is in charge of the girls. I was thinking only that you would be here and play cards with the men as I hear you did when you were here with Hollister. I would pay you well, and you would keep half of what you win besides."

Lizzie searched his face and knew she should not trust this man. Yet, if he was willing to pay her for playing cards and nothing else, she could not pass up this opportunity. As things were, the food in the house was gone, there was no money to buy more.

"All right," she said with sudden enthusiasm. If she didn't take that position, she would be forced to resort to a far different one. She recalled the other offer she had had to work in a saloon. "All right, but I want two-thirds of what I win and no questions asked about how I win it."

"Two-thirds?" he gasped, startled by the change in the lady, suddenly a sharp negotiator.

"You'll be pleased with your share."

He nodded with a slow return of his smile. "Very well, Lizzie. Two-thirds it shall be, plus I'll pay you what I pay Gilbert Palmer, my bartender. You'll continue paying the four bits a day rent I was charging Hollister. Is that satisfactory?"

"Yes," she answered quickly, hoping she could mask her shock at his generous terms. "When do you wish me to start?"

"Tonight." He laughed and reached across the small table. His gigantic fist swallowed her dainty fingers. "I think you and I will work just fine together."

She pulled her hand away from him. "Jerry, I don't recall that anything like that was included in my job requirements."

"Of course, Lizzie," he said, but he did not meet her eyes.

More than ever, she knew she would have to remain careful with this man. If only she could earn enough to take Pete farther east, they might find someone who would help them. With what he was offering and a deck of doctored cards, she could earn what she needed by the time spring made travel easy.

"I'll need money to start."

"Have Gilbert give you what you need." He waved his hand as he said magnanimously, "This first night, I won't charge you for your starting money. Next time you come to me for money, I'll charge you interest on it."

She smiled as she stood up. "You needn't worry about that, Jerry. I don't intend to lose."

"How—?"

"No questions, remember? Don't worry. I will make this very profitable for both of us."

His eyes followed her feminine figure as she went to the bar. She leaned forward to explain to Gilbert what she needed. As she stood on tiptoe to speak to him, Jerry enjoyed a hint of slender ankle revealed beneath her gown. His eyes slid along her. A beauty. Far prettier than his widow on Churchy Street. Soon she would be totally dependent on him. Then he would renegotiate his business deal with Miss Lizzie Buchanan.

Cliff was sure his hunch would prove foolish as he shoved open the doors to the Trail's End. That Stella had caught a glimpse of Lizzie running out of the house dressed in an elegant gown did not mean she had come here. He asked himself as he walked to the saloon where else she could be going in that outfit. Everything on Churchy Street closed at sunset except the assayer's office. Here on Hellbound, all entertainment centered around the Trail's End.

The reek of whiskey and cheap tobacco greeted him as he pushed his way through the smoke. He kept his hat down low over his brow. Until he learned what he wanted to know, he chose to stay inconspicuous.

He recognized a light laugh through the blur of conversation. His head swiveled in the direction of its origin. A jealous rage that was too painfully familiar swelled through him as he saw Lizzie dressed in a beautiful gown he had never seen. She was playing cards at a crowded table of miners. When one of them put his hand on the bare skin of her slender shoulder, Cliff did not pause to think.

In one swift motion, he leapt across the

room. He grasped the man by the back of the shirt and spun him around to face him. Cliff's fist impacted with a dull thud against the man's jaw. The miner collapsed back onto the table next to the one at which Lizzie sat. The men seated there shoved the senseless man to the floor but did nothing else as they watched the spontaneous entertainment.

The other men sitting with Lizzie quailed before Cliff's ferocious gaze. When she stood up to demand an explanation from him, he whirled her away from the table and led her to a shadowed corner of the saloon.

"What in hell are you doing?" he demanded.

She pulled her arm out of his grasp. Awkwardly she rubbed the reddened spots. She continued to hold her cards in her hand. "What does it look like I'm doing? I'm managing!"

"Is that what you call it, honey? You looked as if you were lining up customers."

Coldly, she smiled. "How else can I feed Pete and myself after you desert us? Don't deny it. It's just a matter of time now, isn't it? Pete is feeling better, and you're ready to leave."

"Lizzie, listen—"

"No," she interrupted. "You listen for once. I'm not a child. I know what life is available for me in Garland Creek, and I am going to survive. You know I can satisfy a man."

At her candid words, Cliff swallowed

harshly. Into his mind came the images of her love-softened face beneath his as he shared the sweetness of her slender body. To think of someone else tasting the honeyed textures of her skin and stroking her warm curves sent a bullet-sharp pang through him.

"You're lying to yourself," he argued. "You can't act the whore. Could you have given yourself to me if I hadn't won your heart?"

"Why you arrogant, egotistical—"

His laughter interrupted her. Rage exploded in her as he mocked her honest emotion. Uneasily she watched him. One thing she knew. She could not trust Cliff Hollister to say or do as she expected.

"Honey, you're lying, and we both know it. Did it ever occur to you that I woudn't find it so hard to forget you? You've made it clear that you don't want to be mine."

"I've heard this speech before," she said slowly.

"I know, but if you're sincere about not wanting me, I won't force myself on you." He ran a finger along her neck. "It's too bad about the gold dust being mud. I could have used it to buy me companionship guaranteed to give me the satisfaction I can't have with you."

Outrage stripped her of her voice. Not only was he comparing her with whores, but he was saying she had less value. She stared at him, frozen by her fury. Alice's words taunted her. She began to believe he had indeed told the harlot what she'd said he had.

"You've said what you came to say, Cliff. Why don't you leave and let me get back to work?"

"Work? Don't you know what you're getting yourself into here?"

She nodded. "I know exactly." When he stared in disbelief at her cool acceptance of her fate, she sighed. "Speechless, Cliff? You're abandoning us without looking backward. I must look forward too, although I am grateful to you. Without you, I wouldn't have known how—"

"Shut up!"

His shout echoed through the low-roofed room. Among the tables, conversation died. All eyes turned toward the two in the shadows. A large man moved in their direction.

"Is this man bothering you, Miss Buchanan?"

Cliff snarled, "Get out of here, Whittaker!"

The bull-necked man would have fulfilled the threat he had made when he helped throw Hollister into the street, but Miss Buchanan stood between them. Jerry had given very specific orders on how this woman was to be treated. Whittaker considered those orders only a temporary inconvenience.

"You'd best leave, Hollister."

"When I'm done talking to Lizzie."

A third male voice entered the conversation. "You're done now, Hollister."

Lizzie glanced up to see Jerry. His head barely cleared the rafters of the saloon. Possessively he took her hand in his and pulled her away from Cliff.

"It's all right," she said smoothly as she felt Cliff's anger approaching the detonation point. "We're simply talking about things."

"If you don't mind me saying so, I think you and I have some business we might want to discuss," was Jerry's rejoinder.

She was given no chance to respond. Cliff stepped between her and the huge man. "She's not going to be one of your overworked whores, Riggins, slaving to make a dollar."

"I didn't know you had a personal interest in her any longer, Hollister. Why don't you just go home to your kid and leave this to us? Unless, of course, you've come up with a bit of gold. Then you may want to find Alice for another tumble." His smile returned as he added, "Lizzie, why don't you explain it to him? You know I've asked you to do the kind of work I know is fit for a lady like you, since I offered you a totally different position."

"Such as? A spot in your bed?" demanded Cliff.

Lizzie put her hand on Cliff's arm. This sudden surge of chivalry did not appeal to her. She did not want to be defended against the roughness of the world. Simply because she was dressed elegantly, she did not want him to act as if she had become something other than the Lizzie he had seduced into his bed and was now ready to abandon.

In a stilted voice, she said to Cliff, "I think this is none of your concern, sir."

"None of my concern?" His gray eyes sparked with fury. "I brought you this far, and—"

"I am grateful, but now our paths are parting." She stepped toward the other man. "Now, what is it you wished to discuss with me, Jerry? I think the gentlemen are anxious to complete the game Mr. Hollister interrupted."

Cliff watched in unspeakable shock as she walked away with the owner of the saloon. By the elephantine man's side, she looked as delicate as a child's china doll. His gut tied in knots when he saw that every man in the room had his eyes glued to Lizzie's feminine curves. And not only the men—the whores appraised her, wondering if she was going to be competition for them.

He could not understand what had happened. All the time he had been sitting with Pete, overwhelmed with guilt and searching for a way to heal the breach between Lizzie and himself, she'd been plotting to leave him. He could not pull his gaze away from the form he knew so well. Knowing there was no way he could remain inconspicuous, he stormed across the room to take a seat not far from where she was playing cards. All night he sat there, silent and refusing all offers of a game or a drink. If she once glanced in his direction to acknowledge him, he did not see it.

CHAPTER SEVENTEEN

STELLA MADE IT A HABIT TO RISE IN THE EARLY morning twilight to meet Lizzie when she returned from the Trail's End. She greeted the tired woman with a treat and a cup of tea sweetened with honey. When Lizzie dropped with a sigh onto the settee, the housekeeper would sit with her and share with her what had happened in the house since she left for work. Most of the conversation centered on Pete.

The older woman always excused herself if Cliff came into the room. The way the man treated Lizzie disturbed her. He taunted her for working for Riggins, although Lizzie had no other choice. Only because Pete clung to him, sensing the gap that was destroying their family, did he delay leaving.

Lizzie fought to maintain her calm as she listened to his vindictive words. She could not

deny them, since they were true. To provide for
the child, she was using the few talents she had.

At the end of her first week at the Trail's
End, she proudly gave Jerry his third of her
winnings and accepted her pay in return. When
he counted the gold she gave him, he couldn't
hide his astonishment at the tremendous amount
she had won. She simply smiled when he gasped
out words of praise.

As she began her second week at the Trail's
End, she found she had become accustomed to
the strange hours she worked. She went to sleep
as the sun rose and woke after it had set beyond
the mountains in the early winter darkness.

Bathing in the tub in the warm water Stella
brought upstairs, she swiftly dressed for work.
She always left enough time to spend an hour
alone with Pete. At first he had been awed by her
transformation into an elegant, fashionably
dressed woman, but he soon accepted it with his
normal flexibility. Eating a quick supper, she
would prepare to leave. Her twelve-hour shift at
the saloon left little time for anything else.

When Cliff came into the foyer as she was
pulling her shawl over her head, she saw unhappiness in his face. She longed to bring laughter
back to his volatile eyes, but she knew anything
she did would be futile. He threw all her attempts
at reconciliation back in her face until she no
longer tried. She could not remember saying
more than hello or good-bye to him in the past

week.

"Good-bye, Cliff," she said too casually. "I'll see you in the morning."

"No, honey. I don't think so."

She turned to look at him. Her face, haloed by the crimson wool of her shawl, was expressionless, but he knew her well enough to see beyond the mask. As much as it did him, their final parting would rip her apart.

Dampening her arid lips, she asked, "You're leaving?"

"I have only a few months to get back to where I'm to meet the next wagon train of fools who are California bound. I have to round up a team to help me." He shrugged with studied nonchalance but would not meet her eyes. "You're doing fine at the Trail's End. You've made more money this week than I could hope to make in a year."

"So now that I'm not dependent on you, you can't bear to be near me." Her sense of desolation changed to the anger she found easier to express. "Is that what you wanted, Cliff? A child who must come to you to get your approval of every decision?"

He laughed shortly. "That was never you, Lizzie. You always managed to do everything your way and succeed."

"And that galls you?" When he didn't answer, she sighed. "Than if that is what you want, look for it elsewhere. I am not going to be any man's kept woman." A smile curved her lips, but there was no joy in it. "If you want the truth, I've been keeping you in grand style for the past week."

Her words shattered the remnants of his pride. "Dammit, woman!" he shouted, taking her by the shoulders. He pulled her close to him. The light scent of her lavender cologne floated over him. The aroma lured him, despite his frustration with her. He pressed her to him and captured her mouth beneath his.

Lizzie did not struggle to escape his pained fury as he kissed her again and again. Neither did she capitulate to his desire. To do so would be to lose herself totally within a love he no longer wanted to offer her. She longed for the first days when they had been partners, snarling at one another but respecting their pooled strengths. Nothing existed for them now.

He lifted his lips from hers as he felt the heartbreak she would not share with him. Pushing her hair back from her face, Cliff whispered, "You'll never change, will you, Lizzie?"

"Never."

"Then I guess that was your farewell kiss."

"I guess so."

Her coolness angered him until he looked into her eyes and saw the sorrow there. He couldn't blame her for not trying to convince him to stay. From the time she had come west with the wagon train, he had hurt her again and again. It was usually unintentionally, but there had been . . . He sent the troubling thoughts from his mind as his fingers touched the softness of her cheek. He pulled his hand away as he felt a surge of yearning to caress all of her loving body.

"Take care of yourself, Lizzie."

"Oh, I will." A watery smile played on her lips. "You know me, Cliff. I always manage to land on my feet. Good luck on your trip east."

He waited for her to add more, but she simply smiled again and walked toward the door. There was desperation in his voice as he called, "Lizzie?"

"Yes?" Expectancy lightened the single word, sending the sound soaring through the room.

"Next year, if I come by way of Garland Creek, is it all right if I stop in and see Pete and you?"

She forced back the pain that swept over her. Even during their farewells, he put her nephew before her. It told her more than anything else how little she mattered to him. She had offered him love, and all he wanted was fun.

Emotionlessly she answered, "Of course, Cliff. If we are here, we would enjoy seeing you again. Farewell. May God bless you."

He watched as she went out the door. When it closed, he leaned his arm on it. Resting his head on his arm, he pounded his other fist against the sturdy wood. It didn't help. All he got was a sore hand to go along with his shattered heart.

Jerry smiled as he looked across his saloon. Business had improved tenfold since he had hired Lizzie. Although other barkeeps in the settlements along the river valley were considering adding such a lady card player to their saloons, the Trail's End had been the first. Men from miles away vied to sit next to the pretty woman. Dressed in the silk gowns he had ordered for her, she drew the miners as surely as gold had led prospectors to the western coast.

Many hours he had watched her playing faro with the men. Although he could not determine how she did it, he knew she cheated. Only that would explain her consistent good luck. She allowed the miners to win often enough to keep them happy. Jerry doubted they would complain even if she took every bit of their gold. The men crowding around her table loved to hear her sultry voice and sharp humor. He had heard more than a dozen men propose to her, but she always refused with such gentleness the man was not offended.

As he stood next to the bar, his eyes followed her soft profile. She was talking brightly to her customers. More times than he cared to remember, he had hinted to her that their relationship did not have to be purely businesslike. She would ignore his words or laugh them away in the same kind manner she refused other offers.

Never did she take a man home from the saloon. As far as he knew, the only one she had shared her house with was Hollister. Jerry was begining to wonder if there had been anything between her and Hollister other than their agreement that he would take her and the boy east.

Even after a month of working for him, Lizzie Buchanan remained an enigma to Jerry. She had eyes as hot as a campfire and an exterior that warned off the most amorous drunk. A lady. That was the only definition he could find, but he was growing tired of waiting for her to understand she had other obligations to her employer.

"Lady Lizzie holding court again?" came a sly snarl next to him.

Jerry looked down at the scowl on Alice's face. "Don't be jealous. It doesn't sit well with your customers."

"Customers? What customers? All of them are busy panting over your royal virgin." She reached into the bodice of her gown and drew out a nearly empty leather bag. "See how little I've made tonight."

"So? Wiggle yourself over to a miner and make him an offer in exchange for his gold." He shrugged aside her concerns. His third of Lizzie's winnings equalled more than the four prostitutes could earn for him. "Gilbert! A bottle!"

"Coming, boss!" Gilbert replied jovially. He placed the dirty bottle on the counter. "You gonna join Lizzie?"

"Everyone else has. Now if I want to talk with my friends, I have to go to her table."

Gilbert ran a damp cloth over the top of the bar as he watched his boss walk to the other side of the room. With Jerry in such a good mood, things ran so much more smoothly in the saloon. That suited Gilbert just fine.

Lizzie smiled at her employer as he sat down opposite her. He declined the opportunity to wager. The other men chuckled as he explained jokingly that he saw no reason to lose his money to her when he was paying her for working there. She didn't lose her light expression as he teased her, but she was concerned by his sudden appearance at her table. In the four weeks she had worked there, he had never approached her during work hours.

She had learned to hold her thoughts inside her as she dealt the cards and collected the losing bets. In the days since Cliff left, she had tried to find something to fill the emptiness in her life and in her heart. Although Stella and Pete helped to ease the bereft feeling, she could find nothing to seal the aching void in her soul.

That she and Cliff could separate as they had after all they had shared seemed ludicrous. She fought the truth, wanting to believe it was all a nightmare. Each night she longed to hear his voice or see his hat on the peg by the door when she entered the house. In addition to her pain, she had to deal with Pete's sense of abandonment. He clung to her screaming before she went to work each night. Everyone else in his life whom he had loved had left him without warning. He feared she would do the same.

Damn you, Cliff Hollister! she thought as she smiled sweetly at the miner on her left. *You had no right to hurt us this way. Pete trusted you. I trusted you.* She handed a winner coins to match the gold he had wagered. *I loved you. I love you still.*

Slowly, slowly the miners drifted away, heading back to their claims, broke and satiated with the many pleasures of the saloon. When most of the chairs in the room were empty, Lizzie stood up and stretched. Hands settled on her waist. She whirled to see the black shirt Jerry always wore. Whether he had more than the one, she was not curious enough to ask.

"It was a good night," she said as she stepped back and put the chair between them. She tried to keep her eyes from the hard muscles revealed by the open neck of his shirt.

"Yes, very good." The thick, pungent smell of whiskey flowed from his mouth as he spoke, and she averted her face. "You've proven to be far more profitable for the Trail's End than even I expected, darlin'."

Knowing she could not put off the inevitable, she turned to face him. "Jerry, I'm going to quit at the end of the week."

"Quit?" he roared. Instantly he recovered his aplomb and apologized for his outburst. In a lower tone he asked, "But why, my dear? You're making a good living here. You have a home for your kid."

"I know, but I also have enough money to pay you the rent through the winter, with enough left over to take Pete and me home." She smiled with gentle regret. "I'm sorry, Jerry. You helped me when no one else would, but this is not my life. Pete needs me. I need him."

He grasped her slender fingers. When she tried to tug them away, he simply pulled her toward him. He did not put his arms around her as she feared he would. Instead he just stared down into her eyes. In a yearning voice, he said, "It ain't easy for a man like me to beg. Stay, Lizzie. You have to be here for the winter anyhow. Please stay here at the Trail's End."

"I can't," she whispered. She closed her eyes as she wondered how much longer she could listen to Alice's taunts without exploding. She did not know how many more nights she could endure the coarse pawing of men who left dirty fingerprints on her dress and choked her with the foul odors of their rancid breaths and more fetid bodies.

"If I make it worth your time. . ."

"It's not the money, Jerry."

"Keep all you win at the table, sweetie. Come into work an hour later. That will give you time with your boy as well as the money to buy him what he needs."

Suspicion warned her to be cautious. "Why are you doing this for me?"

He laughed. The sound ricocheted off the ceiling. "That's the first foolish thing I've ever heard you say. I want you to stay because I like to look at you. I like the money the men spend so freely while you entertain them. You ain't going nowhere, darlin'. You might as well take advantage of the situation you're in."

Although a warning bell clanged in her head, she saw the common sense of his words. They would not be leaving until spring. At the rate she was collecting winnings at her table, she would be able to buy a house in the best section of Louisville or anywhere they wanted to live. Lately she had been thinking of Natchez or New Orleans. There she could open her own gambling hall and live well for the rest of her life.

But not happily.

She forced the stray thought from her head. Cliff Hollister had ruined her past. She would not let him have any impact on her future.

"Very well, Jerry. I'll stay. Until spring."

His too-wide grin stretched across his full face. When he reached to hug her, she put her hands up to halt him. Although he wanted to do far more, he simply kissed her on the cheek. She allowed his lips to touch her skin for only the barest second.

"Good night," she said pointedly. "I'll see you later tonight."

"You'll be in an hour later than your usual time then?"

She nodded and smiled. "An hour later."

Jerry kept his eyes on her as she left the nearly deserted saloon. The first lessening of the dark had not yet turned the sky gray outside. Sunrise would be in an hour. He went to check the cash register. Lizzie Buchanan was proving to be expensive, but he expected she would be well worth it.

The street was emptier than the saloon. With the ease of long practice, Lizzie stepped over a derelict sleeping under the bench by the saloon door, his feet stuck out onto the sidewalk. Such sights no longer shocked her. She had become inured to things that had turned her stomach in Hopeless.

Her feet shuffled along the boards. Each night seemed longer than the one before. When she arrived home after a night's work, the house felt emptier than it had been the previous day. Although she tried to lock her pain deep inside her, it oozed out to torment her. She could not keep her heart from believing Cliff would return, although she knew with each day's passing that it was less and less likely.

When a pair of hands reached out of the darkness beyond the lantern's glow, she could not elude them. Memories of her beating in Joplinville gave strength to her flailing hands and feet. The man holding her grunted in pain as one of her pointed toe boots made contact with him. A fist struck her, and she screamed.

A hand settled over her mouth, silencing her abruptly. "Shut up, Lizzie, or you're dead! Do you understand? Another peep of any kind, and I'll slit your throat. Do you understand?"

He loosened his grip on her enough so she could nod her head. She realized he had dragged her into the solitude of an alley while he spoke. Keeping his hand over her mouth, he shoved her against the wall of the building behind her. An involuntary puff of air exploded from her lips as his rough treatment knocked the breath from her.

Her eyes widened in terror as he growled at her. In the growing twilight of the dawn, she recognized the man as Whittaker, Jerry's errand runner. She had suspected he did far more violent things for Jerry, dealing with unpaid bets and old favors. That part of her employer's business she wanted to know nothing about, for she did not want to be sucked into it.

None of that did she think about as she stared at the man who rivaled his boss in size. His wide hand on her mouth covered her nose as well, making it nearly impossible for her to

breathe. When she felt his fingers slipping down
inside the collar of her dress, she instinctively
tried to shove his hand away. Her efforts proved
as useless as trying to scrape gold from the
mountain walls with her bare hands.

The dress ripped, revealing the lace of her
corset cover. He laughed as he bent to put his mouth
against the curves uncovered above the chemise.
She was unprepared for the violence of his attack
as his teeth sank into her sensitive skin. Her cry
of pain and frustrated rage erupted into the night
before she could halt it.

"I told you to be quiet, woman!" He
removed his hand from her lips. The crash of his
fist against her cheek threw her to the ground. He
leaned over her to strike her again.

Lizzie curled up into a ball as she tried to
protect herself from his insane fury. He did not
seem to care where he hit her. She moaned as his
fist landed near the vulnerable spot on her ribs,
where Cliff had feared one had been broken.

The heavy fists ceased pounding her. She
peeked from beneath the arms over her head to
see Whittaker standing over her. His legs straddled her, and he was reaching for his belt.
Clawing the ground, she fought to get to her feet
and away from his madness. With a laugh, he
stepped on her wide skirt. She used both hands to
try to tug it away. When he reached for her, she
gripped the torn waistband of her dress and
ripped the skirt totally from the bodice.

Leaping to her feet, she heard his bellow of anger. She did not turn as she fled, not caring where as long as it was away from the crazy man waiting to abuse her.

When she bumped into a solid body and felt arms go around her, she screamed again and fought to free herself. Only when they were repeated a third time did she understand the words her captor spoke.

"Lizzie, Lizzie, it's all right now. Look at me, darlin'. Jerry won't let anyone hurt you again."

"Jerry?" she whispered through bruised lips. "Oh, Jerry." She pressed her face against his shirt and felt her legs buckle.

Over her head, he shouted orders, but she did not listen. He scooped her up in his arms just as dark oblivion claimed her. As he carried her to the adobe house, she did not awaken. Although he wished the circumstances were different, he savored the feel of her slender body against him. Through the thinness of her petticoats, he could stroke the lithe line of her leg.

Inelegantly, he kicked on the door. Stella opened it. "Senor Riggins!" she gasped. She could say nothing else.

"Where does Lizzie sleep?"

Not knowing what else to say, she answered truthfully, "Upstairs, first door. The boy sleeps in the second room."

Jerry smiled grimly. "Don't worry, old

woman. I have no intention of waking the kid by raping his aunt. This is someone else's handiwork. I just want her to rest now. Tell her to take an extra hour longer than we agreed on before she comes to work tonight."

"Tonight?" exclaimed Stella as she glanced at the senseless woman.

"Work is the best thing for her." He placed Lizzie on the bed.

In spite of his best intentions, his breath caught in his throat as he saw her clothed in lace. Her soft curves tempted his fingers to caress them. His gaze traveled down her legs sprawled across the covers, and he wondered how they would feel entwined with his.

The not so subtle clearing of the housekeeper's throat brought him back from the fantasy just as he was about to touch the satin-smooth skin displayed before him. He ignored Stella as he bent closer to Lizzie to see the bruises already forming on her face and the teeth marks embedded in her skin.

With a growl, he ordered, "Take care of her. Have her at the Trail's End by eleven. In her blue gown."

"Senor Riggins, that dress—"

He paused in the doorway and raised his sausage-shaped finger in Stella's face. "I know that dress well. If you want to continue working here for Miss Buchanan, make sure she wears that one!"

"*Si*," she mumbled. She added nothing more as she went to the ewer to pour onto a cloth some of the warm water that had awaited Lizzie's homecoming. "Hush, *niña*," she whispered as she gently pressed the cloth against the darkest of the bruises. The pain brought the young woman out of her swoon.

Lizzie glanced up to see Stella tending her. She was home. Just now it didn't matter to her how she had gotten there. In a broken voice, she asked for a glass of water. When the housekeeper handed her a glass, she took a sip and spewed it across the bed.

"Water!" she choked. "I said water!"

"Whiskey will help more. It has already," stated Stella in her most sensible, don't-argue voice. "Are you hurt other than these bruises?"

"That's enough, isn't it?" Lizzie demanded acerbically. Suddenly she relaxed and stared at the canopy of the bed. Tears rolled unchecked down her face. "I'm sorry. I'm fine, Stella. I think I'll get some rest. Perhaps a quiet day will help me get this out of my mind."

"Senor Riggins said you did not have to come in until eleven o'clock."

Lizzie sat up and stared at her friend in astonishment. "He expects me to come to work tonight after—"

Going to the armoire, Stella withdrew the royal blue gown. She draped it over her arm to take it downstairs to be brushed and ironed.

"Yes, and he left very explicit instructions that you were to wear this tonight." Keeping her eyes on the tiled floor, Stella walked out of the room.

Lizzie's hands covered her nearly bare breasts. She did not have to look down to know her assailant had left his mark on her. In that dress, each indentation would be showcased. She shivered as she thought of what Jerry might be intending to do. Although he was far kinder to her than she had any reason to expect, he ran his business with an iron hand. She was sure he was planning something tonight, and he obviously wanted her to be the centerpiece.

Desperately she looked around the room. Her fingers dropped to clutch the covers. Her world had gone insane, taking her with it. The man she loved had deserted her, and another had tried to rape her in a garbage-filled alley. A third coveted her but insisted she parade the signs of her abuse before the patrons of his business.

She trembled again. Jerry controlled her now far more than Cliff ever had. Although he let her have her way in small matters, everything he did was calculated to keep her at the Trail's End. For the first time, she wondered if he would let her leave when spring made traveling safe again.

Burying her head in the pillow, she moaned with the pain of her beaten face. Hot tears scorched the cuts in her skin as she sobbed for the woman she never would be and the dreams two men had effectively stripped from her.

By the time she had to face her nephew, Lizzie had devised a tale about fighting off bad men in the saloon. With mock heroics that would have made Cliff envious, she spun Pete a story about how she had saved the Trail's End. He delighted in her tale and insisted on acting out her wholly fictional feat of swinging through the air from a rope on the stage to protect the cashbox from robbers.

More slowly than usual, she dressed for work. She would not look in the mirror. The tenderness of her face and the memories of her reflection in the looking glass after the beating in Joplinville told her how hideous she must look. She made no attempt to cover the black and purple marks with face powder. Nothing could hide them.

She tugged at the neckline of the blue gown, being careful not to rip it, but she could not cover the telltale bruises on her breast. Taking her rose-colored shawl, she tied it at her right shoulder so that it draped across her and covered the worst of the tooth marks.

When she reached the door of the Trail's End, it swung open. A miner doffed his head and bowed. "Please enter, Miss Lizzie."

"Thank you, Ebenezer." Her brow wrinkled as she wondered what was happening within the saloon.

She gasped as she saw all the miners leap to their feet and clap when she stepped beneath the light of the first lantern. Her heated flush lessened the contrast of the bruises against her skin.

Jerry stepped forward and took her hand. "Welcome, Lizzie. We've been waiting anxiously for you."

"What is going on?" she demanded.

With a grim smile, he said, "You'll soon see."

The timbre of his voice warned her he was pleased with what was about to happen. Renewed fear raced through her. This Jerry Riggins seemed like a stranger. She said nothing of her disquiet as he led her to a seat closest to the stage. When she sat there alone, he jumped onto the raised floor. The bright lanterns highlighted the planes of his face, turning it into a grotesque mask.

"Be seated!" he shouted. "It's time for the trial to begin."

Boots stamping and wild applause met his words. Lizzie glanced over her shoulder to see the faces of the miners distorted with eager anticipation of whatever Jerry had planned. She wanted to leave, but she knew none of them would allow that. Crossing her arms over her chest, she hugged them to her.

Her cry of horror was lost in the renewed shouts as Whittaker was dragged on stage. His face was swollen almost past recognition and both eyes were blackened. From the tatters hanging on his body, she feared he had suffered more than she. Heavy iron shackles bound his hands and feet. A hand on her shoulder kept her in her chair as she was about to leap to her feet.

She glanced up to see the disturbed visage of Gilbert Palmer. In her weeks of working there, she had come to like the gentle bartender. He whispered, "You can't leave, Miss Lizzie. Jerry is determined to go through with it."

"Go through with it? With what?"

Her question was not answered, for her boss shouted again to his enthusiastic audience. "This is the bastard who tried to hurt Miss Lizzie." He leaned forward and lifted her from her chair, ignoring her cry of dismay. His eyes dropped to the shawl she wore. "Untie it!" he ordered.

"Jerry, please don't do this," she begged.

He put his face close to hers. She could see the lust for revenge wiping all sanity from his eyes. "Do it!"

With hands trembling with despair, she slowly undid the silk shawl. He pulled it from her shoulders with a flourish. She flinched as his fingers settled presumptuously on the curve revealed above her dress.

"There!" he shouted. "See for yourself what Whittaker did to our Miss Lizzie. Your verdict, gentlemen?"

"Lynch him!" one voice near the back of the

room answered. Instantly the others took it up as a refrain. "Lynch him! Lynch him! Lynch him!" Feet stamped in rhythm with the shouts.

"No!" cried Lizzie, but no one listened to her.

Jerry pulled her back against him as the miners swarmed onto the stage to grasp the manacled man. Mob fevor ruled. She called for them to halt before they ripped the man apart in their frenzy to drag him outside.

"Stop them, Jerry," she pleaded.

With a laugh, he demanded, "Why? He received a fair trial. He was judged by his peers. It's less than what he deserves for touching my woman." In the excitement of the moment, he dropped the pretense that he was keeping her in the bar simply because she could make money for him.

His eyes glittering with bloodlust, he crushed her to him. The fire on his lips augmented her alarm. The crashing of chairs and tables as the miners dragged the doomed man from the saloon did not concern Jerry as he stroked her intimately. Fear gave her a strength she normally would not have been able to summon.

Breaking his grip on her, she spun away from him. He reached out a long arm and caught her. The sound of her palm striking his face was lost in the swell of noise in the tavern. When he raised his hand, she cowered away from him.

Instead of striking her, he grasped her arm and led her to the door. He handed her the shawl. Tightly, he ordered, "Put it on. It's cold tonight. This may not be over quickly."

"Jerry—"

"Be quiet, Lizzie. You must watch Whittaker swing. He must see you as the rope chokes him."

"I'm going to be sick," she moaned.

"You're going to watch."

The cold air slapped her face harder than she had hit Jerry. Tightening the shawl around her shoulders, she concentrated on keeping her stomach from embarrassing her. She kept her eyes on the ground.

Even then she could not escape. The sounds of the men at work and their shouts told her what they were doing. A thick rope was obtained and flung over the branch of a tree that grew at the edge of the street. Cheers sounded as the noose was slipped over Whittaker's neck. Sitting on a horse, Whittaker, surrounded by torches, had a clear view of his executioners. His curses were muted by his swollen jaw, broken by his boss earlier in the day.

Jerry's broad fingers tilted Lizzie's face up as he shouted a command to the men. More than a dozen pistols pointed skyward. She flinched as they fired all at once. The horse whinnied in alarm and raced into the night past the men, who nimbly leapt out of its way.

The pale smoke from the guns faded in the sky, leaving only the sound of the creaking rope in its wake. More huzzahs were shouted, loudly enough to rouse the honest citizens of Garland Creek on Churchy Street. When Jerry yelled that everyone who had helped would be paid with a free drink, the men surged toward the bar.

He turned the quivering woman toward the opposite end of the street. With his arm around her shoulders, he steered her along the boardwalk. Lizzie leaned against him, fighting her rebellious stomach. Only when they paused did she realize that he had brought her home.

"Tomorrow night, regular time, darlin'."

"Yes, Jerry," she whispered.

"Wear something to cover those marks," he growled. "I don't want to see them again."

"Yes, Jerry."

"Go to bed."

"I will." So sick was she that she was ready to agree with almost anything he said, just to escape from this perversion.

He kissed her chastely on the forehead before he opened the door and shoved her, not ungently, through the doorway. Lizzie clung to the wall as the door closed behind her. She did not look up as she heard Stella's footsteps running toward her from the back of the house.

"Lizzie?"

"I'm going to be sick." Lizzie reeled to the backyard. Kneeling on the frozen ground, she gave up the battle with her stomach.

When the final retch left her weak and trembling, she felt a kind hand under her elbow. She let Stella lead her back into the house and to the parlor. Compliantly she reclined on the settee. A cool cloth on her forehead brought a smile of gratitude to her quaking lips.

"That feels wonderful," she murmured.

"What happened? I heard shots. I thought—"

She closed her eyes and sought the strength to form the horrid words. In a whisper so low Stella barely could make out the words, she said, "They lynched him."

"The one who hurt you this morning?"

Her nod of affirmation made her head ache worse. "They gave Whittaker a mock trial in the Trail's End. Then they took him out in the street and hanged him."

Stella dropped into a chair. Leaning her head on the arm propped on the chair, she murmured, "I'm not surprised—No one dares oppose Senor Riggins. He rules this town, although he's not on the town council. What he wants, he never fails to get."

"He called me his woman," Lizzie said with a resurgence of the terror that had stalked her all day.

"Oh, *dios*! You must leave Garland Creek, Lizzie. If he wants you, the only way you can prevent it is to run."

Painfully Lizzie cried, "But how? The snows have started already. The high passes may be closed or too dangerous to travel through. I can't go with just Pete. No one else would accept my money to help me out of here if Jerry is as powerful as you say. And as I saw tonight." She put her hands over her face and moaned with more than the anguish of her bruises, "How did I ever get involved in this?"

"Cliff Hollister should not have abandoned you here. He should have guessed what Senor Riggins would do."

Lizzie wanted to deny Stella's furious words, but she could not. Cliff had more than guessed. He had known, but he had let her blithely back herself into a corner from which there would be no escape.

Damn you, Cliff Hollister! she thought as she had so many times. I hope you're having a good laugh over this. I hope you rot in hell!

Aloud she said only, "I must think of something, but I can't do it tonight."

"Go upstairs and go to sleep. Maybe tomorrow. . ."

Fatalistically, Lizzie asked, "How will tomorrow be different from today? I'm afraid there may be no escape for me this time."

CHAPTER EIGHTEEN

LIZZIE SOUGHT OUT GILBERT IN THE BACK ROOM of the saloon. She had to speak to someone who knew Jerry well, and she trusted the bartender as she did no one else at the Trail's End.

"Am I interrupting you?" she asked quietly as she opened the door.

He whirled in surprise. "Lizzie! I thought you'd have gone home by now."

"I wanted to talk to you. This is the time you're least busy."

"Come in." He pointed to a box. "Sit down and tell me what's bothering you." Before she could speak, he asked, "It's Jerry, isn't it?"

She grinned wryly. "Is it that obvious?"

"No," he drawled as he leaned against the shelves behind her. Unmarked boxes were jumbled together. He ran his fingers through his thin hair. "I know Jerry, and I'm getting to know you.

447

I doubt if anyone else has taken the time to notice. Not many people care about anyone but themselves in Garland Creek."

"Is it true that Jerry rules this town?"

His lips drew into a straight line. "Are you just learning that? I guess the lynching must have tipped you off. No one came to ask why Whittaker's body was left to hang all night and most of the day." He put his foot on another of the cases. Placing his elbow on his knee, he said slowly, "Jerry came to this town late. He knew he couldn't make a fortune digging for gold, so he decided to take the gold from those foolish enough to spend all their days in the hot sun and their nights in trying to find ways to waste what they found. By loaning money at outrageous interest rates and foreclosing on those who couldn't pay, he's gotten hold of half the valley and intimidated those in the other half."

"And me?"

"You're lucky, Lizzie. He likes you."

She swallowed convulsively. "It's more than that."

"That comes as no surprise. Jerry has a weakness for blonds. Pretty blonds like you make him do crazy things."

"Like paying me so much for working here and doing anything to make sure I don't leave?" When he nodded reluctantly, she rose to pace the room.

Although she had known the truth, she had

tried to escape it by turning her back on it. Now she had no idea what to do. To leave would be suicidal. To stay, insane. When Gilbert urged her to sit, she perched on the very edge of the case.

"If Jerry intended to force his way into your bed, Lizzie, you would have known that by now. He thinks of you as a rare commodity in this state. A lady. Keep up the perfect manners you've shown him till now, and he'll react as he's been doing." He raised his empty hands. "That's all I can suggest. No one will challenge Jerry's claim to you, so it also works to protect you from the miners."

"I can't believe this! Just months ago I was dressed in denims, traveling with Cliff and pretending to be my boys' older brother."

He chortled with delight at the image her short explanation created. His imagination had difficulty dressing her in the uniform of the miners. "Don't let Jerry hear of that."

"I won't!" she vowed fervently. She took Gilbert's work-hardened hand in hers. "Thanks."

"You bet!" He grinned as she laughed.

Lizzie emerged from the storage room feeling much better. Her faith in Gilbert's common sense had not been wasted. He had showed her that her future remained somewhat in her control. If she was smart, she might be able to avoid what she feared Jerry had planned for her.

As she stepped around the bar into the

taproom, she heard the slap of a heavy hand on flesh. A scream sent shivers of horror along her spine. She clutched the bar as she stared aghast at the scene before her.

Jerry was rebuttoning his trousers. His four-inch-wide leather belt was draped loosely on either side of his hips. On the floor in front of him, Alice was lowering her raised skirts with one hand as the other one pressed her left cheek. She spat a curse at him, and his hand struck her again.

"Be silent, woman!" he roared.

"Why?" she taunted daringly. "I'm tired of serving as a substitute for that blond so-called lady you're letting ruin you. If you want her, take her, Jerry. Lady Lizzie could use some heating up to loosen the ice around her."

His blow knocked her back to the floor. "I said, be silent. I don't want to hear her name on your filthy lips." His boot pushed her away from him. "Get out of here."

She struggled to her feet. "You'll be sorry, Jerry Riggins, that you've kowtowed to her. She—" Alice hesitated long enough to take a deep breath as her eyes locked with Lizzie's. With a broad smile, she continued, "She's pining for Hollister, who didn't have to beggar himself to share her bed."

"How do you know she slept with him?" Jerry had come to accept totally his belief that Lizzie's first lover would be himself.

"Hollister told me."

"When you took him drugged and senseless to your bed?" He laughed. "Even he didn't believe that he chose to sleep with you, woman. That was a foolish idea you talked me into. I convinced him that he lost the money, but he never accepted the story of him sharing your bed."

"You bastard!" she snarled. "If you don't believe Hollister, why don't you ask her?"

Lizzie paled to a sickish gray as Alice's pointed finger led Jerry's eyes to her. She wished she could move or think of something to say to relieve the horror of the moment. But her brain remained as frozen as her feet.

Jerry moved toward her slowly. He finished cinching his belt as his eyes pinned her to the wooden surface of the bar. "How long have you been here, Lizzie? I thought you had left for home." His voice was deceptively calm.

"I-I-I was talking with Gi-Gil-Gilbert," she stammered. "I-I just c-c-came in. I'll go now."

His hand gripped her upper arm. "Not yet, darlin'. How long?"

"Just a minute. I didn't mean to eavesdrop on your conversation with Alice."

He smiled coldly. "I'm sure you didn't. Get the hell out of here. Don't ever stay later than your regular hours. Do you understand, Lizzie?"

"Yes," she whispered. All the comfort she had felt from speaking with Gilbert had vanished. "Good night, Jerry."

"See you tonight, darlin'."

She did not answer as she fled from the tavern. Even as she ran out the door, she heard Jerry bellowing for Madge. Her lurid imagination came up with many reasons why he would want to speak to the madam, but she felt she was not depraved enough to comprehend the true Jerry Riggins. She feared she soon would learn enough to do so.

Lizzie leaned over the piece of paper spread across the dining-room table. It crackled each time she moved. Her finger traced a sinuous blue line. "This is Garland Creek. We came this way, through the pass called the Golden Door. Here." She glanced up at Stella with a smile. "I'm glad Mr. Blake made such good maps."

The older woman smiled sadly. "Senor Blake was a fine man, intelligent and kind. His only weakness was gambling. He allowed Senor Riggins to draw him into that disgusting saloon." She choked on the last sentence as she glanced guiltily at Lizzie. The blond had made the same mistake.

"Where is Mr. Blake now? Did he go back east?" asked Lizzie gently.

"He's dead. Killed himself after he lost this house. He went up on the ridge above town and unloaded his pistol into his skull." She sighed as she moved to pour two cups of tea from the kettle steaming on the buffet. " 'Twas a shame. Him being such a good man and all."

"I'm sorry."

Stella shook her head. "Don't be, Lizzie. He did not want to live after he lost everything he had worked so hard to gain. Just before he left to go up there, he told me to remember him fondly. I have."

Not knowing what else to say, Lizzie turned her attention back to the map. Her fingernail traced a shadowed line. "What is this?"

"That was a trail Senor Blake was sure would lead to another lode like the one found here in '49. He never explored it after the first survey.

"Where does it lead?"

She shrugged. "He did not tell me. It looks as if it goes through the mountainside to lead to the lowlands beyond the Sierras."

"Through a mountainside?" She clapped her hands with delight. "If that's possible, it would mean the path won't be snowbound. We could leave any time."

"He did not map it fully. You could be taking yourself and the *niño* to a sure death."

Lizzie's enthusiasm tempered as she stated coldly, "And what do we have here if we don't leave? There are enough supplies in the house to get us through the mountain without needing to buy extra. To go to the general store and purchase those things now would show Jerry what we have planned." She paused. "Do you want to come with us, Stella?"

"No, but I must." She smiled to soften her words. "I have grown fond of the *niño* and of you. You speak of opening your own gambling saloon in the east. You will need someone to watch Pete for you. I can do that."

Lizzie flung her arms enthusiastically around her friend's neck. She realized all that had happened in Garland Creek had not been horrid. When she saw that Stella was embarrassed by her effusive behavior, she bent over the map once more. Her brow furrowed.

"What is that?"

"What is what?" Stella bowed over the yellowed pages.

Lizzie struggled to decipher the words. A pang went through her as she realized Cliff must have used these maps before her. On them he had marked in Cal Feathersong's hut and other similar notations farther east. She guessed he had been plotting his journey and planning to visit his friends.

"Nothing," she answered quietly. She rolled up the map and put it back in its leather-bound holder. "Keep this handy, Stella, but out of sight. Just in case."

"When do we leave?"

"As soon as the weather looks as if it will be clear for the two days it will take to get to the opening in the mountain. I don't want to be caught in a snowstorm in the high reaches."

The housekeeper nodded as she took the map case. "Last winter, a party of surveyors was killed by a snowslide up there. We would be wise to wait as long as we can, toward spring."

"I don't think we have much longer." She bit her lip as she looked out the window of the house, which had become a prison. "Jerry's behavior toward me is changing. I think his patience with my act of pretending I don't understand what he wants is coming to an end. I'll let you know more when I get home in the morning."

Lizzie hurried out of the dining room before Stella could ask any more questions. She did not want to speak of the things she had seen at the saloon in the five days since the lynching.

Jerry had lost his genial-host attitude. The miners tried to avoid him and his sharp tongue. Madge's girls cowered each time he came near them. More than one wore bruises darker than the ones fading on Lizzie's face. She had heard rumors of his rampage through the saloon in the hours after she was banished to the charming house down the street that night.

The thing scaring her most was the alteration in Alice Seeger. The prostitute no longer went out of her way to belittle Lizzie. If they chanced to meet in the bar, Alice mumbled a greeting or scurried away in silence. Her actions convinced Lizzie that Jerry had continued at a later time the conversation she had interrupted.

All this lay beneath the surface of the desperate gaiety of the saloon. Outwardly most things remained exactly the same. The miners came to her table to lose their money and spill their drinks on her gown. The entertainment on the stage was as untalented as before, and the piano player as incapable of playing the simplest tune without gross errors.

Lizzie put her fears from her mind as she entered the Trail's End. If Jerry suspected she was as terrified as she felt, she was afraid he would put his plans into immediate action. Time was her most valuable asset. If she could delay him until blue skies replaced the bank of gray that presently concealed the sun, she, Pete, and Stella could flee and put the depravity of Garland Creek behind them.

"Hello, Gilbert!" she said jauntily to the bartender as she went to draw her starting bank from the cashbox. She kept track of how much she took each evening and paid it back before she left in the morning. "Small crowd tonight."

He nodded as he wiped a glass ceaselessly. His eyes roved around the room. "Don't like it, Lizzie. Something is brewing among the boys. Mayhap it's that rumored strike up near Amador City. The boys don't like the idea of preachers finding all that quartz in the ridge."

"The combine has been working Minister's Claim for more than a year." The claim had gotten its name because a Baptist clergymen and his fellow men of the cloth had found the lode. It irritated the more experienced miners that these amateurs had made a strike they had missed.

"Rumors of a new lode. Already some of the boys have left their claims or sold out to head north."

She grimaced. "Fools! By the time they get there, all the best claims will be taken. they may end up with less than they have here."

Gilbert leaned closer to whisper conspiratorially, "They're also talking about being free of someone's interference in their lives."

Nodding, she took out the amount she needed and walked to the table that had become hers. Although she had many men anxious to play, they were more interested in talking about the supposed strike. She tried to hide her disbelief as the figures of the anticipated take from the ground grew with each retelling of the story by tongues loosened by cheap whiskey. More than a half dozen men vowed to her that they meant to leave with the sun to head north.

One put his arm around her. "Will you miss me, Miss Lizzie?"

"Assuredly," she answered lightly as she pushed him away. "I'll miss the gold you bring to this table."

"Marry me, Miss Lizzie," urged another. "Let me take you up to Amador City and build you a golden palace. I would treat you like a queen."

She smiled. "When you have that gold, come back and I'll give you my answer."

"She's a picky woman. You'll need more than gold to win her heart," came a voice from behind her as broad hands settled on her shoulders.

Instantly all the men sat back in their chairs, leery of being too close to her when her employer stood by her chair. Their smiles faded and then returned, tighter and far less sincere. A half-spoken jest fell heavily into the silence.

Jerry acted as if he did not notice the change in the men at the table or in Lizzie, who sat unmoving. Beneath the table, she clenched her fingers together as she tried to act unconcerned about the stroke of his hands on her bare skin. When a single finger traced the crescent of her ear, she needed all her strength not to leap up and race away in disgust.

Bending, he rumbled in her ear, "I've got to speak to you later, darlin'."

"About what?"

"Later, darlin'," he repeated. Patting her on the head, he walked away to play the host of the saloon.

She craned her neck to follow him with her eyes. Fear ate at her. The sand in the hourglass had flowed to the bottom. She could delay no longer. Whatever the weather proved to be, she had to leave with the dawn—unless it was already too late.

Excusing herself, she rose from the table. She placed her winnings in her pocket and took them to Gilbert. Silently he accepted them and secured them in the cash box. He looked up and asked, "Something else, Lizzie?"

"A whiskey. Please."

"Are you sure? You don't drink that rot-gut."

In a stronger voice, she stated, "Gilbert, a whiskey, please."

He poured barely enough to cover the bottom of the glass and handed it to her. When she glanced from it to him, he smiled sadly, "Start all new bad habits in moderation, Lizzie. That's enough to get you started."

"Thanks."

She put her elbows on the bar as he went to serve a customer. Staring into the mirror, she did not lift the glass. She merely held it in her hand to comfort herself. She was sure that what Jerry planned to discuss with her would be a renegotiating of her oral contract. The terms might prove very difficult for her, but she could not tell him no. She had seen enough of his power in Garland Creek to warn her that outright defiance would be stupid.

"Whiskey, Lizzie?"

"Alice!" she gasped as she turned. At first she had thought it was Madge speaking to her. That Alice Seeger would talk to her in such a pleasant voice shocked her.

"Have a minute?"

"I'm taking a break."

The prostitute put her tray on the bar. "Good. Come with me. We have to talk."

Fearing she was being foolish, she went with Alice to a back staircase. No one noticed as the black-haired woman opened a door beneath it after taking a lantern from the wall. She entered and gestured for Lizzie to follow. With a twinge of disquiet, Lizzie went into the darkness.

When she had closed the door, Alice took Lizzie's hand. "Watch your step. These stone risers are slippery sometimes."

"What is this place?"

"Jerry's other office," came back the cryptic answer with a hollow echo that indicated they were in a large area.

The scratch of a flint preceded a feeble flare. Lizzie blinked in the sudden burst of light. She looked around and saw that her nose had not betrayed her. Dampness clung to the walls and ran along the floor.

"One of the old claims," answered Alice before she could speak. "We can't stay here long. Jerry would easily kill us if he found us here." She smiled coldly. "Even you, Lizzie!"

"Kill us?" Lizzie glanced over her shoulder in horror. "Then why are we here?"

As if there were no danger, the black-haired woman stated, "Because I wanted to tell you something."

"What is it?" Lizzie asked suspiciously.

Alice twisted the hem of her stained dress around her fingers, suddenly looking far younger than her hard life made her appear. In a soft voice, she said, "I don't like you. I'm not telling you this because I've become one of the admirers of Lady Lizzie, our resident virgin." Her mouth twisted as she added bitterly, "I just want to pay back Jerry Riggins for the abuse I've been suffering since you came here. It's all your fault."

"I'm sorry," Lizzie said inanely.

"Hell, you can forget the ladylike act with me, Lizzie. I know you ain't the maiden Jerry thinks you are. Cliff told me he was sleeping with you." She grasped Lizzie's arm as she turned to walk up the stairs. "Hey, let me finish."

Tears glittered brightly in Lizzie's dark eyes. "I've heard enough of your lies, Alice Seeger!"

"That ain't a lie. He did tell me that, but," she added in a rush, "he never slept with me. Jerry set him up from the beginning. Giving him the house, letting him win big, cheating him out of everything."

"Why?" Lizzie asked, although she was thinking only of Alice's admission of what she, Lizzie, had known all along in her heart. Cliff would never have betrayed her like that. Sneaking away to love another woman was not his way. If he had decided to cheat on her, he would do it openly.

"That I don't know, and I don't particularly care. What I brought you here to tell you is to get the hell out of here. Go back to Cliff or find yourself another sweetheart. I'm tired of suffering because of you. Jerry wants you so bad, he's punishing the rest of us because you keep refusing him."

"But, Alice—"

Alice put her hands on her full hips. "Look, Lizzie, I don't care about your problems. I just want to keep my head from being knocked off my shoulders every morning after you leave. I'm giving you this warning. Either be out of here by the end of the week, or I'll have a friend who owes me a big favor go hunting with his rifle for pretty blond ladies."

Determined not to betray her own plans for leaving Garland Creek, Lizzie stated coldly, "I'll leave when and how I want to. You and your threats won't influence my decision."

"Think about it, lady. I mean what I say." She blew out the lantern. "C'mon. Let's get back before we're missed."

By the time Lizzie returned to her table, the men had become restless waiting for her. She told them a weak lie to satisfy their curiosity of where she had been. Glancing about the room as she dealt the cards, she saw Jerry in deep discussion with a man she did not recognize. She bowed her head over the cards when he looked toward her. Although she was sure no one had seen her and

Alice go to the hidden door, she did not want her face to betray her.

The hours of the night passed too quickly. She tried to tease the men into staying longer, afraid of what Jerry would say after the customers had left. It was futile. They were anxious to get back to their claims or to begin the journey north to Amador City.

Trying to appear calm, Lizzie yawned as she rose from counting the money she had won. Several of her admirers had given her a present of extra gold before they kissed her good-bye. She wondered how many would return within a few weeks, poorer and desperate for any gold they could find in a frozen river or along a canyon wall.

She waved halfheartedly to Madge, who was leaving to make sure that all the girls were properly occupied in the rooms reserved for their customers. Tomorrow, Lizzie meant to take Pete to the general store to buy him some new clothes. That would not arouse Jerry's suspicions, but he needed heavier things for the journey. Her old buckskins and denims would have to serve. She did not know what Stella planned to wear. They would have to discuss that as they watched the sun rise.

"Lizzie?"

She pasted a fake smile on her face as she looked at her employer. "Hello, Jerry. It was a good night, wasn't it?"

"Most of them have been since you started here. You draw them like kids to candy." He put his hands on her shoulders and massaged the tight muscles with surprising gentleness.

She tensed immediately as his hands left her shoulders and moved along the bare skin of her arms. "Jerry, I don't think—"

As easily as if she was a child, he lifted her from her chair and turned her to face him. His wide palm cupped her face and held it steady as he bent to kiss her. Instinctively her hand rose to strike him, although the thought of his retaliation terrified her. He caught her wrist in his other hand.

"Jerry, no . . ." Her voice faded into a moan as she saw his face near hers. Closing her eyes, she steeled herself against the assault she expected. She could not stop this massively powerful man from doing as he wished with her.

When his lips lingered briefly against her cheek, she gasped in shock. Her eyes met the hooded emotion in his. He released her and sat on the nearest chair.

"I understand. I should have known a woman like you would never want a man like me."

"A woman like me? What do you mean?"

He smiled sadly. Even while he was sitting, his eyes were not much lower than hers. "You're a lady of class, Lizzie. I'm just a saloon owner, catering to the needs of men tired of eating the dust left over after the blasting. It was just a dream."

Lizzie's heart flipflopped. Here was her chance to speak the truth. Maybe he would listen. "Jerry, I did not intend you to think I wanted anything more than employment here. You're my friend, and I cannot thank you enough for what you have done for me."

"Then marry me, Lizzie."

"Marry you?" she gasped. That was the last thing she had expected. That the desire she had seen in his eyes was an offshoot of true love she had not considered. Neither did she believe it. He hoped to appeal to her in this way, but why he wanted to make her his wife, she could not guess.

When he pulled her closer to him, she wanted to flee. He smiled broadly as he forced her to sit on one of his stump-sized legs. Her wide skirts flowed over him as he tilted her mouth beneath his.

Lizzie put her hands up to break his hold. When she touched the naked skin of his chest revealed by his open shirt, she started to draw them back. He tightened his hold on her until she could not move out of his grasp. He leaned her back against the sharp edge of the table so his mouth could travel along the skin bared above her dress.

"Jerry, no!"

He glanced down into her frightened face. "I hope that wasn't the answer to my marriage proposal. Darlin', from the moment you walked in here, I haven't been able to get you out of my mind. I admit it was to keep you here that I offered you this job."

"And it has proven profitable for both of us," she said. "Why don't we just leave our business partnership as it is? It's worked well so far."

His eyes twinkled with amusement. "And that's why I want you to stay with me, Lizzie. With your talent at the card table and my business sense, we could own half of California within a year."

"I don't want to own California. I want to go back east where I belong." She clung to the old tale. "I can't marry you, Jerry, for many reasons. I do appreciate your kindness in asking me, but I must tell you no."

His face contorted with rage, and his fingers squeezed her cheeks between them. "So you still love Hollister?"

"I don't know if I love Cliff, but I don't think I care enough about you to marry you."

He lifted her off his lap but didn't release her. As he stood up, her eyes followed him to his full height. He regarded her coldly. "I suggest you go home and look at that child you're so fond of, darlin'. I recall he was sick a while back. It would be a true shame if he had a relapse."

"Are you threatening me?" she cried. "You would use Pete to force me to marry you?"

"Not force, Sweetie. I just want you to see the facts as they are. The choice is yours. I'll let you have until tomorrow night to give me your decision. The parson will be here then, and it would be nice to have the bride here as well."

Lizzie stared at him, speechless with shock. She had not anticipated he would want to marry her. Prepared to deal with his plan to make her his mistress, she knew she had no more time to think of how to escape Garland Creek. She had to leave now.

"Think about it," he urged when she did not speak.

Silently she nodded. Anything she could say would enrage him. She had a day and a half to escape. They would have to be careful, for she guessed Jerry would keep his spies watching her all the time. Perhaps tomorrow night when she took her break from the card table. She could sneak out of the saloon and meet Stella and Pete. No one would expect her to leave then.

She smiled tightly. "I'll think about it, Jerry. I promise you that."

With a roar of victorious laughter, he swept her to him again. As he kissed her, her mind fought to solidify the plan she would have to make perfect. They would not be granted a second chance.

CHAPTER NINETEEN

FURIOUS ACTIVITY FILLED THE HOUSE AS THE TWO women tried to pack all they could carry for the desperate journey. Food and warm blankets were stored in the small closet off the kitchen. They tried to keep Pete from guessing what they were doing. With his young innocence, they feared he would inadvertently betray them if someone came to the house. Keeping him busy with the project of stacking kindling in the parlor, they scurried to do their tasks.

Lizzie checked her funds and realized she had left the week's winnings at the Trail's End. That morning Jerry had so upset her, she forgot to take her money from the cash box. That problem could be solved easily. She had overheard him speak of an important meeting that would keep him busy all morning. She would go and get the money while everything was quiet in the saloon. If someone noticed her, she would use the lie that she needed it to purchase things for her upcoming wedding.

"Be careful," warned Stella needlessly.

"I will." The heartfelt vow revealed her fear more loudly than any other words.

The ceaseless cold wind swirled her skirts as she walked along the street. Her velvet mantilla was not sufficient for this cold, but her only other winter clothes were the buckskins Cliff had purchased for her. They were packed in the small closet with their supplies.

She bent her head into the wind and held the hood close to her chin. If she passed anyone on the street, she did not look up. Everyone either stayed inside or did their business as quickly as possible on these raw days.

Inside the saloon, she drew back the lace-trimmed mantle so that she could see. She didn't unbutton the cloak over her shoulders, for she did not intend to stay long. Going to the bar, she reached over it for the cash box. Her fingers found nothing.

With a curse, she asked herself how she could be so stupid. Jerry would not leave that money unguarded here in the saloon. She wondered if he kept it in his office. Perhaps Gilbert would know where it was. She guessed he would be working in the back room.

"Hello, Lizzie. Imagine finding you playing hostess in a saloon!"

She whirled as she heard the sarcasm in the drawling voice. Her hands gripped the bar behind her as her eyes met those of Sam Winchester.

"How—how did you find me?" she whispered. "We thought you were going straight to Missouri."

He swaggered toward her. The streaks of light from the shuttered windows created a pattern of stripes across his face. His red hair gleamed in the thin winter sunshine. His smile broadened as she moved away from him in time with his steps.

"I have been nearly there, gal. Hollister's friends sent me back on a chase to find you four." He licked his lips as he lustfully appraised the curves visible beneath her short cape. "You sure do look good, Lizzie. I always figured there was more under those rags you wore than anyone else saw."

"What do you want?" she glanced desperately around the room, but at this time of day no one came into the saloon.

He grinned as he saw her expression of horror as she discovered he had backed her into the far corner of the bar. "Why gal, you know what I want. I want you, Lizzie Buchanan. You owe me for making me look like an ass before my friends."

"You are an ass, Sam!" she snapped recklessly.

Ignoring her comment, he asked, "It's still Buchanan, isn't it? Hollister never married you, I guess."

She tried to edge past him, but he put out a muscular arm to block her path. Knowing her best course of action was to delay him in carrying out whatever he had planned, she smiled coldly. "No, Cliff and I chose to part ways."

"He got what he wanted from you and left you here?" Sam laughed heartily. "Just like everyone said he would. Hell, Lizzie, I thought you at least would get out of California before he convinced you to share his bed. Where is your dear friend?"

"I don't know," she said without a sign of the pain she was feeling. "He's been gone for several weeks. We're doing fine without him."

"You cut your hair."

"I didn't think I needed your permission." She tried to look past him. If Gilbert was in the back room or Madge in her office, one of them should hear voices in the saloon and investigate.

Sam's fingers smoothed the curls on her head. When she tried to pull away from him, he gripped her at the nape of the neck. His voice became heavy with rage. "Where are the brats?"

"Pete is at home with my housekeeper. Tommy is dead."

"Dead?" He paused as he prepared to spit an insult at her. As much as he detested the children, he had not expected one to be killed on this aborted journey east. Shaking himself, he smiled. That made it much simpler. In his gloating voice, he asked, "You have a house-keeper, Lizzie? No wonder your skin is so soft. You have someone to do the work you'll be doing for me."

She laughed, but only bravado fueled her voice. "You've been out in the sun too long, Sam. Go home. I won't go back to Hopeless with you. I wouldn't cross the street by your side."

With a growl, he pulled her head back. His mouth captured hers as he wrapped his arms around her slender figure. So tightly did he pull her to him that her skirts belled out behind her. The sensation of her warm curves against the travel-hardened line of his body urged him to do as he had desired too long.

Lizzie fought him, but with his arms clamped around her, she could not free herself. When she tried to turn her mouth from his, he used one hand at the back of her head to press it bruisingly against him. She screamed when he pushed her against the rough wall so he could free his fingers to explore her. The shrill sound was muted by his mouth.

"Let her go!"

In astonishment, Sam glanced over his shoulder. He smiled as he saw Gilbert standing behind him. In the slim man's hand rested his favorite pistol. Releasing Lizzie, Sam acted as if he would allow her to move past him. When she stepped around him, he wrenched her in front of him. A bare blade appeared before her eyes.

"Lizze is where she should be," Sam snarled. "Now why don't you get out of my way, so I can take her back where she belongs?"

Gilbert retorted, "I don't know who you are, Mister, but Lizzie belongs here at the Trail's End. Let her go."

A sharply hissed warning in her ear ordered her to stop moving or he would slit her throat. Lizzie froze, afraid Sam would do as he threatened. He smiled broadly as the hand around her waist moved upward to caress the softness of her breast. In Gilbert's eyes she could see the reflection of her own revulsion, but she didn't dare to move.

"Who are you?" demanded her captor."

"Gilbert Palmer. I work for Jerry Riggins. He owns this place." His voice grew less hard as he saw the pain on the face of the woman. "Lizzie works for him too."

"Palmer, I think you'd better put that gun on the floor very carefully. You seem like a nice man. You wouldn't want to be the cause of me having to kill this pretty lady, would you?"

"Listen to the man, Gilbert."

Lizzie felt a swell of hope bursting within her as she looked across the dark room to see Jerry coming from the shadows. His obvious lack of fear of the man holding her comforted her. Jerry would protect her, if for no other reason than he wanted to abuse her himself.

Cursing under his breath, but knowing he had no other choice, Gilbert did as his boss directed. He hesitated when Jerry ordered him out of the saloon but hurried away as the huge man stepped toward him.

At the door he paused. "Don't let him hurt her!"

"Lizzie will be fine." Jerry laughed as the door closed.

She stiffened in Sam's arms when he began to laugh with Jerry. He drew his knife away from her throat and placed it in a sheath on his hip. One strong hand still held her arm. He leaned casually against the bar but didn't release her.

"How are you doing, Riggins?" he asked in a friendly tone.

"Just fine. Business is brisk, mostly because of Lizzie here."

No longer could she remain silent. She looked from one smiling face to the other. There could be no doubt. These two men knew each other. All her hopes died, but she could not let them act as if she was incidental to their meeting.

"Jerry!" she cried. "Tell him to let my arm go. He wants to take me back—"

"Hush, woman!" Jerry snapped, using the tone in which he spoke to his other employees but never had to her. He turned his eyes back to Sam. "Where's my money?"

"About that, Riggins, I think we have to

renegotiate."

The large man's face twisted with rage. He raised his stone-hard fists threateningly. "Look, Winchester, I've done all the work on this. I got rid of Hollister and kept her here. She's cost me dearly. Every time she threatened to leave with her kid, I increased her wages until she takes more than she brings into the Trail's End."

Lizzie listened to his words in complete disbelief. She had never suspected Jerry of such subterfuge. Egotistically, she had been sure he wanted her simply to bed her. She had allowed him to trap her in her own foolishness. Why he had done all that she still had no idea.

A growl in her ear wrenched her from her inner thoughts of self-incrimination. Sam stated, "You just said she's helped your business. I think you've gotten all you deserve from my woman."

"Don't let him do this," begged Lizzie. "Jerry, you said you wanted to marry me. If you care at all for me, don't let him do this!"

"Marry her?" Sam's growl became a roar. "Were you going to double-cross me?" He released Lizzie. She started to race away, but he caught her arm again. She screamed as she saw he had his pistol in his hand. With a sharp jerk, he brought her back against him.

Jerry froze as he saw the weapon. Sam ignored his warning to be calm and not do something stupid. The man holding Lizzie simply laughed louder as the saloon owner's wide face washed clean of any color.

"Shall I do to your new lover what you once threatened to do to me?" Sam taunted with a guffaw of outrageous glee as he aimed his gun lower."

She shook her head and murmured in a quivering voice, "Don't kill him, Sam. He's not my lover. He is—was my friend."

"Like Hollister?" When she didn't answer, he stepped toward the door. The gun never wavered.

Jerry's eyes remained on the pistol as he held his hands up and away from his gun belt. He knew how little were the chances of aid. All the miners would be stuck on their claims during this inclement weather. He had made sure no one would be here today during the time this meeting had been arranged. That Lizzie had come to the saloon was the one thing he had not planned.

"I'll go with you. Don't kill him," repeated Lizzie as she saw the gun rise to take aim on the unarmed man by the bar.

The explosion richocheted off the low beams to crash over her and again. Sickness filled her middle as she watched Jerry slammed against the uneven surface of the bar. He leaned drunkenly on it and gaped stupidly at the blood flowing from his stomach. She moaned as he fell face forward to the floor. He did not move as Sam pushed her through the door.

Along the street shouts sounded as the

townspeople reacted to the single shot in the saloon. Sam did not hesitate as he lifted her into the saddle of the waiting horse. He mounted behind her and kept her from escaping. With a roared order to his steed, they raced along the street. People coming to see what had happened at the saloon leapt aside. Several pointed at the captive woman, but the riders were out of sight before anyone could do anything.

"Cheer up, Lizzie. After all, you don't have to marry Riggins now."

She glanced at Sam and then away. Her face was tight with frozen tears. She could not pretend she had loved Jerry. Toward the end, she had not even liked him. But dying that way was not what she would have wished for him.

Wrapping her arms around herself, she stared at the campfire. In her thin dress and mantle, she was slowly freezing. She knew better than to mention that fact to Sam. He would be sure to offer a suggestion of how she could be much warmer.

From her study of the map, she guessed he was taking the most direct route across the mountains back to Hopeless. They had been traveling without a break since they'd sped out of Garland Creek. Even when darkness fell, Sam did not stop until he had found this overhang to protect them from the wind.

Lizzie had not moved far from where he had

placed her by the fire. Although Sam had
snowshoes he could use, she knew how impossible it would be to navigate the snowdrifts that
would be higher than her waist in many spots.
She thought of the dangers she had discussed
with Stella as they planned their escape from
Garland Creek. Over and over they had reassured themselves by saying that at least they
would not have to travel into the highest snow-
fields.

"Don't you want to ask me how I found
you?" Sam jeered.

She shook her head. "I'm not particularly
curious."

Angrily, he pushed his face close to hers.
"Your games won't help you this time, woman.
You're mine now. No Hollister is around to help
you. I've been halfway across this continent
looking for you, and I won't be goaded into
letting you escape me this time."

"What are you doing?" she demanded as he
grasped her wrists and pulled them behind the
tree she had been sitting against.

"What does it feel like?" He laughed. "I'll
be much happier if I know you're not going to
run away again."

"I'll freeze if you leave me out here all
night!" She struggled to keep him from tying her
hands together, but he managed to do so with
little difficulty.

He shook his head as he stood up and

looked down at her. "You'll be fine, dearie. A bit cold, but that'll teach you to obey me."

"Sam!" she cried as he walked away from her. He sat down on the far side of the campfire.

Lizzie watched in silence as he made a meal from the supplies he was carrying on the back of his horse. It did not surprise her that he didn't offer her any of the warm stew. The smell drifted toward her. She heard her stomach grumble, but she tried to ignore her hunger. Sam would not let her freeze or starve. He intended to break her to his will with his cruelty.

Within minutes her arms began to ache. He had tied them far tighter than necessary. She was sure he had done so purposely. Bringing her knees up, she rested her forehead on them until her back cramped with pain. She straightened up and leaned her head back against the prickly bark. Even that position was comfortable for no more than five minutes.

When Sam glanced in her direction and chuckled, she bit her lip to restrain her desire to shout curses at him. She would not beg him to release her. The cost of that would be too high. Why he had not raped her yet she didn't know, but she would not bring the horror upon herself any sooner than necessary.

She listened as he spoke. "I don't think we'll stop in Hopeless. I think we'll go directly to San Francisco. It'll be a good place for a honeymoon."

"Honeymoon?" She could not understand why Jerry and now Sam wanted to marry her.

"Why not?" He laughed as he held a large piece of meat on the end of his knife. Chewing it inelegantly, he mumbled around it, "That'll give you a chance to prove to me that I should keep you around. If you don't, I can sell you for a good price into one of the bordellos there. They would all be interested in a pretty blond like you. I could get a good price for you if I held an auction."

"I'm not your slave! You can't sell me!"

He chuckled. "You haven't been to Frisco, honey. Anything is possible there. The owners of the brothels will be intrigued with you. Whichever one buys you will figure out a way to keep you so busy you'll have no chance to run away." He laughed again. "If you doubt me, I can prove it to you soon enough when we get there."

Not answering him seemed the safest thing, so she lowered her eyes. His chortles surrounded her, taunting her with his triumph. Her confusion continued to grow. Sam showed little interest in her but had chased her since she left Hopeless.

Why?

He wouldn't tell her, and she couldn't guess. Leaning her head back against the tree, she squirmed until the mantle and her skirts covered her as best they could. Although they afforded little protection from the cold, they were the only things she had. She did not share Sam's optimism that she would not freeze to death there.

She sighed. She had been afraid there would be no escape from Jerry. About that she had been wrong, but her release had brought her only into a more horrible captivity. Separated from all her allies, she wondered if she could devise a way on her own to flee.

Sam woke Lizzie as the sun glowed rose on the peaks of the easternmost mountains. He unbound her hands, shoved some dry cornbread into them, and then retied her wrists in front of her. Before she could take a bite, he lifted her onto his horse.

"Cause me trouble, Lizzie," he growled, "and you'll be very sorry."

Irritably she snapped, "I'm sorry now." She had not been able to sleep until late into the night. Her head ached with a steady pulse that resonated throughout her body. The ropes around her wrists had made her skin raw.

When the horse lurched into motion, she grasped the saddle horn. She clutched it all during the long day. Sam led the horse slowly along the snow-thick trail. He used his snowshoes but carried a stick to test the depths of the drifts. More than once he cautioned her to silence as they passed an area ripe for a snowslide.

Lizzie did not fight him on that one matter.

She wanted to emerge from this nightmare alive. Foolishly getting them killed would not help Pete. She thought of him often, comforted that Stella would safeguard him until Lizzie could find a way back to Garland Creek. The higher they went into the mountains, the more she feared she would never see him again.

For four days they traveled in the same manner. Usually the sun shone, but often the wind would ship the loose flakes into a blinding tempest around them. More than once, Lizzie could not see Sam ahead of her on the trail.

Each night he tied her to a convenient tree after allowing her a quick meal. She became accustomed to the cold and the discomfort but longed for the opportunity to be warm again. She wondered if she would ever be able to thaw out the center of her bones.

She continued to be surprised that Sam did nothing but verbally abuse her. Although he could have subdued her at any time, he showed no desire to do so. When he spoke to her, it was of the fine life they would live in the city. How he planned to finance that life, he refused to tell her. He would laugh and turn away each time she tried to discuss it.

With her head against the tree trunk, she counted the stars she could see between the bare branches. She had submerged the true Lizzie beneath the desire to survive. Even though the food Sam gave her was often burnt or raw, she ate it. She knew how important it was to maintain her strength. Sam would not hesitate to kill her if she caused him too much trouble. He had made that clear from the onset of their journey through the high passes.

Slowly, as she counted the twinkling lights, her eyes closed. Sleep had become a precious commodity. Never could she get enough. That night she was so exhausted, it did not take her as long as usual to fall asleep in her cramped position.

"Lizzie?"

She woke to star glow as she heard her name whispered. Raising her head, she looked in every direction but saw no one. She told herself she'd head the familiar voice only in her imagination and leaned back against the trunk again. A hand on her shoulder brought a gasp of shock from her lips. The fingers moved to cover her mouth.

"Hush, half-pint."

Her whisper of "Cliff!" warmed his palm as he emerged from behind the tree. She nodded when he put his finger to his lips. Looking beyond him, she saw that Sam had not moved in his bedroll.

Although a thousand questions boiled in her brain, she waited patiently as he slit the ropes binding her. She held out her hand for the knife. Without asking her why she wanted it, he placed it in her hand. A few quick motions cut the thickness of her skirts and petticoats. Then she lashed them to her legs with the sliced pieces of rope. Only in that way could she run through the trees and thick snow without creating the noise that would signal her escape.

Cliff smiled his beloved, irreverent grin as he held out his hand to her. Rising, she let him lead her through the moonlit trees. She slipped the knife into her belt to use if she had to readjust her skirts.

She had more difficulty than she expected walking through the deep snow. When they reached the frozen surface of a slumbering creek, he gestured to her to step carefully onto it. She smiled as she realized how he would keep Sam from trailing them.

In the snow their journey was marked by each footprint. On the ice there would be no telltale signs to show where they had gone. She watched silently as he walked a few feet in one direction, then backward toward her.

"Maybe that will fool your boyfriend," he whispered with a soft chuckle.

She wrapped her arms around him and pressed her face to his night-chilled buckskins. "Cliff, I can't believe you're here with me."

Tilting her face up, he kissed her lightly. "Later, half-pint. Let's put some of this godforsaken real estate between us and Winchester."

Lizzie wanted to sing out her happiness as she walked with him toward the east. He cautioned her to take small steps and not to make slide marks that might be seen by an observant tracker. She followed his method of walking nearly on tiptoe. Although she was exhausted, the joy of discovering that Cliff had returned for her set her adrenaline going and gave her the strength to continue.

As the rising sun colored the sky, he did not pause. They followed the twisting course of the river, although it no longer led directly east. He constantly looked from one shore to the other, but she did not know what he sought.

"Finally," he breathed as the morning sky was turning blue. He paused by the huge boulder. "Listen, half-pint. This is very important. See the rock past this one? Step from this one to that one and on to the one after that. We don't want to let Winchester see where we left the river."

"I understand."

"I thought you would." He caressed her cheek, rosy with the cold. "You always were a damn good partner on the trail, half-pint."

She smiled as he lifted her onto the stone, which stood as high as her shoulder. Nimbly she negotiated the course he had pointed out. She waited on the last boulder until he caught up with her. They were now more than fifty feet from the ice. Only the most trained eye could follow them now. They gambled that Winchester would not get wise to their trick.

Silently she watched as he stepped on the

snowshoes he had worn on his back. Involuntarily she gasped as he swung her into his arms. She placed her arms around his neck and leaned her head against his chest. As if she weighed nothing, he walked easily through the trees.

Her eyes widened as she saw the shelter made from branches. Cliff chuckled as he said, "Welcome home, half-pint. It isn't fancy, but I imagine it's better than anything you enjoyed with Winchester.

"How long have you been trailing us?"

He smiled. "I caught up with you yesterday when Winchester's horse balked fording the creek. I simply waited until nightfall to collect what is mine. While you rode on ahead, I built this lovely abode for us. Don't you want to see the inside?"

"Is it warm?" she teased.

"I can be very, Lizzie." His eyes glowed with love as he lowered his mouth to cover hers.

As if the weeks of separation had never happened, her desire leapt into life as she touched the skin at the back of his neck. Slowly he lifted his lips and smiled. She stroked his cheek, rough above his beard.

"I'm sorry for everything, half-pint."

"Me too. Cliff, Alice explained how she and Jerry—"

"Hush, honey. It doesn't matter. All that matters is that you're here with me."

She shivered as a cold gust swirled around

them. Pertly she asked, "Can we continue this conversation inside?"

"We can continue whatever you wish inside."

He lowered her to the snow. She sank in nearly to her knees. As she struggled to reach the shelter, he laughed. He followed her into the shelter. Unhooking his snowshoes, he stuck them in the snow by the entrance, which was covered with a blanket.

Lizzie was impressed by the small shelter. Cliff had dug into a snowdrift so there was enough room inside for them to stand upright. The floor was about eight feet across. In the center was a fire pit where embers still glowed. She dropped to her knees to hold her stiff fingers to the heat.

"Oh, that is so wonderful!" she exclaimed. "Sam never let me near the fire."

Hands stroked her upper arms as he said softly against her ear, "What did he do to you?"

"Nothing."

"Nothing."

She laughed. "You don't have to sound so disappointed."

"I'm not disappointed. Simply shocked." He dropped to the ground next to her. He put a few sticks of kindling on the fire and stirred it till it burned a little brighter. "If I had you to myself in these mountains, I—"

"Don't, Cliff!" The pain in her voice cut

through him.

He brought her to rest against him. "Sorry. Let's talk of something else. Are you hungry?"

"Yes," she said enthusiastically.

"I don't have much, but we can survive until we get down into one of the valleys."

He offered her a slice of stale bread. To her, it tasted like the greatest delicacy. While she chewed the dry meal, she asked, "How did you find me?"

"Easy. Winchester didn't try to hide his trail."

She thanked him for the cup of warm water, then said, "That's not what I meant. Why, Cliff? Why are you here?"

His fingers reached to caress her cheek. "I was five hundred miles east of here before my anger went away. It took two hundred more for me to realize how empty that open country was without you by my side, half-pint. I turned Shadow around and headed back to Riggins' Saloon."

"Jerry is dead?" She couldn't help making it a question but knew how foolish her prayers had been when he nodded.

"Even Winchester couldn't miss at that range. Palmer identified the man who took you as Winchester. I went to the house and found Stella watching over Pete." He frowned as he mused, "She didn't seem surprised that I was at the door. Just told me what had happened and in what direction Winchester was heading when he galloped out of town with you. Palmer will watch over them until we get back there."

She smiled as she brushed crumbs from her ruined dress. "She'll never admit she didn't think you would come back."

"And you? Did you doubt me?"

"Yes," she whispered, "I doubted it. I've never loved anyone as I love you, Cliff. I had been afraid to risk my heart, but this time I gambled on you. It was a wager I thought I had lost."

Drawing her into his arms, he leaned her back onto a blanket on the floor. "Half-pint, I've never known you to bet unless you'd arranged the odds purely in your favor. You must have sensed my love for you."

"I think I suspected it once or twice." She laughed as he licked the half-moon shape of her ear. "That tickles!"

"I would be glad to tickle every inch of you, my love."

She stroked the thickness of his dark beard. "I love you, Cliff Hollister."

"Marry me, Lizzie?"

"Marry you? Just like that?" Her sharp questions covered her shock at his proposal, about which she had fantasized since she met him. So many times she had thought it would never be reality.

His eyes glittered like dark jewels. He

renewed his intimate acquaintance with her lips. When he felt the sweetness of her desire, he smiled. Between fiery kisses along her skin, he whispered, "Do you want a long proposal on bended knee, my love? How much nicer it is to lie here with you in my arms and speak the words with our bodies entwined! Marry me, Lizzie. I love you, and you know I love Pete."

"You loved him before you loved me."

"Not true." He laughed. "I loved you from the moment I saw you, half-pint. I simply spent the past three years trying to forget the one woman I wanted and let elude me." His voice softened as he said again, "Marry me, Lizzie, and be with me forever."

"Yes," she whispered before he stripped her breath from her. She melted into the fire of his kisses and knew she had found everything she wanted. If they could escape the cruely of the mountains, they would collect Pete and Stella and be a family again.

CHAPTER TWENTY

THE SUNSET TURNED THE SNOW THE SAME BLOOD color as the sky. As the wind dropped to a teasing breeze, a chill settled on the mountainside. Lizzie had changed into the buckskins Cliff had brought from the house in Garland Creek. She smoothed the thick material against her and enjoyed the ease of movement the outfit provided her.

Securing the knife on her hip beneath her long shirt, she pulled her boots on her feet. Her satin slippers had disintegrated after she'd taken a few steps in the snow. Cliff wandered in and out of the shelter as he made preparations for the next leg of their journey. Each time he entered on a puff of cold air, he paused to kiss her.

"Are you sure you need to come in so often?" she teased.

"It's cold out there," he retorted. "A man needs something to keep him warm on a night like

491

this."

"How about a woman?"

He leaned her back on the floor. The blanket was rolled up and in his pack. "I thought my kisses warmed you as well, half-pint."

Opening her mouth to reply, she halted as she saw a figure move beyond Cliff. She struggled to sit up, but he thought she was only teasing him. He laughed until she cried, "Cliff, it's Sam!"

Cliff rolled over to face the barrel of Winchester's gun. His curse resonated through the shelter. When he moved to put himself between Lizzie and the weapon, the click of the trigger sounded loudly in the small building.

"Move, Hollister. Give me a chance to put an end to your miserable life." Sam grinned at Lizzie's colorless face. "Dearie, you're going to have to learn that you're mine."

"I—"

"Shut up!" he commanded. "Shut up, or Hollister is dead now!"

Lizzie clamped her lips closed. Her wide eyes watched as Sam came into the shelter, overfilling it. He ordered her to take a piece of rope he tossed her and bind Cliff's hands, warning her he would check her work. If she did not tie him well, she would have a chance to practice on his corpse.

"In front of him!" Sam snapped. "I want to see where his hands are at all times."

She looked into Cliff's eyes as she straddled his legs to do as Sam ordered. "I'm sorry if this hurts," she whispered.

"Don't worry. Take care of yourself."

"Cliff—"

Sam interrupted her by grabbing her shoulder and dragging her away from Cliff. Warning her to sit quietly, he kept his gun trained on the other man. He knew he could control Lizzie best by threatening Hollister.

"The great hero," he taunted. "That's what you wanted to be, isn't it?"

Cliff smiled. "With you playing the role of the villain, I have had plenty of opportunity. Why do you want Lizzie so badly? Sure, she's pretty. Sure, you wouldn't mind having her share your claim, but why chase all the way to Missouri for her? There are other women. What makes her different?"

"One hundred thousand dollars." He smirked as he reached into an interior pocket. Withdrawing a folded paper, he laughed. "She's worth one hundred thousand dollars."

"One hundred thousand dollars?" repeated Lizzie. She leaned her head back against the tree trunk that made up one side of the shelter. "Sam Winchester, what are you talking about? I don't have that kind of money."

He tossed the paper into her lap. Motioning with the gun, he urged, "Read it."

She lifted the page carefully. In the dim light of the sunset, she held it close to her eyes to make out the flowery handwriting. Her lips moved as she struggled through the words; then her eyes widened.

"Where did you get this? This is Zach's will."

"The miner you sold your claim to discovered

it underneath a floorboard. He tried to get the money for himself, but the banker in San Francisco wouldn't listen to him. Knowing he couldn't get the money, he brought the will back to Hopeless. He was going to offer it to you, Lizzie, for a share of the money. Unfortunately, he met with an accident. It was left up to me to bring it to you."

"Lizzie, what does it say?" asked Cliff softly. That Winchester had murdered more than once did not surprise him.

In a hushed voice, she read it aloud. The page was more than a will. It told the story of an obsession money could not satisfy.

Shortly after arriving in Hopeless, Zach had made a trip to San Francisco for some supplies that were unavailable in the small settlement. He had met a friend from his keelboat days. Three days and nights of gambling in the saloons netted them a small fortune. The friend used his to buy a mountain claim, but Zach left his money with a banker to be invested. Once a year, the man in San Francisco sent him a report on the value of his money. The winter before he and Whitney died, when they had been eking out a meager living on the north ridge, the report came that the properties bought in the city had increased in value to well over one hundred thousand dollars.

" 'If something should happen to me and my beloved wife,' " she read, " 'the property must go to Lizzie Buchanan. She will take care of our boys properly. Lizzie, I know you have hated California since you arrived. This is my way of paying you back, for it was the cash left to you by your father that got us here and helped us stake our claim. God bless you. With all my love, your brother, Zachery Marcus Greenway.' "

"You're a very wealthy woman, Lizzie," said Sam as he snatched the page from her hand, "but you need someone to help you manage those riches."

She didn't listen to him. Instead she was thinking of the sacrifice her sister had made by going to work for Delilah. While Whitney sold herself to buy them food, there had been plenty of money in a bank on the western bay. In confusion, she gazed at the ground, wondering why they had fought to survive when they could have been living in comfort.

The answer was simple. Zach had never lost his burning desire to steal the gold from the ground. Even wealth obtained in other ways was not good enough. All that mattered to him was striking it rich by himself. His dream had destroyed his wife, his son, and his own life as well.

A hand under her chin brought her head back harshly against the wall. She groaned as she focused her eyes on Sam's superior smile. She tried to stand up and move away from him, but his wide hands held her to the ground.

"You'll never see a copper of that money!" she spat.

"Really?" He stroked her face, ignoring the growl of the man behind him. "I see you in a fine house on one of the hills of San Francisco. You'll sleep in a bower of scarlet silk and be waited on by a bevy of well-trained servants." His hand slipped along her neck to the neckline of her shirt. A single finger loosened the ties holding it closed. "You'll have nothing to do, Lizzie, but pleasure your man when he comes home from overseeing your holdings."

She batted his hand away. "You're insane! I won't marry you."

Sam chortled with glee. "Marry? I've decided not to marry you. I don't want you forever, woman. Only as long as it takes to convert those properties into cash and enjoy it."

"If you don't marry her," said Cliff softly, "you can't touch her money."

"Cliff!" She stared at him as if he had become insane. Why was he trying to convince Sam to marry her? Forced to be his mistress would be horror enough, but she could hope for escape. If she became his wife, she would never be able to flee from his cruel domination.

Pinching her cheeks between his fingers, Sam forced her to look back at him. Although he glared at her, his words were directed at Cliff. "I don't have to marry her. She'll sign her property over to me." He raised his gun and pointed it at the other man. "You will, won't you, Lizzie?"

Quickly she nodded. "It's yours, Sam, if you release Cliff and don't kill him."

"You'll sign it over to me, won't you, Lizzie?" Her eyes followed his as he glanced from his gun to Cliff.

She didn't hesitate. "Tell me what to do, and I'll sign it now."

Sam laughed victoriously. "I didn't think you'd agree so readily. One hundred thousand dollars is a high price for Hollister."

"Just give me the paper," she ordered.

He took her outstretched hand and tugged her against him. He ignored Cliff's rage as he forced Lizzie's lips into possession. With the sound of straining fabric, she struggled out of his arms. His broad hands caught her and held her against the side of the shelter.

"It ain't that easy, honey. You have to come to San Francisco with me and tell the banker you don't want the property."

"And Cliff?"

"That's the problem," he said slowly.

Cliff grinned demonically. "Sorry to trouble you, Winchester. It's a real dilemma, isn't it? Kill me now, and Lizzie will never cooperate with you. Release me and take her to Frisco with you, and you're a dead man. You know I'll trail you. What's left? Taking me with you?" He laughed. "We'll have a lot of fun traveling together."

Sam scowled as he glared at the two smiling faces. Pulling out another strip of rope, he ordered Lizzie to place her hands in front of her. He raised his gun and pointed it at the other man when she didn't obey him.

Lizzie slowly extended her arms. She gasped in pain as he wrenched them viciously. Abuse flowed from Sam's mouth as he taunted her. When he had bound her, he tied the other end of the rope to one of the trees at the edge of the shelter. He glared at Cliff.

"Get near her, Hollister, and I'll give you the best seat in the house to see me enjoy my new mistress for the first time."

"I understand," Cliff said reluctantly.

"I'll be just beyond the door, getting my pack off my horse. If I hear any sound that makes me think you're trying to escape . . ."

"We understand." Cliff's frustration seeped into his tight voice.

Sam laughed as he crawled out of the shelter. They could hear the noise of his passage through the thick snow. He made no attempt now to mask his steps.

"Half-pint?"

She raised her head. Only the movement of Cliff's head distinguished him from the other shadows of the night. Involuntarily she glanced toward the door.

"Are you all right, Cliff?"

His smile could be heard in his voice. "I've done better." In a more serious tone, he whispered, "Under no circumstances let him fire that gun."

"Of course not! Do you think I want to get you killed? I—"

He cut off her blustery voice. "It's not that, half-pint. The sun was hot today. The snow is heavy. Such a noise could bring that mountain of snow down on us."

"Cliff, what can I do?" she gasped. She had thought Sam was their greatest threat.

Shaking his head, he realized she could not see him. "I don't know, half-pint. We have to delay him until the snow hardens again. We're going to have to play this carefully. When she laughed suddenly, he asked, "What is it?"

"Just follow my lead, Cliff. I think—" She silenced herself as she saw Sam's boots peeking through the door flap. Her eyes could not hide the joy in them, but she was careful to keep her face bland.

Sam grinned as he stirred the fire higher. Both of his captives had obeyed his orders explicitly. Perhaps he would take Hollister to the coast with him. Plenty of sea captains needed strong hands on their ships. He tried to imagine Hollister in China and chuckled.

He sat down next to Lizzie and leaned his rifle against his knees. "Surprised?"

"At my newfound wealth? Of course! At your nefarious treatment of us? Not at all." She ducked as he raised his hand, but he paused as he heard a movement on the other side of the shelter.

He ignored Lizzie's cry of dismay as he raised the gun. "Move again, Hollister, and I'll do as I threatened."

Cliff sat back on the ground. "I'll cooperate if you don't hit her. I know Lizzie well enough to tell you that's not the way to keep her in line."

"Thanks for the advice," Sam grumbled as he placed the gun back on the floor.

Silence settled uncomfortably on the shelter. The last light of the day dissolved into night. Lizzie made and discarded a dozen plans to implement her idea. If Sam was suspicious of her ulterior motives, he would halt her gamble before it started.

Finally, in a soft voice she said, "Sam, I think I have a solution for your problem of what to do with Cliff."

"Do you?" He snapped, "I do too! A life at sea would agree with him just fine."

"You know you'll never get him to San Francisco," she said quickly, trying to allay the fear in her heart. She could not let it tint her words. "How about a game?"

"A game?" he repeated.

She leaned forward as far as the rope would permit. "Cards. If I win, you free Cliff and I go with you to get the money."

Slowly he smiled. It would be a long night. Gambling always helped pass the time. He reached into his pack for a deck of cards. Trust Lizzie to know he never traveled without them. She must have been familiar with his reputation as an avid gambler in Hopeless.

"Cut me loose."

"Wait a minute!" Cliff rose to his knees. "Don't I get to say something about this?" He was sure he knew what Lizzie had planned, but he had to portray himself as ignorant. "Half-pint, if you think I'll let you go with this poor excuse of a—"

The rifle pointed directly at him. "Sit down, Hollister. Sit and be quiet. This is none of your business."

"It is my—"

"Shut up!" Sam roared.

Cliff dropped back to the floor. He could push their captor only so far. If he went too far, they all could die horribly. He watched as Sam released Lizzie's ropes. Every motion they made, Cliff noted. He doubted she would have much time to make her move to save them when the time came. He must be prepared to help her.

"I don't know why I let you convince me to do this," Sam grumbled. "The money is mine anyhow. You've agreed to sign it over to me."

She watched as he shuffled the cards with easy assurance. "Not necessarily."

"One hand of poker?"

"No, more than one. The first one is for Cliff."

He paused as he was about to deal the cards. In shock, he asked, "You'll really gamble for his life?"

"If you will agree to release him if I win. Then we'll play for the money."

Sam's eyes glittered with malicious delight. He grasped her wrist as she reached for her cards. Twisting it, he forced her face close to his. "If I win? He dies, Lizzie."

She nodded slowly. Although she fought the impulse, she couldn't keep from looking at Cliff. He grinned at her and winked.

The game took little time, since they didn't have to go through the formality of betting. They knew the prize and the cost too well. Lizzie asked to be dealt two more cards and she discarded two. Sam took only one. He grinned as he saw her reaction to his bold play.

"What do you have, Lizzie?"

Lizzie lowered her cards to the ground, spreading them to reveal her hand. The two queens

and the pair of fives overshadowed the fifth card.
She smiled triumphantly. Two pair would beat
almost anything he could have drawn.

"Very nice," Sam said. "Very nice indeed, but
the question remains, is it good enough?"

He laughed as her smile faded. With painful
slowness, he placed two tens on the ground, then a
king and a deuce. All different suits. As he saw her
eyes begin to glow, he dropped the last card on the
dirt.

Lizzie's cry of horror masked the sound of his
boots scraping the ground as he reached for his
rifle. She flung herself across the damning card,
which matched the pair of tens, in an attempt to
halt Sam's arm from rising. Easily he shook her
off.

"You wagered, Lizzie. Three of a kind beats
two pair. You lost. Now Hollister loses."

Fighting the desperation within her so she
could speak calmly, she stated, "First we finish the
game. You want the money, don't you?" She must
keep him from firing that gun.

He laughed. "You're a competitive woman,
Lizzie. All right. We'll play for the money. High-
stakes games are fun. One hundred thousand
dollars on the turn of a card."

Lizzie dealt the cards silently. She looked past
Sam's exultant face to Cliff's tense one. So slightly
it was barely perceptible, she motioned with her
head toward the left. If he moved toward the door,
they might be able to escape when the game was
over. He nodded his understanding.

She kept up a steady patter of senseless

conversation as she picked up her cards. With Sam's attention divided between her and the hand he held, she hoped he would not notice Cliff's furtive movements.

"How many?" she asked.

"Two."

She dealt them easily and said, "No cards for me. I'll play these."

He laughed. "Have it your way, Lizzie. What do you have?"

"You first. I went first last time."

With a grin, he placed a pair of kings on the floor. She laughed with the same victorious sound he had used. The three queens and two sixes overlaid his cards.

"You cheated!" he shrieked.

"How?" she asked reasonably. They're your cards. Just the luck of the deal. Don't you think if I was going to cheat I would have done it on the last hand?" She smiled. "I have the money. You have Cliff's life. Nothing much has changed. Shall we play one game for both?"

Sam exploded from the ground. Knocking the cards from her hand, he grasped his gun. He swore as he dicovered Hollister had moved, but he swung the weapon in the direction of where Hollister was. Lizzie jumped in front of Cliff. Both men shouted at her at the same moment. Their orders for her to move aside were identical.

"I won't let you kill him! Shoot me, and you lose the money."

Even as she jumped in front of the gun, she had drawn the knife from under her shirt. She could not let Sam see what she was doing. Carefully her fingers sought the ropes binding Cliff. The sharp knife must cut them but not his hands. He lifted them to rest under the blade. She began to saw furtively on the hemp.

Sam shoved her away. The knife flew from her hand to disappear in the shadows. He followed it with his eyes. In the moment he was diverted, Lizzie jumped away from the bound man.

"Outside," he ordered. "Go, Lizzie. You too, Hollister. I don't know what you were trying to do, but we're getting out of here before you can try something else."

Lizzie crawled out of the hut first. In the dark, she sought along the ground for a weapon. She could see nothing. Sam slammed her back against the shelter as he stood next to her and pointed his gun toward the doorway. Cliff emerged from the building last. Whether it was so difficult for him with his hands bound or he simply wanted to delay whatever Sam had planned, she could not tell.

"Over there!"

Cliff did as directed. Sam commanded him to stop when he stood about ten feet from them. Desperately Lizzie tried to think of how to save the man she loved. When she clenched her hands against the side of the shelter, it moved. With a flash of inspiration, she slowly withdrew one of the heavy branches.

On the other side of the clearing, Cliff smiled. "Think you can shoot me from that far away, Winchester? Maybe you want to get a little closer. After all, you never got a practice shot last time you aimed at me." With his eyes holding Sam's, he gauged his opponent's reaction to his insult. A miscalculation now could prove fatal. He flexed his hands and tried to hide his reaction.

"Hollister, you . . . Good riddance to you!"

Lizzie raised the stick to crash it against Sam's head. Something must have warned him—a narrowing of Cliff's eyes, the involuntary upturn of his lips, the tensing of his muscles. Sam spun to face her. In the moonlight, Lizzie's ashen face glowed palely. With a growl, he aimed the gun at her.

The crash as she dropped the branch was swallowed by the explosion of the gun. Pain seared the night. Lizzie crumpled to the ground, clutching her upper right arm with her left hand. Blood spewed through her fingers, tinting them scarlet.

"That was just an example of what I'll do to you if—What the hell?"

Struggling to lift her head, Lizzie saw Sam freeze. Through the pain ringing in her head, she could feel a rumble like the loudest peal of thunder ripping apart the summer sky. She tried to form the word of warning in her mind, but it would not reach her lips.

"Avalanche!" came a scream in a voice she thought was Sam's. "Good-bye, Hollister!"

Hands reached out of the agony to grasp her. She screamed, but the sound was lost in the escalating screech of the elements. Struggling against the hands seemed useless. She did not want to go with Sam and leave Cliff there. If his hands were bound, he might not be able to escape the oncoming tons of snow.

"No, Lizzie."

"Cliff?" She trembled and tried to focus on his face. He put his arm around her shoulders to lift her to her feet. When she shrieked in pain, he slipped his arm around her waist.

"Run, half-pint."

She leaned on him, but found her feet moving impelled by an instinct for survival she did not have to think about. The ground beneath her feet was molasses thick with snow, but moved as if there was a quake. The sound surrounding them threatened to shatter their ears.

Somehow she kept her legs moving. She fought the desire that threatened to hold her captive before the avalanche. Terror drove her forward.

Pick up one foot, then the other. Run. Run. Save your life.

Whether she actually shouted the words aloud or only in her mind, she did not know. When Cliff shoved her forward, she scraped her face against a rock. His body was heavy over hers. She couldn't breathe. Suddenly her screams were swallowed in the maw of pandemonium. She pressed her hands over her ears and clung to the rocking earth.

She did not know how long it was before the sound ended. Her ears were buffeted by the echo of the noise. Only when gentle hands turned her to face the night sky did she open her eyes.

"Cliff?" she whispered. Her voice was hoarse from screaming.

"It's over, honey." One side of his body was

crusted with clouds of snow that had been driven before the avalanche. It created a strange harlequin effect on his face.

"Sam?"

Slipping his arm under her shoulders, he lifted her gently to see over the riverside rock that had sheltered them. A virgin expanse of snow looked deceptively innocent as it surrounded the sheared-off trees that were covered with white on one side as Cliff was. Nothing was where it had been. A pile of boulders rested where she guessed their shelter had stood.

"He went in that direction." He pointed toward the path of greatest destruction.

She closed her eyes and grimaced as the renewed pain of her arm shot through her. She savored it, simply glad to be alive. Maybe later she would feel something else. Now just to be alive seemed glorious. Cliff's gentle fingers wrapped his handkerchief around her arm. She looked at his scratched face and whispered, "Then he's gone."

"Along with your inheritance from Zach Greenway." He explained quickly as she gazed at him with pain-blurred eyes, "Winchester had the will. Without it, that banker will never believe you're Zach's Lizzie Buchanan."

"I still have the miniatures of Zach and Whitney. I kept them after I gave you the frames. If I showed him those . . ." Her words faded into a sigh of rapture as he pressed his lips to hers.

Careful not to hurt her wounded arm, he pressed her to him. No one would deny him the woman he loved. For her, he would give up his free life on the road to share the beauty they had found in these unpredictable mountains.

"Don't worry about it now, half-pint. We have a long walk." He helped her to her feet. "Do you think you can manage?"

Her smile held a spark of its former brilliance as she retorted, "Don't I always?"